Daughter of the Ageian

The Dragon Wars Saga Volume One

By Marius H. Visser

DRAKE
PRESS

Published 2022 by Drake Press

ISBN: 9780645092226 (Paperback)
9780645092295 (Hardback)
9780645092233 (ePub)

A catalogue record for this
work is available from the
National Library of Australia

Acknowledgement

This novel has been very long in the making and now finally I had the opportunity to finish it. To all my friends and family that supported me throughout this project, I am blessed to have you in my life. Thank you.

To my brilliant cover designer, Andrei Bat, I thank you for indulging all my requests and creating these amazing covers for this series. https://99designs.com/profiles/bandrei

To my fantastic editor Floyd Largent, thank you for all the work done. This book is a better version, thanks to you.

You guys were great and made the book look beautiful.

The next novel is already lurking around the corner, so I hope you are ready.

Foreword

Thank you for picking up Daughter of the Ageian. I really hope you enjoy this novel. If you have a moment, please leave a review on your preferred store as this will allow me the opportunity to write more books such as this. I will really appreciate it. Reviews are especially critical in today's world. Help other fantasy readers and tell them why you enjoyed this book. Thank you!

* Leave a Review here:

https://www.amazon.com

Want to stay updated with news about my books?

* Join my mailing list at:

https://www.mariushvisser.com/contact

* Like me on Facebook:

https://www.facebook.com/mariushvisserbooks

* Follow me on Instagram:

https://www.instagram.com/mariushvisser

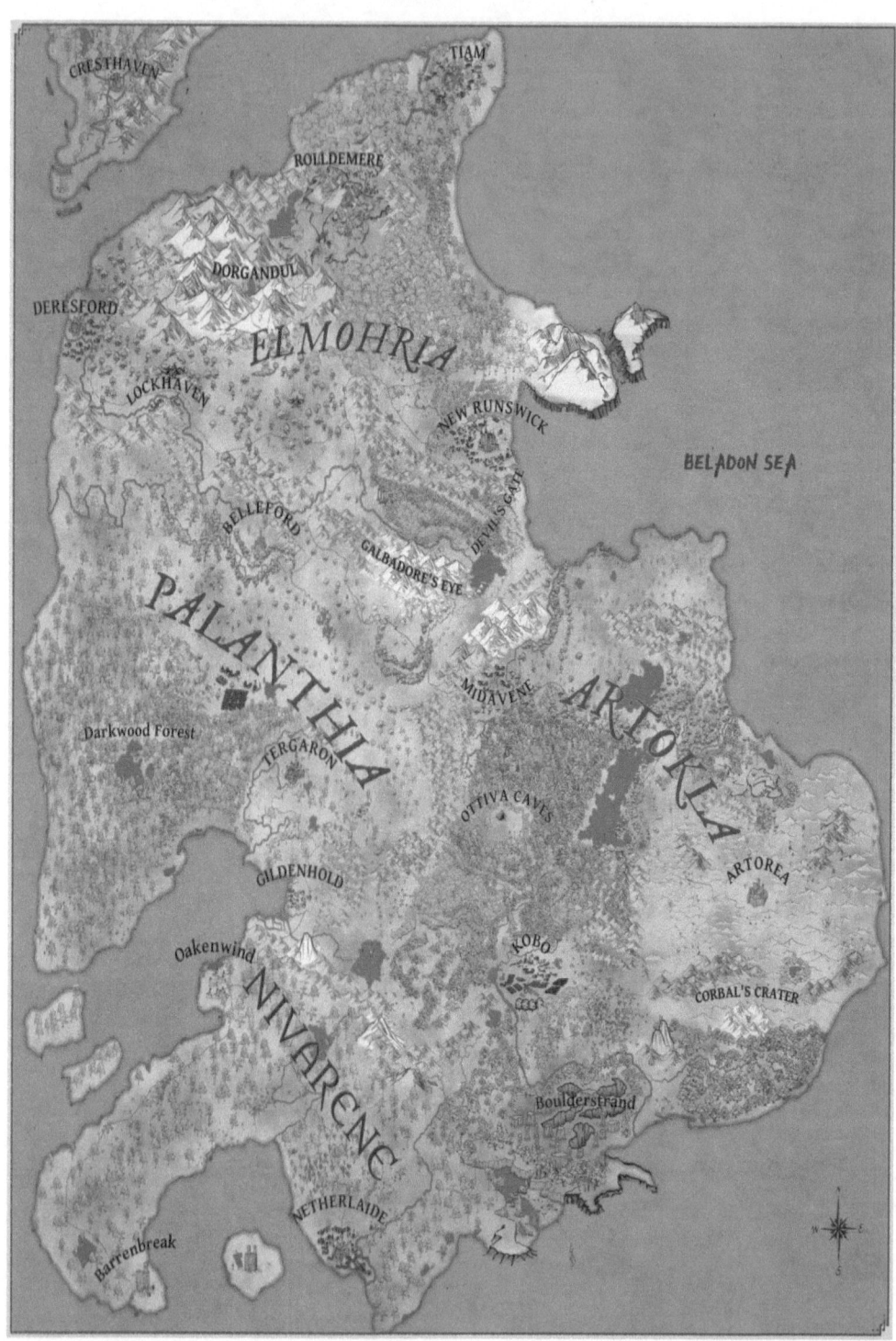

Chapter One

The blood of King Madock was still hot on his hands; the taste of victory lay naked before him. Galvos reached down and gripped the hand of the dead king as he repeated a phrase over and over. '*Entou ta kamien a saldjien.*' The body of the king spasmed; his muscles pulled taut, making him seem animate once more.

As the chant continued, a mist of blood flowed from every orifice of the dead king. Larger and larger it grew, until a sphere the size of a man's head circled above the warlock — beautiful to behold, the colours swirling and misty, as if a war were being waged inside the sphere. Finally, he dropped the dried-up corpse, drained now of all bodily fluid. With a heave and a sigh of agony, Galvos got to his feet, his legs trembling from exhaustion, making him stumble as he took hold of the hovering sphere with his gloved hand.

But this day was not yet at an end.

Galvos walked from the dais through the corridors of the large, ornate palace towards the gardens. The smell of hot iron and piss from the dead and the dying stung his nose, but there was another smell that he recognised above all else: the stench of sorcery. Standing in the hall of the dead king, he focused his gaze and hearing on the supernatural in the air. The hairs on his muscled arms were suddenly erect, like the hackles of an alarmed dog. He swung his axe down, seemingly at nothing — yet it stopped in mid-air, as if hitting a solid wall. Slowly a bladed chain appeared, wrapped around the axe, cutting deep grooves in the wooden haft and holding it firm. Sweat ran down his face as a dark, hooded apparition materialised in front of him. Using all his strength, he stepped in to slam the axe into the face of this new adversary. The weapon shook in his hands as it hit a wall of magic, sending the apparition skidding backwards on its feet. Already weakened by the ritual of removing the blood orb, the warlock's energy was fading fast. 'You're not of the king's company. What do you want?' he demanded.

A slow, steady laugh greeted the warlock as the apparition removed its hood to reveal a woman with long black hair, braided to the back and left flowing further down, her eyes the colour of night. She glided closer and replied, 'Now why would I tell you all my dirty little secrets? All you need to know is that I need that orb. I don't care for your squabbling.'

A low snort escaped his mouth as he said, 'It's a little presumptuous to think I have this orb you're referring to.'

Cocking her head to the side, she said, 'Do you mean to say that you *don't* have it? That it's not in that sack at your side?'

Galvos shrugged and continued, 'No, I just said it's presumptuous of you to assume.'

'Arrogant, even in the face of danger. I like you; you have balls. But I don't like to be toyed with. I'll destroy you if I must.'

With blinding speed, the chain lashed out to wrap around the warlock's left arm, cutting deep. In agony, he screamed as he gripped the chain with his right hand and pulled with all his might, sending her flying into his grasp. Suddenly, she was dangling in the air as he held her by the throat.

Shocked at the turn of events, she quickly drew some symbols in the air.

The warlock's arm started turning red, his veins burning from the inside. Fighting to calm his mind through the pain, he chanted steadily. Archaic symbols appeared on his arms as if seared by fire, the burn slowly subdued by his defences. The sorceress twisted the chain farther around his arm and snapped it down. Blood sprayed as the blades from the chain cut deeper still. Any lesser man would have lost his arm. In torment, Galvos let her go and reeled back as she stumbled to the ground and said, 'Well now, warlock, that was an interesting turn of events. Tell me, what are you planning to do with the orb? Or as my people call it, the Balamuth?'

Galvos staggered back to catch his breath, then pulled a cloth from the sack and quickly bandaged his arm as he said, 'You mean witches, right?'

She chuckled. 'You're interesting, I'll give you that. No, I mean people. I am no witch.'

The chain snapped out in a succession of strikes, left and right, and the warlock stumbled back, defending his life as the attacks came unabated. From his left, he heard shouts as his Kamatayon warriors ran into the hall. Seeing their captain in trouble, they rushed to his aid. The sorceress cursed and ran from the hall in the other direction, disappearing through the doors at the rear that led higher into the palace. Galvos shouted to his men, 'Go after her and bring me her head!'

Five warriors gave chase as the rest remained in the hall, should she circle back.

The blood was running freely down his arm, and he could feel his strength fading. Galvos stumbled forth through the hall and out to the garden, watching as soldiers fought in the courtyard, then used his axe to cut some branches from a tree before he stuck them into the ground in the shape of a large square, about the size of a horse cart, around him. He cut three more and placed them in the square in the shape of a triangle. Pushing the blade of the axe into the ground, he dragged it from branch to branch, connecting them to each other.

'What are you doing, Galvos?' came a shout from his lieutenant, Ganda'har.

'Destroy it. We have to destroy it.' Tired beyond comprehension, he continued with the lines on the ground as his muscles burned with fatigue.

'Stop that! You can't destroy it; we need to take it back to the city!' Underestimating the warlock's ability to fight under such circumstances, he grabbed hold of the axe in Galvos' left hand, but an unanticipated thunderous right came from below, striking Ganda'har full in the face, stunning the big warrior as blood sprayed from his nose. He staggered back and gripped his nose, swearing as he said, 'Aggh! You broke it, you bastard!'

'I told you, we need to destroy it. I'm still the commanding officer in this squadron, so you will obey my orders!'

The air was growing tense. King Madock's Deraset warriors were still putting up a fight in the losing battle to avenge their king and save what they could of their city. As Galvos pulled the orb from the sack, he heard a shout to his right: 'Get him, we need that orb!' A grizzled warrior, tall and muscled, advanced on the warlock, his fellow soldiers joining in the charge.

Mumbling more than speaking, Galvos looked at his lieutenant as he said, 'Please, you need to stop them from getting to me.'

Shocked at the pale visage of his captain, Ganda'har merely nodded, then turned to shout aloud, 'Kamatayon, form up, we defend our own!'

Warriors from all sides converged on Galvos, dust clouds kicked up as the warriors raced towards their prize. The first to reach the defending line was the Deraset warrior, who suddenly flew through the air as Ganda'har used his momentum against him and lifted him into the air, impaling the warrior on the spear of another Kamatayon. The warrior slid off the spear as it was swung to the left, crashing into another attacker and falling to the ground. His end was inevitable, and soon he lay still, eyes glazed. The fighting grew more intense as the others converged around the square.

Galvos placed the sphere in the centre of the triangle and stood at the foot of it. Carnage surrounded him as he saw young men and women dying to defend him in this hour of need. With his palms together, the warlock spoke with authority, sending a prayer to Kelcai — the warrior turned legend, ascended to become a god amongst mortal men. 'Be with these brave soldiers today; guide their sword arms. Make their blades swing true. Protect them.' Then he closed his eyes and chanted.

Soldiers on both sides were tiring, but the bodies still piled up, for the fighting would not cease until the orb was recovered or destroyed. A fierce battle cry sounded as one of the Deraset broke through the line of defence and dashed forth into the square, to plunge his dagger into the warlock's stomach, then rib cage. In the state of trance Galvos was in, he did not stop the incantation, but continued through the bubbling blood he spat up. A distant sound echoed in his ears.

'My name is Sukayi Kavali. Remember me as you die, demon,' the man said as he plunged the blade into the warlock again.

Blood flowed down Galvos' chest at an alarming rate. Sukayi Kavali pulled the dagger out, readying for another thrust, when a sword slid through his back to emerge at his stomach. Looking down, he reached out, felt the cold iron, and laughed hysterically. Ganda'har ripped out the sword, and the warrior fell to the ground clutching his stomach, then scrambled for safety as the earth beneath him quaked. Cracks spread from the sides of the square in the ground, large enough to fit a man's foot into and expanding quickly.

Ganda'har shouted to his men to push the fight farther away, and leaped across a growing crack as a bright light stabbed up into the air, blinding everyone for a few heartbeats, followed by another, then another, and another until all the branches in the ground lit up. With a thunderous crack, an immense force rushed down from the heavens through the pillars of light until it reached the ground, spreading outward, throwing all the warriors from their feet. Soldiers clung to trees and walls, anything firmly rooted. As the winds died and the warriors slowly rose, they saw the orb was gone and the warlock lay unmoving on the ground, ten feet from where he'd stood, blood still spilling from his wounds. Everyone was silent and astonished; there was nothing left to fight for. Ganda'har ran to his captain's side.

The Kamatayon warriors that Galvos had sent after the sorceress emerged from the palace with a scared servant girl clutching her raggedy clothes in fear. They stared down at the lieutenant as he held Galvos' head off the ground and said, 'We found no witch, sir, just one of the servants.'

Ganda'har looked up at her and said, 'What's your name, girl?'

Stuttering from fear, she said, 'B-B-B-Beuneth. P-p-please don't kill me.'

The big man looked at her with deep sadness in his eyes, then back down to his dying friend. 'The killing is done for the day, girl; you need not fret. You will be safe with us back in Artorea.'

Ganda'har whispered in the warlock's ear for a while as the blood bubbled on the man's lips, then rose and shouted, 'Get a wagon here! Now! We ride for home, and we ride hard.' He rose from the ground and stared at the surrounding soldiers, the Kamatayon and the Deraset alike. He could see the eagerness to do battle still burning in their eyes. 'There is nothing left to fight over! Go home, those of you still alive. Go to your families and hug your children. We did not come for *your* lives, just the king's.'

A man wielding a broadsword stood a few feet from Ganda'har. He could see how the man struggled internally to accept this offer; then Ganda'har sheathed his blade and shouted, 'Kamatayons! Sheath your weapons.' One and all, their blades slipped into their scabbards, axes and hammers placed back on their belts, spears lowered to the ground.

The other man was fuming, jittering as he looked about, gripping his broadsword tighter in his hand. A shout suddenly burst forth from the man as he charged at the lieutenant. Before any other soldier could react, they saw a flash of metal in the sun and the charging man sagged to his knees a few feet past Ganda'har, who was standing with his sword in hand. A sigh escaped the lieutenant before he sheathed the weapon again.

Gurgling noises came from the soldier as he collapsed, his throat cut through.

'If there's anyone else who wants to join this man in death, step forth! Or let us pass.' A clangour of steel echoed as the Deraset warriors dropped their weapons to the ground. Relieved for the moment, Ganda'har shouted, 'Get the healer here, quickly!'

* * *

The march back home was a sombre one, with nothing to show for their victory but the dead at their backs, burning on their pyres as they left Tergaron. The smell of burning flesh finally left their nostrils as they put more distance between themselves and the city. After a week of travelling, they had passed the glades of the Nakurothi and were now in the thick of the northern forests of the Baga — indigenous tribes that had claimed the area as their sacred hunting grounds. From here, they would still have to make their way across the mountains of the Chimna dwarves before finally venturing through the vast desert of Artokla to their city of Artorea, the Heart of the Desert. Their king, Naka II, had wanted the source of Madock's sudden boom in power and zeal. Instead, they came home empty-handed, with wagons filled with injured soldiers, an outcome he would not be pleased with.

King Naka had known King Madock for years and found the man to be ostentatious, but not one to sack kingdoms for his own gains. He knew something else must be at play, something supernatural, forcing the sudden explosion of tyranny from Madock, as well as his drive to expand his empire. Two other kingdoms to the far northwest had already fallen to his madness. The next could have been Artorea, but King Naka would not sit idly by. He acted swiftly and without mercy. As Madock's occupying forces moved farther west to capture more lands, they left their king vulnerable in his palace, with a diminished force to safeguard against intruders. The Kamatayon legion slipped into the city of Tergaron with the help of spies on the inside. With reinforcements far away, Galvos and his force of Kamatayon warriors sneaked around in the dead of night, taking their positions to ambush the remaining guards. The Kamatayon struck like lightning to a tree. An alarm bell sounded, and the fighting ensued.

Now they bore fresh scars as they returned home.

Farther down the train of soldiers walked the servant girl, Beuneth, keeping a keen eye on the wagon transporting their injured captain. With every chance she got, she inched closer to the wagon. Eyes continually tracked her movements, but every so often they would get distracted with conversation or become lost in their own thoughts, and soon she was only a few feet from the wagon. Once in its cool shade, she closed her eyes and breathed deeply from the relief of being away from the sun's harsh rays. A horse's hooves beat on the ground moments before a man rode past towards the lieutenant, catching the attention of the men around her. She quickly slipped into the back of the wagon while no one was watching.

Beuneth stared down at the bleeding man barely clinging to life as ragged breaths came from his mouth, then moved to sit next to him. Coarse sutures closed his wounds, but one had already torn free, leaking blood over his chest. The healer was not talented. She spied a small box in the corner and collected it.

* * *

Ganda'har was quiet as he rode his chestnut gelding, contemplating the reactions of the king once he found out they had failed to procure the source of Madock's power, when one of his men pulled up alongside him and said, 'Lieutenant!' With a start, Ganda'har jerked his head up and looked at the man. 'Sorry, sir, but you haven't responded to any of my calls. We need to rest the horses. Everyone is tired, and morale is low.'

Shaking his head, trying to clear it, Ganda'har spat in his hands and worked his fingers through his oily black hair. He sighed as he said, 'Fine, Gailan. Find a clearing in the forest and let them rest.'

Gailan stared at the man, then said, 'We lost too much, sir. I know you were close to Galvos; I'm sorry for your loss.'

'He ain't dead yet, soldier, so I don't want to hear that from any of you again. We fought side by side for many a year, and we always came out on top.' Grinning at a fond memory, Ganda'har chuckled as he

12

continued, 'I remember once when we'd just come back from the Battle of Ormondeo, the king wanted to see us immediately. Galvos really needed to "go" and wasn't happy about it at all, but kept his composure. The sounds of his bowels rumbling could have drowned out the royal bard's most boisterous songs. The king walked with us through the palace as we recounted the battle, as if telling a story to a child before bed, his eyes full of wonder and excitement. Galvos had saved my life that day as he had done many times before...' Bursting out with laughter, Ganda'har said, 'As soon as the king turned his back to leave us, Galvos dashed into the closest chamber's outhouse to drop one. Turns out it was the king's. Outhouse, that is!'

The sound of laughter from the two men rang out over the silent troops. Here and there, heads lifted from their march, joining in with a chuckle. As Gailan called for the train to halt, Ganda'har motioned for him to join him as he walked over to the wagon's rear and flung the flap open at the back. 'Gods, girl, what are you doing in here? Get out!' Ganda'har shouted as he climbed in and grabbed her by the wrist. He hurled her from the wagon, causing her to fall to the ground. Gailan was on her quickly to restrain her hands as the lieutenant climbed back out.

'I was just cleaning his wounds! I wanted to help him. He needed water!' Beuneth shouted, with her head pressed to the ground.

'If you did anything to that man other than what you said, I will cut your throat,' Ganda'har said as he climbed back into the wagon. By now, some of his men surrounded them, waiting for the order to string her up.

He ducked his head to clear the low timbers as he made his way to Galvos' side and examined his friend. A strange odour hung in the air, musky and sour. The thick leather armour and shirt had been undone to reveal the wounds on his chest. Blood was smeared, as if she had tried to mop it up. He saw the bloodied rag on the floor of the wagon as he looked around. The big wound higher on his chest had been closed for a second time. He saw the previous thread and tear marks. A poor job, but he bled less now. He took hold of Galvos' hand and said, 'Hold on, my friend, we're going home.' As he climbed out, he gestured to Gailan to release her and continued, 'She tells the truth. She stitched the wound and cleaned him some. I apologise, girl. Can't be too careful, you know.'

She shoved Gailan aside and wiped her face with the back of her hand, then said, 'Yes, I know.' Beuneth walked away to sit under the shade of a tree, breathing deeply to calm herself.

* * *

Shouts and cheers of elation were heard as the warrior train moved through the gates of Artorea. Flowers of all colours serenaded the sky and covered the roads with their beauty. In the front rows of the crowd, a big man pushed his way through and rushed to the warriors, calling out, 'Father! Where are you? Ganda'har, where's the old man?'

The lieutenant walked up to the big man and embraced him fully as he whispered, 'I'm sorry, Khan. Your father was gravely wounded in battle. The carts with the injured came in ahead of us through the Western gate, heading straight to the healers' hall. Prepare yourself. I don't know if he'll pull through this time.'

Khanaseri paled, his hands and legs trembling as he sought to wipe the sweat from his brow. Unable to say another word, he turned to run as fast as his legs could carry him through the crowds, shoving people out of the way to get to the healers' hall. The knot in his stomach pulled tighter and tighter the closer he got; then he saw the queue of carts with injured soldiers on them, waiting to get into the hall.

Dust plagued the air as oxen stamped their hooves, eager to move forward. He slipped past the waiting men as the healers in their white robes shouted at him to slow down. Pulled from his work, a healer spun around as the big man grabbed him by the arm and asked, 'Where's my father? Where's the captain?'

Before the healer in his grasp could answer, an old man with no hair and a crooked stance shuffled towards him and said, 'Oh, dear man, he's in the back room. We thought to give him some privacy. Go to him. Don't dally.'

Everywhere he looked, he could see blood-soaked rags strewn on the floor of the hall. Khanaseri pushed through the indefatigable workers as they carried the dead out to the back and piled them on carts as the healers frantically ran around trying to save others. Finally reaching the room at the back, he leaned on the door to move in, then stopped to steel himself. With a heavy creak, the old oak door swung open, and he saw a well-dressed man in a red silk tunic and green trousers with an elegant sword hanging from his belt leaning over the bed.

A weak hand waved him closer as Galvos lay in the bed, the stink of infection rancid in the air. He spoke with a garbled voice, 'Khan, meet King Naka. Show some manners, my boy.'

Khan dragged his gaze away from the form that was his father and looked at the king, bowing slightly as he said, 'Father, you are unwell and need to rest.'

A sudden cough wracked the warlock. Blood spewed from his mouth as he struggled to wave his hand, then pointed a finger at Khanaseri to silence him. King Naka grabbed Galvos' hand and whispered, 'He means no disrespect, my friend. He's merely concerned for his father. I can't fault that. Now spend some time with your son before the day is done.'

Galvos locked eyes with the king and slowly let go of his hand. Turning to leave, the king lay his hand upon Khanaseri's shoulder. 'Your father will be in our thoughts this night.'

'Thank you, my king.'

As King Naka left the room, Khanaseri pulled an armchair closer and clenched his teeth as he muttered, 'What does he demand from you now? More blood?'

Blood seeped from the warlock's mouth as he tried to speak, the words coming slow and spaced out: 'You...are...too fast...to anger.'

Khanaseri grabbed a cloth from the bowl by his side and wiped his father's mouth, dabbing at the dark blood staining his beard and chest. The old warlock's eyes suddenly turned inward, showing only the whites as his body pulled tight and vehemently convulsed.

'Someone! Please help!'

Two healers came through the door and pushed him out of the way as they turned Galvos on his side. Another came running holding a small vial, the contents a deep orange. Holding his father down, they pried open his mouth and poured the liquid down his throat, then held his jaw closed. A few pounding heartbeats later, the seizure passed.

Khanaseri looked at his father in this state of dying and thought back to a better time, a time when he'd been full of life, trying to teach young Khanaseri how to wield an axe. With the stance and glare of a general, his father would walk up and down before the boy, speaking as to his troops before a battle, a cold, stern face with little humour hiding behind his deep blue eyes, saying, 'Both hands! Now swing left! Swing right! Move forward! Straight down!' The small wooden axe usually slipped out of Khanaseri's tired little fingers by this stage and went flying to hit his father in the face. The sudden, short-lived curse that was followed by his father chasing after him as he clutched his bruised nose always improved his day.

But the fond memories of youth were quickly being replaced by the truth of adulthood. The world was fast growing to be a bitter one.

A creak from the door behind them made them turn to see Ganda'har stroll into the room, followed by a tall, gaunt man wearing trinkets around his arms, legs, and neck. His sleeveless black kaftan revealed letters and symbols inked into his arms. The lieutenant walked over to the injured warlock as the nurses moved out of his way and motioned to the man to come closer, then said, 'Stilts, see what you can do for him.'

Khanaseri stepped aside and let the man pass without a word. Stilts laid his gangly hand upon Galvos' head, then took a dagger from his belt and cut his finger just enough to bleed. He chanted as he drew a symbol that looked like the sun, with its brilliant rays shining outward on the old warlock's forehead. The blood caked instantly, and the man nervously looked at Khanaseri and took a step back before he said, 'Get over here.'

'What's wrong?' asked Ganda'har before Khanaseri could ask the same.

'He...or something, is resisting me, my blood.' Stilts picked up the rag from the chair next to him and wiped off the dried blood, then continued, 'Hold out your hand.' A swift, slight cut and Khanaseri's finger bled. Stilts grabbed his hand to draw the same symbol as before on Galvos' forehead while chanting.

Khanaseri felt a tingling sensation course through his legs and up his spine. He breathed deeply as the hairs on the back of his neck stood erect. Stilts lowered his hand, gesturing him to move away as he continued chanting. The blood did not dry up this time; instead, a thin trail of smoke – almost invisible – rose from the old warlock's head before the man stepped back.

'What's wrong?' Khanaseri asked as he took a step closer again.

'I can't be certain why...' Stilts looked up at Khanaseri, then at Ganda'har, and continued, 'I'm afraid he's beyond any warlock's help, unless they're blood of his blood. Some might do more, but I can't help him. I'm sorry.' Stilts turned to leave the room and placed his hand briefly on Khanaseri's shoulder as he passed, then disappeared through the door.

A groan sounded from the chair, and Ganda'har tensed his muscles as he leaned on the back, squeezing the frame until they heard a loud snap. Everyone jumped around to see Ganda'har holding the backrest in his hand. He gazed at them, then threw the piece of timber on the floor before storming from the room.

Khanaseri dipped his head, keeping his eyes closed as he thought about what Stilts had said, then turned and left the room without a word.

* * *

The days slowly progressed as Khanaseri sat by his father's bedside most of the time, be it to bring water or food, or simply to stare at him as he slept. People from all over, people he didn't even know, started confronting him on the streets wherever he went, proclaiming their sympathy for his loss, or saying how sorry they were to hear about the news of his father. *He's not dead yet!* he wanted to yell at them, but kept his mouth shut. Truth was, he wasn't sure how long his father had left. Every night he went to the temple to pray, then to the archives to search through the *Acronodium*, the book that held all information about the warlocks and their gifts, hoping that he might find something to bring his power into the light and help his father. But he was yet to find anything.

The nights passed in a blink of an eye as he stood practising everything he'd learnt in the book...but nothing came of it. He was his father's son, but he hadn't inherited Galvos' abilities. Days blurred together as sleep eluded him. Exhausted and plagued by hallucinations caused by sleep deprivation, his mind bent the truth of the world. Up was down and down was up; he was constantly forgetting what he was about to do.

Rounding the corner to the bakery across the street from the infirmary, he stopped to buy half a loaf of wheat bread for his father. A sudden feeling of being watched swept over him — the feeling of being spied upon. He snapped his head around and watched as people made their way in various directions, walking up and down the gravel road hurriedly to get to their destinations, but he saw no one paying him any special heed. Smells from the freshly baked bread filled the air and pulled his attention back to the bakery, and he entered the shop. Wandering around, he reached for a loaf, but upon touching it, he stopped and stood, frozen in time. In a daze of sleeplessness and worry, his mind had shut down any non-essential thinking. He didn't wonder about what people were doing around him, or what they thought when they saw him in his current state of unwash, wearing clothes that hadn't been changed for days. Muffled sounds, as if he were underwater, echoed in his ears, getting closer and louder, yet remained unrecognisable.

'I said, are you going to buy something or just foul all of my bread with your touch today?' The old baker snapped his fingers next to

Khanaseri's ear repeatedly. Annoyed, he finally cuffed Khanaseri on the head with the flat of his palm and said, 'I'm speaking to you. Are you well?'

Snapping out of the trance, Khanaseri looked around as he came back to reality, and said, 'Uhm, yes. Sorry, I'll take this one.'

'You okay? Been coming in here a lot of late, and every time you look worse than before.'

He took the bread and held out the coins to the baker as he said, 'Yes, I'm fine, thanks.'

'You're the great Galvos' boy. Well, can't really say *boy*, now can I? You're as big as a horse! How is he doing?' he asked, ignoring the coins before him.

At first, Khanaseri wanted to turn and run from the shop, not wanting to speak with another fake sympathiser, but turned back as the old baker said, 'Your father came into this shop almost every day, ya know. He's one of my best customers. Ya know, he swore to me he would never buy bread anywhere else. He had a standing discount here, and today I think he earned his free loaf. Tell your da Oloff sends his blessings.'

The old baker tossed the loaf over to Khanaseri, who snapped it from the air and said, 'Thank you, Oloff, he's spoken plenty about "the old baker." Now I can at least put a face to the title. I'll tell my father you send your regards.' Khanaseri sighed as he pushed open the door and walked through.

Once outside, he looked around again. The crowds had thinned, and the noise had died down. *How long was I in that shop?* Staring at the door of the infirmary across the street, it felt as if the weight on his shoulders had doubled. Suddenly, it was hard to breathe or swallow with the lump caught in his throat. Uncontrollable breathing forced air rapidly in and out of his lungs as black spots engulfed his vision. His heart thundered in his chest. His hands shook, and his mind started bending time and the world around him. He wanted to cry out for help, but no sound came from his lips other than his panting breaths. People walking around him were speaking to him. He could see their mouths moving, but he couldn't hear them. A nauseating feeling surged through his body, as if something were clawing its way from the inside, trying to get out. Suddenly, he collapsed on the road as a fit warred through his body. His eyes turned back in his head. All his muscles pulled taut as his body went into shock. People on the street ran to his side, screaming for help from the infirmary.

An old man came running as fast as he could and knelt at the young man's side, then shouted, 'Help me turn him on his side!' After they turned him, the old man soothingly spoke to him. 'Hold on, Khan. Calm down. You'll be okay, just calm down.'

A scream of absolute horror escaped Khanaseri's mouth, terrifying those around him. The sky grew darker as clouds quickly formed in the heavens. Gusts of wind blew through the city at great strength, and unexpected lightning came crashing down all over, sparks flying as it hit ground and metal. A tree burst into flames as it exploded from a strike to their right. Sudden rain poured down in large drops, quickly creating puddles on the road and making it slippery. People were falling all over as they ran to find shelter from the sudden storm. The old healer laid his frail, old body over Khanaseri to protect him. 'Wake up! We need to get to cover! Wake up!'

The spasms lasted a while longer before Khanaseri's eyes turned back, blinking rapidly as his body stopped spasming. The old healer shouted loudly to be heard over the storm, 'You'll be okay, don't fear! We need to get to shelter. Has this happened before?'

Khanaseri looked around at the people moving away to seek shelter, and then to the old man who was helping him up, and muttered, 'N-N-n-o-o.' Minor tremors, like the aftershock following an earthquake, made him tremble all over in quick succession. Feeling ashamed and humiliated for being so weak, he scanned the crowds hiding under awnings, huddled together to wait out the sudden storm. The taste of iron in his mouth made him even more nauseous as his stomach churned, the contents begging to be released into the world. And so it was. Hunched over, the bile spilled from his mouth to the curb.

The old man, however, still stood close by, lending a hand to

Khanaseri. He quickly shuffled into the bakery to reappear with a glass of sweetened water and said, 'Here, drink this! It will soothe your stomach.'

Khanaseri found the sweet taste of the sugared water almost euphoric as he downed the glass and walked with the supporting arms of the healer to a spot under the roof of the bakery. Feeling better, he said, 'Thank you, sir. I don't know what happened. It was the worst feeling — as if I were being attacked from the inside.'

With a sigh, the old healer placed his hand on Khanaseri's shoulder and said, 'I've seen this before. You put too much burden on yourself. You must learn to calm yourself. Repeat after me. Close your eyes.'

'Close your eyes.'

'No, actually close your eyes. Good. Now, breathe in. Hold it.'

'Breathe in and hold.'

'Don't repeat what I'm saying, man. Do what I say. So, breathe in. Hold. Hold. Hold. Now breathe out. Do this a couple times until you feel your heart relaxing.'

Steadily breathing out the long breath, Khanaseri said, 'I've been coming into the infirmary for weeks, and I don't even know your name. I'm ashamed of my behaviour.'

'Oh, come now. You have more important things to worry about than finding out this old fool's name.'

'That doesn't excuse me for being rude.'

The old man eyed him and released a long breath before he said, 'Fair enough. I'm Gantris.'

Gripping the old healer's arm, Khanaseri said, 'Thank you for everything.' The gusts of wind had softened their angry howls, and soon died down. The storm ceased its raging torrent, abated, and calmed as the clouds overhead dispersed and the two men headed across the street. Together, they walked through the infirmary in silence to reach the door to his father's chamber. A momentary seed of doubt made the young man pause as his fingers touched the doorknob, and he said, 'I don't know if I can do this; I'm not as strong as he is. I'm no warlock. I'm a...disappointment.'

An old, bony hand settled on his shoulders as the old healer sighed and said, 'Close your eyes. Breathe in. Hold. Now breathe out.'

The creak of the door was deafening to Khanaseri as he slowly pushed it open. Afraid he might wake his father, he stopped opening the door, then opened it quickly, hoping it wouldn't creak as much. But it did. Scowling at Gantris, he asked, 'Can't you get this fixed?'

The old healer simply shrugged and mumbled, 'Cutbacks...'

Moving through the room, he leaned on the bed and sighed as he looked down at the figure before him. Frail, thin, and grey, his father's body was deteriorating fast. Sweat covered him from head to toe, and the smell of rancid flesh hung in the air. 'Why isn't he getting better?'

Gantris had his hands in the sleeves of his robe as he said, 'We've done all we can medically. *He* needs to fight this now.'

'Father,' Khanaseri said as he shook Galvos lightly. 'You need to eat. I brought you some bread from your friend, Oloff. He sends his regards. Father! Why aren't you waking up?'

The old healer moved closer, placed his fingers on Galvos' neck in search of a pulse, and said, 'His heartbeat is weak, but he's still hanging on...although he seems non-responsive. Nurse, bring me my bag!'

After some time, a helper came running in with an old leather bag and handed it to Gantris, who muttered, 'Thank you.'

'What's happening?' Khanaseri demanded, but the old man didn't answer. Instead, he rummaged through the bag and pulled out a vial filled with a yellow liquid, along with a large syringe. He drew the liquid out of the vial and injected it into Galvos' neck.

Instantly going into shock, Galvos' back arched as his arms thrashed about. 'Hold him down!' cried the old healer.

Khanaseri leaned on his father to push him back down and held him steady as the thrashing continued, and said, 'What did you give him, Gantris?'

'A cocktail to ease him. It's not supposed to do this!' Looking back at the young Khanaseri with dread in his eyes, he continued, 'This reaction seems spell-bound.'

With a puzzled look on his face, Khanaseri squinted his eyes and said, 'Do you mean he did this to himself?'

Sighing, the old man said, 'I rather hope so, son. Because if he didn't, then someone else did.'

* * *

The cold, damp cavern taunted Galvos as he slowly made his way from chamber to chamber in search of something. Exactly what, eluded him. The echo in the cave made it near-impossible to place where a sound was coming from. Bats squeaking, slow-flowing water dropping from a height in the distance to splatter down on rocks below, and the distinct sound of a mocking laugh in the dark taunted his ears and mind, although he wasn't sure if the laugh was real or just in his head. Alone and unarmed, he felt the presence of someone, something, following him, stalking him. The darkness was all-consuming, sending the warlock stumbling into ruts and rocks. Cursing, he slapped his hands together and shouted, '*Asvaniante!*'

A light burst into being in the cup of his hands, trying to escape as he slowly opened them, and said, 'You will obey me today. Follow me!'

Like a dog on a leash, the light followed him around, but it wasn't bright enough to see everything in these vast chambers, merely enough for him not to stumble down a cliff. Shadows danced on the walls and floors, playing tricks on his mind. The mocking laughter sounded out loud to his left, moving past him at great speed. Jumping around to face this nuisance, he said, 'Who are you? Why am I here?'

'Warlock, I implore you to bring me the Balamuth. There is no need for violence here today.'

Galvos studied the cave, watching the movement of the shadows on the walls. 'You will never get this Balamuth. No one should have its power. That's why I sent it away.'

'You misunderstand, warlock. That Balamuth belongs to the one I love. Without it, he is nothing but a soulless husk. I need it back. It chose him.'

'I've seen what that thing does to people! It's too much power for one person to wield. You will never have it!'

He caught the chain that flashed from the darkness and yanked on it. The woman stumbled into the light from the other end. A harsh backhanded blow threw her off her feet. Quick as a lion attacking its prey, he was on top of the sorceress. Her throat felt so soft, so thin under his calloused hand as he squeezed the life out of her.

Searing pain ripped through his right side as the sizzle of burning flesh filled the damp air. Enraged, he screamed as he dropped her and spun around, searching for the threat, but there was nothing. He spun to his right, then looked back down, and she was gone.

Her voice echoed from the walls: 'Just know I didn't want this.'

Galvos recoiled as more pain ripped through his left side, the stench of his burning skin making him sick. Lifting his shirt, he saw blood leaking from what looked like deep, burnt claw marks on his sides. 'You will pay for this! Where are you?'

The omnipotent voice sounded from everywhere as it said, 'You, warlock, are in *my* world now. Help me, and I'll help you.'

Thousands of small eyes reflected the light back to him, following his movements as he made his way deeper into the cave.

* * *

Beaded with sweat, muttering sounds escaping his mouth, Galvos was restrained to the bed to ensure he didn't hurt himself or others as he thrashed about. Khanaseri was frantic but utterly helpless, and resorted to wiping his father's face with a wet cloth as he spoke to calm him, telling stories of his youth to bring him back. Screams of pain erupted from Galvos as the smell of burning flesh filled the air. The blanket covering him turned red with blood as it seeped from his side. Panicked and afraid for his father, Khanaseri stood frozen. Shock filled him as he saw the claw marks appear on the old warlock's sides.

Gantris shouted aloud, 'He's being attacked, and there's nothing I can do to aid him! He needs a warlock who is of his blood, and you — I'm sorry.'

Khanaseri pulled out an old book from his pack, one with a green emerald on the cover. Astonished, Gantris looked upon the old book and said, 'You aren't supposed to have that! They'll hang you!'

'Borrowed, Gantris. I'm going to return it. Now hold him down.'

He flipped through the book and found the page he was looking for, then started reciting the words, '*Ilk anon Senovat!*' Over and over, he recited them, but nothing happened. Launching the old book across the room in a fit of rage, he shouted, 'See, Gantris! I'm useless!'

The old healer hurried to pick up the book and scanned through the pages, then said, 'No, there's something in you that's blocking your ability. You have the magic in you. Normal people, like myself, can't see anything written on these pages. You can! Don't you see? Try again. Hold on to your father's arm and really focus. Force yourself through the blockage.'

'Can you really not see anything in the book?' Khanaseri asked, perturbed by the idea.

'I promise you, young man, I cannot. Now go!'

He grabbed his father's arm and focused as he shouted, '*Ilk anon Senovat! Ilk anon Senovat! Ilk anon Senovat!*'

A burgeoning light appeared in his mind's eye. He could feel it growing, thrashing at the blockage that was stopping his abilities. He imagined the blockage as a dam holding back a vast quantity of water and increased his chanting, visualising it exploding to release a flood.

A burst of pain shot through his head, lighting his brain on fire. Blood gushed from his nose, and he gagged through the liquid, gurgling as he barely kept his focus on the incantation. 'Senoc's balls!' the old healer shouted as he grabbed a rag and wiped the blood from Khanaseri's face.

Khanaseri drifted away from the pain he felt in his head and thought, *Am I dying?* He opened his eyes and saw a fire in the strangling darkness a distance away. Another world surrounded him. Sounds of footsteps and shouts of rage came from the direction of the fire as shadows danced about. Khanaseri steadily moved closer to investigate.

'Father!' he shouted as he ran to the man. A burning branch swung at him, and he dived to the left to avoid the blows, then pleaded, 'It's me, Da! Khan!'

Galvos took another swing as he growled, 'You idiot apparition! I stopped my son from using magic! I blocked his ability! You can't fool me!'

Khan stumbled back, and his foot caught on a jutting rock. Sharp stones cut through his hands as he stopped his fall. He looked at his father, eyes wide with shock, and said, 'I broke through, Da. I had to. You're dying.'

The warlock advanced on his son, and Khan saw the terror in his eyes as he demanded, 'You broke through what, exactly?'

Scrambling back as his father took a swing at his head, he said, 'Through your block! To save you! I went through the *Acronodium* – I could read it, Father! I've been practising since you came back from the battle. Today I finally broke through when I saw you in need.'

Galvos relaxed his fists, and said, 'What do you mean, you saw me in need? I stand here in front of you now.'

'No, Da, you're in a dream state. You're lying in bed, frail and weak. Blood is leaking from claw marks that appeared on your sides, and the healers are trying to save you, but I'm afraid they'll fail.'

Pointing to a small scar on his forehead, Galvos asked, 'Where did I get this?'

'When I was five, my little wooden axe slipped out of my hand as you were training me and hit your head. Almost took out your eye, but luckily it didn't.'

'Slipped, huh? Still sticking to that story?' Extending his arm, he reached out to pull Khanaseri up from the ground, then sighed deeply as he continued, 'You probably have lots of questions, but you shouldn't be here. Just know that I took your magic for your own safety. Not that it lasted, apparently. You must be stronger than I anticipated.'

A voice from the shadows said, 'What is this I see? An uninvited guest! You shouldn't be here, young man.'

The smell of sorcery stung Galvos' nose. His eyes flared wide, and he reacted as quickly as possible, jumping forward to crash into Khanaseri as a bladed chain whip whizzed past the younger man's face with terrible force to slice into Galvos' side. A scream of agony filled the air as she ripped the whip out, blood spurting from his side and onto the ground. Coughing up more, Galvos slowly got to his feet as he watched their assailant draw closer. A sense of triumph radiated from her.

The dark-hooded figure stood facing the old warlock, the whip a blur as she spun it with tremendous precision and grace. In a fight to keep his intestines on the inside, Galvos clutched his side as blood oozed from his wounds, spilling over his hands.

The assailant angrily stated, 'If you'd just given me the Balamuth, none of this would have been necessary! Look, I'm not unreasonable; I desperately need the Balamuth. If you get it back to me, I'll spare you and your son.'

The old warlock glanced at his son as he said, 'Why should I trust you?'

She moved back and caught the whip, then said, 'I don't want to murder you or anyone else. I'm not doing this for fun or out of spite; nor am I a crazy old wench who just wants to sow chaos. I'm here to find the Balamuth because I need to set things straight. Lives hang in the balance. But know this: all who stand in the way of my quest will fall.'

'And you expect me to believe this?'

'Do you have any reason not to?'

The question sent doubts through his mind, and the warlock preferred not to answer.

'In fact,' she continued, 'If you help me, I'll save your life right here, right now.'

Hearing this, Khanaseri shouted, 'Save him, please! Come on, old man, give her what she wants and be done with it. Don't be so stubborn!'

Galvos, without taking his eyes off her, shouted back, 'Stay out of this, Khan!'

For a heartbeat, Khanaseri thought his father was about to charge the woman when the warlock suddenly wheeled around, running straight at him, the deadly whip following close behind. Galvos slammed his hand to Khanaseri's forehead and shouted, '*Exvele!*'

It all happened so quickly. The last thing Khanaseri saw was the whip slicing into his father's back repeatedly, just before things went dark.

'No!' The scream erupted from Khanaseri as he jumped up from the infirmary's floor. Bewildered faces stared at him from the corners of the room as he looked about and got to his feet, then hurried to the bed and grabbed his father's hand. Foam and blood flowed from the old warlock's mouth, his body stiff and shaking as a fit overtook him. He watched his father being torn apart from the inside. The utter uselessness he felt crawled deep within his heart and soul, branding him forever. Vowing that he would never feel like this again, he unsheathed the knife at his side and brought it up to his father's throat.

'What are you doing? You mean to murder your own father now?' Gantris shouted as Khan looked into the frightened eyes of the healer.

Khanaseri looked down at his hands and said, 'He's being tortured to death, Gantris! What would you have me do? Let him suffer? Let my father endure more of this horrific violence? He's going to die, whether I ease his suffering or not. At least this way, it will be quick!'

An unnatural shout erupted from Galvos, shrieking through the room as he suddenly sat upright in the bed, eyes wide open and bloodshot. Foaming at the mouth, he grabbed the knife from Khanaseri and stuck it into his own throat, twisting the blade before pulling it out.

Everyone jumped back from the grisly scene, unable to comprehend what they had just witnessed as blood flooded from Galvos, causing him to die moments later.

* * *

'No! You weren't supposed to die! Can't you do *anything* right?' Pulling her hair, the hooded figure fumed as the grasp on the Balamuth stretched farther from her fingers. In a fit of rage, she flung everything from the desk and cabinets, shattering glass ornaments and scattering documents all over the floor. She grabbed the nearest piece of paper to wipe her hands on, then realised the blood had already dried and forwent the effort to rub them down.

'*Now* look at this, you imbecile. How am I supposed to walk out into the streets?'

The lifeless, twisted, obese man sitting in the chair opposite her stared with unseeing eyes as she screamed at him, the blood still pumping slowly from his cut throat. She rolled up the chain whip and placed it back on her hip as she said, 'At least I know now he has a son with some magical abilities. Hopefully, all is not yet lost. Can't you see I don't want to *do* these horrible things? But no one wants to help me in my quest!' Raging on as she yelled at the dead man, she raised her hands in the air, surrendering as she said, 'You shouldn't have tried to have sex with that little girl! You might have been alive now! So don't blame me.' Beuneth looked up at the little girl sitting on the staircase, shaking with terror, then said, 'Get! And stop whoring around!'

She glanced back at the dead man with a smirk, then looked down at her bloodied hands and left the little house.

* * *

Trembling with anger and anguish, Khanaseri walked through the deathly silent infirmary, oblivious to all the eyes following him. In a complete trance, he closed on the door and reached for the handle. Time passed as he stood in front of the big unmoving door, pushing and pushing, but nothing budged. The hall suddenly felt so very small, as if the walls were closing in on him. Sweat ran down his face. He felt like a deer being hunted, the hunter close by, chills running down his spine. A cornered animal. He grabbed the handle with both hands as he shook the door, pushing on it with all his might, when Gantris appeared out of nowhere and grabbed his arm as he said, 'Calm down, Khan. Brea—'

'Valoush!' Khanaseri shouted. The earth quaked from the explosive force that followed. The door was torn from its hinges and thrown into the street between the passers-by, striking down a woman in the crowd. Rubble and dust fell from his jacket and pants as, coughing, he got to his feet. His face was stained red from a shallow cut to his temple. His head pounding, he looked around and saw that everything and everyone that had surrounded him was now lying scattered on the floor.

'No, no, no no no. What have I *done*? I didn't mean to do this!' Running outside, he saw the carnage caused by his actions. A little boy's screams tore through his very being, sending him into a frenzy, running to help people up from the ground. Some bled a bit from their ears, others held their heads, but luckily, there were no lost limbs — so far. In the distance, he saw the broken door of the infirmary, a slender arm protruding from underneath. The sight of the unmoving body under the door sent shivers through his soul. As he ran to the door, he saw more people hurrying from all directions to see what was going on. He grabbed the door on one end and heaved, flipping it over and off the woman. The cut marks on her face and arms looked superficial. As he gently tore away the dress over her stomach to check for more serious injuries, she gasped for air and sat up, frantically grabbing at nothing as air rushed back into her lungs. Bewildered and shocked, she was unsure of where she was and what had occurred. Realising that a man had torn her dress, she feared for the worst and immediately scratched and kicked at her assailant.

'Wait! Stop that! I'm only trying to help! Wait!' Khanaseri grabbed her arms and held her tightly as she tried to bite him in the face and neck.

A vicious strike from a knee found its target, crashing into Khanaseri's testicles. Losing all ability to hold on to her or his breath, he dropped to the ground, gripping his privates. More vicious kicks rained down on him as the woman screamed at the top of her voice, 'You filthy fucking bastard! Taking advantage of a woman when she could have been dying, you worthless swine of a human being! How do you like me now, you piece of shit? Not so fun when I can hit back, huh?'

A crowd started gathering, seeing the brutal assault on Khanaseri, but none intervened. A few more kicks followed before he reached out and grabbed her foot, twisting it to make her lose her balance. Hitting the ground, she spun to see him staring down at her with his hand extended to help her up and heard him say, 'Please, I wasn't doing what you think. I was trying to see if you had any serious injuries on your stomach. With all the blood on your dress, I thought you were badly hurt. I'm Khanaseri.'

One man from the crowd shouted out, 'Heya girl, ya need us to call the guards on him?'

Looking around, she saw all the attention they had attracted and reluctantly accepted his hand as she said, 'Well, don't expect an apology from me. I'm sure you deserved it, one way or another. I'm called Beuneth.' She turned to the crowd and said, 'No, it's okay. Just a misunderstanding.' Opening the torn section of the dress, she looked at her stomach and said, 'Seems like a lot of minor cuts; nothing deep, luckily. What happened here?'

'Well, uh,' Khanaseri stuttered, then remembered the old healer being very close to him when all this had occurred. Eyes going wide, he shouted, 'Oh no, I need to check on Gantris! I think he might be hurt!'

'Wait!' Beuneth shouted, and followed him as he ran back into the infirmary.

He saw a charred half-moon burned into the floor as he entered. Beds were flipped, and some of the patients still lay on the ground, with others being helped back to their beds by the nurses. Arms flailed about as Gantris groaned from under a bed, then gasped as Khanaseri lifted the heavy frame from the old man's chest. The healer shouted, 'What have you done, boy?!'

At that very moment, guards ran through the doorway. One shouted to the others, 'Arrest him!'

Guards charged in at Khanaseri as he said, 'Wait, I didn't mean for any of this—'

A guard swung down a baton, hitting him over the head. A sudden explosion of pain, then darkness followed.

* * *

Creaks sounded, echoing in the cavernous prison as the heavy wooden door swung slowly open. King Naka entered the small gaol cell, pulling his face into a sneer as the rank odour stung his nose, then said, 'You know, the only reason you're alive today is because of the years of service your father devoted to this kingdom.' Shrugging, he continued, 'Well, that and because I will it so.'

A snort and brief laughter followed from Khanaseri as he said, 'Oh, I see. So I should be thankful that I'm basically drinking piss and shitting in a bucket in the corner of my "lodgings".'

'Yes, in a manner of speaking. Better this than being strung up by the neck or having your head lopped off with a blunt sword, wouldn't you say? The crowds wanted blood for the devastation you caused, not to mention the Keeper of Archives. What were you thinking, stealing the *Acronodium*? That alone is punishable by death.'

Shifting around on the dirty bed, Khanaseri lowered his head as he said, 'My father was being attacked by sorcery. I was his only hope. He didn't die naturally.'

'And so you were able to cast a spell from the book and enter his mind? That's what you would have me believe? You, a man who has shown no magical abilities? You know warlocks show their abilities from a very young age, right?' Moving around the small cell, King Naka dragged a chair from the corner with his foot. Sneering as he looked at the chair — grime all over it — he kicked it back to the corner and continued, 'For all the years of service your father gave me, I would really like not to kill his son. Please give me something to work with and get you out of this.'

'I'm telling you the truth, Your Majesty!' Khanaseri cried as he lunged up from the bed.

King Naka stood unflinching with his hands behind his back and said, 'Well do something. Create magic for me, or control it, or whatever it is warlocks do.'

Khanaseri walked past the king, and said, 'Fine, I'll blast this door off its hinges, the same as I did the one in the infirmary.'

'Oh, come now. I spoke to Gantris myself, and he assured me that the door was really old and the hinges were worn. You merely kicked the door hard enough to break it off the hinges.'

'He only said that not to get me into more trouble, I'm sure.' Mumbling under his breath, Khanaseri turned around to face the door, poised for the blast.

'Anytime you're ready,' King Naka said as he looked through the little barred window to find the sun, then continued, 'It's getting a bit late, and I would like to get back to my duties. You know...as king.'

With his eyes closed, expecting a big bang, Khanaseri shouted aloud, '*Valous!*'

Laughter rang out from behind him, and in between breaths, the king asked, 'Was that it?'

Ignoring him, Khanaseri shouted again, '*Valous!*' But nothing happened.

From over his shoulder, he heard the king say, 'Performance issues? Hey, you know, I have a remedy for that, but don't tell anyone. Bambil horns...changed my life, I tell you.' King Naka strode forward, and Khanaseri moved aside to let the king pass as he said, 'Guards! Open up.'

The door swung open, and King Naka strode gracefully through, then turned to say, 'Honestly, if you want to get out of here, you'll need to give me a reason. And well, the best reason would be magic. We could use more warlocks. They're a dying breed.'

Embers burst into flames in Khanaseri's head. Rage filled him, the sort that could devour the world. The heavy door creaked as it closed, the latch falling into place as the guards turned the key. The monolithic rage, fuelled by agony and hate for himself and everyone around him, burned brighter and brighter. Grabbing his head, Khanaseri felt ripples of energy flowing through him. Power tried to claw its way out, the yearning to be released tremendous. *Why does this hurt so much? What's happening to me?* Vision blurring, unable to see clearly, he looked around the room as it started morphing into a cave, the walls changing shape, almost disappearing altogether. Turning round and round, the beast still trying to fight its way out, head pounding, skin on fire, round and round... The hooded figure who killed his Da was suddenly right in front of him, reaching out to grasp hold of him.

He staggered back, tripped over the edge of the bed, and fell to the floor, hitting his head. The cave disappeared. His vision swam. Sweet darkness...

* * *

Unnerved, shaken, she stared down at her blood-soaked hands, remembering the feeling as she twisted the bladed chain around the fat man's neck, pulling it tighter and tighter, the blood running down and over her hands and chains, spilling to the floor; but she had only noticed the heat of the blood at that stage, blocking out the rest. Thrusting her hands into the bowl of warm water before her, she scrubbed and scrubbed to get rid of the red stains.

Finally satisfied that her hands were clean, Beuneth slumped to the floor, her breathing ragged, the rasp of the inhale and exhale making her clamp her hand over her mouth to stifle the sounds.

The room suddenly went cold, the hairs on her arms rising like the hackles of a beast. Alarmed, she jumped up as a tear in the fabric of space opened in front of her. Seeing Khanaseri in the goal cell, she reached out to grab him. He staggered back, and the rift closed instantly. With her adrenalin surging, she didn't realise that the wound in her side had opened up again, turning the dressing red. Her long black hair was caked with blood and pulled at her clothes, then only did she feel the stickiness of the blood on her arm. Beuneth removed her shirt carefully to examine the wound, standing naked while she pulled the bloodied strands of hair away in disgust. Bruises covered her left flank, with a big stab wound just below her kidneys. She ran her fingers over the stitches in her back and breathed a sigh of relief that they still held. Thinking back to the fight, she muttered, 'You were truly a great warlock. I'm sorry I had to do what I did.'

Chapter Two

Kremaghshi,

 We have taken losses. Two died in a tiger attack at camp, with two more wounded. We were ambushed by a hunting party of rogue goblins as we trekked the pass of Galbadore's Eye. Our Master Bowman took an arrow to the heart. We sustained minor injuries once we engaged in combat, but Ladriana will be sorely missed. She was unmatched by any other archer. There was nothing we could do. We also lost another at night when the idiot stepped into a wolf trap; snapped his leg clean off and bled to death. I have sent the injured back on a wagon with a host of four soldiers, including some horses.

 We have word of an old mine, abandoned by the dwarves long past. I think there could be a burial site there, although there are several suspected locations. People seem not to know their history well. Heading west to Serenity Peak. We could use reinforcements for the men we have lost.

 - Lanik -

* * *

Rolling up the small parchment, Lanik took one of the carrier pigeons from its cage and placed the message in the little bag on its back. Warm gusts of humid air blew through the forest as he walked out of the tent and released the pigeon. He then turned and sauntered through the encampment. The clearing was filled with tents, fires with cooking pots hanging over them, and soldiers standing about, some fighting and more drinking. He walked among the tents, searching the grounds for one he knew would be alone. Angry and frustrated as soldiers fell in his path, he grabbed a man by the back of the collar and said, 'Tapesh. Where is she?'

Almost dropping the tub of water he was carrying, the soldier cursed and shouted, 'Get your stinking hands off me!' He wheeled about and stared at his assailant. 'Oh, s-sorry, sir. Thought ye were someone looking for a pounding. Ye know Anavi, always alone. Scary that one. She be by the stone formations up on the hill. Should I go get her for ye?'

The tall man was suddenly limp in his grip; a high, dark ponytail bounced around on the top of his head like a fountain spewing water, the shaven sides marred by sores on his scalp. Drool dripped down his chin through the missing teeth from the tobacco plant he was chewing. He stank like an old whore who hadn't bathed for a year. Lanik shoved him aside and said, 'Nah, don't bother. I'll go to her. You, soldier, can take a bath with all that water you have there.'

The rise before him was virtually lifeless and barren of vegetation, except for a few weeds and a snake he noticed slithering in the distance. As he reached the summit, he saw her sitting cross-legged in front of the stone formation, just staring at it as if waiting for some unanswered question of eons past to be laid bare before her, to witness its revelation. With a body that swayed at the hips and wearing those ridiculously high-heeled boots, Lanik couldn't fathom how she was able to be a soldier. Long brown hair flowed over her shoulders, complementing the dark leather attire she usually wore over her voluptuous body, leaving very little to the imagination. Eyes of a tigress glared deep into your soul, rending at your heart if you stared a moment too long. A sharp face, a little too much so for Lanik; bony, it would seem. Anavi Tapesh was no hag, and deadly with any blade.

He cleared his throat and moved closer. 'They say these stone formations are evidence of a former race, you know. Once believed to be their last stand as they waged a battle with terrible beasts. Both now extinct. Or rumoured so, anyway.'

Without turning, Anavi muttered, 'No. That is not the case here.'

'Oh, and why do you say that?'

'They're not extinct. They just moved on. Speaking of moving on, when are you going to be done with all this sneaking around and move on with your life? How has Xylac not realised you're the one who orchestrated the betrayal of the Desert Dogs?' She gauged his movements and waited patiently for his reply.

Lanik groaned as he sat down on a rock, rubbed his hands to get rid of some small stones and sand stuck to his palms, and said, 'Soon, but not yet. I told you I'll break these Dogs piece by piece, even if it takes me years. Anyway, now he has us searching for this Gatekeeper's tomb. What is that even supposed to be? He hasn't given me all the information on this new charade. I fear he might suspect something.'

Unwavering, she crossed her arms as she asked, 'What is it you seek of me, Grey Cloak?'

He could hear birdsong in the distance, and rose from the rock with a sigh. 'It seems our esteemed leader has bitten off more than he's letting on. I'm not convinced that he knows what he's involved in.' He moved to stand before the hieroglyphs on the stones and studied them as she gazed at him from the back. 'Anavi. I need you to keep close to Xylac, and find out what he's up to when we're not around. Can you do that for me?'

'Of course, Grey Cloak. Consider it done.' She gazed at the glyphs beyond Lanik and continued, 'If you ever seek valuable allies, try to find these "dead civilisations".'

A chuckle sounded from Lanik before he asked, 'And just how do you propose I go about finding them?'

'Must I spoon-feed you with everything? Follow the stories laid out on the rocks.' Her brief outburst over, she rose and left the mountaintop to head back to the Ottiva Caves.

The Desert Dogs had been around for over a century, and most envied them their freedom until the day of their desertion at the Battle at Ormondeo. Xylac had offered the services of the Desert Dogs in the fight against the foreign Corlithians, who were rumoured to have magical devices capable of great destruction when thrown. It was during this war that the cowardice of the Desert Dogs was displayed. Shunned and banned from all cities, denied entrance to any event, they had a say no more; they existed to the world no more. The tale of their desertion spread like wildfire throughout the nation. No one wanted to hire them anymore. Thinking back to the day of the battle, Lanik found his emotions toying with him.

The echoes of the grenadier's charges rang in their heads; the smell of the explosive powder hung over the field of battle. An arrow dangled from his shoulder, and still he stood to fight beside his Kremaghshi, if only to see the look on the man's face when the time came. Lanik drew forth his sword with his left hand and charged with all his warriors beside him. A detonation went off in their midst; blood, body parts, flames, and in the distance, he saw a platoon riding away with the white-on-black, upside-down crossbow flag of the Desert Dogs held high. He looked over at Xylac and saw the shock register on the man's face. Crude, but effective. Lanik laughed...then darkness. And so, the Desert Dogs took the fall for cowardice that was not their own. The fall from grace was quick, the knife's edge sharp. It went off better than he could have hoped...

* * *

Cold and dark, the cavernous path had a rank odour due to the constant moisture in the air. A terrible stench of rotting plants stung their little nostrils. Squirms and the shuffling of tiny feet echoed throughout the corridor as the children were herded along, chains rustling around their hands and feet as it scraped on the cold rock floor.

Terrified, the little girl glanced back as a soft voice whimpered a few kids back, 'I want to go home. Why can't I go home?'

'Shh! Keep quiet — you're going to get us in trouble,' came another voice from down the line.

A thunderous crack sounded to her right moments before searing pain lanced through her back as the whip came down. A scream of agony erupted from the little girl as she fell to the ground. The woman carrying the whip moved closer and shouted, 'I said no talking!'

'But I didn't talk!' the little girl shouted back at her assailant with tears in her eyes.

The guard cocked her head and said, 'Does it look like I care? Now get up and move!'

The little boy behind her helped her back to her feet as the line started shuffling down the corridor once more. Lanterns hung on the sides of the rough rock walls, casting hideous shadows that danced in the gloom, sending shivers down her spine. Fear overpowered them into submission enough to continue forward.

They walked for what felt like a lifetime through the cave. The cold, damp air made their noses run, making them sniffle throughout the ordeal. Constantly chafing on the chains, they rubbed their wrists and ankles raw and were bleeding, leaving a long trail of blood spatters down the corridor. They approached a large black door with rust stains running down it. Shimmering lights reflected off the damp door, and the little girl could see the pattern of flow the moisture took when it ran down to the floor. The pit of her stomach was telling her one thing: *run!* But there was nothing she could do except whimper as the four women with their whips moved past them to open the door. Unable to cope with the stress, her eyes rolled to the back of her head as she collapsed to the ground, convulsing.

'You have *got* to be kidding me!' one woman shouted as she ran to the girl's side and forced the folds of her jacket into her mouth, so she didn't bite off her tongue. A child with no tongue was useless to them. As the fit eased, she picked up the girl and threw her over her shoulder, then marched through the door. Without hesitation, she threw the kid onto the first of the many beds lining the walls of the carved-out room and shouted, 'Okay, move along! Come through and get yourself a bunk.'

The young ones walked into the room, greeted by the stares of more kids a little older, huddled in the back. As the children stood next to their beds, the four women, who were dressed in all-black attire, stood in a line before the door and one announced, 'The room is yours, Vandalor!'

The mood in the room suddenly changed as the lanterns on the walls were snuffed out by a powerful gust of wind that seemingly came from nowhere. When the four women relit their lanterns, a fifth stood before them clad in red leggings and a black woollen gambeson, her black lips stretching overly wide as she excessively rounded her words. 'Good day, children, I am Vandalor. I am the one all problems come to, as in if *you* are a problem.'

As she stared at the new batch of children, one of them shouted, 'I want to go home! I miss my mommy!' Immediately, one of the bigger kids in the room closest to the little girl clasped his hand over her mouth, whispering, 'Keep quiet!'

Resuming, Vandalor looked at the little girl with long, deep-black hair where she lay on the bed. 'What's wrong with this one?' she asked with a sneer.

One of the four women moved forward and said, 'She got out of line in the corridor, so I whipped her. The wound isn't too deep. She then had a fit outside the door. I had to carry her in. I fear she'll be useless to us and needs to be disposed of.'

Kneeling at the little girl's side, Vandalor said, 'Oh, dear little one, we can't have you having fits and the sort. You'll draw far too much attention, and we don't like attention. Now, what is your name?'

Sniffs and whimpering escaped the girl's mouth before she squeaked, 'Beuneth.'

'Oh, that's a pretty name. Look at me, child.' Vandalor moved the girl's hair out of her face to behind her right ear and saw a nip at the top, then stared deep into her bottomless black eyes. As if some untold emotion haunted her, Vandalor quickly looked away, then said, 'Will you show me where you were hit with the whip?'

A brief nod came from Beuneth as she turned around and raised her shirt to reveal her back.

Vandalor removed her gloves and brushed her hand across the child's back as she gazed at it and felt the soft indentations of older scars. 'Astonishing.' *What is this feeling I have as I look at you, child? This feeling of pure – no,* raw *potential. Power, maybe...*

Vandalor rose from the bed and had almost made her way to the four women when another child ran to her side, grabbed her hand, and shouted, 'Please let us go home!' Without even the slightest thought to it, she pulled back her hand and swung it down hard, slapping the child off his feet. The little blond boy skidded into a bed a few feet away. Everyone gasped. Sounds of muffled cries filled the chamber as some of the younger ones wailed in the cups of their hands. Turning to regard all of them again, Vandalor said, 'I am now your mother! Don't run from me! You're worth nothing to your parents! They sold you to me for so little they almost had to pay me to take you. That's how little you meant to them. Now. Here with me, you will at least have a bed, food, clothes, and purpose. Without purpose in life, we are all worthless, just husks stealing precious air from those who *have* purpose.'

Turning towards the four women, she demanded, 'Was she whipped hard enough to have bled?'

The one who had whipped her moved forward again and said, 'I believe so. I didn't hold back.'

'Keep an eye on that one. Let nothing happen to her. Are we clear?'

'Yes, Vandalor,' came the four voices in unison.

The air before Vandalor suddenly tore open to a new place beyond; she stepped through and vanished from their sight as all the lanterns were extinguished again, and this time, they remained so. The door swung closed as the four women left the chamber.

Impenetrable darkness surrounded them; sounds of scuffling and whimpers could be heard before one of the older boys lit a match and walked to the closest lantern, saying, 'Welcome to Alcaroah. Don't get too comfortable. We have rules here, and you will all abide by them. Number one. No more crying.'

* * *

In one fluid motion, Beuneth sat up in the bed as a dagger flew from her hand. A few squeaks quickly followed the dull thud before silence returned. 'Guess I'm having rat for breakfast,' she muttered. Through a tear high in the cave roof, the sun's deep orange rays were already peeking through. *I still can't believe she sold me to that woman. How could my mother throw me away like that? One day, I'll track her down and find out.*

Beuneth scowled as she retrieved her dagger — the rat skewered through. With her prize in hand, she walked through the cave and headed for the entrance. Tents were pitched haphazardly around the grassless area out front. The Ottiva Caves were notorious for their surrounding deadness. Few things grew in the immediate vicinity, save the hardiest of weeds. Beuneth surveyed the barren lands before her as a lean, balding man, his few remaining hairs greased back — most likely with spit — sauntered towards her, ogling her body as he neared. 'What do you have there?' he asked, spitting to the side.

'What does it look like, Xylac? Breakfast. Send one of your goons with some firewood, would you? I'm starving.'

Xylac looked to the cave, then back at Beuneth as he sat back on his haunches. 'How can you sleep in there? I mean, I've had my fair share of sleeping in caves overnight. But I don't choose to sleep there every night.'

'Just send someone with the wood.'

He worked something loose in his mouth with his tongue and stood back up, making sucking sounds as he did, and finally let out a whistle and waved a man closer. Glaring at the man as he strolled up to them, Beuneth clenched her teeth, her jaw muscles working back and forth in frustration. *Oh, I cannot wait to be done with these idiots. But they serve their purpose for now.*

As the man eventually arrived, Xylac slapped him on the head and said, 'Move faster, you dimwit! You're keeping the lady waiting.'

She handed the skewered rat to the man, and said, 'Skin it, clean it, and grill it over a fire, then bring it to me.' Turning around, she moved back into the cave to enter a chamber with a map sprawled open on a table, the ends pinned down by some rocks and a candelabrum. She still stood over the table when the Kremaghshi entered the chamber. 'Update me on the search,' she ordered. 'I have plans dependent on their findings.'

Xylac strolled over in a lazy saunter as he said, 'Aw, missy, don't you worry so much about the little things in li—'

Before he finished his sentence, he was dangling in the air and experiencing the fury in the eyes of the sorceress, raw power radiating from her. A cut to his leg from out of nowhere sent blood spurting to the stone floor as she said, 'Don't you ever test me with your childish provocation again. Do you understand me? I'll kill you where you stand — or hang, as the case may be. You're nothing to me. A worm that slithers its way across a barren field is worth more than you.'

A strangled gurgle came from the man. 'Forgive…me…my queen.'

'Queen? I am not your *queen*, nor do I want to be.'

With a thump, he fell to the ground, gasping for air, coughing and spitting until he could speak. 'We received word this morning. The search continues. They haven't found the tomb yet. But I'm confident that they will soon. If I may ask, what do you hope to achieve with this tomb? What's buried there?'

'A key.' Beuneth turned her attention back to the map and continued, 'I need you to clear out of the area. Join the others for the search or go back to your hideout. I don't care. I can't have you seen here.'

Getting to his feet, Xylac spat against the wall and left the room.

* * *

Room with a view, he says. I can be glad, he says. Idiot. Squeaking sounds came from his right. Without looking, he tore off a piece of the bread in his hands and dropped it on the floor. The little mouse scampered for the prize. Hanging his arms outside the barred window, he sighed and muttered, 'I'm sorry for failing you, father.' A terrible cold suddenly enveloped the room. He hugged himself with his big arms as he turned and demanded, 'What in the...' The heat returned to the room as a note appeared out of thin air, drifting down to his feet. *Where did this come from?*

He picked it up, slowly opened it, and read in a whisper, *'Valoush.'* The slip of parchment was ripped out of his grip and torn in two. He shook his head in disbelief as he stared down at his hands, then moved to the door and planted his feet firmly on the floor, extended his arms — half covering his face — and shouted, *'Valoush!'* Bricks, mortar, timbers, and iron bars flew through the corridor as the explosion rocked the room, throwing him from his feet. His ears were ringing, but he could still hear the alarm bell in the distance, and got up from the floor in haste. Coughing from the dust, he moved through the strewn rubble as a guard closed in with spear in hand, shouting, 'Hey, you! Stop right there!'

The guard stepped in and swung the spear to knock him down, but missed as Khanaseri sidestepped and ducked under the swing. He sent a fist to the guard's face, breaking his nose and knocking him out cold. His heart pounded in his chest; his hands trembled as he moved his long, dirty black hair out of his face. *I guess I am doing this, then.* More guards appeared to his right, charging at him with batons. Ducking and weaving, he slid past the first attacker's blows, grabbed the guard from behind, and hurled him through the air to crash into two other guards, taking them all to the ground like a bunch of bowling pins. The fourth guard rushed in with a short sword, slicing up, down, left, and right. *Must be a recruit; that's the very first move you learn in training.* Stepping left, stepping right, he tucked and rolled up to the guard and thundered an uppercut to his jaw. The guard's eyes rolled back as he fell to the ground.

The rest of the guards were getting back on their feet as he ran for the door.

Khanaseri rounded the corner to go down the stairs and ran straight into a guard coming up. The momentum drove them both tumbling all the way down. The world spun as he tried to focus on his whereabouts. He found that a vicious cut on his forearm was bleeding profusely. He then saw the blood on the sword lying loose in the guard's hand. A groan sounded as he rose from the floor clutching his arm, then looked down at the guard. The man's neck was bent on the last step, and he knew it was broken. *Shit, that wasn't part of the plan. I'm sorry, friend.* 'How am I going to get out of *this*?' he wondered aloud.

Quickly tearing off the hem of his shirt, he tied it round his arm and opened the door. *Walk calmly. Don't draw attention to yourself.* Strolling from the prison door as casually as a merchant in a fruit market, he headed for the gate. *Come on, just a little farther.* From his left, a shout came, 'Oi! You there! Stop!' *Oh, balls.* Khanaseri ran for the gate as the guards gave chase.

'Stop, or we'll shoot!' came a shout from the gate, which was lined with guards equipped with bows and arrows. Luckily for him, a tear in the fabric of space opened up right in front of him, swallowing him as he sailed through and vanished right before the guards' disbelieving eyes.

* * *

All light seemed to vanish as he fell through the portal, the soft sand replaced by wet rocks, sharp and unforgiving to any skin that came in contact with it. Slipping and sliding, he stumbled through the dark, straight into an iron bar. A harsh clang sounded as a bolt fell into place. Khanaseri knew that sound all too well from his time in the gaol. 'No!' Turning, he squinted to gauge where his captor might be in the dark. He squeezed his eyes shut and opened them for a bit, then slowly made out some outlines, seeing a vague figure moving around slowly, observing him.

'Who are you? What do you want from me? I have no coin!' he shouted, but the figure wouldn't answer. Standing back, he said, 'You asked for it. *Valoush!*' He opened his eyes one at a time, expecting a blast, but nothing happened. Again, he shouted, '*Valoush!*' Adjusting his stance, he moved closer and uttered, '*Valoush.*' *I don't understand.*

'It won't work in there.'

'You? I know your voice! You killed my father!' Charging at the bars, he slammed his body against them. The thud to the iron reverberated throughout the cave. He reached out to grab hold of the figure, but it was a futile effort. Lowering his arms, he demanded, 'Answer me! Why did you kill him?'

The silence grew, spanning a lifetime as the figure walked about the dark cave. With the snap of fingers that echoed in the chamber, a blue flame appeared in a lantern that hung from the wall. Then another, and another. Slowly, the room was lit, revealing the breadth of the cave and the massive pit to the side. Before him stood the most beautiful woman he had ever seen, with her long black braided hair swinging halfway down her back. He stared as she walked closer, the sway of her hips in her tight black pants irresistible. 'You?' Khanaseri muttered, his eyes wide, his mouth hanging open. He stood as he said, 'You were at the infirmary. Beuneth, right? *You* killed my father?'

'That wasn't my intention. I pleaded with him to help me instead. But he wouldn't listen to reason. In the end, it was him or me. So I chose me.'

'I should kill you where you stand.'

'I *can* kill you where you stand. Remember that. But I'm also choosing not to.'

'Well, maybe you should!' Enraged, he slammed his palm against the iron bar and felt a bit of movement. Again, he slammed his palm against the bar, and again.

'Stop that! What are you doing?' Beuneth shouted as she readied herself. A loud clang sounded as the iron bar broke out of place to hit the ground. Instantly, Khanaseri rushed at her, reaching for her throat. Unexpectedly, a chain whip wrapped around his wrists and flung him through the air. He hit the wall with tremendous force, the wind knocked from his lungs. He gasped for air as he righted himself. This time, he came at her with more caution. '*Valoush!*' he shouted, sending the blast wave hurtling towards her. Thrown off-balance by the force of the blast, he rushed in as soon as he could move.

Beuneth waved her hand, dissipating the blast; but she reacted too slowly, and Khanaseri tackled her off her feet. With blistering speed, he rained down blow after blow. Beuneth, finding cover behind her arms, knew she would not last long against this assault. The big man towered over her, picked her up, and launched her into the air. As nimble as a cat, she spun as she sailed toward the wall, righting herself and landing on her feet, skidding to a halt on the stony floor.

The whip was a blur as it spun around her and she advanced on Khanaseri. With a quick turn, the whip shot out in an arc, heading for his head. As he dived as fast as he could to the left, it came swishing past, missing by a mere hair's-breadth. The speed and fury with which the chain came at him was relentless. Missing with another throw, the blade tip thundered into the timber struts of the cage, almost splitting it in two.

Spinning through the air, her foot caught him in the face and hurled him to the ground. *Dammit, I think she knocked a tooth out.* Groggy, he tried to rise, but before he could, he felt the chain wrap around his arms and neck, constricting him, the blades biting deep. Even though he was stronger, she had him in a death-grip. The life was being choked out of him. Strained gasps escaped his mouth as he struggled to breathe, unable to break the chain.

Screams of fury erupted from her as she pulled on the chain. Flashes of her fights with Vandalor seeped into her vision, her hatred burning bright. She shook her head when she felt no more struggling beneath her and finally eased her grip on the chain. She dropped it and backed away, breathing deeply to catch her breath. Khanaseri rolled to the ground in a heap, his lips turned blue from the asphyxiation.

'No, no, no. Not again. Beuneth, you idiot.' She quickly turned him over and locked her lips to his, blowing air into his lungs. Tears ran down her face as she slammed on his chest with her fist, over and over, then blew more air into him. 'Come on, breathe!'

With a mighty gasp of air, his eyes flared open. Shocked and confused, he looked around and, between breaths, ordered, 'Stay away from me.' Leaning against the wall, he lowered his head. 'Why did you save me?'

'Like I told you, I never wanted to kill anyone! I need your help, just like I needed your father's help.' She moved closer and pulled a wineskin off the wall, and threw it to Khanaseri as she said, 'You might want to know that *I* didn't kill your father. I might have had a part to play, but I didn't draw the knife.'

Khanaseri frowned as he said, 'What do you mean?'

'He mistook my enthusiasm for wanting the Balamuth, thinking I wanted it for something bad, for myself...I had him beat, and he knew it. So he did the only thing I didn't plan for...'

'He killed himself.' Stunned, Khanaseri bowed his head, then drank a huge gulp of wine before he said, 'I can't believe it. I thought it was sorcery.'

Beuneth settled on her haunches. 'I wouldn't have killed him. I was actually going to heal him once he agreed to help me. From the little I know of him, I admired greatly. And for what happened, I'm truly sorry.'

'My father died keeping you away from this Balamuth. What reason is there for me to help you?'

Beuneth rose and cried, 'He died for the wrong reasons! Please, I beg of you! Your blood connection to your father is the only way to find out where he sent the Balamuth. It could be anywhere!'

'What makes you think he didn't destroy it? From what Ganda'har told me, that was his aim, after all.'

'I don't believe it was destroyed. Your father would have had to use all his power to destroy it, and with him stabbed several times, there's no way he would have been able to pull it off.' With her index finger drumming her mouth, she said, 'You fight well enough. What training do you have?'

'First Infantry, corporal. I've served in the army for just over three years, and I'm damn good at it. I was recently promoted, so they gave me

some time off before I had to start my new duties. You know the rest.'
He threw the empty skin to her and said, 'So what now?'

'If you're willing to help me retrieve the Balamuth, I'll teach you all
I know to help you master your abilities. You'll feel a power unlike any
other.'

'Tell me more of this Balamuth, and why you need it so badly.'

* * *

Guards were running around the yard, trying to restore order after the
chaos caused by Khanaseri's breakout. Some limped away with the aid of
other guards, making their way to the healer's hall. King Naka walked
the grounds, looking at the officers shouting orders, then called for the
nearest. As the man jogged up to the king, his short, stocky body
reminded King Naka of the pigeons outside his bedroom window every
morning, with their chests all puffed out. *Oh, how I hate those things,
always shitting on everything. And so noisy.* The man's red hair flopped
around as he ran, irritating the king even more. Unwilling to make eye
contact with the man, Naka demanded, 'What happened here?'

Bowing awkwardly, the guard said, ''Twas that prisoner Khanaseri,
Yer Highness. 'Scaped his quarters somehow. 'Splosion rocked the
whole yard. Felt it a mile away.'

The king sighed, trying his best not to look at the man. *Oh, why
today? He even speaks like an idiot.* 'How did he escape, man?'

Flustered, the officer awkwardly bowed again and continued, 'Oh,
yes. Apologies, me Lordship. Vanished right before our very eyes, sir.
We'ze were stationed at the gate, saw him running straight at us. We'ze
drew our bows and then poof, gone. Nothing.'

Finally meeting the man's eyes, King Naka said, 'Get me Lieutenant
Ganda'har. And shave your head, soldier.'

Saluting, the guard turned around and ran away, greasing his hair
with spit as he did.

* * *

'Your Majesty,' came a voice from behind as footfalls drew closer in the vast, empty hall. Taking another grape from a table filled with an abundance of food, the king turned around to see the lean, tall warrior kneeling before him and said, 'Rise now as Captain Ganda'har, and get yourself something from the table. The grapes are exceptional.'

Ganda'har's emotions toyed with him, as the promotion was something he had wanted for a while, but not at the expense of his friend's life. 'Thank you, Your Majesty.' Ganda'har stepped over to the table and plucked a few grapes and some cheese. 'You're right, Your Majesty. These grapes are good.' Ganda'har stuffed a piece of cheese in his mouth, enjoying the rich taste melting on his tongue. Not wanting to look barbaric, he turned away from the table and said, 'What service do you require of me, Your Majesty?'

The king's long, flowing robe dragged over the polished marble floor as he moved to sit on the throne in the centre of the room, gesturing Ganda'har closer. 'I have a matter of urgency for you to attend to. Galvos' son escaped from the dungeons. It seems he has his father's gifts, and—'

'They imprisoned *Khan*? For what?' Shocked by the news, he didn't even realise that he had interrupted the king.

King Naka gestured with his hands as he said, 'He injured people in and near the infirmary by means of magic, and stole the *Acronodium*.'

'What? That's crazy! That's punishable by death. Why would he do that?'

'I can't blame him. He wanted to help his father. But that's not the point of this conversation.' Drawing a deep breath, King Naka continued, 'I would never execute him. He's been through enough. I actually wanted to see if he had his father's gifts and promote him as squad warlock if so...but he broke out before we had a chance to really talk.'

Shocked by this news, Ganda'har reeled back as he said, 'I've known

Khan since he was a babe. He's like a son to me. Why wasn't I told?'

Tilting his head, the king frowned as he said, 'Remember to whom you speak, Captain. Now, I have this for you. I believe the person who attacked Galvos is after Khanaseri to find the orb. So if you find him, you find the person who killed Galvos, and hopefully, the orb. Kill the bastard and bring back Khanaseri as well as the orb. Your priority, though, is the orb. Be very clear on this, Captain. We can't have a warlock roaming about freely with no allegiance to the kingdom, harbouring ill will. If you can, bring him back; if not, kill him. Are we clear?'

The room was suddenly hot, the walls closing in. Ganda'har merely nodded and said, 'Yes, sire. It will be done.'

'Good.' Rising to his feet, King Naka wiped his hands together, brushing crumbs to the floor. 'He was last seen in the gaol yard before he vanished. I would start there. Take a squad of Kamatayon with you. We don't know if they've found the orb, or how many men you could be facing.'

Barely bringing up his hand, Ganda'har saluted the king and headed for the door, walking as fast as he could to get out of the hall. Once outside, he bent over a bush and vomited. He wiped his mouth with his sleeve and spat once more, cursing before he continued to the gaol.

* * *

Very far away, across the vastness of the Beladon Sea, a man named Ozo — a vision of ambivalence — floated around the village market of Sethinai, unsure of what he wanted, or where he wanted to be. Reaching the temple of Teros, he ambled into the centre of the prayer hall and sat down on the floor, crossing his legs. The aroma of rabbit stew filled his nostrils — the only part of his face not discoloured by ink — as it was being prepared in the back for the hungry and the homeless.

He looked up at the statue that was Teros portrayed, then snorted and blew snot from his nose through his fingers to the floor. For the last few weeks, visions of his riddled past had haunted him, confusing him even more. To his left, people prayed to their god, while to the right, some stared at him in disgust, but he didn't care. Rather, he pulled at the loose, weathered skin on his biceps and muttered to his fellow worshippers, 'I have seen it with my own eyes, you know. They were chasing him, hunting him down in the forest. I was a distance away, watching from behind a tree. Just when they did not see, he changed. Veered into a nasty, big grey wolf. It is unnatural.'

The tattooed man rose and raised his voice when no one wanted to listen, louder and louder until it was a scream, sounding out over the serene humming of the temple dwellers. 'There is going to be death in this world the likes of which you people have not seen!' Frantic, the village guards came rushing in to subdue and restrain the man. A shout rang out from one guard. 'Calm down, Ozo, dammit! Relax.'

Receiving a slap across the face, Ozo stiffened and stared at the guard with contempt. Young and lean, with a face he knew well, the man looked back into his eyes. Suri said, 'Please, Ozo, relax. You know what the punishment is for causing a disturbance in the temple. They'll behead you if you don't quiet down.'

With no other possible outcome, Ozo relaxed in their grips as they escorted him out, and said in a low voice, 'One would think that the merciful god they portray him as would be just that.'

The guard lowered his mouth to Ozo's ear and said, 'That is the *god*, my friend, not his people. We are infinitely crueller.'

* * *

The sun was beating down, but little heat reached the land. Winter was fast approaching, and Ozo felt the chill running through his skin as they moved higher up the mountain towards his cabin overlooking the valley. Only Suri still followed him up the path; the rest of the guards had turned back. Mumbling away, the darkly tattooed man halted and turned to his escort, saying, 'Thick-headed, the bunch of them, I tell you! Do you believe me, Suri? Do you believe what I saw?'

Suri shrugged to state his indifference, which only enraged Ozo even more.

A large rock flew through the air as Ozo launched it and screamed his irritation about everything. 'You young, uncaring, selfish, self-obsessed little shits of today's world! I feel like wringing your necks! Grow a pair and start giving a crap about something other than yourself for a change!' He turned around and stomped off, leaving a trail of dust up to his cabin, and slammed the door shut.

Suri sighed and turned around as he said, 'Goodbye, Ozo. It was nice seeing you too.'

* * *

'Choose your weapon.'

Khanaseri stepped forward, picked up a short sword, and swung it in an arc, up and down. Feeling the weight of it, he frowned and placed it back on the rack, then moved to the next: a long wooden spear. He moved back a step and started swinging it around. The swoosh of the long timber echoed in the cave. Stabbing and twirling it through the air, he jumped up, bringing it down with tremendous force, splitting the spear in half as it hit the ground. 'Well, I can't have that happen during a fight...'

'True, but that's not the weapon's fault. You need to be more flexible and sensitive when working the spear. It's not a sword.'

Staring at the woman in the cave's corner, he put the broken spear back on the rack and took up a crude battle axe. With a smirk, he said, 'My father had a battle axe like this, but better.' The weight of the weapon made him smile, and he ran his hand over the sharpened blade, then the spiked end on the other side. 'I've always wanted to fight with it. Why can't I go back to Artorea?'

'I told you, they're hunting you for killing that guard.'

Angry, he stormed forward with the axe pointed at her and said, 'That was an accident!'

'All the same, the man is dead, and several others have severe injuries. Do you think they would take kindly to the man who killed one of their brothers?' Cold air formed in the cave, the wet rocky surface and wall freezing over as the cold expanded. A heartbeat later, Beuneth was gone.

In the void of the cave, standing in solitude, memories of his father training him filled his mind as he spun the crude axe in his hands. He chopped down, up, side to side. *What did she say again? Think what you want to let happen and speak the words.* He said, 'Belavos, et siliate!' Nothing happened. *Oh yeah. I forgot; some sorcery needs to be targeted.*

'Three should be enough for now,' he said as he moved the tables in the cave to form a square before him, then took up the axe again and stepped back from the first table. Focused and ready, Khanaseri charged forward and swung the axe down with all his might, shouting as the axe made contact, 'Belavos, et siliate!'

The blade sank into the table's frame, breaking rather than cutting a piece off the furniture. It rebounded and was ripped from his hands, making a swooshing sound as it scythed the air to hit the rock face some distance behind him. Sudden pain lanced through his right hand, and he brought it up to stare at. A large gash had opened on his palm, a tear more than a cut. His hand trembled, and he quickly bound it with a rag from one table. 'Blistering balls in a vice! That hurt! So that's what she meant when she said, "magic bites".' *What did I do wrong?*

Khanaseri retrieved the axe from the wall and lined up before the tables again. The axe ricocheted off the surface as he brought it down, barely leaving a mark as it flung back, hitting Khanaseri full in the face with the flat of the blade. Blood seeped from his nose and he cursed as he rubbed his tender face and stamped his foot, glancing about to see if Beuneth was around to witness his shameful failure.

He picked up the axe again and closed his eyes as he lined up, saying the words over and over in his head as he visualised the tables before him. The hairs on his arms prickled as he focused on his task. 'Belavos, et *siliate!'* he shouted as he charged and swung the axe down to make contact with a thunderous crash. Split in two, the first table flew forward and shattered against the wall; the second cracked and fell to the floor in half. The third had a tear running two-thirds of the way through to the end. Laughing, he brought the axe down and chopped the last third of the table to see it crash to the floor.

'Oh, boy. What else can I practice on?' *That felt good. Father, how I wish you were here to see.*

'You're smiling.'

Snapped out of his thoughts, Khanaseri's smile faded and was replaced by a sneer as he returned the axe to the rack. 'Yes, well. No thanks to you.'

'Let's go outside. We need to begin your training. Take this with you.'

He turned to meet her eyes and saw the massive axe in her hands, its silver-winged tip resting on the ground. Quickly walking to her, he took the axe from her reluctant grip and said, 'Now *this* is an axe. My father fought countless battles with it. How did you get it?'

Reaching out, Beuneth restrained herself and pulled back her hand. 'You should be careful with this weapon. It has great power. See the symbols etched into the blade? They draw power from its wielder.'

'Then it's good that I have so much of it.' With a smirk, he continued, 'Didn't you see what I did to those tables with a normal axe?'

'Don't be a fool!' The unintentional shout slipped out before she could stop herself. Memories of prison rocked her mind. The pain they had bestowed upon her. No sunlight for years. Breathing deep, she slowly walked towards him and pointed to the bed in the corner, saying, 'I brought you some clothes from your home.' As she made to pass him, he grabbed her arm, and she flinched in pain, muttering a curse.

His hand slipped from her, slick with blood. In the dim light of the cave, he hadn't seen her injury. 'What happened?' he asked as he looked at her.

With an icy stare, Beuneth said, 'I told you they're looking for you. Turns out they were waiting at your home. When I came through the portal, they attacked without question. I'll be outside shortly. Just give me a moment alone.'

As Beuneth turned, he saw the slash across her left arm and back, her shirt and flesh ripped open by a vicious sword cut. Blood dribbled down, dripping to the floor as she slowly made her way to her room. She reached under the bed and pulled out a small bag, her hands shaking from the pain as she readied the needle and thread to pierce her skin and close the wound, when Khanaseri walked in.

'That will get infected if you don't clean it first.'

'What do you care? You'll have your vengeance then.'

'Just give it to me,' Khanaseri said as he sat behind her on the bed. *Focus.* With a snap of his fingers, a small fire danced in the palm of his hand, and he smiled. Holding the needle over it for some time, he then quenched the flame and threaded the needle through her skin. 'It will take some time to heal, but you should be okay.'

Her head dropped in her hands as she said, 'Thank you, Khan.'

* * *

Ozo sat on the windowsill overlooking his vegetable garden. The tomatoes were ripening, the tops of carrots were sticking out of the ground, and the cabbage was growing wild. The unexpected heat of the early morning sun was increasing at a rapid rate. Sweat trickled down, stinging his eyes, and forced him to close them. *The village was under siege...* Quickly opening his eyes from the fright of the vision, he shook his head and closed his eyes again, forcing them shut to see the blood of that day.

Fire and lightning rained down from the sky as soldiers died around him. There was someone behind him. He felt their presence, but couldn't turn to see who it was. Someone broke his arm then, and he could remember the pain. Then darkness. A thrill arose in him, coursing through his body as he opened his eyes and looked at his garden, then placed his hand upon his chest. The beating of his heart had turned into a thunder, now slowly calming as he said to himself, 'What happened that day? I think a walk through the forest would do me good.'

Why does it feel like I'm being watched? Even if I'm the one doing the watching. Something feels out of place. It has for a long time. Where do I come from? Who was I? Who am I? The years have gone by, and yet I've made no effort to find out. I simply am...

Time, they said, would reveal my secrets to me, but alas, nothing. I have to start looking, but where? What was the flash I saw? Was that the preternatural event that caused me to forget?

Walking in a haze, Ozo soon discovered he had wandered deep into the forest with no recollection of how he'd gotten there. It felt like a mere heartbeat had passed, but the sun was almost gone. Defeated by his own thoughts, he muttered, 'Oh, hell. I'll never make it back to the cabin before nightfall. Best I look for a place to make camp.' He gathered some branches for a fire as darkness slowly crept in. The cooling air brushed his skin, giving him goosebumps, sending a wave of enjoyment through his body. Suddenly Ozo felt as if he must have been very busy during his past life, as if he hadn't taken enough time to smell the roses, as they say. Then depression took him by surprise. Sighing deeply, he resumed his twig collection, then cleared an area for camp.

'I do love the solitude of the forest; I just wish I had someone to enjoy it with.' Talking on and on, Ozo took some twigs, laid them out on top of each other with dry grass stuffed in the middle, and rubbed two twigs together with great fervour. Soon after, smoke trailed. As he gently blew on the spark, the fire took shape and the crackling of wood started. *A sweet sound.* He pulled out a knife and cut his nails, falling back in thought. He sat close to the dancing flames and, with a slip of the knife, cut deep into his finger, sending curses through the forest. Blood spurted out onto the flames — and a sudden eruption threw him off the rock. More curses followed as he lay on his back, coughing.

'What in the bloody name of all that is not well with this world was that?' came a voice from the woods, and two figures emerged from the gloom. Ozo quickly sat up to meet their eyes, then rose when he saw they were carrying long knives.

'Now, now, fellas, I don't want any trouble. I don't even have anything with me here. You're welcome to join the fire, but other than that I have nothing to offer.'

Advancing on Ozo, the fatter of the two men said, 'I think you should come with us. Pa would want to skin a witch!'

With a quick dive round the fire, old Ozo squeezed on his finger, sending a large spurt of blood through the flames, causing another eruption as the blaze sprayed all over the fat man, igniting him completely. He ran through the forest screaming in agony, dropped and rolled, but the flames wouldn't die. Sudden silence and a pungent stink of burnt flesh and clothing hung in the air. Ozo looked for the second man, but saw nothing. Tension rose in him as he sensed the man behind him, but it was too late to act; a strike to the head, and the smell of dirt was the last thing he remembered.

The smell of burnt flesh...a sphere... Blood...more so on his hands...yellow eyes, a serpent's hiss... Death.

Chapter Three

Leaves rustled as the wind sighed through the trees, bringing a sense of calm to the area as Khanaseri sat cross-legged in the woods with closed eyes. Serene, his thoughts drifted away with the sounds of Beuneth's chants before him. The ritual had been going on for quite some time as she sat, stirring the bowl of fox blood with her fingers. The constant drumming of the chant sent Khanaseri's senses into disarray, pulling him away from reality. His mind wandered, letting go of its ties to the world.

'Open your eyes,' said Beuneth, as she rose to her feet and looked over a vast plain of rolling fields. 'We're here.'

His eyes fluttered as he tried to focus, then looked around and said, 'Where exactly is *here*?'

'Let's just say that time doesn't matter as much here. This is where you will train. Think of an opponent and he'll be here to fight you. Just don't go too far with your ego; if you get hurt here, you get hurt in the real world.'

'So, the same trick you pulled with my father.'

Caught off guard, Beuneth stammered, losing her words before Khanaseri interjected, 'Don't worry. I didn't mean it like that.'

She stared into his eyes, the deep greens not revealing any emotions.

Those eyes; they remind me so much of Mother. 'In that case, yes, it *is* the same spell I used. He fought me for what felt like days.'

On the field of long grass, they turned to face each other. Beuneth closed her eyes for an instant, and a whip materialised in her hands as she said, 'Now, we'll start with the three most important basics: breathing, control, and focus. If you can't master them, this is pointless.'

'Pff, I've been trained. I'm not some fresh recruit on his first day at boot camp.'

A slap fell across his right cheek. 'Yes, you're right. Very trained. Now listen to me! The first time I saw your father, he was casting the spell on the Balamuth. He was so entranced, he didn't even flinch when a man jumped over the line of defenders and stabbed him twice in the chest. *That* is focus.'

'Sounds like him. Stubborn till the end.' The earth felt rich and moist as Khanaseri took a handful to rub over his arms and hands, then said, 'I've been practising the incantation to home in on this Balamuth. It keeps pulling me to the west, but it feels very distant.'

Beuneth uncurled the long whip, her head cocked to the side and her eyes darting over the field. She looked back up and said, 'Makes sense it would take you to the area your father sent it from. That's where the connection was severed. So we'll ride for Tergaron and get as close to the city as we can; but first, we'll train until I believe you're ready.' Working her feet to stand firmly on the ground, she continued, 'Enough talking. Now, focus on the incantation. Create a ring of fire around us. Do *not* lose your concentration. If the fire dies, I hit you with the whip. Sounds simple, right?'

A mighty crack from the whip sounded right next to his left ear, and he dived to the right, cursing as he did.

'I *said*, don't break your concentration.'

The whip snapped again, this time on his back. Khanaseri shouted, 'Okay, okay! Give me a moment.'

Beuneth pulled back the whip and lashed out again and again as she said, 'Do you think an enemy is going to give you a moment to get ready?'

The whip came unabated, left and right, the leather point leaving red marks all over his body as he tried to evade. *This isn't working. Come on, Khanaseri!* Rising to his feet, he winced as the whip cracked on his stomach, but didn't move. *Focus.* Chanting, he saw the flames slowly rising around them. Another crack fell on his back. Losing concentration, the flames went out. A barrage of strikes followed. Seeping back to life, the fire rose higher and higher. Beuneth cracked the whip next to his face, his body, and from behind, but he kept chanting, ignoring everything around him with the fire burning high, until a sudden searing pain ripped through his chest. He staggered back and saw Beuneth standing a distance away with a sword in hand, then saw the blood flowing from the cut in his chest.

'Are you crazy?!'

'Lesson Two. Never get so focused that you don't know what's going on around you! You should be able to fight even while performing your incantation. If your father could have done that, he wouldn't have been stabbed by that assassin and might still be alive today.'

Khanaseri shook his head as he said, 'Wait. Assassin? I thought he was just a soldier.'

She sighed and said, 'I believe he was there for me. He harbours great hatred towards our kind. So when he saw your father, he took his opportunity. Enough on that. Now chant, damn you! And I don't want to see the flames go out, or any blows hitting their mark.' She charged in...

* * *

Sunlight lit up the red sands and rocky outback as the sun rose above the peak. To the far west, he saw the trees standing scattered, as if placed by a game of chance, providing minimal but valuable cover for those in need. Lanik was sitting under a deadwood tree, carving a small statuette of an elk from a fallen branch with his dagger, when he heard footsteps to his right.

'Always the artisan, eh? You shouldn't be in this line of work,' came the soft-spoken voice, gentle only to him.

'Nor should you, Ladriana, and I've made certain of that. Hate me for it if you must.' Lanik rose to meet her eyes, his spiked ash-blond hair making them of equal height.

'What have you done, Lanik? Xylac will have your head for lying,' she demanded as she gripped his arm.

With a snort, he continued, 'Mph, I don't think he's even in control anymore. Someone else is pulling the strings, and our esteemed leader couldn't care less about his followers. I sent a message to him that you took an arrow to the heart and died during an attack by some goblins. You can't be seen here anymore.'

Turning around, she shrugged as she said, 'To be honest, I thought I would be angrier than I am. But I think I've been done with the Desert Dogs for a while now. Come with me. We can leave together.'

'We'll meet up soon enough. But I have to finish a few things here first, otherwise he'll hunt me down.' A gust of wind caused her fiery hair to drift in the wind, exposing her neckline and face. 'You are one exquisite creature,' he said as he handed her the statuette, then sighed as he continued, 'Please leave. Go to The Flying Squirrel in Kobo, speak to the man who runs the tavern, and give him this. Call him by the name Kelvos, and you'll have his attention. He'll know who it's from, and for what reason. Trust me, there's no point in staying here any longer.'

Tying her bow to her horse, she thought of the time they'd spent in service to the Desert Dogs and said, 'What happened, Lanik? The Desert Dogs were respected and feared, and they used to have a code, some honour. But since I joined, it's been nothing but secretiveness, and we steal and plunder. The Dogs used to fight for those who couldn't fight for themselves — at a price, of course...but they never backed out of a fight.'

A scorpion lay in wait for an approaching lizard under the bole of a rotten tree on the ground. Lanik watched as it pounced to nab its victim, and said, 'Those days are gone, and so is the man who led them during those times. This Kremaghshi isn't him. His body and soul have been tainted.' He caressed her cheek, then drew her close as he kissed her. 'Please, take care not to be seen leaving camp.'

Ladriana reluctantly loosed her grip on him and mounted her horse to ride away, leaving him alone once more.

* * *

'For your crimes, you shall be crippled and flung down the bottomless pit; do you object?' Wearing a great red dragon's hide as armour, fire coursing through its very existence, the king's voice echoed throughout the square.

The dream blurred, then snapped into focus in his head.

The king gave one last insult as he slapped him across the face and said, 'Your time is up.'

He tried to hold on to the memory as it faded.

Fever-stricken as pain assaulted his mind, he watched in horror as the hammer came down with brutal force. Another sickening crunch sounded. The pain... Oh dear gods, the pain! Please take it away! The guard rolled him over the edge of the pit with his foot as he said, 'One last sting to remember me by,' then only darkness as he fell and fell.

One after the other, he opened his eyes. His head throbbed, and he reached to the back to feel a lump the size of a chicken's egg standing proud, sore to the touch. Groaning, he sat up slowly, taking in his surroundings: an old wooden hut with little more than a bed and red-painted wooden blocks that lay scattered about on the floor. What monster lives here? Escape. Must escape. He grabbed the closest things to make a weapon and lashed out as someone entered, landing a solid blow to the ribs. The man reeled back as he raised his hands in the air and protested, 'Wait, Ozo, it's me! Suri.'

The heavy pillow thudded on the floor as Ozo dropped it, then covered his mouth, and blurted, 'Oh dear! I am so sorry, son; I thought you were one of them.'

With a groan, Suri nursed his ribs. 'I think you broke one. What was that?'

'I stuffed the pillow with a bunch of those blocks — sorry. What happened back there in the forest? I thought they had me for sure.'

Creaks sounded as Suri sat on the little bed, still clutching his ribs. He reached down for the pillow and stated, 'They did. Lucky for you, I was nearby when I heard the commotion.'

The older man surveyed the room again, this time with no fear hovering over him; small, colourful, and filled with toys. Picking up a little wooden horse, he said, 'I didn't know you had a child. You're so young.'

A deep sigh came from Suri as he took the little wooden horse and said, 'Senri. A brave little boy. He's not mine, though. I'm merely his guardian, not his father. I found him near Bardow, in one of the surrounding villages. His mother, a whore, was killed by an addiction to the ruby leaf. His father was hunted down by thugs to whom he owed some gold. They took their time with him, made Senri bear witness to their cruelty. I will never forget those eyes...

'Walking into the village that day, I was so tired. My horse had broken its ankle two days earlier in the middle of nowhere. I just wanted a place where I could lay my head and sleep for a while. So I went to the inn at first, but they turned me away, wanting more than I offered. I kept walking until I reached the very end of the village, where a more secluded home was located, and headed for the stables. There was some hay in the corner, and I fell asleep almost immediately as I lay down. Don't know how long I slept for, but when I awoke, Senri sat across from me with those enormous eyes, just staring at me with a smile, and said, "You sound funny when you sleep. You sound like a dragon." We talked for a long time after that before he ran off.

'A while later, I went back into town for some supplies. The sun was halfway down when I saw a man running past me in fear, falling as he stepped into a ditch on the muddy road. He was quickly on his feet and off again. Shortly after, four men raced past as well. For the better part of the night, I was busy, and found this man selling these wooden horses. I bought one for Senri to say thank you for not telling his parents I'd slept in their stables. I remember walking back to the house, thinking how I would tell his father how I'd come to know his son and why I'd bought the toy for him. But as I was about to knock on the door, I heard his screams from inside.

'So I did what any man would do. I kicked down the door and grabbed the first man wielding a knife. There was no other way; it was them or me, so I thrust his own knife into his throat. The second came running clumsily with a piece of timber. It was easy to take it from him, so I cracked him over the skull. Somehow, I pulled the knife free from the first man's throat in the process and let it fly to the third, sinking it in his chest. The last thug came at me with a pair of pliers, but I had some training with my fists, so a few sidesteps and jabs were exchanged before he landed a blow with the pliers, cutting my face open. Seeing an opportunity, I swung my fist up so hard, teeth exploded from his mouth as I made contact. I shattered his nose as he fell over and rained down punch after punch after punch until there was no movement under me.

'I saw, as I looked up, Senri staring at me; then I saw his father, all bloodied in the chair. He had died during the fight. There was nothing I could do. His father was the man who had come running past me earlier that day, the one who fell in the mud. I could have saved him if I was willing to step in, but I was a coward, not wanting to get involved. So Senri came to stay with me. On that day, I decided to join the guards.'

With some grunting sounds, Ozo cleared his throat and placed his hand on Suri's shoulder as he said, 'I think you're much more than just a guardian to this boy. You care for him; you clothe and feed him. You educate him. No Suri, you *are* his father now.'

'You really think so?'

'Yes, I do. Now tell me what happened in the forest. What were you doing in the woods all the way out there?'

'I could ask you the same question... I was hunting and lost track of time, I suppose. Luckily for you, I might add. I heard some noises and saw the fire, then heard the screams of that man burning. I saw the other one hit you over the head with a piece of lumber from behind and intervened as quickly as possible. What I don't understand is how you set the fat one ablaze.'

Taken aback, Ozo rubbed his beard and sat up straight on the bed, saying, 'Oh, that? Well, that was a silly thing, actually. That fat tub of lard ran at me and tripped over a vine of a tree. Landed face first in the fire. Stupid, really. 'Twas the other one that caught me off guard.'

With narrowed eyes, Suri mumbled, 'Uh-huh, is that so? Then what was the explosion of fire I saw?'

Nervous under the scrutinising stare, Ozo rubbed his hands and stood as he moved to the door. 'Don't know, I'm afraid. Must have been his clothes. I thank you for your hospitality and heroism, my friend. I need to be on my way, though.'

'Come, I'll walk you home. Senri is off playing with some friends anyway.'

* * *

The warlock opened his eyes to a new world. His senses were brimming with possibilities. Across from him, Beuneth also opened her eyes. He no longer felt the impulsive nature of the young pulling him in every direction. No, he felt...measured. Calm, even.

'We need to eat and drink. We've deprived our bodies of water for too long. The training is taking longer than expected, and there's much I still need to teach you.' Beuneth extended her arm and grasped Khanaseri's hand to rise from the ground.

The warlock winced as he rose from the ground, clutching his sides as he said, 'How long have we been gone? My insides hurt.'

With a careless gesture as she walked away, she said, 'I would say around two, maybe three days out here. A couple of years in there, though. How do you feel?'

Khanaseri followed her. 'I don't really know how to answer that.' He looked at his right hand and saw the newly healed scar where the sabre-tooth cat had bitten through years ago in his mind. The scar felt old in his palm as he rubbed at it. 'It's a strange sensation, this, being older than one's body.'

'Yes, I understand. You'll get used to it; the feeling will fade. You'll feel a bit disjointed for a while, but soon you'll feel more like yourself. Come, let's get some food and water, then get our gear together. Tonight, we'll sleep in beds to replenish our strength, and tomorrow we'll train some more. If all goes well, we should be done with training in the next two days, then we ride for the Dikunabi and spend the night. I know the chief; he's a good man. We'll go forth from there.'

* * *

Warm ale ran down her throat, the liquid not helping to quench her thirst, merely occupying her mouth and hands as she eyed the burly man with the apron round his waist. The curly red hair on the sides of his head amused her some; she smirked at a thought. A short, stubby nose too wide for his face seemed as though it was the cause for his eyes being pushed too far from each other.

From table to table, he slipped across the room, always sitting down with someone and listening to their problems or boasts of bravado, being very pragmatic in his approach of giving advice. After some time, he wandered in her direction, then planted himself across from her with a heave and sigh that would bolster his size, just eyeing her as she stared back, not making a sound. He cleared his throat and ran his hand through his thinning hair and said, 'So... Ye trouble, lass?'

Sipping more of the ale, she replied, 'Why would you ask that?'

'Well now, lass, there's the bow hanging on yer side, which ye don't part ways with, and the arrow ye keep boring into my table. Then there's the fact that youse been drinking that hot piss all night. Care for another? Oh, and not to mention the looks youse been giving my customers. Have ye noticed this half of the inn seems a tad vacant?'

Putting down the arrow, she asked, 'Are you a good man, Kelvos?'

The surprise of that name gave him such a fright that he jerked his head around, almost tearing it from his thick neck, seeing if anyone had heard, but they were all out of earshot. Focusing on her again, he demanded, 'Where in the blazes did youse hear that name? And don't ever mention it again. Not in this town, nor anywhere else! Ye hear?'

He'd angrily shoved the chair out from under him and started for the kitchen when she tossed the statuette on the table, asking, 'What should I call you, then?'

As he gazed upon the wooden elk statuette with a glazed look in his eyes, deep in thought and far back in memory, he slowly sat back down. 'Ye can call me Magnus.' Upon taking the wooden elk, he looked around, embarrassed, and pulled out a pair of spectacles from his shirt's pocket, then looked at the intricate designs formed all over, inspecting it with great care. 'Ye were careless with it... Ye let it fall. It got nicked. Lucky for ye I can still make out the inscriptions.'

Scowling, she put away her arrow. 'So you recognise this, then? I don't have to explain anything?'

'No. I mean, no, ye don't have to explain.'

'Very well, then.' She twirled her hair as she looked at him, then continued, 'So please, can you tell me what in the balls of the black abyss is going on?' She was shouting now. 'Who are you, and why am I here?'

Abruptly, the innkeeper slammed his fist against the table, splintering the wood on the sides. The sudden motion stopped Ladriana in mid-rant.

'Now, now, missy, I will not condone yer foul mouth here. Do ye understand? Now get upstairs and leave these people in peace. I will come fetch my coin from ye soon. Better have it! Now go!'

Gathering her bow and arrows, the inn silent for the first time today, she softly intoned, 'We shall talk about this later.'

Avoiding her gaze, he said, 'Aye, we shall.'

* * *

'Still pacing the floor through, I see.'

The sudden voice in her room made her jump. 'What? Oh, only

you, then.' Staring at the big innkeeper, she was impressed at how quietly he had walked into her room without her noticing, then said, 'What's going on, Magnus? I dislike being left in the dark, and in this case, I'm completely in the dark. First Lanik tells me to meet with you and give you that stupid toy, then you go all glazy-eyed when you see it. How do you know Lanik, and what is this secret between you two?' Frustrated, she dropped to the bed, her shoulders slumped.

'So *that's* the name he uses now. Interesting.' He mumbled some more incoherent babble, but she couldn't hear it clearly.

'What?'

'What's what?'

'You know what I'm talking about. What you just mumbled, "So that's the name he uses now".'

'My dear, I can honestly not tell ye what I do not know. What I can tell ye is that if he called in this favour for ye, then he truly must love ye.'

Sitting upright now, attention focused on Magnus, she said, 'What kind of favour are we talking here? Gold aplenty? Protection? What? Being shipped off to some godforsaken isle where the crows don't even go?'

He fumbled about with his fingers. 'In a manner of speaking, yes, yes, and, well, yes, though I believe there to be crows, and it's not an isle. My dear, youse are about to become queen of New Runswick.'

With arms folded and a sneer to match, she said, 'Oh, piss off, old man. This is no time for jokes.'

'Well, youse won't be seen as a queen with that mouth o' yers.'

'How? That's impossible—'

'I can't tell youse all the details, but it's very possible. I believe yer Lanik has a couple of secrets he doesn't like to share.'

Stunned to near-silence, it baffled Ladriana just how little she knew of the man she knew only as Lanik, only to find out that wasn't even his real name. 'So where is this New Runswick?'

'A few weeks' travel north, northeast of here, through the icy mountains of Galbadore's Eye and past the far-reaching plains, beyond a beautiful land of green and colourful flowers known as Butter Valley.'

'Will he join us there? What did he say on the toy?'

Rising, Magnus wiped his hands on his shirt. 'Yes, eventually.'

A stern look came from Ladriana as she stood with her hands on her hips. 'What do you mean, eventually? It's easier to pull my own teeth than to get an answer out of you!'

'I suppose...he said he has to take care of something, but he didn't mention what, I'm afraid. But for the matter at hand: we have to get ye to look and act like a lady before we can go. So first thing in the morning, we'll get ye some proper clothes.'

'Hey! What's wrong with my clothes?' Ladriana scowled as she pulled on the tight brown shirt and frayed, green-edged dress.

Magnus shrugged his shoulder as he said, 'Oh, nothing, if youse want to run around the forest like a hairless elf and live under a bridge with the animal folk.' He wagged his finger as he continued, 'But 'tis not fit for a queen.'

* * *

The old man sat next to the fire, deep in thought, glaring at the dancing flames. The crackle and smell of burning wood entertained the night's sky. Earlier, Ozo and Suri had walked back to his cabin with little in the way of conversation to aid their march. As they neared the cabin, Suri had turned around, wishing the old man a good night and telling him to stay out of trouble before walking off. But Suri did not go far...

Ozo pulled a knife from his robes as he stood closer to the flames, muttering to himself as he stared at his hands.

From behind a tree, Suri crept a little closer to get a better view. The dark of the night concealed his whereabouts as he crouched a few feet from Ozo. 'What are you doing, old man?' Suri muttered under his breath. Dangerously close to the flames, Ozo took the knife and cut the palm of his hand with a vicious slash. Blood flowed down his arm to pool between his feet as he spoke to himself, or it might have been to his god; Suri was unsure. Ozo grasped a nearby twig, smeared his blood over the tip, and reached for the flames with it. In anticipation, Suri stood silently watching as the twig made its way toward the fire, then with a sudden crackle, the end of the twig was set alight. *That wasn't even close to the fire.*

A violent blue flame burned at the end of the twig, brighter and much hotter than the flames from the fire. So engrossed with the flame was he that Ozo didn't realise just how close it was getting to his hand, and he jerked as the sudden heat burned him, letting it drop into the pool of blood at his feet.

A mighty explosion rocked the area, hurling the old man through the air, engulfed in flames. The force of the blast threw Suri to the ground, hard. Deafened, he rose and scanned the area for Ozo. The night air was profusely hot, with blue flames licking the night sky, burning high and bright where the old man had stood. The blast had incinerated the outhouse close by, with the burning body of the old man lying some thirty paces away. *Bloody fool.* Suri started running towards the old man, then stopped halfway as he saw the body rise to its feet. He jumped for cover behind a tree, too afraid of this unholy sorcery to be a part of it.

Dazed and unaware of the flames engulfing his body, Ozo shook his head, then looked down. Screams of agony erupted from him as he fell to the ground, rolling as he tried to extinguish the flames; but nothing would quench them. Terrified and tired, believing death would come soon, he fell silent and awaited the inevitable — but death did not come. And yet he still waited and waited. *When is this going to end? I really thought burning alive would be worse than this.* Only then did he realise there was no pain and never had been.

Tired beyond reason, he closed his eyes. Sleep took him instantly.

Standing watch in the distance, sword clenched in his hands, Suri watched the blue flames slowly die as Ozo slept, the rhythmic movement of the old man's chest the only sign of life until soft snores were heard. He neared the sleeping man and saw soot covering his body. All his clothing had been burned away, but there were no actual burn marks on his skin.

Suri looked up and saw that the flames covering the outhouse had also died. Silently moving back to the forest, he sent up a prayer and ran for the village.

* * *

The candlelight flickered and fluttered in the dark abyss that was his chamber. Sitting at his desk, unmoving, he silently contemplated his next move. For anyone who dared to observe him from a distance, it would have seemed that time had frozen him in place. For the better part of the day, he did not move until a voice came from his doorway. 'Knock-knock.' Only then did he look up.

As she moved through the open chamber, the smell of roses drifted through the air and flowed into the nostrils of the Kremaghshi. He looked upon the deadly Anavi Tapesh standing before him with her hands on her hips. 'What do you want, Anavi? I'm busy, can't you see?'

Folding her arms, she said, 'Yes, I can see that. So busy that you don't see those who conspire against you.'

His distracted face quickly turned to glare at her. 'What did you just say?' He rose and moved around the table to stand mere inches from her with clenched fists. 'Be very careful of your next utterances, Anavi. My men are as loyal as dogs. They know all too well what will happen if they aren't.'

With the cool demeanour of a lioness in a jackal den, she turned her head to the side and said, 'Have you ever watched a dog when he thinks you're not around?'

A swing from his left hand sent her bowed over and gasping for air. Coughing, she muttered and laughed, 'Didn't think you had it in you to hit a girl.'

Another fist came at her. But while Anavi had given him the first attack, this one she wouldn't allow. She spun past his badly aimed blow and grabbed her two daggers — the hilts, curved dragon talons — as she ducked and cut Xylac's thigh just deep enough to seep blood. Before he could even scream his outrage, she was on top of him, her legs locked over his neck, driving him to the ground.

Blinking, he stared up at the end of a dragon dagger hovering just in front of his left eye and felt the other at his throat, pressed hard enough to cut.

The assassin lay on top of her appointed leader and said, 'I'm not the one you should fear. Not today, at least. On my count, we're even now. So try nothing stupid again. Next time I won't be so gentle.' She spun her legs and was quick on her feet to sheathe her blades, then lowered herself to the chair before the desk. Gazing at the items in the room, she found there was little in the way of good taste. A half-broken vase stood in one corner, a portrait of a man in uniform shouting orders hanging skew on the wall. The old, rusted knife-set on top of the desk was the best thing to look at.

Xylac groaned and cursed under his breath as he came to his feet, embarrassed at what had just transpired, and thought about the best way to deal with it. He took a bottle of liqueur from his shelf, poured them a drink, and said, 'I should kill you for what you just did.'

'Yes, you should, shouldn't you? But then again, I'm worth more to you alive than dead. I mean, who else in this worthless group you call warriors has taken you down as quickly as I just did? Or had the guts to try? And besides that, I know of a plot against you. Someone is scheming in the dark to get rid of you. And then there's the fact that I want to bed you because I find you so irresistibly delicious.'

'Do you now?' Twirling the glass in his hand, he continued, 'They say the men in Cadence Valley have a certain plant they grow to prolong their ability to make love. It is said they can go on for days without end. I don't think I would need such a plant tonight.' Xylac took her by the hand as he walked to his bed, throwing her down roughly. The clip of his belt fell away with a click, and he dropped his pants before climbing on top of her.

* * *

'Beuneth! Welcome. You are still as beautiful as the day we met.' Chief Cairn embraced the woman, lifting her from the ground as one would a long-lost daughter. Beuneth's laughter flowed through the air as he swung her round. Finally setting her down, his eyes fell on Khanaseri, his visage suddenly dark as he said, 'And who might you be?'

Men and women, soldiers all, emerged from the forest, spears and bows in hand, ready to kill with a snap of the chief's fingers. Khanaseri looked down at the dark-skinned chief, the man's multitude of tawdry silver and gold facial piercings reflecting the sun's light like little mirrors. He saw the annoyance in the chief's eyes as he approached. *Guess he doesn't enjoy needing to look up.* From the back, a man ran by and clubbed Khanaseri at the back of the knees, sending him to the ground.

Beuneth jumped forward and shouted, 'No, Cairn. Please. Don't do this.'

Chief Cairn turned to her and stated, 'This is my village! I do not tolerate miscreants! And he looks like a miscreant to me.'

'I am Khanaseri, son of Galvos Brathos. And I mean you no harm.' On his knees, his head cocked down and arms raised to the heavens, he waited for the chief's reply.

Shocked, the chief whistled. More soldiers moved in to encircle Khanaseri, pushing Beuneth out of the way.

Beuneth shouted again, 'Cairn. Stop this, or I will be forced to stop it for you!' Lightning surged from her hands, scorching the earth as she neared.

Chief Cairn chewed on the inside of his gums and said, 'Why are you with him? He comes from a monster! Destruction follows wherever that man walks!'

'He's—'

'You know, that's hilarious,' Khanaseri said as he rose from the ground, then walked up to press his chest against the spear of a warrior and continued, 'My father — who is dead now, by the way — told me stories of you. The great Chief Cairn. The man who brought the tribes together, back from the verge of extinction. Because you all wiped yourselves out with your petty differences. My father had respect for you. Was he wrong to have it?'

'Your father also killed more people than I could ever count!' The chief pointed his finger and shouted at Khanaseri, making his warriors anxious.

Anger flaring, Khanaseri pushed forward, the spear's point cutting into his chest. 'My father only killed during war! He never pillaged, never raped. He stood by his principles throughout his life. He had his faults, but he was still a great man.'

A thunderous crack followed as lightning arced to the clouds that formed above. The Dikunabi soldiers and their chief dived to the ground as the blinding arc illuminated the surroundings. In a flash, the lightning disappeared, but the dark clouds lingered. Defiant, Beuneth stood towering over the cowering Dikunabi and Khanaseri, also back on his knees, then said, 'Now you have measured your cocks, and you were both found wanting. So I suggest we end this nonsense and all get along...quickly.'

The Dikunabi chief stood. 'Yes, of course.' He looked down at his cowering subjects and shouted, 'Well, why are you still cowering on the ground? Get up! We have a feast to prepare.' He extended his arm and helped Khanaseri up from the ground, nodding as their eyes locked, then departed.

Khanaseri ambled over to Beuneth's side, watching as the Dikunabi dispersed. As most of them vanished, some into the forest and some running to get food ready for the feast, Beuneth suddenly collapsed onto him. Her face paled, her strength sapped. Catching her, he steadied her frame as she slowly regained some composure. 'You need to lie down; you don't look well,' he noted.

Breathing deeply, she lifted her head and said, 'I'll be fine. The healing of the wound on my back and creating the training realm has taken more out of me than I expected. Come, we're to be dined. I'll be fine.'

Chapter Four

Towering flames rose high above the bonfire, the heat intense. Khanaseri shielded his eyes from the blaze as he sat next to the Dikunabi chief, drinking wine and eating grapes as men and women danced around the flames to the beat of the tribal drums. He looked at the chief as he heard his name called in a thick, guttural accent.

'How do you know Beuneth?' Chief Cairn pressed on the chair's wooden armrest, leaning in to hear better.

She's the cause of my father's death. You would probably love that, you fat bastard. Choosing his words carefully, Khanaseri said, 'She helped me get out of prison.'

The silence that followed between the two men grew as the chief kept staring at him. 'No, she did more than that, but I respect your choice not to talk about it.' Pulling his face into a sneer, the chief looked away as he said, 'I'm sorry for what I said about your father. I knew him very well, actually. And we were friends of a sort. So I'm sorry to hear of his passing.'

'It's fine...'

'No, let me finish apologising for my poor behaviour. He was a ruthless man, but he was also a man true to his word. And once you made a friend of him, he would burn the world to the ground for you. I respected him for that.'

'Thank you for your kind words, Chief Cairn.'

'Did you know Beuneth was also imprisoned once?'

Khanaseri brought his head back up, shaking it as he looked at the chief and said, 'She's mentioned prison before, but never explained. Do you know why and how?'

'Well, as for the why and how, you'll need to ask her, but for the story of how she escaped, let me tell you...'

* * *

A clatter of teeth sounded through the room, the cold sending shivers down her spine as she sat in the corner of her cell, hugging her knees. The last two years hadn't been kind to Beuneth. Signs of madness were looming as she constantly shook her head, as if seeing someone who wasn't there.

A loud creak came from the door as it swung open. A guard moved through with a plate of slop and water in a cup. Scowling, he cursed as the rank odour of piss and excrement hit his nose, and said, 'Beuneth, there's a bucket for that! Stop shitting wherever you please.'

Her dark-ringed eyes followed him as he moved through the room. As he placed the food on the stand in the corner, she said, 'Oh, Humly, you've been so kind to me during my time here. Come a little closer so I can reward you properly.' As sensually as she could muster, Beuneth pulled her raggedy top off and threw it on the little bed in the corner. She moved in closer to the guard, hips swinging, bare-breasted and filthy, only to see Humly nervously retreat and stumble over the little wooden stool, then turn to run for the door.

With Beuneth right on his heels, he slammed the wooden door shut as he passed through. Screams erupted from the other side, the door shaking as she pounded on it.

Sounds of laughter filled the long corridor as a passing guard bent over and clutched his stomach. 'Whew, she almost had you this time, Hum. She take her top off again?'

Still shaken, Humbly said, 'Y-Yes. It was too close.'

'You are such a puss-puss. Tell you what, tomorrow you give *me* her meal to deliver. Let me show you how I drive my enormous cock into her, ripping her apart from the inside. Make her actually go crazy.'

Blinking at the tall, slender guard as he waved his long, golden hair from his face, Humbly said, 'By all means, Artus. I'm done with her.'

Footsteps echoed down the corridor, and Artus rapped his knuckles on the wooden door. 'You hear that, honey? Tomorrow I'm coming for you, and I'm bringing a *big* friend for you to play with.'

Laughter followed Artus as he continued on his patrol, disappearing around the corner of the corridor.

* * *

She stood before the imaginary window she had drawn with a piece of coal, overlooking the valley beyond the city, the lush green of the forest, the rolling hills, and the clear blue sky. Beuneth twirled her hair, remembering her last few days with Blanka. She rolled her tongue in her mouth — her teeth feeling loose from the neglect of the past few years — until she found one that made her reel at the touch. The rot had set in. *Why did it have to be a molar?* She closed her eyes and stuck her hand as deep in her mouth as she could, to get the best grip possible on the tooth. Nerve endings ground against the root as she yanked on it. Faint sounds of pain escaped her mouth, but it would not relent. She took a deep breath as she viciously twisted the tooth and pulled. Stamping her foot on the ground, her hands covered in blood, she spat in the cell's corner. A spatter of red covered the wall, dripping down to the floor. Her hands trembled from the pain as she stared at the molar, its massive sharp root decayed, the stench horrible. Closing her fist, she clutched the tooth as the door to her cell swung open.

'Well, well, up and about early today, I see.' Artus put the tray of food on the stand and turned back to her, unbuckling his pants as he said, 'Now how about me and you have some fun? I mean, you must be lonely, having no one else to play with.' Laughing, he sauntered over to Beuneth and grabbed her left hand, forcibly swinging her around. 'Look at me when I'm talking to you, bitch!'

She turned and brought her hand up fast.

A sharp pain lanced through his neck. Confused, he lifted his hand and felt the blunt edge of the molar sticking out.

She began, 'I wouldn't pull—'

With a tug, he yanked the large tooth out of his jugular. A sudden burst of blood gushed down his neck and clothes. Wide-eyed, he stared at her in disbelief.

That's right. Let it sink in. I just killed you with a tooth. 'Never mind. Hey, don't blame me. I was just having fun, like you wanted.'

Artus tried to run, but Beuneth jumped on him, holding tight until he sagged to the ground as he paled, his limbs growing numb from blood loss. He tried to stem the flow, to no avail.

With a sigh, she stepped over him, and said, 'At least, I *thought* that would be more fun.'

A few lanterns clung to the side of the long, dank corridor; shadows danced on the opposite wall. With no guards in sight, Beuneth ran as fast as she could for the door at the end, which led up and out of the dungeon. As she reached the stairs, she heard voices moving down towards her. She jumped to hide behind the stairs in the shadows, waiting for them to pass. Afterward, she dashed upward, hyperventilating, the rapid breaths threatening to take her vision as she ascended the spiral staircase two steps at a time. Shouts from down in the dungeon caught her attention and made her stumble as she looked back. *Shit.* Back on her feet, she reached the top quickly and shouldered the door open. Her frail body, thin and wiry, almost wasn't strong enough to move the door; she nearly broke an arm against its frame. Finally, sunlight burst forth and touched her skin for the first time in nearly two years. Laughing out loud, she marvelled at the bright blue sky.

'Hey, you! Stop right there!' Guards ran at her with weapons drawn. Briefly, cold air flowed as she opened a portal and stepped through.

* * *

The market area was unusually quiet as the guards searched the vicinity for the escaped sorceress. People moved about cautiously, not bringing attention to themselves. Most started moving away when the air grew colder; the life sucked out of the area as the portal opened. A short scream was heard, followed by a dull thud as Beuneth fell from the sky, hitting the middle of the cobblestoned road. Slowly rising, she looked up and said, 'I know I'm a little rusty, but that was ridiculous.'

'There she is!' came the shouts from the guards, giving chase as she ran through the market and into the alleyway. A short crossbow bolt flew by her head, the hissing sound sending a cold rush through her body. Black spots filled her vision as she ran, her legs trembling from the sudden exertion. Cold air burned her lungs as she inhaled the most and cleanest air she had in a long time. *They're catching up; I won't make it.*

Heading up Lancaster Hill, the crowded street made it difficult for the guards to fire their crossbows, having to push their way through the mob of people. She took the next left and ran straight into the city square. The memories of that fateful day came rushing back to her. Tears streamed down her face as she headed for the great pit. *I'll see you soon in the great beyond, Blanka. Wait for me.* Guards came in from all corners with weapons raised. Crossbow bolts flew past, hitting the trees and stone benches with enormous force. *So close. Why can't they just let me die in peace?*

A few feet from the pit, a bolt hit her in the back, ripping out from her side. A clean hit, through and through. *It doesn't matter anymore. I've made it.* With no hesitation, Beuneth flung herself over the side of the pit, smiling as she fell. *The end is near.*

Utter darkness enveloped her as she fell. *I'm going to bleed to death before I hit the bottom of this pit. How much more? Wait, what is that light?*

Unceremoniously flung through the air, Beuneth found herself cast out of the pit. She kicked the air as she fell back to the ground, dust swirling up around her from the impact. Coughing, she rolled over, then sat up to stare at her surroundings. The domed ceiling of the cave was very high above her. Bats fluttered about from the intrusion, squawking and squeaking their anger at Beuneth. *What's going on? Where am I?* She clutched her side as the bleeding continued and started walking.

* * *

Joining the two men, Beuneth sat down and said, 'Regaling him with my tales, are you?'

With pursed lips, Chief Cairn said, 'Sorry, Beuneth. It was not my tale to tell.'

'No, it wasn't, but I was tired of keeping it to myself anyway. So just as well it's out now.' Turning to Khanaseri, she continued, 'I walked for days after that, with no idea where I was or where I was going. All I knew was, I felt ten years older, and when I finally found a mirror, looked it as well. As I walked through these forests, Chief Cairn's men surrounded me. Delusional from all the blood-loss and weak to the point of keeling over, I couldn't cast any spells. I just watched as they jumped from the bushes and pinned me to the ground. Tied down like a hog for a feast, they brought me into their camp and placed me before Cairn to decide my fate. I was lucky, though. As my fate was being decided, a band from a rival tribe attacked them. I promised to help bring the tribes together if they would let me go. At first Cairn laughed at the idea, wondering what good a half-dead woman could be. But with my last morsel of strength, I summoned the skies to darken on a cloudless day. It didn't last long before I collapsed, but he saw my potential and saved my life instead. They patched me up and fed me. If it weren't for him, I would be dead. After that, I searched for Blanka for a while, but found it futile. He could have been anywhere, if not dead already. So I resorted to searching for the Balamuth after helping Cairn with the tribes. I figured it would be much easier to follow the trail of a powerful object than a man nobody knew. I'm hoping that if I find the Balamuth, it will lead me to him.'

Khanaseri stared at her, realising just how strong this woman was, and found himself smiling at her for the first time. 'May I ask why you were imprisoned?'

Opening her mouth to speak, Beuneth stammered and closed it again. Cairn quickly shot up from his chair and shouted, 'Tonight we celebrate friendship. Let us feast and drink in each other's company!'

When Khanaseri looked for Beuneth after the commotion, she was nowhere to be seen. Sighing, he sat back and stared at the fire and the dancing Dikunabi.

Chief Cairn hung over the side of his chair as he leaned in toward the warlock, shouting to be heard over the loud festivities of the night, 'Tomorrow, you ride away with two of my finest horses, Bellombi and Flintlock. Take great care of them.'

* * *

Looking down, he saw the hand thrust into his chest, feet dangling, lifted off the ground with so much power...

'Aaaghhh!' Ozo sat up as he screamed, clutching his chest. Scanning the area, he saw the multitude of beds in the long, open hall, healers running about, and faces staring back at him. From a distance, he saw one of the apprentice healers quickly approaching. *I think his name is Broken or something like that.*

'I am Bronek. How are you feeling, sir?' The apprentice asked it in a very slow and irritating manner, suggesting that he was speaking to the ancient, the deaf, or the dumb.

Clearing his throat, Ozo said, 'Young man, I guarantee you I'm as fit as an ox, not deaf, not dumb, nor dead. Nothing wrong with me. I just don't know how I got here. Explain this to me.'

'Sir? We found you outside your cabin. Half of it was up in smoke, the other half disintegrated by what seemed like an explosion. We found you covered in soot with a very weak heartbeat, not to mention that you were nude. We thought you were injured, especially after we tried to wake you. Garnet even slapped you across the face to see if you would wake, but nothing. Not even a stir. So Garnet threw you over his shoulder and carried you into town.'

'Oh, so I should actually be grateful to this Garnet?'

'Well, and me,' Bronek muttered under his breath.

'What was that you said?'

Scratching his head and looking about, Bronek turned before he left and said, 'Oh, nothing. Nothing at all.'

Not entirely sure what had occurred the previous night, Ozo quickly gathered his belongings and left the healing hall before anyone else could interrogate him. *"The old fool,"* *that's what they used to say.* *"Mad old fool, you must be dreaming."* *Well. Now they'll see. Once I show them what's going on, they'll have to believe me. I will not be cast out again. There's strangeness in this world, and I know it now for sure. But first I need to find out what's going on with me. Hopefully, I'm not possessed, as that child was a few years back.*

He'd just rounded the corner to the temple of Teros when, out of nowhere, Suri ran up and tackled him, putting him down hard on the ground as he pressed his dagger against Ozo's tattooed throat.

'What are you?' Suri demanded while holding the old man's head to the ground, looking around the alley to see if anyone else saw them. 'Speak quickly!'

Pleading for his life, Ozo spread his arms as he said, 'Please don't do this, Suri. Don't kill me, please.'

Anxiety was clawing at Suri as he lifted the old man to his feet. 'Move it! We're going to your cabin. Then you'll tell me everything, and I'll decide what to do with you.'

* * *

At the edge of the cliff, Ganda'har bent down and picked up an old arrowhead from the sand. It was nearly invisible, the rust camouflaging it in the red of the soil. His thoughts railed: *Where have you gone, Khanaseri?* A scout reined in close, rocks skidding against the captain, angering him as the man blurted, 'Captain, it seems Khanaseri was definitely here in their camp. We overheard a woman talking about a warrior with a female who accompanied him.'

From behind them came the screams of an elder as he dangled over the edge in the grip of Untara, a giant of a man. Upside down, looking at the rocks sticking out from the sides of the cliff, Chief Cairn cried, 'You lie, you wretched creature! You tortured her for the information, made her tell you what you wanted to hear. He was never here! I don't know what you want!'

Before him lay the beautiful vista of the valley below. Ganda'har sighed and slowly turned his gaze upon the chief. 'Sometimes I wish I could live here in the forest, like you do. You know such beauty, whereas we know only sand. Cairn, do you expect me to just take your word? Just because we've shared a meal and a laugh or two in the past? I'm not happy with the way things have turned out today, but you know better than to get in my way. I need to find him and bring him back to Artorea. Now, where did he go? And how long ago did he leave?' Looking over his shoulder, he saw all the eyes staring at him, pleading for him to stop and pull back the old man from the edge. The Kamatayon stood in a half circle before him, protecting their captain from any attack, and beyond them stood the Dikunabi: men, women, children, all caught unaware by the sudden outbreak of violence from the elite company.

* * *

On arrival at the camp the day before, Cairn had personally ridden out to greet Ganda'har as they neared. The Dikunabi were well known for their ambivalence towards most, and the slightest of reasons given them to doubt your intentions would cause you to reap the inevitable point of an arrow in the forehead. A feast was prepared in honour of the guests. Throughout the day, they drank wine and ate the best meats, enjoyed the company of women and men, carrying on late into the evening before they turned in for the night. Ganda'har had sat at the table making jokes with Cairn whilst drinking his wine, every so often being slipped a note or a signal from afar.

Early morning while the sun rose over the forest, a chill left a freshness in the air, invigorating to those already awake. Cairn lay in his bed on the verge of waking up, trying to push it aside a while longer when, in the hut's silence, a voice rang out, 'Come now, Cairn, I don't want to be in this shit-hole all day!'

Alarmed, Chief Cairn sat up in his bed and stared at Ganda'har as the captain cleaned his nails with a huge dagger and demanded, 'What are you doing in my house? And why did my guards not stop you?'

'Oh, they tried. Don't you fret about their allegiance or bravery now, you hear? I have some questions, and you'd best be giving me the right answers. All these charades of last night, the wine, the dancing, the women...did you really think me that stupid? To bed a woman and just forget why I've come all this way?'

The elder man got out of bed and dressed as he said, 'I don't know who you think you are. You know there's a treaty between Artorea and the Dikunabi. Do you really want to be the man who starts a new war?'

Laughter burst from Ganda'har as he knocked on the door, signalling two of his soldiers to come in, and said, 'Take him to the cliff.'

Dragged outside, Cairn saw his guards in the street: five dead, six more tied up together. 'You will regret this, Ganda'har. What do you want from us? We have nothing to offer you.'

'Oh, don't play coy with me, Cairn. I know Khanaseri was here, and I know you're trying to throw us off his scent. What I don't know is why you're trying to help him.

'On second thought, I actually don't care why you're helping him. All I want to know is, when did he leave and in what direction? I'm at a bit of a crossroads, and I would hate to go in the wrong direction. It would be a tedious exercise.' Ganda'har stood in the winds buffeting the cliff face, then looked down and continued, 'You know what's the worst thing about falling here? You would probably survive it. Which means I can go down, scoop you up from the blood-spattered ground with your broken legs and arms, bring you back up, and do it all over again. But I also see that threatening your life won't make a difference to you. So let's see who we have in the crowd. Ah, there's one.'

Still hanging upside down, Cairn watched as Ganda'har walked into the crowd, pushing men and women aside to lift a young girl with dark curly hair to his shoulder.

'No! No! Ganda'har, put her down! Damn you! This has gone far enough! She's just a child. Have you no morality, no honour?'

'Oh, I do, Cairn. Do you? For it isn't my morals or honour that come in question here, but yours. Would you rather let me throw this innocent young girl over the cliff? Or are you going to tell me what I want to hear?' The girl was screaming, clutching at Ganda'har's arms as she also dangled over the edge. 'Please don't let me do this, Cairn. You would never forgive yourself.'

The elder dropped his head in surrender, saying, 'Fine. You win, Ganda'har. I'll tell you what you want to hear. But first, bring her to safety.'

The little girl sagged to the ground as Ganda'har put her down, trying to regain herself as urine ran down her legs. The captain signalled Untara, the beast of a man, to bring Cairn back to solid ground, and said, 'You'd better speak clearly and truthfully, now. You've wasted enough of my time.'

Chapter Five

In the dead of night, with no moon in the sky and very little visibility, Anavi sneaked through the camp's defences, dressed in all black, silent as an assassin. She stopped in her tracks as she saw a guard sitting by a fire to her right with a mug in his hand, waiting for his meat to be cooked. *They've rearranged some stations. Got to be more vigilant, Tapesh.* A sudden realisation struck her: she sounded just like her father when she wasn't paying attention. He'd died years ago, laid to rest on their farmstead. Those words were so drilled in, they would haunt her forever.

She remembered the day her father was busy bringing out the new stallion from the stable to break him in, when she ran up and said, 'Please, Papa, let me break him!' Against his better judgement, he gave her the reins, as he had promised her so many times before.

With the lead attached, the stallion started at a canter, circling Anavi in the bullpen. Every so often, the stallion would buck to the side at the slightest of noises, his ears flicking back and forth as his eyes scanned the surroundings.

A piercing cry from above made Anavi look to the heavens to see a great eagle soar up high in its graceful glide.

'Keep your eyes on him, Ana—'

The stallion yanked the lead from her hand and reared up on its hind legs to tower over her, its front legs scything the air. Anavi stumbled back from the magnificent black beast and caught her foot on a rock. Sprawled on the ground, she used her hands and legs to push herself back, then covered her face with her arms and closed her eyes as the stallion's legs came down.

Just in time, her father had rushed in, shouting at the horse and taking its attention away from Anavi. Its big hoof crashed to the ground next to her legs before the horse turned to run to the other side of the bullpen. He helped her up, eyes red with worry as he shouted, 'You must be more vigilant, Anavi Tapesh! He could have killed you!'

A smirk came over her face as she returned to reality. *I'll go and visit you, Papa, soon.*

With as little noise as possible, she moved into the tent, creeping closer to the far corner. In the dark of the tent, she could finally make out the bed and moved closer. *Two feet away.* She paused as she felt the tip of a throwing knife prod the small of her back, gently pressed, but with enough force to take it seriously. Without turning, Anavi whispered, 'It's me, Lanik. We don't have time for games. Lower the knife.'

As he pulled the knife away, she spun around and said, 'Get out of camp immediately.'

'What? Anavi, what's going on?'

Pacing before him anxiously, she said, 'The best way to have gained Xylac's trust was by giving up the one person he thought I would never go against. You.'

An icy chill ran through him as numbness spread through his legs. 'What are you talking about, Anavi?'

Grabbing some of his things, Anavi threw them on the bed, saying, 'I gave you up as the traitor. You won't have long before I officially ride into camp, coming for your head.'

Lanik grabbed his bow and trained a nocked arrow on her as he said, 'Why would you do that? They'll hunt me down and kill me.'

'I know. But not if we kill them all first. I'll keep you alive. We have to make our way out of camp and run for the hills to the east. I have a horse waiting for you there. A little while after you depart, I'll ride into camp, demanding your presence and execution so they don't suspect me of colluding. Then, in three nights' time, meet me at the old bridge going to Kelvos. We'll talk there.'

'I asked you to watch him and report back, not this!' Lanik grabbed his gear and stuffed it in a pack. As quiet as thieves, they made their way out of the camp for Lanik to jump on the waiting horse and ride off in the dead of night.

* * *

'Why are you doing this, Suri? Haven't I always been kind to you?' Ozo pleaded as they walked up the mountain.

Suri kept a close eye on the older man from the back. The kind, humble geezer he knew now seemed a monster with every glimpse, an unnatural creature. A thing that should not be. 'What are you? I watched you the night of the fire; it scared me witless.'

Ozo froze on the spot, cold sweat running down his spine. 'What do you mean, you watched me? Sounds a little stalkerish.'

'I was hiding in the bushes. I watched you light up that cabin with an explosion of blue fire. Fire so hot it melted the metal pots you had a distance from the house. I saw you thrown from your feet, engulfed in those very flames. Yet here you stand, untouched by them. Explain this to me! Why are you not dead?'

As they stood staring at each other, Ozo felt tears well in his eyes and quickly wiped his face as he spoke with his voice stuck in his throat, 'I, I don't know what I am.' He collapsed to his knees on the dusty road and grabbed his hair, tearing it out, tufts at a time. Blood ran down his face, and his screams echoed through the woods. Animals in the vicinity dashed away from the tormented sounds in fear.

'Don't you see? I thought I was dying, Suri! Being burned alive! My life flashed before my very eyes! Only, it was half a life. I can't remember anything prior to me waking up half-dead. Memories cloud my mind, but I can't make sense of them. Those of being born, but not knowing when or where, of fighting, yet not with who. I remember dying, yet not an eternal death.'

Shocked by all this, Suri just stood, watching the old man, then said, 'What do you mean, "not an eternal death"?'

Ozo came to his feet and grabbed Suri by the collar, shaking the man as he said, 'I don't know! I have dreams of what sounds like my execution. I awoke in a bed in an old healer's home. How I got there and what happened, I don't know. Who I was. What I was. Not even where I was heading. I was near-dead, and my legs were crushed. After months of rehabilitation and relearning how to walk, I boarded a ship to scrub the decks for some coin and ended up crossing the Beladon Sea to find this village. After some time of spending my days rotting away as a beggar on the street, the village was attacked by some thugs. We fought them with everything we had, and I saved one of the Elders that day with a bit of luck, really. Since then, they've been lenient towards me. They've taken me in, given me that cabin, been kind to me. I thought all the dreams I've been having were just that, dreams, and nothing more. Now I'm not so certain.'

Suri, still motionless and expressionless, said, 'Okay, calm down. We'll figure out what's happening here. I believe you.'

The only thing Ozo was sure of now was that his days of speculation and madness were finally at an end. Something was taking shape, rearing its head out of the darkness; and although he was confused and scared, for the first time he felt calm — felt that this was supposed to happen.

'See the carnage you wrought on this cabin with just a few drops of your blood? It was something to behold, as none would believe it.' Suri walked through the wreckage, forgetting about Ozo for a short while; and when he turned, he saw the old man crumpled on the ground, foam bubbling from his mouth. Rushing forward, he turned him on his side and talked soothingly to him, trying to guide him back with his voice. 'Calm down, all will be fine. Just relax. Listen to my voice and release the tension. Release the evil...'

So much pain from within, so much pain from without! The news of his crimes had spread, and citizens now called for his head. Caged in the iron cells meant for those bent on committing treason and betrayal to their kind, he felt he did not belong. One such was in the cell next to him, preparing for his dismissal from the realm, unable to keep his mouth shut, speaking to anyone who would listen.

'You know, I did the right thing. They're not what we're supposed to be. Not human. No, no, no, no, no. They are not using their power to help where they can. What do they do? They hide it. Like cowards. Live like kings, and yet condemn everyone and everything who steps out of line for an instant. Who are you to decide? Who are you to give judgement over all beneath you?'

Ozo sat on his bed, chained to the wall, musing over his cellmate, and thought of the actions that had led him to this place. He looked away then and asked, 'What's your name?'

The prisoner stepped closer and looked into his eyes. Deathly chills ran through the prisoner; excrement freely flowed down his sodden trousers as he whispered, 'I can see you... You are one of them. *Why are you here?'*

* * *

Dusk was closing in fast as the sun set below the mountains, its fiery orange still lighting up the clouds above. Cradling Ozo's head in his arms, Suri felt the air change; the dust riding the currents suddenly fell to the ground as if by command, and a tear through the fabric of space opened just a few feet before them. Through the darkness came a rider, jumping clear over the pair as Suri fell on top of the seizing Ozo.

Suri rolled backwards on the ground and unsheathed his sword to meet the rider, struggling to get to his feet. He realised his leg had gone numb. He hobbled forward and readied himself against the intruder as he saw the man dragging his feet with great effort over the sand to stand over Ozo, just looking down at him with no weapon drawn, ignoring Suri completely. Suri's voice broke as he shouted, 'Stand back or perish!

Do not touch that man, or I will kill you!'

Still ignoring Suri, the man knelt down, removing a small pouch from his side. Suri saw that the man was panting as he stuck his thumb and forefinger into his mouth to wet them, then stuck them into the pouch. A yellow paste fouled his fingers as he pulled them from the pouch to draw a symbol on Ozo's forehead. That's when Suri attacked.

Sword swinging wildly, he charged at the unarmed man, fear getting the better of him. With a rocking blow, he felt cold steel slam against the side of his head. Dazed and confused, he fell flat on his arse, dust kicked up by the crash. Thinking he was dead for sure, he felt the side of his head, but little blood was present. The flat of the blade. *By the gods, I'm lucky.*

'No, my friend, you were *not* lucky... If I wanted to kill either of you, you would have been dead already. Now please, let me save your friend's life.'

'Oh, that's enough now,' came another, softer voice from the left. A woman stood next to the stranger, looking down at Ozo, and seemed to find herself unable to speak any further.

The man noticed her sudden silence and rose from the ground. 'Beuneth! Snap out of it.'

'What! Stop that, Khanaseri. I'm not some child you can shake like a toy.' Beuneth stormed off, shouting as she did, 'I'm getting some food for the night! You make sure he's okay.'

Suri grabbed his sword again, but restrained himself as he saw the rider put down his axe and take out the pouch once more.

With no thought to it, the warlock — for surely he was that — drew a symbol of horizontal waving lines next to each other on Ozo's forehead, with another vertical line through the middle of them. At the bottom of the line in the middle, he drew two shorter lines running off to the sides and down. The yellow paste had a foul odour to it, smelling of a dead bird baked in the sun for two days. Khanaseri took a handful of the powder and spat on it, then rolled it into a dough before breaking off small pieces. He fed it carefully to Ozo, ensuring he did not choke. Slowly, the fits ceased in their rage.

'Are you a healer?' Suri asked as he moved closer, sheathing his sword.

A grunt from the rider. 'No, far from it. Just a man on a quest.'

'So, you're not here for us?' Suri asked, his hand still resting on the sword hilt.

'I won't kill an unarmed man having a fit, or a young untrained boy with as much anger in his heart as he has talent to swing a blade. No. I'll save his life, because these seizures will kill him eventually, and spare yours, for it's unfounded to kill you. That woman you just saw did the same for me, so I'm paying it forward, I suppose. So there, you have my reason. I owe you nothing more.'

'Wait, you had fits as well?'

'Yes. It turns out that these "fits" happen when something inside you more powerful than you can handle tries to come out. Your body kind of just breaks for a bit and resets. What I want to know is, what does he have inside him that wants to come out?'

Suri relaxed his sword arm and asked, 'How did you know what I thought? About being lucky?'

'I saw it in your eyes. You thought you were done for. Come on, let's move him into the shade and wait for him to wake up. I could use a break and some supper, seeing that it's getting dark anyway. This trip has exhausted me, drained me completely. You're welcome to join us.'

Suri extended his arm and said, 'I'm Suri. The old man is Ozo. This burned-down house was his until yesterday. We can camp here for the night. Tomorrow we go our separate ways. I'm sure he'd like to meet the man who helped him.' Suri saw the big man stumble a bit as he stood, but said nothing.

Gripping the extended arm, the big man said, 'Khanaseri.'

'Where did you come from? What are you? Why are you—'

'Whoa, hold on there. So you have a lot of questions; I see that,' Khanaseri said as he walked to a rock to sit down, then continued, 'I come from a place called Artorea, very far from here,' he looked around. 'Where I'm from, it's very much summer at the moment. I dislike this cold. As for the question of what I'm doing here, let's just say that I'm looking for something very important. Now, before any more questions can spill from your mouth, let's get a fire started before she comes back. She can be a real—'

'What?' Beuneth walked closer from the left, holding three hares tied with a rope around their necks. Go on, finish that sentence. I dare you.'

'Handful. She can be a real handful.'

In the shade of his burned-out home, Ozo regained consciousness, and leaned his back against the wall, groaning as he did so. Suri moved closer and asked, 'How are you feeling, Ozo?'

'Like a bucket of rattled bolts.' Pale and cold, the older man moved his tongue around in his mouth and spat the horribly foul residue of the paste from his mouth. 'Dear Teros. What in the world is that? Did you piss in my mouth?'

'No. No, not at all, Ozo. A man appeared and helped you. He put that paste in your mouth, and your fit ceased. You got calmer. At first, I thought he was going to kill us both, but it seems he's here to help.'

'He's still here?'

'Yes. I think he went to relieve himself in the bush. He said those seizures would kill you if he didn't give you the paste. So I let him.'

'You just let him? He could have poisoned me.'

'But he didn't.'

Ozo wrapped his arms around his body, shivers racking him when Khanaseri arrived a few moments later, dusting his hands off on his trousers. Cradled in his childlike posture, he said, 'Thank you for your help today. It felt like my mind was going to be torn from my body. What can I do to repay you?'

Beuneth moved in from the side, her eyes locked on Ozo as she demanded, 'What kind of name is Ozo?'

Ozo's head drooped as he said, 'It's more of a title, really. It means something like, "The Forgotten".'

The warlock turned and took the hares from Beuneth, then prepared them for the fire, shouting with his back turned to them, 'What does that mean?' The crunch of the hares' necks snapping sounded, and Suri flinched. Drawing forth a big knife from his side, Khanaseri skinned the hares and gutted them before hanging them over the growing flame.

'It means I don't have my memories. I've lost all connections to my life prior to a couple of years back, when I woke up one morning with nothing but a bloody body and broken legs, left for dead. As if time didn't exist for me before that day.' With a smile on his broad face, Ozo looked up at the warlock and the beautiful Beuneth next to him. *A deadly pair*, he thought. Shaking his head, he said, 'You two make a wonderful couple.'

Without a word, Beuneth turned to leave, her hair waving in the wind as she moved past the warlock. *Of course! How could I have been so stupid? All this time here... Time. Yes.*

Khanaseri grabbed her arm. 'Where are you going?' He stared into her eyes and saw, for the first time, vulnerability, clear as day. 'Are you okay?'

'Yes, of course. Take the old fool with you as a guide to the Balamuth. If he threw your senses off, he'll also get you closer, so protect him. I have to go take care of some things on the other side.'

Brows furrowed, the warlock said, 'We came here for one reason: to get the Balamuth. *That* is the mission, not to babysit some fool. What do you have to do that's more important than this?'

'I just realised that I need the key as much as I need the Balamuth. You get the latter while I get the former. Without the key, I can't go back home,' she said as she pulled away from his grip, then walked a distance from them and started to chant. Opening a portal to move over vast distances requires a lot of effort and preparation.

'Let me know when you need me to bolster the power for the rift,' said the warlock, then turned away as she nodded.

Khanaseri walked back to Ozo, dropped to his knee before the man, and said, 'Well, since you asked, I have a question that I need answered. A while back, King Madock came into possession of a powerful orb. My father, being a great warlock — rest his soul — got it away from him after a vicious battle. He made the decision that no one man should have this power, so he sent it away. Now we need this orb once more.'

Ozo furrowed his brow and said, 'And how should *we* know anything about this orb? We're mere townsfolk.'

'Oh, now, that's not true; we all know this.'

Nervously, Suri grabbed the hilt of his sword and said, 'What do you speak of?'

'If you reach for that sword one more time, boy, I swear I'll cut off your arms and feed them to Ozo. I mean you no harm. I only need answers. Now, as I was saying. When my father cast the spell on the orb to send it away, it imprinted a kind of mark upon it that causes me to sense where the orb is, as I'm of his blood.'

Khanaseri stood and walked over to the horses, feeding them carrots from his pack as he continued, 'So my question to you is this: how is it that when I cast the spell to take me to where the orb was located, it brought me to you two? Now, I can sense that Suri over there has absolutely no energy of the orb on him. But not you, old man. No, you have the residual power of the orb on you. I sense you don't have the orb itself, but that just means that you should know where it is. My problem is this: because of your influence, I can't trace the location and retrieve it.'

Suri stepped forward. 'So that's why you helped him, to get the information from him.'

'Let's just say that it was mutually beneficial for the both of us if I helped him. Where's the harm in that?'

Rubbing his beard, the tattooed old man said, 'I don't know anything about this orb of which you speak. Can you explain to me what it does, or how it could be recognised?'

The hares had been cooking over the fire for some time now, and the aroma of the searing meat filled the clean night air. Khanaseri closed his eyes momentarily as he caught the smell. His mouth suddenly watered as he anticipated sinking his teeth into the soft flesh of the little beasts destined to serve as sustenance. 'The orb itself can be ingested somehow, by an acceptance of sorts,' he said after a moment. 'This gives the person great power.'

Ozo jumped to his feet in a dismal display of aerobatics. His thin arms and legs flew about uncontrolled, almost sending him back to the ground as he said, 'Well, I *have* seen some strange things a distance from here. Seen a scrawny young boy lift a man twice his size into the air.'

'You saw this first-hand and close by?' Khan asked, eager for an answer.

Heart thumping wildly, nervous and flustered, Ozo said, 'Yes, um... Yes. I did! Ha-ha. I knew I wasn't going insane. I tried to warn them. Remember, Suri? But no, they threw me out of the temple.'

'Where did you see this? I need to know.'

Ozo jumped up and ran to his destroyed cabin, climbing to the roof, but soon realised he wasn't going anywhere as he dangled in the air in the clutch of the big warlock. 'Now, where are you off to?' Khanaseri asked, his tone flat. Suri lay on the ground behind them, blood streaming from his nose.

'Oh, no. Don't worry, I wasn't running away or anything, just wanted a better vantage point is all. Come with me to the top.'

'You nearly caused me to kill you, you know.'

They climbed to the top and looked out over the forest to the right, with the tiny village down at the bottom of the mountain to the left. Farther south lay more mountain ranges and past that, more villages, silhouettes of the ranges and treetops their only guide in the dark. Ozo pointed with his finger and said, 'There, some distance into the forest, more to the right, there's an enormous tree. Looks like the roots are on the wrong side of the ground. That's where I saw it. Please take me with you. I need to see this. I can be your guide.'

Khan nodded and replied, 'Fine by me. Just know that I can't protect you at all times. You'll need to pitch in if there's a fight. Or run.'

'Oh, don't worry about me. I'll be fine. I've looked after myself so far, haven't I?'

As they reached the ground, Ozo gleefully ran to wake the unconscious Suri.

Khanaseri moved to the fire and broke the leg off a hare, then walked over to the chanting Beuneth and said, 'We leave in the morning.' He waited for her signal to join in, and soon received a nod from her. He grabbed her hand and joined the chant as the wind picked up forcefully. Lightning erupted from a growing storm up above, and drops of rain could be felt. The cold settled in, and soon the heat from the fire was but a distant memory as the portal ripped open. The warlock extended his hand and said, 'Here, eat this. You must be exhausted. I could barely move after opening it from the other side.'

Grabbing the leg, she took a big bite with her eyes closed, then stumbled forward and said, 'Thank you, Khan. Be careful with the Balamuth. And whatever you do, do *not* touch it. It will try to consume you for its own benefit.' Turning to step through the portal, she stopped and said, 'Oh yeah, I almost forgot to tell you. During my time trying to get the Balamuth, I might have made some promises to some bad people I never intended on keeping, so if they find out you're looking for it, they'll probably start hunting you. So be vigilant.'

'Hey! Come ba...'

Before he could finish the sentence, she was gone, and the portal snapped closed as if it were never there.

* * *

The cling-clang of the shop's bell sounded as the door opened and closed. Beuneth stood in the middle of the shop, unsure of where to begin as she stared at the hundreds of maps displayed on the shelves. Overwhelmed, she sighed and started off to her left, perusing them slowly, when a voice came from behind the counter. 'Sorry, miss, is there something I can help you with?'

'You just might. Are you the cartographer?'

The man rose from his chair to tower two heads above her as he crossed his skinny arms, looking at her over his spectacles. 'You a scholar?'

'What is this "scholar" you speak of? No, I don't think so, but I need to see some maps that stretch beyond the limits of these on display,' Beuneth said as she clutched a map, searching through the names.

He walked out from behind the counter and frowned as he said, 'I'm the cartographer, yes. What are you looking for, precisely?'

She placed the map back on the stand. 'I'm looking for a map of the city of Terenore.'

The cartographer tapped his index finger over his mouth and said, 'Terenore. I'm pretty certain I haven't seen a place called Terenore. But why does it sound so familiar? Give me a moment — I'll be back. Anatole, keep watch for new customers!' He then darted off to the back of the shop.

To her left, on the counter, lay the fattest cat she'd ever seen. Barely able to turn on his side, he begged for a scratch. 'Anatole, I presume?' She heard the cartographer rummaging through papers, then made her way to the back room, where maps lay strewn all over.

The cartographer stopped for a heartbeat in his search and looked up at her. 'Yes, I know. I need a better filing system. See if you can find a brown leather case somewhere beneath these maps.'

Working her way through the maps, Beuneth swept the papers along with her feet until she heard a dull thud as she hit something more substantial. Underneath all the maps, she pulled out a suitcase. 'Is this it?'

Red in the face from bending over so long, the cartographer looked at the case with wide eyes as he said, 'Yes, yes, that's it. Bring it here.' He took the dusty old case from her and unlatched the locks. 'You're in luck. I acquired these ancient maps a while back, and have slowly started going through them.' He flipped through the maps like a man possessed, his voice filled with glee. 'Oh, this is exciting!'

Beuneth could hardly contain herself as the cartographer suddenly stopped, studying one map in particular.

'Yes, yes. This is the one. To the table!' His long legs made his entire frame sway as he jumped over the maps on the ground to run back to the front of the shop. 'So very exciting!' In a rush of exhilaration, he pushed everything off the table: some fine laid-out glass pieces and smaller maps, showcasing his artwork with various layouts — maps with the topography, showing the mountains and valleys, others showing only the roads and so forth. As some glass pieces broke on the floor, he said aloud, 'Oh, don't worry about it, Anatole, those are the rubbish pieces you sell off, remember.'

Frowning at the man's change in demeanour, Beuneth shook her head as she said, 'Well? What is it?'

'There!' He placed his finger near a city to the far northeast on the map and moved slightly for her to see.

'Terenore.' She read the name aloud, hardly able to believe it.

'I'll be back.' His long legs carted him again to the back room, to return a few moments later. He placed a more recent map over the ancient one, lifting the corner from time to time, comparing the two. One city lay directly over Terenore on the newer map.

Finally satisfied with his findings, the man sat down on a chair behind the counter and said, 'New Runswick. That is the name of the city previously known as Terenore.'

'A new name? Why would it have a new name?'

'Oh, I can't recall the tale exactly, but I know something bad happened with one of their kings, and when the new ruler took over, he changed the name to wipe the slate clean. I only know about this since I travelled through there a few years ago to study some of their cultures.'

Tears welled in her eyes and her hands trembled as she said, 'Please, take this for the map and your troubles. The new one, not the old one.'

As she handed the man four gold orlings, he nearly fainted in his chair as he said, 'Oh, miss. This is very generous. But I can't. The excitement alone was worth the trouble!'

'I insist. You've just solved the biggest mystery I've been struggling with for over two years. It's the least I can do.' She took the map and said goodbye to the man, to vanish through the door into the bustling streets of Tergaron.

* * *

The Flying Squirrel stood bare, with a chain around the door and a sign that read, "Closed for Summer." He thought of the nights spent in this inn. If only these walls could spew out tales of the late-night festivities!

A man stumbled to the door of the inn, swinging left, then falling forward and back two steps before eventually reaching his goal. He pounded on the door and yelled, 'You cnt do tis to us! Wee hafno place lse to go!'

The myriad of those who needed a getaway, those who had lost so much that they only had this place and what it served left in this world...he had seen this too many times. The thought hurt him more than he expected, remembering all that he himself had lost.

A whistle brought his attention back to the present. He looked across to the old bridge and started in that direction. The muddy slopes of the banks saw his horse slip and slide as he headed down to the river under the bridge. A familiar voice came from across a fire in its infancy. 'Glad to see you're still in one piece,' Anavi said as she gestured at him to sit.

'No thanks to you. I should have your head for putting a bounty on mine. Do you know how long I worked to gain his trust? To get close to him? Years I've obeyed his will, doing his dirty work. All for naught.'

'You should have let me loose long ago, then. I've done more in these last few days than you could in years.'

Grinding his teeth, he pointed at her as he snapped, 'Watch yourself.'

Finally settling down next to the fire, he pulled a map from his leathers, holding it close to the fire to see more clearly. From the other side, Anavi stirred the fire with a stick as she said, 'You know, Xylac has great love for you still, even after your betrayal. He thinks it must be a mistake. That you did this for a stupid reason, like love.'

'Oh, but I *did* do it for love.'

'You know what I mean; not that kind of love. A recent stupid love, like Ladriana.'

'Don't pursue this subject. It's ill advised. Besides, whoever I want to spend the rest of my life with has no bearing on you. And no, I haven't forgotten them. I do all this for them still, to avenge them. And believe me, I *will* avenge them. Now give me the information.'

'Whatever you say, boss. Anyway, I heard something else. Xylac was pacing as he does after their meetings, mumbling to himself. He was going on about what we were searching for. Called it a key, but I don't think he actually knows what it is. They have a new location to search for this key, and I believe he's sent his people out already.'

Throwing twigs into the fire, Lanik spoke without averting his gaze. 'Where did they go?'

'Why? So you can get yourself killed? He has hundreds of men looking for this key. All of them ready to kill anyone who gets in their way.'

'If we get it before them, we have the upper hand. If he needs hundreds of men to procure and safeguard such an item, it must be precious to them. And I'll bet my life that the sorceress will be *very* unhappy with Xylac if something were to happen to this item. Especially if it were his very own lieutenant who stole it from under his nose.'

Anavi stood, mesmerised by the man's vulnerability, the hatred that roiled within, the desperate need to seek vengeance; not just to kill Xylac, but to maim him constantly first. Lanik was willing to go to the ends of the earth to cause him displeasure. Finally she said, 'Okay. I'll tell you where, but on one condition: I go with you.'

'Out of the question! I need you by his side.'

'That's the deal. Take it or leave it. Besides, I think he's onto me since my recent disappearing act.'

A few moments of silence passed between them, the only gossip being the fire's crepitation.

Lanik sighed, then continued, 'Where did they go, then?'

'You won't like this one bit. They went to a region close to New Runswick. Not to the city itself, but close enough to cause problems, as they will no doubt buy their food and supplies there.'

Shaking his head, he stared at her with wide eyes as he said, 'Ladriana and Magnus must be there already.'

Anavi gasped, choking on her own spit as she tried to rise to her feet. Between wracking coughs, she said, 'What? Are you serious? We have to leave now!' She grabbed her gear and flung the pack on her horse, then doused the fire with river water. Lanik whistled for his mount, as it had strayed a distance to their right, drinking water from the river.

* * *

Under a big willow swung a hammock ever-so-gently, and on it lay a young man whistling to his heart's content. The sky above was blue, the sun overhead cooled by a breeze flowing through the trees. To his left, the animals quieted down. He leaned over to look at the forest surrounding him, then rose from his hammock and moved closer to the area to investigate, carefully making his way through the forest, seeking any sign of life other than a worm or a beetle. No one ventured this deep into the forest, fearing the unknown. Men had tried to prove themselves worthy of the word "brave" by venturing in — more to show a girl their tenacity than anything else — but they soon came running out, wide-eyed and terrified by what they had experienced. Every man had a different story to tell, though, making the consistency of attacks on them unbelievable, causing them to be branded as cowards by the townsfolk and losing their hope with the girl they wanted to impress.

He took great caution not to step on any twigs or brush that would give away his position, but he didn't spy the patch of dirt that looked out of place from the rest. Then, with only a click, the trap was sprung. A thick rope shot up from the ground, hoisting him into the air, trapping him up high as he dangled by his leg. He struggled to free himself as he heard footsteps drawing closer. Two men ran into view. The shorter man, an older fellow with short curly hair, came running up with a strange gait, as if an old injury bothered him, his face tattooed all over, looking back and forth as he pointed at his hanging prey. A big, hulking warrior with a stern gaze followed close by and said, 'So *this* is the terrifying fellow you saw? He looks like he can barely lift a sword, let alone swing it.'

The man caught on the rope looked upon them calmly as he swung, and demanded, 'Why are you doing this? I've done nothing to you.'

Ozo said in a murmur, 'Yes, yes. That's him. Don't be fooled by him; be very careful.' He regarded the trapped man and said, 'We have you now! Finally they'll believe me!'

'Let me out of this trap, and no one will get hurt. I promise. Otherwise, I can't guarantee your safety.'

Khanaseri stepped closer, gazing at the man as he said, 'Who are you, and how did you happen upon the orb?'

The man laughed. 'Happen upon... Well, I suppose that's correct in some ways. It was actually the other way round. I was minding my own business as I walked in the woods, just after I had acquired quite a marvellous piece of jewellery from one of the townsfolk. Admiring the work that went into the piece, I was wondering what I might get for it, naturally — when out of nowhere, this damned enormous ball falls on my head, nearly killing me. It just materialised out of thin air. I thought someone had thrown a rock at me.

'I was out for some time. Eventually, I awoke and heard guards combing the woods for me. I saw the orb on the ground and thought, what the heck, couldn't hurt to take it, right? Little did I know that as soon as I touched it, it would swallow me whole. It felt like my skin was on fire, and my bones were being pulled apart. It was a torture the likes of which I had never felt. But at the same time, I wanted more. Like an addict craving euphoria, I opened my soul to it. When eventually the pain subsided, the orb was gone, and I could do this!'

Suddenly the man transformed into a huge, scaled bear with eyes of a serpent, growing until, eventually, the rope could bear its weight no longer. A loud snap, like the cracking of a whip, sounded as the rope gave out. Khanaseri dived and rolled for safety as the monster hit the ground with a mighty crash, coming down almost on top of them.

The warlock got to his feet and faced the growling bear, which was standing on its hind legs, displaying its teeth and claws. Ozo stood off to the left, too afraid to get closer. A strange pull in the bear's visage occurred, as if something was being rent from his soul, trying to escape him then.

Khanaseri pulled out his axe and rushed forward to attack; but before he could reach the bear, it shifted once more, this time into what looked like a red raven with crippled lizard legs dangling beneath it, and flew off through the forest and out.

He turned to Ozo and shouted, 'You knew of his ability to change?'

Ozo retreated step-by-step and quavered, 'Um, yes. Didn't you?'

A rage overtook Khanaseri then. Shouting at the top of his voice, he walked towards a nearby tree and swung the axe with all his might. What sounded like a lightning strike echoed through the forest as the tree was severed, crashing to the forest floor and sending up clouds of dust. 'This just made my retrieval much more difficult, which means it will take longer! And time is something I don't have at the moment!'

Ozo stepped over the fallen tree and looked down at it: the thickness of two men's legs, cut down with one blow. Unnatural. 'Forgive me. I didn't think to tell you this detail.'

The warlock gazed at the old man, then turned and headed in the direction the oscine bird had flown as he asked, 'Is there a town to the north?'

'Yes, there is.'

'Good. He'll probably head there.'

* * *

The vestiture of the land, fields cloaked with an appealing green grass reaching to a man's ankle, rolled on over the hillside as trees and bush enveloped the area. Soldiers sat everywhere, relaxing after the long day's march, some readying food and fire while others slept on the grass. Ganda'har sighed as he heard the laughter, along with the clangour of pots and pans. He had heard that sound too many a time in his life. The sound of camaraderie — usually the last pleasant sound before a battle.

He saw that the trees to his right were marred, burnt black by the foulness of sorcery. To his left, everything leaned away from him, branches broken and grass flattened, as if he stood at the epicentre of an explosion. Remembrance of the battle they'd fought against the Corlithians as grenades went off seeped into his mind; limbs, guts, blood, and livestock had flown in all directions. Those blasts had made a similar impression on the land.

Stilts announced, 'This is the location where he passed through, sir. We should be able, with some luck, to open this portal again to the location of its previous destination.'

Looking at the young warlock, Ganda'har said, 'I don't want to hear about luck, soldier; do your duty. How long will it take you?'

As skinny and pale as a newborn, Stilts thought as he rubbed the stubble on his chin, then said, 'We'll be ready to go through by nightfall, sir.'

'Are you sure this is the place? Because if you're wrong, I'll skin you alive.'

'There's still some residue of the magic Khanaseri used here. It's like a footprint that fades with time. I'm sure of it. What I don't understand is how he got this good so quickly. It takes years of practice to create a stable portal.'

'What are you getting at, soldier?'

'Can't say for sure, sir. But someone must have trained him well and fast. Meaning we might face two magic users soon.'

Untara shoved Talgar as he pointed at the warlock, and said, 'I think Stilts just pissed himself.' Both men burst out laughing, the bigger Untara clutching his stomach as Stilts walked by.

'What the... Did you just piss yourself laughing, Untara?' Talgar shoved the big man away from him as his trousers stained from the inside.

'What? No! Stilts, you piece of shit! Get back here!' Untara had started running after the warlock when Ganda'har shouted from the back, 'Untara! Let him go! He's our only way through this portal. Unless you've grown any magical abilities to get us through, sit down and shut up.'

'But sir,' Untara protested as he pulled at his pants, 'He made me piss myself! Can't I just hit him once? I promise not to kill him.'

'I said shut it, Untara! Go find something else to keep yourself busy. And change your drawers.'

* * *

'Come, my lady. It's time for morning tea.' The gruff voice of the big man sounded as serene as he could muster, given the constituents of onlookers: guards and crown staff, none of whom fully understood why the pair was allowed in the castle. The throne had stood empty since the murder of the king. No one had been allowed entry other than maintenance staff. But orders had been handed down from the Council very hastily not to confront the new lady and her guardian. They were to be escorted and guarded whenever they left the premises of the castle, and reports were to be provided of their whereabouts daily. The castle was abuzz with rumours running wild.

The pair wandered the halls, then moved down to the courtyard and farther into the gardens, where a table and two chairs awaited them. Her long red dress dragged on the ground behind her, the jewels on her left hand blinding her guardian with every flick of her wrist. Her red-brown hair was rolled up and pinned down, revealing her sensual neckline, where hung a necklace of sparkling green pearls. She marvelled at the garden before her, and could, for that moment, not believe the truth of things. How could it be that a girl, a nobody from a tiny village, could now possibly be royalty? Ladriana looked over her shoulder at her guardian and said, 'Magnus, please tell me everything. How is this all possible?'

With a sigh and a twist of his mouth, he said, 'We've spoken 'bout this already, my lady. I can give youse only half-truths, and youse deserve the whole truth and nothing less. Also, if youse don't like what I says, who's to stop youse from doing something stupid? I will be forced to club youse over the head and drag ye to the dungeons until Lanik returns to explain things. So do youse still want me to tell youse the half-truths, my dear?'

With pursed lips trying to hide a mocking laugh, she said, 'Okay. First, it won't be as easy to take me down as you described, Magnus. And if need be, I can probably still outrun you, even in this ridiculously marvellous dress. Remember that I was part of the Desert Dogs for a very long time. And second, yes, I *do* want you to still tell me the half-truths that you can impart.'

'Aye, I do know. And do ye know that I fought in the Gallian wars?'

Ladriana tilted her head in amazement and said, 'I thought all the warriors who fought in the Gallian wars died?'

'Aye, that's the rumours we spread, yes. But there are a couple of us still alive. But that's a story for another time...'

The roiling in the pit of her stomach made her nauseous, and rightly so. The propitious alignment of fortunate events thus far would run out eventually, and she knew it. It could not go on in her favour all the time, and with all that had gone right, that which went wrong would be devastating. She had learnt the hard way that no matter what, your luck will change, and usually in a turn for the worst. She thought back to her childhood...

Ladriana's father ran errands for a merchant, selling his wares, setting up meets, arranging antiquities and such. It went well for them for some time, but he had a dream of owning his own shop; and so he put all his hard-earned orlings away, but it wasn't enough. Then out of nowhere, a man named Ebron came to see him and wanted to partner up with him to start the business. Father was as happy as a pig in slop, already seeing his dreams becoming reality. The merchant he worked for agreed to let him go and wished him all the luck in the world with his new business venture.

His merchant's licence went off without a hitch. Everyone else moaned and groaned about not being able to get one, but he got his with the very first application. Even acquiring premises was no hassle; he only looked for a few days, and again, first application and all was granted. All went so well they thought Kelcai himself had blessed them. Still a child, only sixteen years of age, new to the world and learning all that it offered, she worked in the little shop during the days, while Ebron looked over the income and her father moved from place to place to sell his wares. Sometimes her father had to go to different cities and villages and stayed away for days, weeks even. It went very well, and they prospered for a time.

One morning, as they were getting ready to head to the shop, a messenger stood by the door as they were about to leave. Taking out a rolled-up parchment with the merchant's guild emblem on it, he read, 'Dear Roahn of the Nuka family. We, in an official capacity as the Merchant's Guild, advise you that your fees have gone up to one hundred orlings. The next payment is due in seven days. We look forward to doing business with you.'

Roahn contested the price hike, stating it was double what he was paying currently, but alas, he could not sway them. In order to just make ends meet, Roahn worked his fingers to the bone, working day and night, almost never seeing his daughter. One morning, as they neared the shop, they found the door hanging on its hinges. Everything not bolted down had been stolen and everything bolted down broken. No one saw anything, and if they did, they weren't talking. Despair set in for the first time in her life. She saw her father fall to the ground as tears streamed down his face, sobbing as he said, 'I have failed you, my child. I tried so hard to give you a good life. But they have ruined me.'

She looked into her da's eyes and said, 'We'll beat this together.' The times were hard on them then. For months they scraped by, barely eating, replacing all the stock in the shop and still having to pay the guild. The darkness slowly dissipated, and light started streaming in for them as their cash flow increased yet again. Not long after, another messenger appeared with another price hike. Double again. The inevitable occurred. They could not pay and went into debt. A few days later, men dragged her father away and threw him in the dungeons, leaving him for dead, never to be heard from again. Men from the Merchant's Guild took her away, putting her to work to pay off his debts. For years, she toiled to pay off the debt until she escaped their clutches.

'I feel as if I need to hunt and kill something,' she said, looking around anxiously.

Magnus' shoulders sagged, and with a sigh of deep, thoughtful anguish released into the encumbered world of pain and sorrow, he said, 'Why do I even bother? This is not ladylike behaviour. Please, can we have a delightfully prepared meal, rather than having to butcher it ourselves and pin it over an open fire?'

Still looking at him with fire in her eyes, she asked, 'Where's my bow, Magnus?'

Another sigh was released. 'In the closet. I will go ready the horses.'

* * *

A soft voice whispered in the wee hours of the night, 'Into the night we go, silent as assassins be, to take a life or three. For what we do, we don't for gold. We only strive for the guild to survive. Honour be as honour should. Honour the assassin lying next to you. This is the oath we live by.'

Five figures moved in the dark, the moon looming over them, dressed in dark blue leathers, their weapons all painted a dull black to conceal them. Hoods covered their faces, only their eyes barely visible. Link ground his teeth as he said to his brothers, 'How is it we five master assassins have been sent to eliminate one man? This is surely not even a job for one of us. They should have sent an initiate.'

Glass slapped him on the back of his head, saying, 'We don't question their reasoning. You would do well to remember that.'

'I've grown tired of lies, Glass. What has this man done to deserve us five as company?'

Taking out his dagger, Glass turned to Link and said, 'All I know is he angered the wrong people. Besides, I'm the only master assassin here. You four will always be my trainees...'

At the far end, one of the five shook his head and said, 'Is that right, old man? I believe in this case that the student has become the master. Remember, with age comes slow response time. But you probably already know that.'

Switchblade whispered, 'By the way, while they sent you across the oceans to laze about in the sun all day, we had to pick up your work.

You owe us an explanation. What were you doing over there?'

Glass unconsciously rubbed his stomach, feeling the scar beneath his garb, sighed, and said, 'Amateurs, the lot of you. A personal matter, Switch. Enough talking. You and Draft move to the right on the roof of that house. Link, you and Sliver move to the left, and find a good vantage point. I'll move about in the shadows below.'

The night's cool breeze caressed their skin as their target made his way through the little fishing village off the shore of the Beladon Sea. The entire village was comprised of only a few hundred homes, a few temples, some shops, a fish market, and a brothel for the sailors coming into port. No guards patrolled, and usually none were needed. They didn't even have a guard on duty until recently, when Carlin Moore chopped up his cousin for sleeping with his wife. Since then, they had appointed some weasel to have a go at protecting the citizens of Belinai. The streets were mostly empty, except for a few roaming cats and dogs, and the occasional drunk lying passed out wherever they found a softer spot for their head.

Moving from shadow to shadow, Glass stalked his target, a big brute of a man walking in the centre of the street muttering to himself whilst holding a blanket wrapped round his shoulders and back. The man stood for some time, swaying back and forth, as though the universe had postulated his coming demise and had frozen him in place. Glass signalled the rest to hang back and observe for now.

Atop the roof where Link and Sliver kept watch, movement caught Link's attention on the roof opposite them.

Draft moved silently at great speed towards his victim. With ease, he leapt through the air, dual sai ready to kebab the target. In a swift motion, the target flung the blanket to the ground and hurled a massive war axe towards the assassin... The kill was quick, splitting Draft's head in two as the axe cleaved his skull. As the corpse spasmed on the road, the big man wordlessly stepped closer and wiggled the axe to pull it free with a sloshing sound as blood and bone caused it to stick.

Silently he waited, staring down the streets, looking for any movement, but there was none. He went to his knee to wipe the axe on

Draft's leathers, then turned and headed down a long alley as if nothing had happened. A dark alley solicits trouble; and on more days than not, it found it. He walked with not a care in the world as the four remaining assassins followed on the rooftops. One could get lost in the alleys quickly; they formed an absolute labyrinth of gargantuan proportion. One fed into another, then two or three connected before splitting off. Glass was in front, keeping a keen eye on the man, when from the back, Sliver said, 'Why didn't we attack back there? We had the numbers. Now Draft is dead.'

For a moment, Glass lost his concentration and looked behind him, saying, 'That was all on Draft. He was careless.' When he looked back, the man was gone.

'Looking for me?' a voice called out, and Glass felt a chill in his bones. *How did he get up here so fast?*

The assassins spread out around the warlock on the flat rooftop as he rested the axe on his shoulder and calmly asked, 'Why are you hunting me? I've done nothing to warrant this attention.'

Glass unsheathed his swords and said, 'I don't really care what you did, except that you just killed one of my men. And therefore, you must die.'

The big man pulled his axe down to rest his hands on the haft as he looked around at the four men. 'Honour! Loyalty! I can relate to that. And I'm sorry about your friend. But I refused to die just for him to live. It was self-defence. You lot came out here tonight to murder *me*, not the other way round. I am Khanaseri. Who are you?'

'Stop talking and die!' Glass charged in, dual swords swishing through the air with grace and speed. Khanaseri blocked the slashes and got in a few of his own, but the assassin was fast, avoiding the blows from the big man with ease. With a flare of enormous power, Khanaseri shouted words unknown and thundered his axe down on the roof, collapsing the beams and sending a section to the floor below. They plummeted downward in a hail of dust and wooden beams. Vision obscured, Sliver and Switchblade cried out in pain, both unable to get up from beneath the rubble. They had held back, wanting to watch the fight between the two men. Neither of them had thought that something like this would happen. Coughing, Link saw Khanaseri rise from the rubble, standing ready with that dreadful weapon, just waiting. Link untangled the chain whip from his neck and legs, watching the patient man before him, then heard him speak. 'You know, if you take any longer, I'll have to fight someone else.'

Damn! How can he be this calm? 'Oh, I'm ready for you.' The dance of death started as he spun the whip, but struggled in the narrow space as his whip hooked onto a beam. He cursed as he heard the man say, 'Is this going to take long? I have somewhere to be.'

With a shake of the whip, it released and began spinning once more. Small blades laced the last section of the whip, and at the very point, it had a blade the size of a tiger's tooth. Working with both hands, Link guided the chain carefully, with sinister perfection at tremendous speed – under his arms and round his body, swinging it like a bo staff and out with enormous force, slicing into Khanaseri's chest before ripping the blades out. Blood spurted, and the chain kept coming. Round and round it went, turning this way and that, snapping out and curling round beams, yanked back with enough force to shatter them. Round his neck it shot out time after time, seeking its target as Khanaseri fell back. Several times he got through, cutting his opponent.

Khanaseri thought back to the fights he'd had with Beuneth, then smiled as he raised his hands to the air and shouted, 'Hold on... Stop! You fight well with this weapon. If you stop now, I'll spare you all. I didn't come here to kill any of you.'

Glass finally made his way out of the rubble and snarled, 'We honour our commitments. So die you shall, demon!'

Khanaseri muttered a few words, repeating the pattern over and over. Glass stumbled on unsteady legs, his energy sapped, until he fell to the rubble.

Looking around, Link saw the other two assassins' heads drooping, their eyes closed. Ready to attack again as fear gripped him, he shouted his frustration at this witchery: 'What is this? What have you done?'

Quietly placing the head of his axe on the ground and leaning on the haft, Khanaseri said, 'Easy. Easy, now. I haven't killed them. Far from it. I've only made them sleep. Go. Feel their hearts beating.'

Link focused and saw their chests moving as they breathed. 'You could have done this from the start. No one needed to get injured at all. Why didn't you?'

Khanaseri frowned and said, 'I needed to gauge my pursuers. How did you find out I was here, though?'

Standing ready with his chain whip, Link nodded as he said, 'A message came earlier from the south.'

'Ah, Suri,' Khanaseri muttered, shaking his head. 'Damned lad must have told the wrong person in his village about me.'

The assassin, unsure of his next move and uneasy about the situation, demanded, 'Why are you here?'

The warlock tilted his head as he replied, 'I'm here at someone else's behest. Don't even know the place. If you're willing to let me go, I could use some information. I'm searching for a young man with red hair and a slash across his neck. Have you seen him?'

Link lowered his weapon as he said, 'No, but if he's hiding, then you should go search the catacombs to the east. The guild won't stop until you're dead, you know.' Link looked around at his sleeping brothers and continued, 'How long will they sleep?'

Khanaseri shrugged. 'Maybe a day.'

'Good. I can work with that.'

Turning around, Khanaseri waved his hand as he strolled out of the room and muttered, 'Boy, am I glad that room was empty.'

* * *

Hunting: the unmistakable act of murdering an innocent victim unable to defend itself, only to devour the flesh for the brevity of sustenance. It felt good releasing the bowstring, watching the arrow buck and weave through the air to find its target a good distance away. There was no desultory act in hunting; everything was done as planned. She looked at the tracks; the animal was moving slowly and steadily to the west. There was no rush, no urgency in the footprints, no branches broken on the path. Stealthily but swiftly moving through the forest, the big cats barely noticed her, unperturbed by her gracious movements. The same, unfortunately, could not be said of the big oaf dragging at her heels, panting like a very ill dog. Every time she stopped to scan the area for more visible signs of the deer, Magnus would stand a few paces back, trying his utter best to stifle the coughs and regurgitating motions his body was pulled in. Running an inn had its privileges, but none of those were exercising. The panting continued as he motioned with his hands, trying to say something, but the only sounds coming from his mouth were, 'Ss. st...' and then he collapsed. Moments later he opened his eyes to find Ladriana hovering over him.

'You really need to exercise more.'

He sat up as the world spun around him, and said, 'You're going to be the end of me.'

'Mmm, I was thinking more along the lines of me being the one trying to save you from heart failure. Just look at all the flab. That's what will kill you, my friend. Now come, we've lost time and need to make it up, quickly.'

Running once more, Magnus was soon drowning in his own spit. Not because there was too much, no, but because it had become so dry; the saliva string hanging from his mouth ran all the way down his throat and would not break even under rigorous circumstances as he shook, spat, and even used a twig to break it off, but nothing, it would not relent. His throat was parched, and there was nothing to quench the dryness. Once more, she came to a stop, scanning the area. Magnus was coughing again, but she lunged at him and thrust her hand over his mouth, and said, 'Quiet! Something isn't right.'

Taken aback, red in the face and still choking, Magnus held everything down and listened. 'I hear nothing except some hammering...'

For a few heartbeats, Ladriana watched Magnus with a wondering gaze of defeat, ebbing with the possibility of regaining victory. Finally, he snapped round with a dramatic look upon his face and almost shouted, 'Goodness me! No one is supposed to be in the king's forest except royalty, and they definitely wouldn't hammer anything; they're far too lazy.'

'Wow, that was amazing to behold,' she said as she slowly set off toward the hammering sound. Magnus, confused by the statement, pulled out his axe and went after her.

The forest was thick, providing plenty of places to hide from prying eyes. Hot and humid, they were bathed in sweat, causing their clothes to stick to their bodies. Nearing the centre of the forest, they saw several men hammering at the solid stone door of King Tolken Venut's tomb, a mammoth structure; within lay his body, encased in a solid marble coffin. Magnus came to a stark realisation and tapped Ladriana on the elbow. He pulled out a vial filled with a crimson liquid hanging round his neck and paled as he said, 'I know what they're after.'

Confused, she asked, 'What is that?'

Magnus turned, holding on to the vial as he said, 'It all happened a very, very long time ago. Terenore was still in its youth when all this took place, a newfound city proclaimed so by Warchief Tolken Venut, after a great many battles fought against the dwarves, elves, demons, and orcs that roamed this beautiful land... It was his very first conquest in Beltokko, the land of many. After landing with their ships on the east coast, they travelled some distance over mountain ranges and forests. He felt the presence of others following their movements, never straying too far away; but never could he glimpse the growing threat. As he summited the Red Mountains, he saw the beauty that was Beltokko, and he knew he had to have it. As far as the eye could see, stretched land so fertile it would never stop giving crops. Winding rivers flowed through the forest and out. It was teeming with life. Immediately, they began construction at the base of the mountain. His men worked around the clock to get defences up as the women furiously started with food production.'

Ladriana cocked her head and whispered, 'I thought this was New Runswick?'

'Aye, it is. They changed the name a long time ago. Now, where was I? Oh yes. That first night, two figures emerged from the forest unarmed: a dwarf and an elf, messengers from their lords sent to gauge the plans of this intruder. They ambled up to the soldiers of Tolken with their hands in the air, speaking a language unknown to them. But the warchief did not see this as a land that could be shared. He didn't even give them the chance to be peaceful. No. He walked up to the two men smiling with outstretched arms, and as he came within reach, he went to his knee, pulled free his sword, and sliced it through the air, disembowelling the elf and virtually decapitating the dwarf. Were it not for their thick necks and strong spines, his head would have rolled. No, there was no peace back then. After his eventual demise, they buried Tolken here in the centre of the forest, and every subsequent king lies beside him. The legend goes that Warchief Tolken, who later became King Tolken, never actually died but ascended; and that whoever drank from his blood would have unnatural strength and longevity of life. When they found him in his chambers on the floor, he was brought to the priests, but he was already dead. So, in order to preserve what they could, they drained his blood from his body and hacked out his brain, heart, lungs, liver, even the kidneys, and stored them all safely away.'

Ladriana stood silently, watching him. Pale, she said, 'Please tell me they buried the blood with him.'

'No, they would never leave it in his tomb. It's too valuable. Why would you say that?'

Sighing, she said, 'Because if it's safely tucked away somewhere in the palace, guess where they're heading next to find it? And I bet they won't ask nicely. We need to leave and warn the guards.'

Slowly they backed away, keeping and eye on the men in front of them, barely a few dozen feet away. There were at least thirty of them that they could see. Moving from tree to tree, they walked as softly as possible, so as not to give away their presence. But suddenly, a loud crack, deafening to the two, sounded under Magnus' foot. 'Maybe they didn't hear,' he whispered with a shrug.

Shouts arose from the men at the tomb. 'Someone is nearby! Go,

118

find them and bring them back here!'

Another group came from the left, and one spotter shouted, 'There, I see them, in the trees!'

Immediately, arrows began raining down upon them. They needed to get some distance between them and their pursuers, so they ran as fast as their legs could carry them. *So quickly the hunter becomes the hunted!* The hunters were soon converging on them from all sides. Ladriana loosed one arrow, then two, then three. As fast as she could, she let the arrows fly from her bow. At least five men went down that she saw, and she hoped it would be enough. The horses were close by now. *Just a little farther.* Ladriana looked over her shoulder and saw some men still running at them. Arrows still swished past. An audible *crunch* sounded behind her, followed by a shout of anguish. She looked back and saw Magnus on the ground, an arrow jutting through his thigh.

Pained, he looked up at her, his face pale as he shouted, 'Go, you idiot! What are you doing?! Get out of here and warn them! And take this with you to the priests! I'll hold them off!' The vial sailed through the air to her, and as she caught it, another arrow pierced his left biceps. They were closing in fast, and she knew she would not make it back to him.

Tears ran down her face as she turned and ran for her horse.

Chapter Six

A thunderstorm was brewing in the south, drawing closer as the day progressed; violent flashes of lightning arced to the ground in the distance as thunder drowned out all other sounds. The walk to the catacombs took longer than expected, annoying Khanaseri even more than receiving the conflicting information about where the actual location of the entrance was. Finally reaching the entrance, Ozo rubbed his hands together as consternation and doubt settled in, and moved in behind the warlock as he said, 'Oh, I don't know if this is such a good idea anymore. It's very dark in there, and he could literally be anything!'

'I don't think it works like that.'

'Oh? How does it work, then? Enlighten me.'

Khanaseri closed his eyes and gritted his teeth as they walked deeper into the catacombs. *Of all the fools in the world, why did I have to be paired up with this one?* The warlock pleaded, 'Can you be quiet, so as not to let him know we're here? If we maintain the element of surprise, there might not be too much blood shed. Especially mine.'

With their eyes adjusted to the dark, they could at least see the silhouettes of things. Many tunnels branched off this main walkway, making it near-impossible to find the man. Ozo pulled a torch from the wall and felt the rag, ensuring it was still wet. He turned to the warlock and said, 'Do you mind? I can't see a thing in here.'

Khanaseri stood for a moment, considering the old man's request, then cupped his hands around the rag of the torch and whispered under his breath. The torch suddenly flared to life, lighting up the corridor. With his battle-axe in hand, he walked through the eerie narrow walkways of the catacombs, followed closely by the doddering old fool with his torch. Old, damp air and the smell of decay flowed into their nostrils, making it hard to breathe. As far as they walked, animal skulls lined the gaps in the walls.

'I don't think he's in here,' said Ozo as he stopped to inspect an item on the wall — a curious little idol made of straw. Dust fell on his face as he turned the idol above him to inspect it from below. Stifling a cough, he drew a deep breath, inhaling the dust through his nose. At first, he bent backwards with a slow heave, and then a mighty sneeze erupted from him, launching an enormous ball of fire down the walkway, hurtling towards the warlock, nearly engulfing him as he dived for cover.

Khanaseri rolled on the ground, making sure he wasn't on fire, then looked at Ozo as he jumped to his feet, his face covered in dirt. 'What the hell was that?!'

Still clutching the idol, Ozo backed up against the wall. 'Sorry, sorry, sorry. It was just a sneeze, just a sneeze. I didn't mean for it... I don't know where that ball of fire came from.' As he spoke, he felt a tingle in his nose once more, and immediately covered his mouth, 'Ha-ha-ha --'

Khanaseri's eyes widened as he backed away and said, 'No! Don't you dare!'

'Haaaaachhhooooo!' Massive fireballs erupted again and again, as Ozo failed to control the sneezes wracking his frail body. Khanaseri dived to the left, then to the right to avoid the blasts.

During this chaos, a hulking lion with a gigantic lizard tail appeared from a tunnel with a mighty roar and a vicious smack to the sternum of the warlock. Khanaseri's back slammed hard into the wall, the lion trailing close after. Half the lion seemed wrong, its face permanently pulled into a snarl, and it was scaled on one side as if overtaken by a sickness. The claws on one foot were overly large, scraping the ground and causing the beast to stumble.

Dazed, Khanaseri lay on the ground, trying to regain his senses, and saw the beast bearing down on him. Massive teeth bit down on the axe's haft as he tried to keep the animal at bay. He was still contemplating his next move when another ball of fire came flying, setting the lion's scaly side on fire. A roar of pain erupted as it threw itself away from the warlock before it scrambled to its feet and disappeared down another passage.

Still lying on the floor, Khanaseri dropped his head to the stone surface, laughing. 'I don't know if I should kiss you or kill you, Ozo. What do you think?'

'Well, I'm leaning towards kiss...but coming from you, even that sounds scary.'

* * *

'This is a one-way trip, sir. Seems Khanaseri travelled a great distance. It will take a few days, weeks maybe, for me to replenish my strength to fashion another gate for us to come back. It will drain me completely. We're ready to proceed when you are.'

Unflinching under the gaze of his men, Ganda'har said, 'So you better not get dead whilst we're over there...'

Stilts shook off the comment, bowed slightly, and moved away as he signalled for Talgar to join his captain. Ganda'har studied the man as he approached and remembered his first days of joining as a recruit. What a transformation had occurred in this man after only a few skirmishes. They had joined at the same time. He had seen Talgar at the training grounds, a skinny, pale kid with long hair and nothing to say, shying away from everyone and always being picked on... Until one day when one of the older soldiers walked past and told him his mom must make for a good ride. An inhuman scream shrieked through the training grounds as Talgar launched himself at the man, swinging a rock in both hands. Blood sprayed from the soldier as he sagged to the ground, a big gash in his head. Reversing his motion, the rock slammed against the soldier's face again, breaking his nose and jaw, fracturing the orbital bones. It took three soldiers to restrain Talgar and get him under control. Turned out his mother had passed away two days prior from a fire that broke out in their home. That rage never left him... Now Talgar was light on his feet, lean and fast. Always lightly armoured, he wielded dual assassin daggers at his side. His head was shaved, with silver adorning his ears. As second in command, his men respected him, for they knew he would stand steadfast between them and death.

Talgar moved among the men, shouting, 'Okay, then. Everyone form a line — we're heading through in single file. Once you reach the other side, set up a defensive perimeter as quickly as possible. Make sure you cover the person coming through behind you. I've arranged for you to go through as pairs — warrior, archer, warrior, archer — for a tactical advantage. We don't know what to expect when we go through, so work together. Cooks and gear come last, so don't forget about them! Is this understood?'

All the soldiers shouted in unison, 'Hu!'

Lightning arced, igniting a tree to their right. Shouts and curses sounded as soldiers scurried for cover. Another arced out. Red bolts streamed from the warlock, tearing the portal open. Stilts screamed as his fingers turned black. Ganda'har rode his horse up to the warlock and shouted, 'What's going on?'

Stilts looked back at his captain. The pain and exhaustion on his face made the captain turn away as the man shouted, 'Move quickly! I can't hold this long!'

The sun was setting in the distance while they were in the mania of the lightning storm that shrouded the portal. Winds howled through the trees as Untara, the first of the warriors, slipped through and disappeared from this place to be whisked away to somewhere unknown. The men and women moved through, one by one, all warriors at heart, every one of them willing to put their lives on the line for the one standing next to them.

* * *

The immense soldier made his way through the crack torn in the world's fabric and sighed as he stared ahead. Those coming through behind him were unsure if it was a sigh of relief or disappointment that no one was facing him with weapons drawn. Dawn was approaching fast on this side. The mountainous outlines to the far west would be the last to be touched by the burgeoning light of the day. They were standing on a barren field, with small, dying, or dead trees scattered around haphazardly. Untara looked around and said to the archer next to him, 'Now, this brings back memories of Artokla. I love this place already.'

Geolas put away the arrow he had nocked, then stared at Untara. 'There's something seriously wrong with you. No one really misses the desert or likes it. It's an unforgiving place with little to no life in it.'

The beast of a man sheathed the long sword he was carrying, and said, 'No, you're very mistaken, my friend. Life is everywhere in the desert; you just need to know where to look. If you had ever in your life been out in the desert at night, and not always cowered up under mommy's blouse, you would know this. I blame your parents, not you...' With a grin, he looked at the archer, who seemed speechless and on the edge of putting an arrow in the giant's forehead.

'At least I wasn't breastfed by a goat...or my pa.'

Stunned to silence, Untara laughed at the witty comeback before walking away.

Warriors were still filing out of the portal as Ganda'har stood a distance away, watching the skyline, trying to get any idea of where Khanaseri might have gone from here. A shout came from the rift as it closed. He turned and ran down the slope to investigate, skidding on the loose gravel as he did. As he neared, he saw Talgar carrying Stilts over his shoulder and settle the unconscious man down on the ground, then shouted, 'Get me a healer!' His second-in-command looked up at him and continued, 'Opening that rift took a lot out of him, sir. He has blood coming out from everywhere. He'll need to rest — if he even makes it at all.'

With a nod, Ganda'har moved away and said, 'See that he does. He's our way home.'

At the front lines, Untara and Geolas surveyed the area while every so often looking back to where the healer worked on Stilts. They knew they would not move out until the man was dead or stable enough to leave in the back of a wagon. The men and women had all enlisted for a mission none of them wanted. They all knew Khanaseri through the stories told by his father, the man he was, and how well he fought. And now that he might have his father's gifts, the possibilities were endless. *Hardly seems right that an entire platoon would go after one man. Then again, it might be the safest way of bringing him back alive.*

Geolas thought back to the chilly morning when they'd enlisted.

Every soldier fought through the cold, shivering from the icy winds, steam rising from their mouths with every breath they took. Looking up from his sparring session with the bo staff, he saw Galvos enter the busy training grounds with a demeanour that deserved attention. The big warlock walked straight past everyone to a man who still had his back turned to him — a big warrior as well, muscled from head to toe, with a long, braided ponytail hanging down his back. Galvos grabbed the ponytail and yanked, pulling the man down with so much force that the planks underneath him broke as his head hit the floor. Everyone stood stunned, not knowing if they should intervene. The warlock strolled up and down in quick passes right in front of the man, who was slow to get up. Galvos said to all watching, 'Let all bear witness to this day! Do not think that you can hide from me if you intend to betray this place or the brothers who stand next to you. This man, Jomein, has been in our midst for some time, trying to learn our ways, our strengths and our weaknesses. But he has failed his employers today, for he shall not be informing them of anything.'

Jomein stood, facing Galvos, then rushed in with a blisteringly fast right hook.

Galvos dropped to his knees and pulled the legs out from under Jomein. The sound as he hit the floor was nauseating. Again he stood, but this time he approached with more caution, and unsheathed a dagger from his belt. A left cut, reverse, right cut. A succession of cuts and kicks and punches followed, all of which Galvos blocked with little effort. Then, with a last right stabbing motion, Galvos caught his arm and reversed it so that the elbow was above his shoulder. He brutally wrenched the arm down, snapping it. Bones jutted from the flesh and blood sprayed from the wound. As Jomein lay there screaming in pain, Galvos said, 'I saw in your notes that you thought my "abilities" were something they could exploit, something that could be manipulated, as if that were my weakness. Well, then. Let me show you how wrong you are.' Galvos grabbed the warrior's head and mumbled a few words over and over. Jomein screamed in pain, but at first, there were no signs of anything happening. Soon after, one could see why he was screaming. It seemed as if all the tendons in his body were pulling tighter and tighter until a succession of snaps were heard. The screams were horrific. Jomein lay on the ground, unable to move any of his limbs, a sack of meat. Everyone stared in silence at Galvos, who then said to no one in particular, 'Take him away. Throw him on the dumps outside the city, for all I care.'

One soldier – Untara – stood and said, 'But he still lives! At least end his misery first.'

Galvos turned to him and said calmly, 'No, leave him alive. I'll visit him later, maybe tomorrow. If he's lucky, the crows won't have taken his eyes by then.'

Geolas shivered as the memory faded. *If Khan is anything like his father, we'll need to be ready.*

* * *

After the debacle in the catacombs, they'd barely said a word to each other for the rest of the day. Ozo made many attempts, but most of the time, he only opened his mouth for nothing to leave it. Earlier, Khanaseri had been brooding and paused as he said, 'I'm going to find something to kill. You make a fire somewhere discreet. I'll find you.'

Some distance from the little town, under an overhang of rock a ways up a mountain, Ozo sat waiting for the warlock to return, and thought on the day's events. *What's happening to me? First it's all the dreams, then my blood is literally on fire, then I don't die from seemingly fatal burns. Now I'm spitting fireballs when I sneeze.*

A loud snap brought him out of the trance as Khanaseri snapped his fingers before his eyes and said, 'Oi! Come back to the living. The whole Malidonian army could have marched up to you and sliced your throat, and still you wouldn't have seen it coming. I've already skinned the fox and placed it over the fire. You didn't even know I was back.' Khanaseri threw out a bearskin rug and lay on it as he said, 'What can you tell me about back there in the caverns?'

'Catacombs...not caverns.'

The warlock took out an apple and cut it up piece by piece with the sharp axe blade, sticking them in his mouth as he did. 'What are you on about?'

The old man sat staring into the flames, refusing to look up, and with a stern gaze said, 'Caverns are just caves.' He gestured around them and continued, 'This is a cavern. Those were burial chambers. Have some respect, you oaf. If you want to beleaguer me and break me down, the least you can do is use the correct words.'

'Whatever. Just be glad I spared your life,' the warlock mumbled as he lay down with his arms behind his head.

Ozo jerked his head up and flew into a rage as he swung his fists through the air, shouting at the top of his voice, 'Spared my life? Spared my life, have you? Well, come on, then. Kill me. I don't care!' Trying to make an impression of the big man, he rubbed his balding pate, saying, 'Look at me, I'm the great and powerful Khanaseri! I can kill anyone whenever I want! There are no consequences if I kill anyone, because I'm an arse! Well, great and powerful Khanaseri, there will come a day that you wish you *weren't* such an arrogant arse. All I hear from you is how great you are, how powerful you are! Well, I have news for you. No one likes you; they probably never did. Everyone only tiptoes around you because you're an egotistical maniac. You don't have any friends. Someone says something you don't like, you kill them. Someone does something you don't like, you kill them. You are intolerable! Come on, then. Kill me! I've said more to you than anyone...ever, I would think. And stop flexing your damned muscles so much, your arms look like they're giving birth!'

'You don't know what you're talking about! I haven't killed even one person since I got here. In fact, I spared the lives of those assassins who wanted to kill *me*.'

'What about the one whose head you split in two? Doesn't he count? What about you almost killing Suri? And you're quite set on killing this young thief for your orb! Don't they matter?'

'Okay, oh yeah, I killed one. One! And it was him or me.'

Khanaseri turned away from Ozo, stunned at the outburst. As he glanced back over his shoulder at the old man, who still paced up and down, itching for a fight, he frowned and thought, *I hope I get this orb soon.* Ozo stood ready, swinging his bony fists in front of him with as much elegance as a turtle in a tree, waiting for the warlock to approach.

Khanaseri rose to his knees and turned his cheek. 'I promise I won't retaliate. If it'll make you feel better, hit me.'

Stunned, the old man stood in silence, contemplating the warlock's reaction, then threw himself down next to the fire, brooding.

Silence reigned for a while before the warlock removed a small salt block from his pack, then shaved flakes onto the meat over the fire, and said, 'I guess I *have* been a bit of an arse. My father died a few weeks ago, and I suppose I've hardened myself with arrogance.'

A nicker sounded from Flintlock as his nostrils flared, his eyes begging for the warmth of the fire. Khanaseri rose and untethered the horse to lead him closer to the heat, then lay down holding the reins. It wasn't long before Flintlock lowered himself to nuzzle against the warlock. 'Okay, okay now. Here, have a carrot.'

Khanaseri fed Flintlock a handful of carrots and turned back to regard Ozo as the old man picked up some twigs to place in the fire under the fox, then turned the meat over as he said, 'Sorry about your father. You know, I joined you on this quest because I'm also searching for answers.'

'Answers to what, exactly?'

A frustrated sigh left the old man. 'My body's been going through some strange changes, and I'd like to understand what's happening. It started a few weeks ago.'

Khanaseri cleared his throat. 'Well, I gathered that much in the catacombs.'

'Yes, exactly. And it's not just changes. There are dreams as well. But I'll get to them. This is more bizarre.'

A dry branch lay off to his right. Ozo walked over to collect it and sauntered back to the fire, shoved the tip in, and undressed as he said, 'Throw me your knife.'

Cocking his head, Khanaseri asked, 'Ozo? What are you doing?'

'Just trust me,' he said as he gestured with his hands, and the huge knife sailed through the air. Ozo tried to catch it, but he misjudged the speed, slicing his palm on the blade, and let it fall to the ground as he winced.

Khanaseri cringed and rose to his feet. 'Ooh, sorry, Ozo. You okay?'

Blood flowed freely down his arm. 'Perfect,' said Ozo as he lifted his hand over his head and dripped the blood from above, smearing it over his body. He pulled out a flaming branch and brought it closer to his chest as he moved away. 'Do nothing. I'll be fine.' A mighty eruption occurred, knocking the warlock to the ground and causing Flintlock to bolt away in fear. There was an instant blaze, the blue flames engulfing Ozo's entire body.

Khanaseri took a moment to recover from the eruption, then moved closer to Ozo but couldn't get too close. The heat was intense. He shouted over the roar of the fire, 'Okay, this is definitely new! How do you put it out? And please cover yourself; that's an image I did *not* want seared into my brain.'

Ozo closed his eyes and calmed himself. The flames ebbed and died. 'You know magic. You must have seen something like this before...'

With his hands in his hair, the warlock said, 'Like this? No. Magic is the bending of the truth or the plausible to make it possible. This is pure. This is your body speaking to you. I have no answer for this. Get

129

dressed. I don't want you giving Flint any more reasons to run away. I'll go fetch him.'

* * *

The night-watch lieutenant was getting frustrated with the woman as she went on and on about a group of people that had attacked them — only there were no visible signs on her, other than some dust on her leggings. Looking at her, he said, 'Lady Ladriana, I mean no disrespect when I say that you need to lay off the wine a little. It's got you all rattled inside. Now, you say that the men who attacked you have this Magnus, and that they're probably busy torturing him right now. Is he your personal attaché or something? Wouldn't want to be in his shoes, then. Being with you is torture enough.'

Trying her best to shrug off the man's comments, she said, 'That's correct, yes.'

'So they'll storm the temple in search of some magic blood and organs from a long-dead king here in New Runswick, will they? Let me guess; soon, the unicorns will fly out and eat the hearts of weary travellers and dragons will rule the world...ha. You should stick to those.'

Ladriana grabbed the lieutenant by the collar and slammed him against the wall of the small office as she said, 'Yes, you incompetent moron. That is *exactly* what I'm saying. Now, I don't give two shits about what you think of me, but know this: if something happens to Magnus because of your inaction, I will cut off your balls and feed them to the dogs.'

Visibly shaken, the lieutenant shook her off and said, 'Fine, we'll investigate the temple and I'll post some guards out there for the night. But know this, you mangy bitch. If nothing happens before the morrow, I'll report you to the council and have you taken away and imprisoned. I knew you were trouble the day you arrived.'

Ladriana stormed off towards the castle as the lieutenant called over a guard to give him orders.

* * *

The humid air made everything feel sticky. Ladriana whispered a curse for getting too comfortable with the fine garments she'd been wearing over the past few days and tugged on the tight leathers now pressed against her waist. She looked up and saw the temple's towers standing high in the centre of the city as a beacon to light the way, lanterns burning brightly in the belfry. To her left, in the distance, she saw the crumbling remnants of the old, fortified walls still intact in some places around the city, but they were of no use now. They had never been rebuilt after the Gallian wars some years back. Guards stared at her as she walked past to enter the temple, and she could hear them speaking about her behind her back. She gritted her teeth as she continued on. Voices were trailing from the back of the hall; then she saw the lieutenant conversing with the priest.

Their voices fell away as she neared, and the lieutenant regarded her with a look of pure bemusement and said, 'What do you think you're doing here?' His eyes darted up and down her body, then scoffed at her. 'And what is that you're wearing? No lady dresses like that.'

Brown leather vambraces covered her arms over the tight black vest and leggings, with boots joined to the greaves covering her legs. The short, black leather skirt was barely noticeable. Ladriana made a mocking bow and said, 'Why thank you, good sir. But I can't let you have all the fun. Regarding this attire I'm wearing, it's standard battle attire for a master bowman.' Drawing closer, she continued, 'I need to talk to the priest, if you don't mind.'

'Master of the bow, are you? Yeah, right, more like mistress of deception...ha-ha. Am I right, priest?'

Before the priest could answer, four arrows had pinned him to the wooden wall behind him, the shafts piercing clothing and narrowly missing his flesh. The lieutenant stood stunned for a moment, then stormed off as he mumbled, 'Fine, get yourself killed. What do I care?'

The old priest spoke drearily from where he was pinned to the wall. 'I'm getting too old for this. Child, please help me off of these pointy sticks.'

Quickly rushing to aid the priest, Ladriana pulled out the arrows and said, 'Sorry, I needed to prove a point.'

Rolling his eyes, the priest said, 'But why did you have to prove it with me? Never mind. I know the lieutenant isn't always the smartest of men, but he means well.'

'Unfortunately, I don't have the luxury of being nice just because he's a good man. We have much more pressing matters to attend to.' She pulled out the vial of blood, and a gasp filled the room as the priest took it from her hand.

He turned the vial slowly from side to side, upside-down and right side up, then sighed as he said, 'Oh, dear. I was worried it might have something to do with this.' He turned back to Ladriana and showed her the bottom of the vial. 'You see, my dear, most don't know this, but it's not the blood that's of significance here. Although it comes from the king, it has no importance. If you were dumb enough to drink it, you would just get really sick and probably die. The thing of significance is the tooth lying *inside* the blood.'

She studied the vial, staring at the small piece of white enamel leaning against the glass bottom. 'What are these markings on the tooth?'

'Ah yes, a keen eye you have. That puzzled everyone, even the magi. Even more puzzling, they figured it must have been done by the king himself, just before his death. Can you imagine pulling out your teeth one by one and marking them? Then, that's not all. Most of his bones have the same sigils on them. The only way to do that was to cut deeply enough to hit the bone.'

Frowning, she said, 'That sounds...painful.'

Beating footsteps echoed through the hall before a night watchman came running around the corner and shouted, 'They're converging from all sides; we can't hold them off for long! We've lit the braziers to summon reinforcements from the coastal patrols, but it will take them a while to get here. We're only a few, milady. I suggest you get out of here and take the priest with you.'

Nodding to the night watchman, Ladriana slung her bow over her shoulder as she asked the cleric, 'Where are the rest of his bones located?'

The old priest shuffled over to the table to extinguish the candles and motioned for her to follow, moving like a man who had led a very hard life, his legs unable to bend at the knees anymore. His robes dragged over the stone floor of the hall as they made their way down a stairwell, heading deep underground. The hall soon turned from the luxurious white of the temple to a wall-crumbling, dilapidated old building. A few small braziers hung along the side of the wall in the distance, barely clinging on with their rusted chains, while others lay on the floor, broken and forgotten. The priest scurried over to the first to light it, then to the next. Somewhere not too far off, she could hear the consistent ear-numbing drip of water. The air smelled stale, like a wet dog. *Is that my heart thumping in my chest? I'm surely not that unfit. Something doesn't feel right. I'm anxious for the first time in a very long time.* The priest took her hand and gave her a comforting smile as he moved forward. For what felt like forever, they walked and walked, until eventually he stopped at a large double door with a rather peculiar-looking lock with three curved sides to it. The priest took from around his neck a short three-pronged key and placed it in the locking mechanism. Turning it, he said, 'This door has not been opened for the past forty years, so cover your nose as you enter.'

Twisting around at the priest's words, she said, 'That can't be. Magnus isn't that old. He was given this after the Gallian wars.'

'I fear he has only told you half-truths, my dear. The man who received this item did so forty years ago. The Gallian war lasted another fifteen years after they awarded him this for his loyalty and bravery for saving the king. He was, if I remember correctly, at that point nearly thirty already. Did you get this from his son, perhaps?'

Shaking her head in confusion, she said, 'Yeah, yes. Must be, right?'

They pushed hard on the door, and with a loud, creaking sigh, it swung open for them to walk through into a massive, dome-shaped room, easily twice, maybe three times the size of the temple above. Quickly turning around, Ladriana leaned and heaved at the door to see it slowly close. A mighty crash followed, sending the door completely off its hinges and flying into the room. Thrown from her feet, she flopped onto the tile floor, rolling to a stop some distance away, a smear of blood left in her wake from a cut in her leg. Dazed, she looked up, her vision failing her as it blurred, causing her to see double. Focusing, she saw a hooded woman move in and pick up the old priest by the neck.

She wasn't perceived as still alive yet. Her chance was now. Lying on her side, Ladriana nocked two arrows and loosed them. The aggressor was quick, dodging the first arrow as she dropped the priest, but the second struck true, plunging into her shoulder and protruding from her back.

A cry of horror sounded as the hooded figure bellowed in pain and frustration, then made sigils with her hands and chanted a few words unknown to Ladriana. The dome shook violently and crumbled. Cracks in the walls and floor appeared, tearing wider as the figure chanted. Another wail sounded, this time not from the figure, but from down in the earth. And it was getting closer...

Exploding through the old, marbled floor, an enormous creature climbed out as debris flew all over. As tall as two men, with four arms wielding dual swords and a bow, a large hairy black mane crested its head and enclosed its throat down its chest. Black as night and as slimy as a hagfish, it opened its maw and let out a roar, revealing fangs that could rival daggers. It glared at Ladriana as she rose, then charged. A stench to obliterate civilisations filled the room.

* * *

Smoke hung in the distance over the trees, the sugarcane fields burning bright and the heat intense. People from all over the city rushed to douse the flames, but more got injured and burned than were able to put the fire out. Anavi looked around to find Lanik missing once more. *Dammit!* She scanned the area and shouted his name for some time before hearing her name called from a distance away. She turned and ran in that direction.

'Anavi! By the trees!' Coughs wracked his body as soot filled his lungs. Desperately trying to move a fallen tree crushing a hapless man's leg, he strained at the weight of the bole. The man had been trying to put out the flames when the ground under the tree gave way to send it toppling onto him. In great anguish, he had already given up when Lanik arrived on scene, and now he said, 'It's no use, friend, it won't move. Save yourself.'

Lanik shouted, 'No! We'll get you out.'

Anavi wrestled at Lanik's arms to pull him away for his own safety, the fire raging ever closer towards them, but he wouldn't relent and pushed her away as he snapped, 'Instead of using your energy to pry me away, be useful and help me get him out!'

'He's done for, can't you see? You'll never move that tree!' The tree was massive. It would take a team of horses or oxen to move it.

Lanik rubbed his head as he said, 'Who said anything about moving the tree? Bring me something to dig with.'

On all fours, he dug under the man's leg. Anavi grabbed a branch and did the same from the other side of the tree, working frantically as the heat grew more intense. After some time, the soil gave way enough for the leg to drop, leaving the tree firmly on the surface. Screams sounded as they pulled the man free, his leg dangling under him like a piñata hanging on a string. Finally reaching safety, the man, beaded in sweat, thanked them as they set off down the road.

The clangour of steel against steel reverberated in the night, accompanied by shouts of anger and pain as the night watch and the Desert Dogs fought for the spoils of the temple. From a distance, Anavi unsheathed her sword and moved with grace into the fray of battle, slicing left, ducking right, slicing up, dismembering limbs to the left. It was a show of pure art as limbs flew from her victims. The night watch were holding their own, but wouldn't last for long as their numbers dwindled. The Desert Dogs outnumbered them three to one still. Lanik was in the thick of it, trying to get to the lieutenant of the night watch near the temple entrance, stabbing left and right with his daggers. The two were thinning the herd as they caught most of the Desert Dogs off guard, coming from the rear.

Reaching the lieutenant's side, Lanik shouted, 'Where's Ladriana?'

As he hacked a man's head from his shoulders, the lieutenant bellowed, 'And who might you be?'

Lanik pulled a cord free from around his neck, holding up a golden ring as he shouted, 'I am Garidan Rourke, son of the murdered King Rourke, and I am your rightful ruler!'

The night watch lieutenant pulled him away from the fight to the entrance of the temple and stared at the ring. Passed down for generations, they had thought the old ring lost since the vanishing of their prince. Now it bore new nicks and scratches as it lay in his hands. He rubbed the blackened ring to rid it of soot to see the symbols below. Heavy-set gold and silver entwined to form a glorious wolf's head. He stared into Lanik's eyes and said, 'How do I know you didn't just pick this up, or worse, killed the prince for the ring?'

Lanik took a knee and unsheathed his sword, pushing the point into the ground as he declared, 'I will uphold justice and mercy in all judgement! Thieves and murderers will have no foothold in the city during my watch. By the divine blessing of the ascended King Tolken Venut himself, I will give my life to protect New Runswick and the greater nation of Elmohria from any threat! I am Garidan Rourke, son of the late King Rourke, murdered by the council members to take rulership of New Runswick — and I had my justice!'

Men within earshot lifted their swords to the sky and shouted, 'The king has returned! Defend the king!' New life pulsed through the soldiers. Reinvigorated, they pushed back at the Desert Dogs with renewed energy.

'Well, I'll be... We thought you dead, sire! I'm glad you've returned, Your Highness. She's deep in the temple with the old priest. I can escort you in, but we're running low on men.'

A Desert Dog came crashing through their defences and headed straight for Lanik, his club swinging left and right. Two knives flashed out of Lanik's belt into the throat of the attacker and the man sagged to his knees, not a single sound uttered before he hit the ground. Retrieving his knives, Lanik said, 'Spare your men; you need them here. Make sure they don't breach the temple. I can look after myself.' As he entered the temple, Anavi joined him at his side, and he saw blood dripping from her tunic. He pulled at her clothing and said, 'Anavi, are you okay?'

'Yes, minor cuts here and there, but I'm still fit for battle. The blood is mostly theirs.'

* * *

Arrows arced across the dome as Ladriana loosed one after another, and the creature retaliated with volleys of its own. There was nowhere to hide and nothing to do but run around in circles until one of them got hit. Staying clear of the creature proved the sensible option, if only to buy time to figure out what to do; to find a weakness, if it had one. *Or is it they who are buying time?* Quickly changing her aim, she loosed a couple of arrows again at the figure in the middle of the room as she neared the sarcophagus, narrowly missing.

Outraged, Beuneth made a few hand movements and lifted the creature from the floor to throw it across the room, close to Ladriana. With incredible speed, it was on top of her, kicking, biting, striking with the bow and slicing with the swords in hand.

Fighting for her life, Ladriana parried everything as fast as she could, but some blows breached her defences. A slice from one sword cut her stomach, another deep into her right arm; and then the creature backhanded her. Sailing through the air, she saw two figures running into the room before she hit the floor and lost consciousness.

A scream of pain erupted from the black apparition as two throwing knives plunged into its left ribcage. Blood oozed out as it pulled the weapons free and threw them on the floor. Anavi charged at the beast, dodging attacks from its dual blades.

More throwing knives flashed through the air as Lanik let them fly as fast as possible. Surprised by the two new assailants, the beast took cover behind its arms and legs as two more knives sank into its limbs, giving Anavi an opening on its flank. Spinning around, she held her sword backwards and slashed its left Achilles tendon; the blade sinking halfway through to the bone.

The beast toppled over, and Anavi scrambled out of its path as it thrashed in pain, still trying to kill her. As it hit the ground, she leapt on top of it and twisted her sword around its neck, severing its head from its shoulders.

Muffled shouts echoed in Ladriana's ears. She slowly opened her eyes and glimpsed Beuneth above her, moments before a fist rocketed her head back onto the stone floor. Then another fist stung her face, cutting open her cheek. Ladriana's head swam. She felt the string break around her neck as Beuneth plucked it, then heard her say, 'So long, bitch.'

* * *

Movement to the left drew their attention away from the beast, and Lanik saw Beuneth standing over Ladriana. One more knife in his belt; he couldn't miss. Letting it fly, he watched the blade spin in the air. All sound fell away for him, save for the swish of the blade as it raced to its victim.

At the very last second, Beuneth flashed out of the way to let the blade fly by and skid on the floor behind her. Distracted, she was looking back at the knife on the floor when an arrow pierced her hand from the side. She shouted in anger and pain, then turned to Anavi as more arrows flew at her. The arrow through her hand suddenly burst into flames, searing the wound closed; the arrows in the air turned to ash, the metal tips melted. For a few heartbeats, everyone stared at each other, waiting for someone to make the next move. Then a rift appeared next to Beuneth, and she stepped through, clutching a large bag, to vanish as it closed behind her.

'Ladriana, are you okay? Wake up! It's Lanik.'

'Wh...what happened?' Sitting upright, Ladriana clutched her head as Lanik cradled her in his arms.

In a soft tone, he said, 'Don't worry, I'll get you to a healer. You'll be fine.'

Anavi drew closer and nodded her head as she said with a smile, 'Glad to see you can still take a beating.'

Ladriana rose unsteadily and walked to the middle of the room, guided by Lanik to the great stone coffin, now lying bare. She scratched at the surface of the sarcophagus, hoping for some kind of false door, but nothing; Beuneth had taken all the bones of the old king, even the tooth in her vial. She suddenly brought her head up and shouted, 'Magnus!'

Lanik tore apart his shirt and tied part of it around her arm to stem the bleeding; the rest of it he used to press against her stomach. 'Let's get you to the healer first, then we can discuss Magnus.'

'No, I'll get myself to the healer. You find Magnus. They grabbed him at the tomb of the king, in the forest to the north. If you don't go for him right now, I won't go to the healer.' *Does anybody in this world still care for people other than themselves? Or does everyone just follow blindly to please their chosen leader, not thinking of the consequence of their actions? The question of morality doesn't weigh on anyone's shoulders anymore. Have they killed Magnus? I wonder... The lust in their eyes for death would astound even the morally challenged. People are far too easy to manipulate. All you need is some coin and a promise, or better yet, the promise of coin and glory...*

Anavi ran from the room as she shouted over her shoulder, 'I'm getting a horse and a wagon. Meet me outside!'

Chapter Seven

The warriors were all poaching in their sweat as they marched on under the desert sun, which beat down upon them with its unrelenting waves of animosity towards all living creatures — or so it felt to Stilts. His heart thumped in his head, his eyes dark-rimmed still from opening the portal, looking like a pale visage of death. Glancing up at the bright ball of fire, he wiped at the dried mucus on his newly formed moustache. *Today you don't heal or replenish strength; today you're not life-bringer, but life-stealer*, he thought, staring at the sun. He stumbled as his feet dragged on the ground and got caught on the smallest of rocks, causing him to fall over. Sharp pain shot through his arms as he stopped his fall against the parched ground. Droplets of blood stained the ground with his heavy breathing and he wiped his nose with the back of his hand to see it come away bloody. He had only regained consciousness a day ago. It had been more than a week now, and still they couldn't get any traction on where Khanaseri had gone. Alone at the back of the column, far away from everyone, he heard the muffled calls to halt the march.

A dust storm was approaching from the south, a constantly building, billowing monster on their heels, ready to devour everything in its path. Orders were being barked out to pin down everything that could go flying. They wouldn't outrun this beast. Everyone scattered about, getting ready for the new challenge that lay before them.

Just another day in the ranks.

Moving away from the noise, the shouting, and the orders, he found himself a more peaceful place a distance away and sat down on the warm soil. Eyes closed, he recited an incantation while drawing in the dirt, his mind's eye guiding him towards his goal. He opened his eyes and saw in the distance to the right the tree he was being guided to. Faltering steps and ragged breathing led him to the tree, the effort almost not worth it. He reached out and grabbed hold of the thick bark-covered bottle tree trunk. Still chanting, he could see with eyes closed all the life connected to the tree: the little creatures that burrowed into the wood, the bird's nest at the top with the new hatchlings inside screaming for food. He followed the roots deep under the earth, where he saw them reach for the water that flowed below. 'You are teeming with life, my friend. I beg of you to share some of that life with me. I will not take it all, only what I need.'

Energy flowed from the tree and every living creature that dwelled in it and nearby. Worms shrivelled up and burrowing creatures dried out; the spiders roaming the treetop turned to empty husks as the hatchlings ceased their cries. Down in the water, the small living creatures gave their last breaths as it flowed into Stilts, healing him. He could feel his energy being replenished. The tree groaned as it dried out from the bottom up, its bark cracking and splitting to reveal a rust-coloured sap running down its sides. Stilts opened his eyes and let go of the tree, then patted its side and said, 'I thank you, my friend. Now heal once more.' He turned to walk to the camp as the dust storm hit.

* * *

A scout came from the east, a cloud of dust kicked up by his horse as he drove his heels into its flanks before reining in near Ganda'har's tent. He slipped off the back of his horse and ran in, saying, 'Sorry for the intrusion, sir!' The young scout stood at attention as he realised he had just burst into the captain's quarters without so much as a thought, and now stood staring at the high-ranking officers in the squad, all huddled around the table, discussing the lay of the land. They had sent four scouts out in different directions to report back their findings, and he was the last to arrive.

Ganda'har dropped the pin in his hands and said, 'Well then, spit it out. What have you seen?'

The scout adjusted his attire a bit and said, 'Hadock reporting from the east, sir. A town, sir. It's about a three-day ride, hence why I'm late, sir. Forgive me, I know you said to turn back after two days, sir. But just when I wanted to turn back, I saw people heading farther east. So I followed them.'

The captain sat down and rubbed his hands over his growing beard, and said, 'How big is it? Can we find supplies there? Does it look like we'll have any problems getting in?'

'It's not big, sir, a few hundred maybe. More farmers, looks like. No defence, really. Not sure about supplies, sir. I headed back as soon as possible.'

'Fine, then. Get me Stilts and be quick about it.'

A stiff salute followed, and the scout turned to leave the tent just as the dust storm hit. Talgar dropped into his chair and said, 'Where did you find that one? He's as green as the day is long here.'

'I thought you brought him in,' Ganda'har said as he frowned at his second-in-command.

* * *

Unperturbed by the raging storm, Stilts walked through the camp, lending a hand here and there as he made his way to the captain's tent, even as sand blasted its way into every crevice it could find. The winds howled and thunder rained from the monstrous dust storm. In the distance, he heard a faint cry for help and ran to investigate.

Hadock hung on for dear life, gripping an ox's horns, straining its neck as the wild winds lifted him to the sky. As Stilts neared the scout, the wind died down in his immediate vicinity and the scout dropped to the ground, laying there sprawled, covered with dust. Stilts helped the coughing man to his feet and dusted off his face as he said, 'Hadock? What are you doing here?'

As soon as the scout saw his saviour, he nearly hugged the man, and said, 'Thank you, sir. I was actually looking for you, to give you a message.'

Stilts stood with a puzzled look on his face. 'I meant...never mind. Yes. What's the message?'

'You need to see the captain in his tent immediately.'

Rolling his eyes, Stilts left the scout and entered the tent. Immediately, the wind slammed into the scout, almost lifting him to the sky as he grabbed onto the ox's horns again.

* * *

The entrance to the crypt stood wide open, with pieces of the stone door scattered about, blown to hell by some kind of explosion. The sun peered over the trees in the distance, marking the day's return and the hope that lay with it. Anavi moved with caution into the dark room, Lanik close on her heels, bearing a lit torch. A big, open room with pillars every few feet to keep the ceiling from collapsing greeted them with a moist chill. Lanik shook off a tremble and was suddenly nauseous as he said, 'At the back of the chamber, that's where the old king's tomb is.'

Silently and slowly they walked, the cobwebs dissolving as the fire of the torch neared. Some unscrupulous, disrespecting spiders jumped onto Lanik as he damaged the webs, causing him to send a shrill cry through the chamber. 'I really hate spiders!'

'Really? I hadn't noticed at all. I thought you just enjoyed making those girlish noises.'

143

'Oh, shut up,' he said as he wiped his face for the umpteenth time. 'I swear it feels like they're all over me.'

Languidly and with the utmost disinterest, Anavi stated, 'Yeah. Well, that's because they most probably are.'

Nearing the end of the chamber, they saw the dais was covered in blood. Anavi felt her heart jump in her chest and tried to calm herself as she took a deep breath, then heard a groan to her right. Suddenly breathless, she ran through the dark with Lanik struggling to keep up with the torch. Twice she fell as her foot caught loose paving or she stepped in ruts, skinning her knees and hands on the rough surface as she stayed her falls. In the chamber's corner, Magnus sat against the wall, barely alive. Her hands trembled as she removed her canteen and brought it to his mouth, tears flowing down her face. She couldn't contain her emotions any longer. 'Please. Drink, my love, please. I'm with you now. All is well.'

Finally arriving by her side with the torch, Lanik saw the body of his best friend poked full of holes by something other than a sword or knife, his left leg was broken at the shin and one of his ears hacked off. As Magnus tried to take the canteen from Anavi, they saw that his right hand's fingers were mangled, most probably broken by using a rock. Lanik stood shocked, frozen in place for some time, until Anavi slapped him across the face to rouse him. 'Get something to make a stretcher! Now!'

Staring down at the man she had always loved but never confessed it to until now, tears streamed down as she dabbed his face with a sleeve she had torn from her tunic. With great care, she poured some water over his face and dabbed at the sticky blood. Streaks of crimson ran down his temple and swollen face. Unable to speak, his teeth loose from the tumultuous beatings, Magnus moved his mouth, but no sound came out. Anavi cut open his shirt to examine the extent of the injuries to his body. She saw that with every breath he took, blood flowed from a hole in his chest. Crying and shaking, she bandaged the hole with his shirt, hoping it would stop the flow. Similar holes were revealed all over him that looked like they were done with a fire poker, but they didn't seem to lose too much blood. *I just hope that no organs were injured. He already had a bad lung.*

Time went by quickly as they tried to put together a support sturdy enough to carry the big man. Lanik had gathered fallen branches from close by and rope from the wagon to create the crude stretcher, and ran back to Anavi. When they had something that would serve, they laid it down next to the injured Magnus and turned him on his side as they shimmied the stretcher under him. Foot by agonising foot, they then managed their way to the exit, carrying the heavy barkeep on the stretcher until finally reaching the exit. Once outside, the sun shone down upon them with its healing rays, giving a bit of hope while they crossed the rough terrain. They stepped precariously over the rocky area to get to the wagon and loaded him in. Jumping up on the front, Lanik whipped the horses into motion and set off. Covered with dirt and grime, her hands and knees raw, Anavi sat in the back holding Magnus' hand, eyes closed, as he barely breathed.

* * *

Xylac paced up and down before Beuneth as she meticulously placed each of the bones on the floor of the inn's room, forming the complete skeleton of King Tolken Venut. Chewing on his nails, he pondered the nostalgia he'd been feeling for the days when he was a young boy playing in his Ma's backyard, overlooking the house with the pretty little girl. Shy glances occurred as their eyes met occasionally, before glancing away, hoping the other didn't notice the ambivalence shown there. Not knowing what to think, what to do, or how to control the impulse that was driving them towards each other as they grew older, he couldn't take it anymore. He had plans, and those plans didn't involve getting shacked up with some girl. She was a distraction. To fight the urge, he enlisted in the guards and was taken away from home for good.

But now he stood in front of this goddess with her sensual hips swaying back and forth as she moved about the room, her breasts inviting him to draw near, the sweet scent of lavender lingering as she passed by him...and then there were her lips. A distraction indeed...and he couldn't resist anymore.

He grabbed her from behind, yanked and tore at her slitted gown, sending her flying to the floor, and was on top of her before she could get up.

Panic in her eyes, she looked up at the vile man and saw the pleasure this brought him. She could feel her undergarment getting ripped and saw him loosen his pants and lie upon her to thrust. The stink of his breath flowed over her as he said, 'Mess with my head, will you? I'll teach you a lesson, you witch!'

As he pulled her near, she grabbed his face and took a full bite of his cheek, tearing it away and spitting out a lump of skin and fat. Blood sprayed all over her as he screamed, still on top of her. Comprehending what had happened, he looked at her and yelled his outrage, 'You bitch!' and beat his fists down on her, landing blow after blow on her arms as she covered her face, before a sudden hot, searing iron shaft thrust through his left shoulder, dragging him back and bending him up off her. Another bar pierced through the other shoulder and curled at the end, keeping him firmly in place.

Xylac looked around with panic in his eyes now, his shoes dragging on the floor as he drifted off the ground. Fixtures from the hearth had come to life at her command, restraining his movements. He begged her forgiveness as she got to her feet and pulled at her clothes to straighten them. Without hesitation, she walked up to him, and a solid thump sounded as she kicked him in the groin with so much force, she heard something pop.

Regaining her stature, she stood watching her puppet as he dangled in the air, unable to comfort his privates as urine soaked his trousers. 'Xylac, I relieve you of duty. There is gold in the Ottiva cave near the pit. Take it and begone from my life, you vile piece of filth. Leave this village immediately.'

His face was a mixture of sweat and blood, as pale as the beaches of Bona Bay. She watched him nod his agreement, then lowered him to the ground as the iron bars pulled from his shoulders, and said, 'I never want to hear your name or see your face again.'

It took some time for Xylac to crawl out of the room to make his way to their infirmary before she continued with her ritual.

She had laid out all the bones in front of her and examined the symbols, finding them extremely intricate. From the skull to the fibula, basically all the bones had markings on them. Whispers left her mouth as she studied them. 'I have searched for a very long time for you, Gatekeeper.' Then, placing dried dabbleweeds all over the bones, she brought a candle close to light the weeds and waited for the smoke to fill the room before she intoned, 'Hear my words from beyond the grave! I summon you, Gatekeeper, to come forth and deliver unto me the key, as I would see you set free from this horrible fate they have forced upon you, my lord. Let me free you of this burden!'

Smoke billowed and built, swirled and swayed until in front of her formed a vague old face in the smog, staring down at her with pure amusement as she knelt before him. He said, 'Child, why have you disturbed my slumber?'

'I beg of you, Gatekeeper. Give me the key to the vault so I can set you free as you deserve.'

The face shifted as if thinking, then waned, and he said in a muffled voice, 'You are all the sa—'

Waving her arms about, she shouted as she ran forward, 'No, wait! Hear me out. I am *not* the same as any other who has stood before you.'

Intrigued, the face re-emerged and with a wizened voice questioned, 'Oh? And how is that, exactly?'

Suddenly, not knowing what to do with her hands, she pulled on her clothes and stood awkwardly there before she continued, 'For one, I don't want to take this from you by force. Unlike those before me who wanted to fight you for it, I'm begging you for it. May I ask what happened to King Tolken Venut? Why did he die?'

'He was a fool to think a mere human could contain the pain of the Ageian Gatekeepers. He had me murdered and performed the ritual of binding, as you do now. Child, do you even know what you ask to bring upon yourself?'

Breathing deeply, she released a sigh. Her head lowered as she said, 'Yes. I do.'

With a frown, the face in the smoke asked, 'What makes you think you'll fare any better than the old king?'

She looked up into the eyes of the veiled face. 'I am daughter to Sir Kai Neth, Son of the Gatherer Cal Neth. My mother sold me after his death to a woman in the mountains. I can't remember a lot about my father, but I believe he was one of the few Ageian who stayed after the Great Sundering when he had fallen in love with my mother.'

The face set sternly, as if in thought, then said, 'The blood of the Ageian flows in you; I can sense it now.'

'Yes, lord,' she said as she stood with her left hand resting in front of the right, waiting calmly for the next reply.

'The burden of the Gatekeeper must remain with the Ageian.'

'I agree, my lord.'

'And what do they call you, dear girl?'

'I go by Beuneth.'

With a languid smile, the old Gatekeeper said, 'Know this, Beuneth: you will know pain for the rest of your life if I grant you this key. You will bear the weight of thousands of souls. All those trapped in the vault will be your burden.'

'I understand, Gatekeeper. And I accept this burden as my own.'

The face in the smoke bowed and swirled in the room, drifting down into the bones once more. All the symbols on the bones moved about, converging at the skull. At first, a soft glow emanated from it, growing brighter and brighter until the room shone like a sun on its own. Sliding back on the floor as the wind picked up, Beuneth grabbed on to the walls to stay upright. The howling winds battered her as the blinding light made it near-impossible to open her eyes. Through slits, she could see the bones fade away and turn to dust from the feet up. Where the skull had been, a golden medallion had formed, now lying in the remains of the old king. The wind died as she picked up the medallion. With a confused look, she held up the piece and said to the empty room, 'Okay. I thought there would be more to it.'

Beuneth bit the piece and stomped her foot as she only hurt her teeth, then rubbed it on her arms and legs. Nothing happened. She released a resentful sigh, and said, 'I'm going to look like an idiot with this thing on my head.' As she pressed it to her forehead, she felt a tingle in her brain. The wind started up again in the opposite direction, but this time, it did not affect her. A tornado developed around her, picking up the furniture in the room, throwing it about. Chairs, a desk, the bed, papers and many other things flew around in the chamber, crashing into each other; and yet she stood untouched. Her eyes turned pitch black as the medallion melted away on her forehead. Symbols appeared on her skin as if some unseen force had seared them all over her body. Pain wracked her as the symbols found their marks, then burned through her flesh and into her bones. To her, it felt like someone drilling into her soul a thousand times over. Beuneth screamed at the top of her lungs and fell to the ground as the winds died. She dragged herself over to the hearth, leaving a trail of blood behind her, then snapped her fingers. Fire jumped to life, heating the cold room. She pulled a cover over her, trembling in pain, then closed her eyes.

A knock on her door was followed by the hesitant voice of the innkeeper. 'Pardon me, miss. Are you okay in there? We heard some loud and strange noises out here.'

'I'm fine, thank you. See that I am not disturbed again.'

* * *

'So wait,' Khanaseri said as his face contorted, and he waved his hands about, perplexed, as he continued, 'You remember nothing from your younger days?'

Swatting at mosquitoes and flies, Ozo looked like a human pincushion, as they had stung him many times during the past few nights. 'That's exactly what I'm saying. How come you aren't being eaten alive by these pestering little critters of death?'

As if Flintlock was also annoyed at this, he swiped his tail into the warlock's face, neighing as he did so. Ozo laughed and stumbled over some rocks protruding from the ground. A quick gasp and some waving arms followed as he nearly fell on his face, righting himself just in time.

Now the warlock also laughed, and said, 'I don't know. Just lucky, I guess. Why don't we move down to the river and do some exercises? I'd like to see if you can control whatever it is you have. We also need to think of a better way to capture this young thief.'

With a smile, Ozo said, 'I'm just glad you bought me a horse.' He turned to look at the skewbald mare with glee.

The serene views of the landscape reflected in the river were magnificent. Ozo breathed deeply, and said, 'Just listen to the water flowing, the calm and peaceful setting before us. Everything is so green.' He took another deep breath as he closed his eyes, then continued, 'Smells of never-ending life. I don't know how long I have left, but to witness this but once in my life and remember it is worth everything I've done.'

Khanaseri stood next to the man, reflecting on his life as he looked upon said beauty. 'Yes. Maybe you're right. One should stop more often to realise what one has in life rather than not.'

Maybe he's not such an oaf after all, Ozo thought as he stepped closer.

Khanaseri broke a dead branch off a tree and drew a big circle about himself in the sand, with a smaller one inside. Then he placed some candles in the smaller circle and called out to the old man. Looking inquisitively at this, Ozo frowned as he asked, 'What are we doing?'

'Oh, don't worry so much.' Without warning, Khanaseri grabbed Ozo's hand and cut his palm with a knife.

'Ouch! You moron! Why did you do that?' Still busy shouting his outrage, Ozo was picked up and turned upside down on the warlock's shoulder like a sack of potatoes, his hand held out and the blood forced out of him with shakes, spraying it all over the ground in the circle to wet the area.

'Almost done. Sorry, Ozo.'

The world still shook for Ozo after he was put down. A momentary wave of nausea came over him before he curled over and vomited to the side, then hawked and spat to rid his mouth of the remaining content, and said, 'Great! Why did you have to cut the other hand? You could have just asked, you know.' He rose and collected a cloth from his saddlebag, then wrapped it around the fresh cut and walked back to the warlock.

With as much patience as a nun in a brewery, Ozo stared at the warlock in the centre of the circle, chanting away. Since nothing happened immediately, Ozo was of a mind to leave the warlock to his own devices, and turned away. A powerful hand grabbed him by the wrist, holding him in place as everything suddenly went dark. Moments later, a hall of stone and mortar surrounded them, easily twenty men in height. A steel door as thick as the length of Khanaseri's axe stood close to them. Shaking his head, Ozo stood dumbfounded and said, 'Is this real? How did we get here? What is this place?'

The warlock looked around and tapped on the steel door, hearing the echo ringing in the great hall, then said, 'Well, you tell me. This place definitely exists, that's for sure. *Where* this is, I can't say. I've just brought out a deep hidden memory that you couldn't recall.'

Footsteps rang out, the echoes running through the hall getting closer and closer. Squinting his eyes, Ozo saw two men walking towards them in the distance, one old and grey, the other a young man. Anxious, he grabbed the warlock. 'Can they see us?'

'No, they can't. Remember, this is a memory.'

Calmed, Ozo moved closer to the approaching men with his jaw hanging slack, and said, 'I'm pretty sure that's me, but different. Younger, with hair. Hey, I looked pretty good.'

The young Ozo, dressed in black, neared the big steel door as the old grey man lay his hands on it.

Khanaseri pressed his tongue against his cheek as he watched the scene unfold. Suddenly, the young Ozo grabbed the older man, held a knife against his throat, and forced him to enter the vault as the door swung open. 'Whoa, Ozo. What are you doing?' Khanaseri asked as he scratched his beard.

Nervously standing next to the warlock, Ozo said, 'Maybe it's not as bad as it looks.'

When the door fully swung open, Khanaseri couldn't believe his eyes. He rubbed them and looked again. Thousands of Balamuths lined the walls, the floor laden with weapons, armour, gold, silver, and so much more.

The old man stood in the vault with his hands folded as he said, 'You cannot escape, young man. And they will not allow an uninitiated boy to be bonded and made a Kingsguard. They will kill—'

'Enough, old man, I need to think.' Pacing up and down, the young Ozo continued, 'How does this work?'

The old man scowled at him as he lowered himself to a golden bench and said, 'Look around, take the gold, the diamonds. *That* they might let you live for. But not the Balamuths.'

Ozo spread his hands, pleading with the old man, 'Look, what do you care if I live or die? I have no need for jewellery and gold. I need this. Now, please.'

'It will be your pyre that burns in the night. Go stand in the centre of the ring and don't be afraid.' The old man cleared his throat, then said loudly, 'Heed my call, all Balamuths. I, the Gatekeeper, summon you to seek the heart of the next follower. Find him just, find him worthy of the bond, and bind with him to be one, forever to roam the lands again. Find him unworthy, and burn his soul into damnation, to roam the world lifeless, never to be whole again.'

From all over, voices filled the chamber, speaking an unknown tongue. Young Ozo looked around, confused, and shouted to the Gatekeeper, 'What are they saying? I can't understand them!'

'Oh, they are deliberating your fate. Some seem to think you have courage. Go figure. Some think you are nothing but a thief. Others feel your heart is pure, but broken. Interesting.'

One voice rang out, silencing the rest of the Balamuths, and the sphere floated up to hover before young Ozo. A swirling mist flowed through the ball of red and black. Moving closer, Ozo reached out to the sphere...

Darkness suddenly swallowed the scene and pulled them back to reality; they stood once more next to the river. Khanaseri's eyes were wide as he looked upon Ozo, then said, 'What did I just witness? Here I am, worried about *one* of those Balamuths, and somewhere out there,' pointing out to nowhere in particular, 'there are literally thousands of them stored in a vault!'

Ozo stuttered, 'Uh, um, ye-yes. Well, well. Uhm. It *is* an enormous door...' He cleared his throat then, and continued, 'What I meant was—'

Khanaseri sat down on the sand and laughed. 'Get a fire going, and I'll get food. This is getting more interesting by the day.'

'What do you mean, what did *you* just witness? What did *I* just witness? Why did you end the spell? I wanted to see what happened!'

The warlock shrugged and said, 'I'm sorry, Ozo, that was as far as I could see. We'll try again in a bit if that's what you want. But I need to rest a little; I feel drained.' He looked down at his hands and saw them trembling, then muttered, 'Just how old *are* you?'

* * *

In today's life, you cannot simply be a soldier anymore. You have to provide daily for your wife, your children. I mean, you need to have a steady income, not one where if you don't get hacked up on a field of battle, you get your wages, but if you do, your next of kin gets double. It's like an incentive to get killed... When this is over, I'm quitting the Kamatayon. Thinking of his little Fraya back home, Geolas couldn't wait for this to be done. He looked at Untara as the big man sat, amusing himself by spitting at passing lizards, laughing when he covered one with his mucus. Geolas picked up a fallen leaf and sliced it in half with one of his arrows' blades. With a contented smile, he placed the arrows back in the quiver, then folded the cloth back over the whetstone before placing it in his pack. *Talgar is barking orders again. Are we finally going somewhere?* In the distance, Talgar walked among the soldiers, clapping his hands to put pressure on them, shouting at them to get ready for...*what is he saying?* Straining his neck, Geolas couldn't make it out, and moved closer.

'We need to move to the hill on our right and begin fortifications, men. That's where we'll make our stand should things go wrong in town. If you see anything strange, brace for a fight. I want you all ready and awake.' Talgar continued talking about layout and position, and where the food and supplies must be stored. He had a good head for things like that, being a superb tactician.

From the distance, Talgar turned to Geolas and shouted at him, 'I almost forgot. You and Untara need to meet the captain at his tent. You're to guard his back in town. I hope you understand the importance of this job.'

The two soldiers nodded and made their way to the captain's tent, where he waited on horseback, ready to ride, and looked at them with disapproval. 'You're late. Come, let's ride.'

Geolas and Untara looked at each other with grins and raised brows. Both knew what the other was thinking...

Three travellers going into town seeking refuge from the blistering sun — that's all they were. The ride was silent. No one spoke. Geolas pulled his hood a little farther down as he locked his eyes on the evening sun, a beautiful, enormous sphere of pure light setting over the mountains in the distance. It was bigger than he remembered it being.

On the main road, as they rode in, they slowed their horses and studied the town. Dirt roads led in a myriad of directions. Ganda'har scanned the area, saw a couple of people to his left, and said, 'Excuse my interruption of your conversation, gentlemen, but can you please guide me to an inn where we can get some food, and a market where we can buy supplies? We're desperately hungry, as we've travelled far.'

One man, an ill-looking bald fellow, thin as a reed and wearing clothes suited for someone three times his size, walked over to the captain, gazing at the horses and weapons they carried. He laughed, revealing rotten teeth as he asked, 'Youse goin' a-huntin' fur some drag'ns? What y'all got 'ere, 'nyways?'

Ganda'har looked to Geolas and Untara, who just shook their heads, unwilling to comment on the proceedings as the old man started dancing next to Ganda'har's horse, flicking his arms up and down as a skeleton on a string might. Before the captain looked back at the old man, he saw Geolas' eyes widen and mouth gape open in alarm, but he was too late. The idiot had grabbed the sword from the sheath hanging over the horse's back, and with great speed and considerable strength, yanked Ganda'har off the horse. As the dust settled, Ganda'har stared up past the point of his own blade into the eyes of a much younger man with short red hair, who said, 'Tell your men to stand down.'

With a motion of Ganda'har's hand, they lowered their weapons, and the redhead continued, 'Very good. I'm the guard to these parts, and I don't trust you because I've never seen you before, and I've seen everyone here. Now tell me why you've come and where you're from.'

Ganda'har cursed at himself for being duped so easily, and as he lay under his own blade, he said, 'We aren't here for you or anyone else. We're searching for a man we believe came this way. We need to bring him back to our city, Artorea, tucked away in the desert of Artokla.'

The man didn't relent; instead, he pulled in closer and said, 'Oh, is that right? And what about all those men you have camped a distance from here? Do you expect me to believe they're all here for one man?'

'Well, yes. He's no ordinary man. It will be hard to bring him in, especially alive.'

For some time, the man stared into his eyes without flinching, then stood and held out his hand to help the captain up. Reversing the blade, he handed it back, saying, 'People round here call me Tannor. You don't need to stay in the village to find out anything. As I said, I know everyone in these parts, and I've seen no strangers but you. Come, I'll take you to the inn for a drink. We can talk there.'

* * *

Dew-scented morning freshness hung low in the cool air so near the river. Khanaseri opened his eyes, seeing Ozo down at the water's edge. He rose and drank from his water pouch as he neared, and asked, 'What you doing, oldie?'

A line in his hands, Ozo suddenly yanked back, shouting with joy, 'Breakfast, dear lad, breakfast! Go start a fire.' Ozo fought with the big trout as it thrashed about in the water, jumping high out of the river to throw the hook from its mouth. 'Come on, fishy. Easy now. Here we go!' He pulled in his second trout and was beside himself as he jumped up with joy.

Khanaseri smiled at Ozo and said, 'As long as you clean them, I'll eat them.'

Without a word, Ozo grabbed a knife and gutted the two fish, cleaning them rapidly before placing them over the fire. He was in his element.

A little time passed as the fish cooked; soon, a delicious aroma drifted through the air. Khanaseri nodded in approval and said, 'Well done. This is just what I needed.'

Ozo took the knife, feeling the meat of the fish as he smiled and said, 'I think it's ready.'

Sitting cross-legged with his fish on a flat rock on his lap, Ozo slowly and meticulously pulled apart the meat, carefully plucking out the small, sharp bones, as they so easily got stuck in the throat. The scene across from him was a completely different story as Khanaseri sat with legs spread apart like an old whore's, holding the fish by the tail and taking big bites from it. Every so often, he would spit a few bones to the side, growing the pile on the ground. Silence grew as the two continued to enjoy their meal, thinking of nothing else except this very moment.

Finished with their meals, they had packed up their gear when Ozo suddenly reeled and clutched his chest in pain. His face was a vision of terror as he reached out to the warlock and sagged to the ground, then curled into a ball, rocking back and forth as groans escaped his mouth.

The warlock dropped his gear and ran to his side. 'What's the matter, Ozo? Talk to me.'

Eyes closed and his mouth clenched, Ozo couldn't speak as Khanaseri pressed his hand against the old man's forehead, feeling the heat emitting from his frail body. Forcing open Ozo's eyelids, Khanaseri saw his eyes were bloodshot, almost bleeding. A fierce cry sounded from Ozo, with the emancipation of terrifying heat billowing out from his mouth. The warlock was forced to leave his side and move a few steps away to watch from a distance. After a long moment, the cries grew less fierce, and the older man's body calmed.

Focused on Ozo, the warlock did not notice the intrusion at the back of their camp until he heard the voice of the man they were hunting behind him. 'Hel—'

Khanaseri grabbed a rock and threw it at the shifter's head, cutting him off mid-sentence. Blood spilled from his nose as his knees buckled beneath him. The man grabbed his face and swore as he saw the big warlock charge at him.

Khanaseri dived forward, taking him in the midsection and driving him through the air as the man transformed. Growing larger and heavier, a scaled pelt, as hard as iron, pushed at him as they hit the ground, rolling to a stop on the loose rocky soil. Khanaseri didn't hesitate to leap on the creature's back as it lay sprawled on the ground. He flailed about on top of the beast, trying to smother it with his arms around its thick neck while the malformed bear ran for the woods and crashed into bushes and trees to throw him off. It reared to stand up straight, then fell backwards; the warlock had no choice but to release his grip. With a mighty crash, the wind was knocked out of him, and darkness threatened to take over. Off balance as he stood to face the bear, he was too slow to move out of its way as it bore down on him. The bear drove its massive head into his stomach and carried him until he crashed into a tree.

The bear transformed back to a man and stood before the warlock as he lay spitting blood, trying to catch his breath. The thief also spat some blood to the side and said, 'I'm not here to fi—.'

He suddenly staggered back as pain lanced through his head, his brain feeling too big for his skull. The pressure in his head built, and he could feel his heart pounding in his skull. His skin was on fire, his senses a mess. Screams of pain filled the air as Khanaseri rose from the ground, focusing on his chant.

'Please! I'm not here to fight!' The thief looked up as he lay on the ground and saw a big fist heading for his face.

Chapter Eight

Being the minority is infinitely more difficult than not, the three discovered. Geolas leaned in to Ganda'har and whispered, 'How are we supposed to know how many guards are in this town if we don't even know what they look like?'

'Maybe they can't all do that disguise trick he did.'

As they walked through the doors of the inn, the noise of exuberant conversation fell away as the three made their way to a table in the corner, waiting for Tannor to join them. The attention slowly faded as people returned to their own business. Geolas leaned over and whispered to the captain, 'I don't like this, sir. How did he accomplish that transformation? It wasn't like the warlocks we know. He didn't chant or draw or anything. It just happened. I've never seen this sort of witchery before. And we're not even sure if Khanaseri is here at all.'

Untara scratched at his thinning hair, then lit up a cigar as he said, 'Yeah, boss. I'm not one to admit this often, but I agree with Skinny here. Something's off.'

Ganda'har sat back, tapping with his middle finger on the table as he looked around the room. 'Your concerns are noted. I agree, we need to be very careful here, but first let's see how this plays out.'

From across the room, Tannor weaved through the crowd with four tankards filled with a green liquid spilling over the sides as he made his way to them. When he arrived, he slid the tankards over the table. Untara curled his top lip, revealing stained teeth as he stared at the drinks, and said, 'What moose piss is this? Are you trying to kill us?'

Geolas and Ganda'har glanced at each other after the outburst from the brute. 'Untara, manners! Apologies, Tannor, he's used to the military life. I fear it's dulled his sense of civility,' Ganda'har said sternly as he looked around.

Brushing his hand through his sweaty red hair, Tannor said, 'Say, your accent's really strange. I mean, I understand you fine, but there's something to it I can't put my finger on.'

'Yes, we noticed your accent as well. I fear we've travelled farther than we thought.'

Seeing the disgust on all of their faces as they looked at the green liquid, Tannor pointed to the drinks and said, 'Try it. It's good for the soul.'

Ganda'har stared at the man as he rubbed his beard, and said, 'How did you do that disguise trick? Was it magic?'

'No. No magic, my friends — plain makeup. I'm just very good at it.'

All three waited until Tannor took a big gulp of his drink before they too attempted it. Geolas hesitantly took the first mouthful. Instantly, he spat the ale back into the mug, then said, 'Oh dear. We have very different souls, you and I.'

Untara chewed the liquid in his mouth, tasting the subtleties of various fruits as it rolled around his tongue. 'I don't know. I kind of like it.'

Tannor slammed his hand on the table as he smiled. 'I told you.'

Unwilling to show any interest in playing this game, Ganda'har instead pulled a map from his pocket and lay it on the table. He circled a section of the map with his finger and said to Tannor, 'Can you show me where we are?'

Examining the map for some time, turning it upside down, to the right, then to the left with a puzzled look on his face, Tannor looked up at the three with a furrowed brow, then stood from his chair and gestured with his index finger for them to wait. He hustled through the horde of guests and quickly disappeared into the back room with the innkeeper. Ganda'har nervously glanced about, looking for an easy exit, and said to his compatriots, 'If he returns with a weapon of any kind, we go through that window and get out of here.'

A few tables to their right, a fight broke out as two men grabbed each other and started throwing punches. People scurried to get out of the way of the brawlers as tables were uplifted, ale flying everywhere. A fat man with an apron over his belly ran over and grabbed both men by their necks, marching them out of the inn and leaving them sprawled in the street.

'There he is,' Untara pointed out, and continued, 'Looks to be carrying a parchment.'

Tannor lay his version of the map on the table next to their map and circled an area as he said, 'This is where you are. I don't know who sold you that map, but it's complete garbage.'

All three bent over the table to study the map and compare the two. Dread filled Ganda'har as he saw the subtle differences. The continents were all there, but they were shifted, sitting in the wrong places, as if they had drifted closer to one another. Lying back in his chair, he wiped his hand over his face. 'We have a bigger problem than we thought, boys. I need to take this to Stilts, and most likely, kill him.'

'Why are you really here?' Tannor asked as he put his mug on the table.

Ganda'har quickly stated, 'As I said, friend Tannor, we're just searching for a man. Our king has recalled him to service, and he's gone AWOL.' They shared quick glances between the three of them as Tannor looked away for a moment.

'Don't linger too long here, then. I have to report any foreign military presence on our lands to the king. I would leave as soon as possible, were I you.'

Ganda'har rose from his chair, followed by Geolas and then Untara as he quickly downed the last bit of ale, and said, 'Thank you for your candour, Tannor. We'll be on our way, then.'

Tannor followed the three from the inn and shouted as they mounted their horses, 'Good luck with your search!' He then turned and whispered to himself, 'That was so much fun! I wish things like that happened more often here.'

* * *

Frazil ice drifted down like passing fleets in a would-be siege, rising against the current's everlasting abashment to their gods along the streams. Anavi sat transfixed, staring at this war in the stream, her mind drifting, a blank look on her face. Inside, roiling turmoil desperately sought a way out of the cage that was her mind, wanting to lash out at the people who had caused the pain and suffering of the man she loved. *All those times the damned oaf tried to get me to show any feelings for him. The flowers he brought, the way he acted when I entered the room... If anyone dared say anything untoward about me, Magnus was on them. How many times did I berate him for it? Belittle him for being the kind and generous man that he is? And yet, never, not once, did he retaliate; he would just stand there taking it, and then more often than not just apologise and leave the room, not to be seen for days after.*

'I'm so sorry, Magnus.' A constant stream of mucus ran from her nose, causing her to sniff. Startled, she jumped up as someone handed her a handkerchief.

Sword drawn, Anavi wiped her tears and saw Lanik a few feet away as he said, 'Sorry, Anavi, I thought you heard me approaching. You're usually... I'm sorry. Have you been to see Magnus?'

She lowered her sword and looked at him with anguish in her eyes as tears welled up, then muttered, 'I'm scared, Lanik. I've seen thousands of dead and dying. I sat next to my mother as she lay dying of the plague, and although I was sad, I didn't feel this pain in my heart.'

Lanik embraced her, holding her for some time as she trembled in his arms, then said, 'Go to him. The only thing that will give him the courage to fight for his life is you.'

With a nod, she turned and left him on the riverbank.

Anavi passed the temple where the siege had taken place. The bodies were being dragged out and flung onto an oxcart, piled on top of each other with little respect and care — they had a job to do. Blood stained the earth, and the flies and maggots were having a feast in the guts left on the ground. The marketplace was dour indeed, as few wandered out to buy their wares and food. No one paraded around town or took in the scenery today. She rounded the bend to the healer's quarters and felt her heart thudding in her chest, louder and louder the closer she got. *What if he doesn't love me anymore? What if I took too long, and he's moved on? I could have run away with him years ago. None of this would ever have happened.*

One leg in front of the other, she walked, but couldn't remember giving her body the instructions to move forward. Her knock sounded hollow, and her stomach tightened and churned, twisting into a knot as the door slowly opened. In front of her stood an old man with short, curly grey hair, glasses hanging on the very edge of his nose, with an apron smeared with blood. Impatiently, he said, 'Well, what do you want? I'm very busy.'

'I... Magnus is here.'

Her tongue failed her as she tried to speak further, and the old man merely nodded and gestured her inside as he said, 'Take a seat, my dear. I will be with you shortly.'

The old man's house smelled of various herbs, very concentrated versions of them. Anavi tried to figure out the smell as she waited and was sure of ginger, mint, and rosemary. But that last one... *What is that?*

'The blood of the dragon tree. Not actual blood, its sap. But I suppose it bleeds when cut. So, blood.'

'What's that?'

Hobbling closer on his cane, the old man said, 'That's the scent you can't identify. Everyone struggles with it. Follow me, young lady.'

They passed a few rooms, where she saw families huddled together in prayer for loved ones lying at the edge of death. The old man abruptly stopped, and Anavi nearly walked into him, her heart skipping a beat as he said, 'In here, my dear. Please note, his injuries were extensive. He's not safe yet, but he *is* better. At this stage, though, I can't say if he'll ever walk normally again. I'm sorry.'

Uncharacteristic of this fierce woman, she had nothing to say, almost whimpering as she said, 'Thank you,' and moved into the room, closing the door behind her.

* * *

Khanaseri sat on a rock, staring at the gangly man in silent flagellation as the two waited for Ozo to awake after his ordeal earlier. The young man scratched at the old cut across his throat, the memory of the knife cutting deep, still vivid. It was a sullen day; dark clouds roamed above, constantly shifting around, changing shapes, the smell of petrichor in the air.

Khanaseri took deep a breath and said, 'So, who are you?'

The man stopped his incessant scratching and turned to the warlock. 'My name is Arem Toforay.'

'So, Arem, why on earth did you come back to us, knowing that we're hunting you?'

'I told you the orb was in me, but I don't know how to get it out. It was great at first, being able to turn into some deformed creature; but as of late, it feels like my insides are being torn apart. My head is on fire, and I keep being drawn back to you two. That's why I'm here.'

A moan sounded from the left as Ozo rose from the ground, holding his head and his chest. Khanaseri called out from the rock he sat on. 'Easy, now. Slow and steady. Join us when you're ready.'

Ozo cursed as he stood and walked to his horse, taking out the water pouch and drinking deeply before he said, 'Us?' Out of breath and pale, he moved closer to see the young man sitting across from the warlock. Too tired and sore to care, he asked, 'How long was I out?'

'Half the day has gone. We have been waiting for you to come around before we start.'

Ozo joined them and said, 'Well, I'm here now. Continue.'

The young man cleared his throat. 'As I said, my name is Arem Toforay. I'm a collector of sorts.'

Breadcrumbs rolled down Khanaseri's jacket as he took another bite of the loaf and said, as he chewed, 'You mean you're a thief.'

With a quick look, the young man said, 'Like I said, a collector.'

The warlock stood and shoved another piece of bread into his mouth. 'Awe you no a wit oo all...'

Outraged, Ozo shouted, 'Stop talking with a mouth full of food, you damned oaf! We can't understand what you're saying!'

Swallowing the dry bread, he said again, 'I asked if you're not a bit too tall to be a thief?'

Arem rolled his eyes, muttering, 'It's not as if there's a height requirement, you know. Besides, you try reaching high ledges if you're short.' A rock skidded across the river after he launched it, then he continued, 'It was great to have this power flowing through me. The ability to become something else in a blink of an eye... And I believe there's still much to learn from it.' He looked at the warlock. 'But lately, something has changed. Every so often, I'd be besieged by it, as if it wanted me to go somewhere. It was tearing at the walls of my soul, wanting out. And every time I felt this way, you two were close by. I can feel it clawing up my throat to get free even as I speak. It hurts so much, like a fire burning in my throat.'

Khanaseri picked up a branch and drew archaic symbols on the ground, enclosing the symbols in a square. Frowning, the two men watched him prepare the scene next to the river as they approached. Finished with his bread and with the symbols, the warlock pointed at Arem and said, 'Get in the square.'

Unsure, Arem looked at Ozo, who just shrugged and said, 'I'm old. What do I know?'

The warlock gestured with the stick in his hand as he said, 'We don't have all day. I promise, I'll try to keep this as painless as possible.'

'Have you done this before?'

Annoyed, Khanaseri walked over to the thief and picked him up as

Arem squirmed in his grip. Shoved face-first into the sand, Arem heard the chanting start as he felt the big hands on the back of his head, holding him in place. A red veil of fire illuminated the square. Over and over the warlock repeated the phrase, 'Estas pory as tas kurjiel onto mei! Estas pory as tas kurjiel onto mei!' As if it were being swallowed by the young man's subsequent screams, the fire faded as it rushed down his throat.

Arem wailed as the heat threatened to burn him from the inside out. He could feel a battle being waged in his insides, as if the warlock were tearing whatever it was in him out. It felt like great talons ripping him open from the inside as they were dragged from his body. His eyes turned back in his head and he felt the grip of the Balamuth weaken.

Ozo covered his mouth and paced back and forth, seeing blood seep from Arem's eyes, ears, and nose. It looked as if the man's face was getting even thinner. Unable to take it anymore, he shouted at the warlock, 'Stop it! You're killing him! Can't you see? Please stop!'

Khanaseri could feel his grasp on the orb. To let go now...well, he couldn't. Blood flowed freely now as a mist streamed from the young man's every orifice. *Almost done.* The sphere materialised before him and he smiled.

A loud thump on his head, then nothing.

Immediately, the viscous crimson liquid poured back into the man, tearing Arem's mouth open as it rushed towards safety and salvation. Lying on the ground trembling, the young man watched Khanaseri get back to his feet, dazed, shaking his head as he shouted, 'What was that? I almost had it! Now I have to start all over again!'

Ozo scrambled back as the warlock approached him and exclaimed, 'You were about to kill the boy! Just give me a chance with him. I have a feeling.'

Rage was building in the big man. He threw the stick to one side and said, 'Fine, but if you fail, we do it *my* way. Got it?'

Arms in the air, Ozo sneered, 'Sure.'

Arem glowered at Ozo as he approached with an outstretched hand, shivers still racking his body. The old man helped the young man up and said, 'I'm having similar episodes, yet I don't have an orb in me. The only difference is that it feels like it's calling me. Wanting me to open myself to it. And until recently, I wouldn't have done it. But now, I feel a sort of peace as I stand before it.'

The warlock sat on the rocks, watching the two talk from a distance. Ozo crossed his legs and sat as straight as he could, then said, 'Clear your mind, Arem. Think only of the orb. Try to commune with it. Urge it to leave freely. Be respectful of it, as I believe it to be alive. Take your time; don't be forceful.'

For quite some time, they sat with eyes closed as Arem's hands rested on top of the old man's.

Ozo felt a slight tingle as they made contact. Words formed in his mouth. 'Worthy shall I be. I place my life with thee. I shall seek you if lost. Protect you if you have fallen.' Ozo felt the Balamuth respond to his voice, to his calling. Loosening its grip on Arem, it coursed through the veins of the man, releasing his soul and moving towards Ozo as he continued, 'Separate, we are alone, weak and afraid. But now we are one and we are strong.'

A small, almost unnoticeable flicker of light passed between the two in a blink of an eye. Ozo gasped for air, his eyes fixed on the heavens. A wealth of information came rushing in, flooding his brain with all his lost memories, the years that had passed, the life he had lived, why he was here and how he got here. Visions flashed by his eyes so fast, and yet it felt like a lifetime of remembrance as the events unfolded. His skin was on fire; the cells in his blood electrified and sped up, regenerating his body.

Khanaseri watched as the older man's features turned back the clock, becoming less wrinkled as youth clawed back the lost years. His hair grew out and his voice changed as he screamed from the pain, becoming deeper and full of life. And yet, Ozo wanted more...

Khanaseri ran in and grabbed him by the shirt. 'No! You were supposed to get the orb out. Not take it!'

Ozo fell to the ground and shuffled closer to a tree, resting against it as the warlock went on with his rant, the sounds muffled to his ears, his vision blurry. The ringing in his ears subsided gradually as he moved his head up and down, and said, 'Sorry, Khan, but I couldn't let you kill the boy. This Balamuth belongs to me. You can't deny what you saw in my memories. I had to take the chance.'

Arem stood up, his legs wobbling beneath him. Astonished to see the transformation in Ozo, he said, 'I appreciate what you've done for me. I truly do. But if it's all the same to you, I'll leave now.'

Straining his face as he coughed, Ozo smiled and said, 'Of course. It's only natural that you would want to get away from the people who nearly killed you.' He looked at Khanaseri, now sitting on a rock a few paces away with his back turned to them, unwilling to meet his eyes. Ozo continued, 'Anyway, be a good lad and try not to get into trouble.' Quickly grabbing Arem's shirt before he could get away, Ozo pulled him closer. 'And by that, I mean stop stealing other people's belongings.'

Arem pulled away with a smirk on his face, then left the way he came.

* * *

'What do you expect me to do now?' Khanaseri asked as he wrapped his belongings and shoved them into Flintlock's saddlebag, then joined Ozo at the fire. Silence answered him.

The day was ending as the sun set over the mountains in the distance. Reflected in the shiny blade of the battle-axe was the face of a man Ozo barely recognised anymore, his youth bringing back painful memories of his past. Physically, he felt great for the first time in years. His once-crooked legs had seemed to straighten slowly as the day had progressed. He could feel the uncomfortable fractional movements of his bones, as if some force were constantly pressing at them. He knew the damage done to him was being repaired, but it would take time. Khanaseri gestured to him for the axe and said, 'Can you remember everything now?'

With a heave, Ozo tossed the axe over the fire to the warlock. 'I feel like I have all the pieces, but they're not yet assembled, if that makes sense. As if I'm building a hugely complex puzzle in my head. I believe, given some time, I'll understand more. There are a few things I've remembered. Like, I'm not from here. I somehow ended up here by falling through a portal. I know someone badly injured me. Maybe even tortured me, but I'm not sure.' He stood up and walked to the horses, then continued, 'I remember being treated by an old healer for a long time before I could walk.'

'And your abilities?'

Laughter echoed over the river, and in between the chuckles, Ozo asked, 'Are you afraid I might get away from you? No, not yet. I think I need some time for that as well. I know my actual name now, though. It's Blanka.'

'Wait — Blanka? As in Beuneth's Blanka?'

'One and the same, my friend. No wonder she wanted me to go with you. I don't know how she got to this side.'

Raising his brows, the warlock took his axe as he stood. 'Well, I do, and it's a doozy. I'll tell you if you tell me about some things from your past.'

A loud, fireless explosion rocked the earth as a sudden cloud of smoke obscured their view. Khanaseri struggled for breath as he shouted, 'Get low to the ground. Run for the forest!'

'I can't see a thing!' Blanka shouted back, then saw movement through the smoke. 'Watch out, someone's here!'

Three figures appeared out of thin air, moving with grace through the smoke, as if it didn't affect them in the least. Pain ripped through Khanaseri's left hand, then his right as short crossbow bolts trailing ropes pierced through. The ropes were tightened, spreading his limbs apart, tearing through flesh and bone. Another arrow bolt sliced through his left thigh, then his right. Gaining some momentum, Khanaseri pulled his arms closer together, trying to reach for the bolts in his hands. Two more bolts sailed through the smoke, slicing through his left and right biceps. Again, they pulled tighter and tighter, dragging the warlock to the ground. The bolts were of a clever design, fashioned with barbs so they couldn't be easily removed once they pierced flesh.

Blanka charged in with the warlock's axe and ran at the nearest assassin, swinging the enormous weapon. The weight threw Blanka off his feet, sending him face-first to the dirt, missing his target completely. He looked up at an arrow pointed at his right eye, mere inches away as a voice said, 'Move and die.'

More figures appeared out of the mist, moving closer as they held the ropes to control the warlock. Khanaseri was on the ground, hands stretched out before him. He wanted to cast a spell, but found his mind drifting. Pale from the pain, he shouted, 'What do you want?' His face was pushed to the ground as he succumbed to the pain, drool running down his mouth while they tugged on the ropes over and over.

One assassin stepped closer and said, 'You should have killed us on that roof.' A dart hissed out of a tube, striking Khanaseri in the neck.

The big man's face turned into an illustration of ecstasy, his head bobbing around as his eyes wandered, lost and out of control. All thoughts of the arrows in his flesh had disappeared, as well as the willingness to fight. His head swam in an ocean full of sharks, lashing out until oblivion took him.

Blanka kept his eyes averted as they pushed him to the ground next to the warlock. With his face pressed hard against the rocks and dirt, he shouted, 'Why are you doing this?'

A sharp pain, like a bee sting, burned his neck, then sudden euphoria. Vivid flashes of light danced before his eyes; his mind raced and his heart was a beating drum as voices filled his ears and night took his sight.

* * *

Afternoon sun shone down on the encampment as three riders approached. At the lead, the captain bypassed the initial greeting party and instead headed straight to Stilts' tent at the very back of the encampment and reined in next to it. Ganda'har jumped off the horse and threw the flaps open as he moved in. The room was empty. Storming out, he shouted, 'Where is he!'

A soldier nearby, busy shaving, said, 'He's a ways south, sir. Said something about tracking the warlock.'

Ganda'har's anger flared as his thoughts reeled at this setback. He stormed in the designated direction, thinking about the many days they had wasted here for nothing. 'Stilts! Get over here now!' Seeing a figure rise in the distance, he assumed this to be the veritable dead man and marched in his direction. Heat waves rippled across the scorching sands whilst every so often, the cry of a crow could be heard in the distance. A tremble rushed through Ganda'har that made him stumble. Regaining his footing, he turned around and could see no one, not even his encampment. Turning round and round, there was nothing. *Surely I didn't walk that far.*

'Stilts! Where are you, boy?' He covered his head with his hands as he walked, trying to keep the sun away, then in the distance saw a figure sitting cross-legged, and ran towards him. Anger flared in his head. His fist broke Stilts' jaw; then another cracked his skull. 'Stilts, you son-of-a-bitch!'

He was still holding onto the man's tunic, now limp in his hands; but the man was suddenly gone. Ganda'har shook his head and stammered as he said, 'W-what?' He looked up and saw Stilts running towards him. Anger flared again, and before he could even think about his actions, his knife had left his hand, sinking into the man's throat. Even as Ganda'har sagged to the ground, screaming for forgiveness, the scene changed and there was nobody again. 'What *is* this?' He picked himself up from the ground and regained his composure.

Seemingly from nowhere, Stilts stood behind him. 'Sorry, Captain, but as I was sure you wouldn't listen to reason before you tried to kill me, I made a choice to give you a chance to act out your desire — twice, in this case — so you could calm yourself. This is all in your mind, sir. Now, when we go back, are you going to kill me, or give me a chance to explain a few things? Also remember, without me, you won't get back home.'

Ganda'har could feel the anger bubbling up as he said, 'We'll talk.'

The sun was still beating down, but Ganda'har woke in the shade of an overhang in the hillside. Stilts sat before him, silently sharpening the blade that had plunged into his throat only moments ago. Parched, Ganda'har cleared his throat and pointed to Stilts' water pouch. 'Please.'

Stilts handed over the pouch and said, 'I believe someone tampered with the portal, sir. But it wasn't Khanaseri. Someone else had a hand in this. But that's beside the point; I have bad news. Khanaseri isn't here; he's not even close.'

Ganda'har threw the map Tannor had given them to the warlock and stated, 'You're damned right. I don't know what to make of this, but their continents don't align with ours.'

Stilts smiled as he studied the map, and continued, 'Incredible. Time is the answer here. We may have been thrust forward or backward in time – a long way, it would seem. So this could be what it looked like or will look like at some point. And now that this has been explained, I have some even worse news. We can't open a portal from this side to get back to our time, place, realm...'

Ganda'har slowly reached for his knife and said, 'Tell me again why I have to keep you alive.'

Stilts watched the steady gaze of the man as he reached for his knife, then quickly added to his comments, 'Because there's another way, sir. I feel a massive pull of energy due northwest of here. If we're lucky, I can use that to open a portal back home.'

* * *

'Come on, Beany! You can do it! Just don't look down! And no magic this time! Oh yeah, one more thing, don't stop at the edge; it's very slippery, and it's a long way down.'

'Would you shut the hell up, Blanka, or is there anything else you'd like to share with the class?' Beuneth shouted back from across the gap between the roofs. The rest of the children were milling around, waiting for Beuneth to take the leap over the sixty-foot drop.

Buffeting blows from the eastern winds made her lose her footing for a second, knotting her stomach before she shook it off and readied herself. Rocking back and forth, she settled into place, concentrating on the edge and where her last step needed to land, to send her flying to the other side. Beuneth looked out over the plethora of buildings so closely knit. For a heartbeat, she was almost happy for their cave dwelling up in the mountain.

'Whenever you're ready!'

'Shut up!' *That's at least a ten-foot jump to get across. What am I doing? Trying to show off, that's what. I've already proven myself to these scoundrels staring at me with their indignant eyes. I don't need to do this.* With all her might, Beuneth pushed herself off the line towards the edge, her footfalls landing perfectly on the treacherous tiles of the roof. All it took was one wrong foot placement and down you went, but she had been running on roofs since she could remember. *Almost there!* The drop towards the cobblestoned road below filled with roaming ignorant pedestrians moved into her view, the realisation striking like a viper to the heart. *No backing out now.*

'I love you!' came a shout from the other side of the gap.

She looked up and saw Blanka smiling as he stood with his arms crossed. A sudden and vicious barrage of pain shot through her leg and foot as she twisted her ankle just before she jumped.

Seeing her in trouble, Blanka sprinted forward and leapt, colliding with her in mid-air between the two buildings, then plummeted to the ground below, holding on to her for dear life. The rope around his waist pulled taut almost instantly, jerking her out of his grasp and sent her slipping down his arm. *I'll have terrible burn marks around my waist tonight. Worth it,* he thought. 'Hold on!' he shouted as she slipped even farther down until, finally, he got a grip on her. He pulled her closer to him as they swayed in the air, and heard people shouting from below, pointing up at them.

Beuneth looked up into his eyes and shouted, 'You asshole! I have my own rope! Bloody imbecile! Why would you do that?' Angry and subdued, she resorted to kicking him on the shins as they were pulled back up onto the roof by the rest of the children, who were laughing wholeheartedly at the scene...

As the dream faded, the pounding in his skull replaced his smile, bringing on a wave of nausea. Blanka spilled his guts on the floor and over his clothes as he hung from iron shackles, groaning at the foul smell in the little room.

* * *

Oh, how this brings back the memory of me being chained in the cell awaiting my execution. Strung up in the air only by their wrists, Blanka turned to see the warlock, head slouched, his snores echoing in the chamber. He looked around the dark room and saw a big iron door obstructing their exit in front of them. There was nothing to the sides and back except rock walls with no windows or discernible weaknesses. He focused on the warlock, squinting his eyes to see his wounds more clearly. They had pushed some kind of herb into the holes to stem the bleeding and hopefully stave off any infection. Swaying back and forth, his arms felt as though they would be pulled from their sockets as he tried to kick the warlock. The distance was too great. He needed more momentum. *Damned muscles. I might look younger, but my muscles have grown weak. No wonder the axe threw me off balance.* He closed his eyes and concentrated on his memories, trying to piece together something that might help them escape. As he worked through the memories, he flicked his thumb against his forefinger repeatedly until he felt a sudden heat in his hand. A smile appeared on his face as he saw the flame dancing on his thumb. He closed his hand and continued his swinging, swaying farther and farther until eventually, he kicked the warlock awake.

Startled, Khanaseri blinked a few times and felt the pain returning to his arms, hands, and legs. His voice sounded groggy and strained as he said, 'Where are we?'

'I don't know, but I don't think we should hang around to find out.'

Just then, a loud clang sounded as the door was unlatched and swung open. The assassin who'd anesthetized Blanka walked into the room, then punched the warlock in his stomach. Blanka pulled on the chains, trying to reach the assassin as he shouted, 'Please stop! What do you want? Look at me!'

The assassin ignored Blanka's pleas and withdrew, then removed his hood as he stared at the warlock and spat in his face. 'Look at me, demon. You will remember me as you die tonight! My name is Sukayi Kavali. I killed another like you not so long ago, a captain of some useless squad! Travelled across the seas for another like you and had the fortuitousness of running into him! Stabbed him over and over in the chest until he lay dying on the ground.'

The warlock's eyes widened. '*You* killed my father!' As he tried to pull himself up on the chains, blood seeped from his wounds, making the floor slippery beneath him.

Glass replaced his hood and laughed. 'Oh, what a fortunate turn of events.'

Another assassin emerged through the door. 'Why have we brought them here and not to the guild?'

The warlock recognised the voice and said, 'Because this is personal. The guil—'

Glass hammered another blow into the warlock's stomach to silence him. He looked back at Link, and said, 'This is the guild's orders! Now take him to the torture chamber. The guild wants answers.'

Link stepped back to let Sliver and Switchblade move by. The sound of the ratchet echoed harshly in the chamber as the chain ran through the cogs of the device. Sliver turned the lever until the warlock could reach the ground with his toes, then tied his legs. 'Gag him, Switch.'

A filthy old cloth was stuffed deep into Khanaseri's mouth. They dragged him from the room as he grasped at the door and the walls. Glass turned to Blanka with a grin on his face. 'Don't worry, I'll take good care of him. Then I'll come for you. I'm curious to know why he's with you.'

Spit covered his face, and a chuckle sounded through the assassin's covered mouth. 'Oh, we're going to have so much fun, you and I.'

The door swung closed, and the latch fell into place. Blanka feared for the worst, thinking quickly of ways to get free, then closed his eyes and focused on his memories.

* * *

Chills ran through her body from the cold, damp rock she sat on as she looked languidly over the valley in the bright moonlight. The silhouetted trees rocked gently back and forth as the winds howled their early morning woes. She looked to her left and said, 'You know sound travels well at night, right? Talking to yourself as much as you do will land you in heaps of trouble one day. People will think you're crazy.'

'I don't care what people think. They're still the best conversations I have in the day,' Blanka said as he sat down next to Beuneth, flinching from the cold rock. 'Mother is...' His voice cracked and changed pitch as he was entering adulthood. He cleared his throat before he continued, 'Mother is thrilled with the retrieval of the amulet. We'll have a generous supper tonight.'

Short, mocking laughter escaped her lips as she said, 'A generous supper...'

'Well, yeah. Very. We might even get some meat tonight, all thanks to you.'

'I'm serious, Blankadu. Is this what we risk our lives for? The possibility of some meat for supper? Do you even realise how sad that is?'

He snapped his head around as he said, 'Whoa! You haven't used my full name since I stole the little doll you had when you were seven, I think.' Silence followed for a moment before Blanka continued, 'Beany, you know you can't talk like that. Kids start disappearing when they question Mother.'

She trembled from the rage in her and glared at him. 'We live in a fucking cave, Blanka. A cave! On the outskirts of Terenore, like a bunch of filthy fucking rats, just waiting for their chance to invade, steal, and plunder. How is this a life?'

'It's the only one you have, Beuneth. It's the only one all of us have, and the quicker you realise that, the better for all of us. Don't you think we all want something better? That I want something better than to do the bidding of Mother?' Taking her hand in his, he continued, 'Just think: they can't run this place forever. We're getting too old and too strong for them to handle. And they know it.'

'I just want us to be free.'

Blanka sighed as he stood and gazed over the valley and said, 'Come on, the sun is coming up soon, and Mother wants you to train with her at first light.'

Begrudgingly getting to her feet, she sighed and walked after Blanka through the forest. As they neared the cave entrance, Beuneth said, 'You should come and watch the training. I'm going to break her vase.'

'Why are you constantly looking for trouble? And you know I can't come and watch, she'd have me flogged.' Beuneth slipped on a wet patch of dirt and Blanka steadied her, then said, 'I'll watch from the shadows. Happy?'

Beuneth smiled then and continued up the rocky path and into the cave mouth. *Our very own little necropolis.*

They walked deeper into the mountain, through the winding halls of the cave dwelling, their only guide being the lanterns on the walls. Up ahead, new children were busy revamping the halls, adding a timber floor and trusses to the side for some walls to be put in. 'Watch out for the nails on the floor!' came a shout from one boy. 'You don't want them in your foot!'

Almost half the rooms and halls had been completed, slowly being turned into an actual house in the mountain. *Now all we need are some windows.*

A voice rang out from a distant room. 'Beuneth, you are late! As always! Training room! Now!'

'Of course, Mother!'

As they entered the training room — a vast hall with artefacts resting on pedestals displayed along the walls — Blanka looked around for a hiding spot and saw some tables and chairs on the far end, moved aside to make space for training. Quickly, he dashed across the room to hide behind a table as Beuneth warmed up for the training, stretching her muscles and breathing deeply.

With no warning, a chain whip sliced through the air, the swish of the chain alerting Beuneth just in time to duck out of the way. She avoided the following bombardment as she dived to the left. Nearing the weapons rack, she grabbed her own chain whip from the hook on the wall and immediately dived to the right as another blow came at her. Skidding on one knee, she bit her lip, feeling the skin tear away, then flicked out her chain and sent it crashing into the oncoming chain. The deadly dance of the chain whips was incredible. Having found her footing, Beuneth pushed Vandalor back, driving her to the wall near the vase.

Pottery flew across the room and smashed to tiny pieces as it hit the ground. The fury of the two locked in battle was relentless as they moved about the room, each preparing to strike yet again. Beuneth stumbled back from the attacking Vandalor as the chain whip swung at terrible speeds, left, right, over her elbows and neck, then with a furious kick that sent the porous clay ball at the end of the chain hurtling into her chest. Beuneth hit the ground hard and brought her hand to her chest as she got back to her feet, spitting out some blood. *How can she be this quick at her age? She must be near forty at least!*

Vandalor moved with ease and grace, her lithe form approaching steadily as she said, 'Daughter, that was a seven-hundred-year-old Balminian vase. One of a kind, you know.'

Loud cracks reverberated through the room as Beuneth cocked her head left and right, then wiped the blood from her mouth. 'Yes, I know full well, as I was the one who stole it for you. They almost captured me that night. The pain of the arrow striking my thigh, lodged there as I ran, is a hard thing to forget. Do you remember that, Mother? Or just the vase? Don't worry, that was a stupid question.'

Vandalor spun on her heels, expertly swinging the chain whip around her neck, propelling it at incredible speed towards Beuneth. Surprised by the speed of the attack, Beuneth dropped her chain whip and shouted, 'Stop!'

Mere inches from her face, suspended in mid-air as if frozen in time, hung the clay ball, waiting to be released to claim its victim. A few heartbeats passed as she gathered herself before Vandalor broke free from the spell. Outraged, the woman marched over to Beuneth and gave her a mighty slap across the face. 'I told you not to use magic during training. You need to be able to defend yourself without it. Now, again.'

* * *

Blanka opened his eyes. The memory quickly faded, replaced by the sounds of whipping as it echoed through the cave, sending chills down his spine. For a brief moment, he closed his eyes and saw that massive hammer coming down once more. The sound of bones snapping, crushed beneath the blow, sent him reeling. He vomited to the side. Shaking his head to dissolve the vision from his mind, he breathed deep, sputtering breaths as he felt the world twist before his eyes.

He realised just how weak he had got. Everything ached. *What have you got to lose, Blanka? Push through the pain, you idiot!* Time crawled by as he continued relentlessly to pull himself up. The skin of his wrists had worn through and blood trickled down his arms when he finally grasped the main chain. The sounds of whipping had fallen away, replaced by the screams of the warlock. Concentrating, Blanka said, 'If you're in there, I need your help to survive this. How do I call upon you or your abilities?'

The voice in his head called out in pain, *'I am still healing, but I will share what I have. You only need to think what you want; I will answer.'*

He saw in his mind's eye the workings of his body, the concealment of the power that lurked just below the surface — still hurting, but willing. Channelling heat from his body, he sent wave after wave through to the chains. His hands grew hot. As he opened his eyes, he saw the red glow on the iron links. With all his body was willing to give, he pulled himself up as high as he could, then dropped back down to stretch open the links in the chain. *I am heavier than I remember, but I will not give up.* His arms burned from fatigue as he pulled himself up. The top was getting closer with every pull. A sudden pain lanced through his arms, causing him to drop. 'Bastard!' Screaming as he strained his muscles, he climbed higher and higher, only to drop back down and do it again.

Under great pressure, one link gave way, snapping up high and his fingers reached out, grasping at air as he fell. While he was sprawled on the stone floor with the wind knocked out of him, an assassin burst through the door. Lungs wheezing, Blanka slowly got back up and pointed at the waiting assassin. 'I'm warning you! Stay back!'

Link raised his hands and said, 'Hold on. You need to get out of here. I didn't sign up for torturing a man just because of a personal vendetta against their kind.'

A momentary flicker of doubt settled in as he looked at the assassin, then Blanka said, 'I don't understand. Why hasn't he used his magic to escape?'

'They've been injecting him with a drug that swallows the mind. He can't think coherently. Your friend will most likely not come out of this alive. But at least *you* can get out of here.'

Running past the assassin, Blanka stopped and glanced back questioningly.

'To the right.'

Out the door he went, turning left and running as fast as he could towards the screams of the warlock.

'I said right! You're heading straight for them!'

'I know.' Blanka heard the footsteps behind him as the assassin caught up with him, grabbing his arm to pull him back.

'They'll kill you!' A few heartbeats went by as Link thought, then said, 'I go in first.' Drawing his hood, he disappeared around the corner. Casually walking up to the two assassins, he spun and thrust his dagger into Switchblade's side. Sliver reached for his short sword as he saw Switchblade sagging to the ground, when a ball of fire crashed into his chest, flinging him through the air and into the wall.

A voice from the other side of the door called out, 'Who's there? I told you, I don't want to be disturbed.'

Glass opened the door and was greeted with a fist to his nose. He staggered back; his vision blurred. Shouting and cursing at Link, he tried to regain his sight as the pain coursed through his face. Link turned to Blanka and said, 'Get your friend out. I'll take care of this.'

Blanka nodded. 'Thank you.'

Glass ran towards Blanka, but was cut off by Link as his chain whip's blades sliced deep around Glass's arm, holding him back. Wincing, Glass turned to fight the other assassin.

Untying the straps around the warlock's arms and legs, Blanka cringed as he saw the wounds. Khan was in terrible shape, barely able to stand or see. With a heave, he let the warlock put some of his weight on him and guided him out of the room. Hearing the two men still fighting, they moved as fast as possible to gain ground, just in case Link wasn't the victor.

The never-ending hallway, used only in times of secrecy, spiralled higher and higher.

* * *

Sparks flew as the two swords missed their mark and hit the stone wall. Link got to his feet and swung the chain whip.

Glass leapt in, spinning through the air, dual swords swishing as he brought them down, narrowly missing Link's neck as the assassin shifted to the left. The chain whip flashed out, wrapping around a sword hilt and Glass's hand, biting deep as a smaller blade dug into the top of his hand, protruding from the bottom. With Link's savage jerk, blood sprayed to the floor as the sword dropped, clanging on the ground.

Screams of anger and pain filled the room, Glass's eyes brimming red with fury. Attacking with his left hand, he was a little slower, and much more vulnerable, but just as dangerous. Link dodged the blows as he parried left and right, shouting, 'I don't want to kill you!'

Glass kept coming, swinging and stabbing as fast as he could. 'Too bad. I'll kill *you*, you traitor! The guild will hunt you to the ends of the earth!'

Parrying another blow, Link said, 'What you're doing is wrong, and you know this. We are not murderers. We kill for the guild, never for personal reasons.'

'Oh, grow up, Link! The guild sends us to kill for *their* personal gain all the time! How is that any different?' A sudden thrust from Glass sliced deep into Link's arm.

Link fell back against the wall, clutching his arm, then saw Glass jump across the torture table, bringing his sword down hard. Scraping past Link's face, the blade cut into the wall as he moved just in time to avoid the death blow. He spun on his heels and grabbed Glass at the back of the neck. Using the assassin's momentum against him, he slammed his head viciously against the wall, and Glass sagged to the ground without a sound.

* * *

Finally, seeing light in the distance, they ran towards it, and Blanka covered his eyes as the sun blinded him. A sudden pull from behind on his shirt's collar sent the two men falling to the ground, hard. Quickly rising, Blanka hurled a ball of fire through the air, expecting Glass with his swords, ready to skewer them. Lying off to the right, Link slowly rose to his feet. Out of breath, he waved his hands at the exit and said, 'Cliff. Death.' He bent over, standing with his hands on his knees, trying to catch his breath.

Khanaseri lay on the ground as soft groans escaped his mouth, his face a pale grey, while Blanka moved to the cliff's edge. Hundreds of feet down, he saw the valley floor with tall oak trees swaying like long grass in the winds. Rivers wound their way across the scene to the right, and to the left in the distance, he could see smoke drifting up from a village. Blanka turned to Link and said, 'How did you get us up here?'

The assassin moved to the edge and looked down as he said, 'There was another way out. As you came up, you should have seen it branch off to the left and taken that. It would have led you out closer to the bottom where there's a path to follow.'

Blanka looked down and took a deep breath. *I hope you're up for this.* Then he looked at Link and said, 'Whatever happens next, attack nothing, and trust that it's not here to harm you but to help you.' Closing his eyes, the dark-haired Blanka dropped from the edge, falling down the side of the cliff before Link could catch him.

With a loud sigh, the assassin looked at the big man on the ground, and said, 'Well, looks like I'll have to drag you out of here myself.'

Extreme gusts of wind were forced into the corridor as a piercing cry sounded, and massive charcoal talons plucked them from the cliff's edge. The sudden force as they were pulled from the solid ground was enough to make Link scream for his life — something he hadn't done in a very long time — as he felt fear grip him in its entirety. Khanaseri hung motionless in the clutches of the dragon as they soared through the sky, magnificent wings beating above.

The vista before them was now dominated by a ruddy hue on the clouds in the distance as the sun set over the horizon. Like an oil painting, the colours mixed with a perfect contrast as the red-orange clouds met the rolling green landscapes below, the blue-grey of the water in the lakes, and the green-brown rivers snaking through to create overall perfection. Link clutched at the beast's claws in fear and awe as he looked up at the black dragon above. Large scales covered its powerful body, with huge horns on top of its head and a long tail swaying in the winds far behind.

They descended to the ground near the village, a short way from a lake in a clearing, taking advantage of the trees to cover their descent.

Link stared as the dragon transformed with a golden refulgence, veering into a man standing before them. Legs buckled beneath a fatigued body, and Blanka fell to the ground. The transformation had sapped all his energy. Quickly running in, the assassin moved to his side and grabbed his arm to steady his frame. Pale and breathless, sweat beading his forehead, Blanka said, 'Thank you. I need to eat. My body is still too weak for the full transformation.'

The assassin stood dumbfounded as he searched for words to reply, then asked, 'What *are* you?'

Blanka stared at the man, seeing the shock on his face. 'I am a long story, my friend. Come help me with him.'

Dragging the unconscious Khanaseri between the two of them, they headed to the village healer.

Chapter Nine

Silence now, after the bell's clangour to honour the fallen in the unwarranted siege. Ladriana sat on the bed, perfectly poised to convey highborn society while Lanik paced up and down the room when she spoke. 'Why were you really with the Desert Dogs? Why would you leave all this behind?'

He stopped pacing and stared at her in wonder, thinking just how lucky he was to get a woman so beautiful and brave to fall for him, then said, 'A long time ago, when I was a young boy, the former council members of this kingdom conspired against my father, and sent for the Desert Dogs to murder us all in our sleep. Luckily for me, the half-wit who was supposed to kill me just reported me dead with all the others, being too lazy to search for me. My mother, my father, and my sister, all murdered in cold blood for political gain.' Emotions toyed with him as he held the ring still hanging from the chain around his neck, then yanked to snap the chain. With an audible sigh, he slid the ring on his finger.

Ladriana rose, wanting to comfort him, but he pulled away, saying, 'And now, the one person who took care of me, who saved me that night and took me to safety, is lying half-dead in a bed a mile away, and there's nothing I can do to save him. He raised me in that bar. We changed our names, and have never been back here officially, other than my visits to those council members a while back. My real name is Garidan Rourke.'

As she closed her eyes, she saw the arrow pierce Magnus again, the pain so clear on his face as he shouted for her to run and leave him behind. Tears streamed down her face as her body trembled. Shaking her head, she said, 'I am *so* sorry, Lanik. I should have turned to fight for him. Then maybe he would've had a chance.'

He sighed and turned to her where she sat on the bed. 'No. Magnus knew the likely outcome. He knew that if you'd stayed, you would both be dead right now.'

She wiped the tears from her cheeks. 'Just tell me, why didn't you kill Xylac long ago? You surely had many opportunities.'

'Yes I did, and maybe if I had, then none of this would have happened.' He nodded and rubbed at the ring on his finger, then continued, 'My plan was a slow and meticulous one, meant to break him down from the inside; I wanted him to suffer. I planned to take him down piece by piece, and during that time, I decided I would learn from them. First was the killing of his second-in-command, so I could move up the ranks. Then I orchestrated the betrayal at the Battle of Ormondeo, making the Desert Dogs lose all credibility. Set the whole thing up. Then I gave away a full treasure chest to an orphanage, claiming someone had stolen it. I was breaking him slowly. Turning his men away from him. For Xylac, we were just gold in his pocket, nothing more. So I stayed on for a few years to learn how to fight, how to spot corrupt people, and how to be corrupt without being spotted. They taught me various skills over the years, and for that, I was grateful. I know it's crazy, but I wouldn't be the man I am today if I hadn't joined them. And then you joined...and, well, I just wanted to keep you safe.'

'And Anavi, how does she fit into all of this?'

'Now *that* is an interesting story...'

* * *

It was a snowy night as a blizzard moved through the region. People scoured the area for warm places to lay their heads, most finding refuge at the inn. Young Lanik was busy playing with his wooden sword, fighting a horde of intruders who had landed ashore and were now busy invading their bar to take ownership of all the ale in The Flying Squirrel. A few patrons who frequented the bar laughed and played along as the boy ran around, shouting orders as the epic battle ensued. *Only ten years old now, and so much imagination,* thought Magnus as he walked past to deliver another round of ale to the falling intruders being hacked to pieces by "Lanik the Great." He was still having a laugh with the men at the table when the door was kicked open. A gust of icy wind and snow rushed into the bar, sending shouts up from everyone to close the infernal door and seal it shut.

Magnus hurried towards the door, properly slamming it shut, and turned around to see *her* standing in front of him. She was no pretty sight. Covered in blood, her clothes torn and reeking of alcohol, she stared at him through eyes that wandered about, unable to focus or comprehend what was going on. Her legs gave way under her, and she fell to the wooden floor without a word. Patrons rushed up to see what was happening. Lanik worked his way through the crowd and saw Magnus holding his fingers to her neck and wrists as he hushed everyone.

'Make way, everyone. Come now. Give her some room!' Magnus shouted, and picked her up. He carried her through the kitchen and out into a room at the back, where he lay her down in his bed, and said to her unconscious form, 'Sorry, deary, but Uncle Magnus has to look and see if youse are injured.'

Carefully cutting away the sides of her torn shirt and pants, he covered her breasts and nether region as he meticulously inspected her body. There were two fairly deep stab wounds to her right thigh, not deep enough to cause any real damage; luckily, they had missed the great artery there. Her eyes were swollen from a beating, and severe bruising showed around her neck, as if someone had been trying to strangle her.

Wonder what else they did to you. Poor thing.

He turned around to get some bandages and saw little Lanik waiting with them already in hand. At first, Magnus wanted to be angry at the boy; but then, what would that accomplish? Besides, he needed assistance. Taking the bandages and the knife from Lanik, they set about stopping the bleeding and dressing her wounds.

The patrons all hushed as he returned to the tavern, and followed him with their eyes as he moved to stand in the middle of the room. One stood up at the back and said, 'Ho, Magnus, you know weez like you, but what if she's a criminal? Wanted by authorities? Weez don't want any trouble or nothing, but maybe it's best to just send her on her way.'

Magnus took a deep breath, turned to the man, and said, 'Aye, Jimmy, she might be a criminal, and it might be less trouble to just send her on her way.' He walked over to the counter and poured himself an ale and continued, 'But what would that make me? What kind of man would I be? Besides, most of youse in here are basically criminals.'

Another man stood and shouted his outrage, falling back to the chair as his legs wobbled beneath him, 'What ya mean 'bout dat?'

'Youse answer me this; how many ales have youse had here that youse haven't paid for?'

Murmurs sounded as the patrons discussed this with each other, leaving Magnus to continue cleaning the bar. Jimmy stood up once more and cleared his throat, saying, 'Weez agreein' with you, Magnus. Weez won't tell nobody.'

With a smile on his face to indulge them, he said, 'Why, thank ye all for that. Much appreciated. Boys, I'm sorry to have to do this, but I think I'm going to call it a night. I have to take care of this situation, so please start headin' home.'

The night progressed slowly as people unwillingly left their sanctum sanctorum, dragging out the inevitability of becoming sober – the only thought that scared these patrons more than death itself.

With the bar finally empty and Lanik to bed, Magnus sat on a stool at the counter and rested his head in his hands. The front door to the inn creaked open as three men moved through. Rising from the stool, Magnus said, 'Sorry, fellas, weez closed for the night.'

The man at the front draped his long coat over the coat rack and faced him. Corlithian leather armour wrapped around his chest and most of his arms, a red woollen shirt visible beneath. He lowered himself to the nearest table as he said, 'Isn't it a bit early for you to be closed?'

Glancing between the two men standing and the one at the table, Magnus deduced that the one sitting must be their leader. He could see swords jutting out from under their long jackets, and as one man moved around the bar, he saw a smallish crossbow hanging at his hip. Slowly moving to the bar, Magnus slipped a knife that was lying on the counter into his pocket as he said, 'Do youse want some ale? I can offer youse only one mug each. But then youse have to go. I'm tired.'

The man at the table laughed and said, 'No, we don't want ale. We want the girl you're harbouring. Bring her to us and you won't be hurt.'

'The only girls I see here are youse three. There are no other girls. Now leave!'

Still laughing, the man at the table continued, 'She's a murderer, you know. Killed five of my men. It was her initiation night to join our guild, and no one was supposed to get hurt. She had a task to complete, and she failed.'

A stern gaze fell over Magnus as he looked at the man. 'Yeah. Because youse laid a trap for her, didn't ye? And when youse caught her, youse tried to rape her. Poured liquor down her throat to make her incoherent?'

Not laughing anymore, the man continued, 'She shouldn't have got herself caught.'

Slow and steady, Magnus made his way to the centre of the room and said, 'So, let me get this straight. Drugged and outnumbered eight to one, she broke free and still gutted five o' your men, and then youse followed her here? Wow, sounds impressive to me.'

'Can I kill him now, sir?' asked the man nosing about the bar.

With a gesture of one hand, the man at the table said, 'Don't say I didn't offer you a better solution.'

Fists raised, the other man walked up to Magnus as he said, 'I'm gonna make him bleed first.'

The first swing landed straight on Magnus' nose and sent the fat barkeep staggering back. As the second approached, Magnus grabbed it with his left hand and thundered a right fist to the throat of his assailant. Bent over and grasping at his throat, the man struggled to breathe as the fat man stepped in around his back and locked his arm round the man's head. A quick jerk of his arms, a sharp *crack*, and the man slumped to the floor.

A crossbow bolt sank into Magnus' chest just below the right shoulder. He dropped to the floor and stayed low, scouring for cover as another bolt flew to thud into the table above his head. The two aggressors moved through the room towards his last position, training their crossbows in his general direction. Rounding the corner, they shot their bows, bolts thumping into the wood. The man in charge gestured for the other to move right as he went left to corner their target.

The second man walked stealthily on the wooden floor as he entered the kitchen area. A loud creak sounded behind him. His eyes went wide as he turned in time to see a full pot of boiling oil tossed in his face, searing through his skin and eyes. The man rolled about on the floor, inhuman screams sounding through the tavern. Footsteps sounded out loud as the last man came running around the other side of the bar to investigate, only to find his friend on the ground, his face swollen with blisters, his skin torn and cooked. It was revolting. His breaths were ragged and shallow as one remaining eye stared at him, lidless. The soldier pointed the crossbow and pulled the trigger. A crack and thud fell on his ears as the bolt sank deep into his comrade's skull.

'I seem to have underestimated you, my friend. Let's just call this even and I'll leave you to your duties, hey? What say you?' Backing toward the door of the inn, he felt a sharp pain lance through his back, making him stop in his tracks; then agony tormented him as the object was slowly pushed deeper, and deeper, and deeper. He could feel the burn of cold steel sliding steadily through him. Blood leaked in a trickle down his chest. Pushing his hand under his leather cuirass, he felt the point of a knife jutting from his ribs to the right of his breastbone. With a vicious pull, the knife slipped out of his back, blood gushing from the mortal wound. Wide-eyed and terrified, the man turned to look upon the half-naked form of the woman he'd sought to kill. Hand extended, he grasped at her as he stumbled forward.

Eyes locked on his, she moved back as he fell to the floor, bleeding out just in front of the door.

* * *

Lanik sank into the long armchair as he looked at Ladriana and said, 'That's how they met. From then on, she was in and out of the inn until the day I confessed my desire to join the Desert Dogs and kill Xylac. I think I was about sixteen at the time. Magnus, obviously, was furious and against it, having none of it. But then Anavi agreed to take me and joined as well for my protection.'

A tear rolled down Ladriana's cheek. She quickly wiped it away as she said, 'Forgive me, I was thinking of Magnus.'

Lanik moved to the bed and hugged her as he said, 'He'll be all right. I'm sure of it.'

'Lanik, I would never have joined the Desert Dogs if I knew this was what they do — slaughtering families in their beds, torturing old men, and leaving them for dead. I grew up with the tales of their glory. Their freedom to choose who to stand with. To be free. I'm truly sorry about your family.'

He leaned in and kissed her on the head. 'I don't blame you, Ladriana. Those tales were mostly true, probably before Xylac took over leadership. But he's nothing but a foul creature seeking riches, and he doesn't care how he gets them.'

A knock sounded and Lanik called out, 'Enter.'

The large hardwood door swung open, and a hunchbacked old man entered, escorted by two royal guards standing at attention with spears in hand. Lanik waved them away and gestured for the old man to come closer as he said, 'Atwood, so great to see you, old friend!' He rose from the bed and embraced the old man, then pulled away, holding onto his shoulders as he said, 'What has it been, twenty years?'

'It has been far too long for sure, young Garidan.'

Lanik stepped aside and said, 'Let me introduce you.'

Ladriana bowed slightly to the old man, and said, 'Ladriana; it's a pleasure to meet you. May I ask how you two know each other?'

Energetically, Lanik said, 'Atwood is one of the remaining members of the council. He's the one who's been feeding me information about what's been happening here in New Runswick. He did all the hard work, following the other members to find out who was involved in planning the murder of my family. Only he and Vehlos are left of the original six who ran the city then. They remained loyal.' He turned to the old man and continued, 'How is the old hunter?'

'He is not hunting anymore, I can tell you that much. His bones would snap if he tried to run.' Atwood laughed and continued, 'He is turning a hundred and three this year.' A groan escaped him as he breathed. 'But I fear this year might be his last. His health is failing.'

Lanik's mood changed, and he smiled no more as he said, 'I'm sorry, Atwood. I know you've been friends for a very long time. I'll visit Vehlos before it's too late.'

An old, bony hand gestured it to be okay. Atwood cuffed his hands in his white robe as he said, 'I am here in an official capacity to welcome back the king and officiate his office. We are to have a ceremony of the greatest proportions. All will know that Garidan Rourke, true King of New Runswick, has returned.'

Lanik turned to Ladriana and took her hand as he said, 'I presume we can fit in a wedding at this ceremony?'

'Oh yes, of course. It will be an honour,' Atwood said with a smile on his face.

Ladriana dropped her head and whispered, 'We can't have the ceremony without Magnus. It wouldn't be right.'

All smiles vanished, and Lanik turned to the old councilman. 'She's right, Atwood. We will have to wait until he's ready to join us.'

Atwood bowed deeply. 'I understand. He is a great friend of mine as well. I will postpone the event for a little while, but please, Garidan, we cannot wait too long. New Runswick needs you now more than ever. Our old bones will not last forever.'

* * *

The journey thus far had been nothing but disastrous. A few nights back, a raging bull elephant set on a path of utter destruction had rampaged through their camp. Soldiers scurried to get out of its path as four of his warriors died during the chaos of the night, trampled by the colossal beast. Then too, one by one, soldiers had been vanishing during the night. Through the ranks, soldiers bore witness to something following them at a distance, never getting too close, giving them only glimpses of its catlike body.

Despair set in as they travelled across the desert wasteland near where they thought Artorea should be, hoping to at least glimpse home, but there was no sign of any city ever being in the area. Days went by before they neared what looked to be an old mine that led through the enormous mountain before them. Three times scouts had been sent out; none had returned. Sending more would be a waste. Not knowing how far or even where the trade routes were to get around this mountain, Ganda'har stood at the vanguard, deliberating on the narrow corridors of the mine. As he sat astride his horse, he glanced back at the ox wagons and said, 'Stilts, how long before we reach this place? Is there any way around this mountain that you can see?'

The pale warlock pulled out the map, studying it for a time as the captain anxiously waited for his answer. Using a piece of string for crude mathematics, Stilts said, 'Well, the map shows the mountains spreading very far, bending like a serpent for many miles to the east and west. I would say, if we wanted to go around, it would take roughly thirty days, whereas if we go through, it would be roughly nine on foot if we kept moving.'

Ganda'har felt his stomach churn as he thought of the dire consequences his decisions could have on his men. Their lives were at the mercy of his choices. He thought back to all the times Galvos had led them through so many battles and sieges to come out on the other side. *We always made it back home safely. I'm so sorry for doubting your choices, old friend. This burden is not for most men.*

With a gesture of his head, he sent Talgar away.

Eyes trailed his second-in-command as he walked past the soldiers, then Talgar shouted, 'Set the oxen and the horses free! Everyone takes extra from the wagons, only what they can carry. From here on, we walk. We go through the mine!'

Murmurs rose from the gathered men and women, doubt setting in about their leader, as their entire journey had thus far proven a failure. Instead of finding Khanaseri and the orb, they had ended up in another time, losing soldier after soldier, and were now giving up most of their food, water, and their wagons to go through a mine they knew nothing about — not even whether it came out on the other side of the mountain.

'Keep quiet, you whining maggots!' Talgar shouted as he walked among the ranks.

Horses ran as they slapped their rumps, the oxen not straying far to feed on the grass under the trees. One by one, they pulled gear, food, and water from the carts before entering the tunnels.

* * *

A strong, pungent smell hung low in the air, waking the warlock as the irritation in his nostrils grew. Khanaseri pushed on the bed to sit up and felt his head sting and his vision drift. Still, he tried to focus on the surroundings. The room was mostly empty, except for an old man wheezing with each breath he took in a bed opposite his. Pain lanced in his throat as he tried to speak. Dry, his voice groggy and hoarse, he asked, 'Where am I?'

No answer came.

He felt a pressure on his chest then, and saw the bandages wrapped around him, stained with blood as it seeped through the now-stitched wounds. More bandages were drawn around his head and feet. Memories slowly returned as he closed his eyes of what Sukayi Kavali — the assassin named Glass — had done to him. He remembered how his hair had caught on fire from the heat as the branding iron melted into his flesh. Pressed again and again over his pate, his left ear and his throat, it left the markings of the assassin's guild: an arrowhead crossed with a sword. His back burned from the flogging he had endured as the whip ripped the flesh from his body. He turned to the side of the bed and made to stand, but fell back down as pain shot through his feet into his legs.

A round man with whiskey on his breath and a smile on his face walked into the room, speaking as he came. 'Those cuts on your feet are deep, friend, nearly to the bone. Oi would try to keep off them for now. Glad to see you moving about, lad. Oi was worried you would never wake. Oi've seen plenty of young men with your wounds not wake up. May have been too much for them. But you be a fighter.'

'Where am I?' the warlock repeated as he unwrapped the bandages on his feet. The wounds were cleaned and stitched and covered with some garlicky paste. The healer approached with new bandages and started re-wrapping them as he said, 'Okay, those needed to be redressed anyhoo, but don't take them off again. Oi will come and do it as needed.'

'How did I get here?'

With his hand on his beardless chin, the fellow said, 'Oh yes. A man carried you in. Yes, two men, in fact. One dark-skinned man with black hair and markings all over his face, and another more ominous-looking fellow in a blue outfit of some sort. They asked me to care for you. And the coin didn't hurt neither. They've been in here a coupla times. They'll probably be back soon. Usually every second day or so.'

Khanaseri shook his head and said, 'Wait, what? How long have I been asleep?'

The healer rubbed his wide, stubby nose and pointed his finger to a chart hanging from the door. 'Hold on,' he said as he seemingly counted, and continued, 'Yes, that would be five an' a half years now.'

Khanaseri felt the blood drain from his face as his heart jumped into his throat. 'Years...'

Completely red in the face, the round man burst out laughing. 'No, son, days. It's been five and a half *days*. Relax and get well soon,' he said as he left the room and closed the door, giggling to himself.

'That was not funny.' Khanaseri laid back down on the bed and closed his eyes.

* * *

The click and clang of the short metal picks hammering away at the stones in search of valuable gems between the heaps of coal rose and fell throughout the paths of the mine. For miles, it stretched on, branching off left and right from the main railway, leading in and out to get the coal being hauled from the corridors. Men and women stained black from the coal-dust worked day and night to provide for their children. How many had died here to feed their young? There must have been plenty of accidents and deaths in here.

Looking down from his thoughts to the skeleton of one of those workers with his torn clothes, still lying with the short pick in hand, Ganda'har shook his head when he saw another not far away with a gaping hole at the top of his pate. Must have been a fight of some sort. As he stepped over the skeleton, he could not help but wonder what drove them to kill each other. *Did one of them find a gem, the other jealous? Perhaps.* Why weren't their bodies removed? Might be thieves? His legs were getting tired, but he didn't want to be the first to say anything, so he kept walking, hoping someone would complain eventually. Down in the tunnel, there was no way of telling what time of day it was. They walked until tired and made crude beds and quarters to sleep for a bit before moving on. They had stopped three times already and soon would mark the fourth.

Talgar and Untara had to break apart some men, as arguments were getting more heated. Water was running low, and food was being rationed. Hungry, thirsty, cold, and wet, with little air this deep under the mountain, it was virtually impossible *not* to lose one's temper over little things. Five fights had broken out between the warriors already over silly things. One accidentally stepped on the back of the boot of the person in front of him, one talked too much, the other didn't want to pass along a torch to someone else, and so on.

Stilts walked at the front of the column with Ganda'har, guiding them to stay on track, constantly drawing from his power. The rocky floor made finding good footing hard in the darkness of the tunnels, even with the torches they carried, the fire making their shadows dance against the walls. With every third or fourth person holding a torch, it made them look like a giant fire worm carving its way through the tunnels. Mining equipment lay scattered as if thrown to the ground, abandoned in haste, and never collected. Old, hardened blood stained some equipment, most of the evidence eaten by crawling critters over the years.

'What happened here?' Ganda'har asked quietly as he stepped over an old lantern and a long rope, rolled up neatly on the floor with a bony arm and hand still clutching it. At the very back of the column, a loud scream erupted, sending chills through the soldiers as fear gripped them. Their training prevailed. Each man and woman calmly drew their weapons as they made ready, watching vigilantly, straining their eyes to see in the dark. Their minds played tricks as every flutter of light and shadow mixed, creating the illusion of movement nearby. Sounds echoed, making it impossible to figure out exactly where they originated.

A ruckus sounded from somewhere in the middle of the column as soldiers called for a halt, their voices echoing in the vast chamber. Talgar darted off towards the disturbance to investigate the matter. Ganda'har saw a rock with a flat top some distance away and moved closer. His feet were burning and his back ached from all the gear and supplies they had to carry. With an audible groan, he sat down and massaged his shoulder as he slumped his pack on the ground. Talgar jogged over and almost tripped over a rock in the faint light, cursing as he neared his captain and said, 'The men are tired, sir; they're collapsing from fatigue. What are your orders?'

Ganda'har looked back at his men and said, 'Make camp. We'll rest here for a bit. Form a circle and set the weapons ready for quick use, should they be needed. We are in the open tonight, so everyone will cover each other's backs. Six men to patrol in a square around us should be fine; rotate them often. I do not want to get them too tired for marching.'

Talgar nodded and ran off, shouting orders as usual, leaving him in silence. 'Mind sharing that rock there, Cap'n? Ol' Talgar really enjoys shouting orders, doesn't he?' Muscles flexed as they pulled tight, Ganda'har jumped as the harsh voice startled him. 'Whoa, quick on your feet there, sir. It's just me, no goblin to drag you into the dark abyss.'

An armoured foot and leg came to rest on the rock next to him as he looked up at the ironclad woman standing before him. 'Stentor, shouldn't you be guarding the rear?' Ganda'har said as he relaxed his muscles.

'Supposedly, but who will guard *my* rear? Besides, there's not much going on in here but for the occasional fight breaking out.'

'Mph, you should learn to follow orders.'

She drew off her helmet to reveal her red hair, then worked her fingers through to free the sweaty, clumped knots. Her open arm revealed inked symbols flowing beneath her garb as she removed the heavy axe from her back and placed the head on the ground to lean against the rock. 'I would, if they were good orders.'

Ganda'har glanced at the weapon as he stood and said, 'Watch yourself, Stentor. You Terenesians have never been an easy breed to deal with, but that doesn't excuse your manners. I'm the captain, and you *will* follow my orders.' He stood facing her at eye level, pushed up close, a mere hand's-breadth separating them. The air was tense for a moment as he thought she would reach for her weapon, but then she grinned and backed away as she loudly said, 'Oh, Captain, of course I'll follow your orders. Never said *yours* were bad.' She picked up the axe and her helmet before turning to make her bed for the night.

He watched as she departed, then looked at his surroundings. They couldn't see very far in this dark with the poor lighting of the torches. He noticed a couple of men run off with torches to place them in the distance, providing some light and warning should anyone – or any*thing* – approach. *Well done, Talgar.* He walked among the men and shouted, 'Right, settle in for a while, get some food going. Eat and rest. I need some volunteers to fetch us some fuel for a fire.' That would have to include bones and rope; there wasn't much wood that wasn't tool handles in this place, but they'd bring that back too. Three men rose, and he gestured for them to leave, saying as they turned, 'Don't go too far, you'll get lost in this infernal maze.'

It wasn't long before a fire was burning, and snores echoed from those too weary to care about food.

* * *

'Wake up! Break camp, we need to move!' Talgar kicked some men's feet as they still slept. Groans sounded as they woke to rise in the cold cave, still tired and sore. Once awake, the men devoured the cold rations and packed their gear, and the fire train was off to work their way farther down the tunnel. Ganda'har chuckled as he heard the loud-mouthed Stentor shout, 'All the way at the back, Cap'n! Just waiting for an order to come.'

For some time, they made their way through the maze of tunnels, following the directions of the warlock, until the captain halted for a moment, feeling as though he was destined to be here. Ganda'har trudged forward as he passed a tunnel branching off to the side, then heard the faint calls of his name in the distance. A glow emanated farther down, enticing him to take a closer look. He halted the column and gestured to Untara and Talgar to join him. Weapons drawn, they walked hunchbacked in the narrowing, low corridor. Ganda'har looked back over his shoulder as he asked, 'Do you men see that?'

Talgar looked around and saw nothing but darkness. 'No sir. There's nothing out here. Let's get back to the group and continue. We need to get out of this mountain soon.'

'It's beautiful,' the captain breathed, in awe of what he saw. He became puzzled and frantic as they reached the end of the corridor, where a wall of mud stood facing them. He grabbed a rock and hammered and clawed at the mud wall, scraping handfuls of dirt while Talgar and Untara pleaded with him, but he did not hear them. Ganda'har could feel someone pull at his arms and spun around, sword flashing through the air as he gripped Talgar by the throat with his left hand, the point of the sword resting gently on the shoulder of Untara.

Shocked by this sudden turn of events, Untara moved back a step, saying, 'Easy, Captain. We're here to help.'

Ganda'har's eyes flickered with madness as he said, 'If you want to help, then dig!' He jammed the sword into the mud and scraped out the dirt, as they reluctantly did the same. Another plunge and another until, at last, his sword and arm went through the hole, his face planting in the mud. He pulled back the sword and stared with mouth agape at the wondrous blue rays shining through the hole in the earthen wall. With his renewed energy, he didn't even realise the other two had stopped digging a while back.

Unsure of what to do, Talgar and Untara stared at each other, then frowned as they looked at their captain. Talgar said, 'Might be too little air. He's hallucinating.'

Finally, Ganda'har said, 'We're through. You two wait here. I will be back soon.' He wriggled through the hole before Talgar could grab hold of his legs.

* * *

A small room, cold and damp, awaited him as he fell through the narrow opening, his eyes glittering with joy as he gazed upon the source of the radiantly swirling blue light, which looked as if it were reflected from some watery surface, only brighter. Moving closer to the object, he gasped as he stood before it.

Entranced, he said, 'I've found you in the darkest hold, the deepest of cracks in the earth. I've searched and proven myself worthy!' He gripped the source of the light and pulled it free from the muddy wall. A perfect sphere rose from his hands, grasping onto his mind and cuddling his soul.

Talons tore at the figurative shell as a powerful, blood-red dragon made its way into his psyche, the clawed tips of its wings scraping at his consciousness as it broke down his barriers. Facing him as it moved closer, he saw that its front legs melded with its wings, like a bat's. When the enormous head dropped to look into his eyes, he saw the horns adorning the crown of its skull. A deep voice trailed in the back of his mind: 'For so long, I have waited to be freed from this prison. This section of the mine collapsed many years ago, when the miners were attacked. I bore witness to it all, but I had no vessel then, and I have waited until now for you, a warrior I deemed worthy to be my vessel. I will grant you great power and an even greater life if you accept. I cannot promise that I will protect you always, but I will give my life when it comes to it. In return, all I ask from you is the same. Do you accept?'

Ganda'har stood at the precipice... yet he wasn't sure if this was real or just in his head. His heart thumped wildly, and his legs felt weak, but his soul felt joy above all. 'Yes! I accept!' he cried. 'What do I call you?'

You call me Ganda'har. For we are truly one.

Chapter Ten

Birds chirped on the windowsill as the early morning sun greeted them with its fiery orange. Anavi was fast asleep in a chair as nightmares plagued her mind. *Dogs snapped at her heels as she ran through the forest, closing in fast as she dodged left and right. A great weight landed on her back as a dog jumped and sent her to the ground hard, knocking her head and spraining her wrist. Within a heartbeat, the dog was tearing at her clothes, pinning her down. Shouts arose from a familiar voice, and the dog's weight was lifted from her as the man said, 'Wake up, dear!'*

Anavi shook herself and looked around, confused by the abrupt awakening.

Propped up on the bed, Magnus sat with a smile on his blue-and-purple face and said, 'Youse was havin' a bad dream.'

Immediately, she jumped up from the chair and embraced him as tears rolled down her face. 'Have you any idea what you put me through, you bastard?!'

'Sorry, my dear, wasn't intended. Besides, I didn't know youse cared anymore.'

'Oh, you stupid, stupid man.'

Anavi pulled back to sit by his side, holding his hand as she looked at his legs. 'You might be crippled for good, you know. The healer says you have a long recovery ahead, and if all goes well, then maybe one day you'll walk unassisted again. But for now, you'll have to use crutches.' Seeing the sudden sadness in his face, she shied away and held her breath as she continued, 'I am so sorry for the bluntness, Magnus. I've been running the scenario over and over in my head, trying to find the best way to tell you. It seems I chose the worst.'

'Now, now, dear. I'd rather you give it to me straight. Sugar-coating does nothing but give false hope,' he said as he wiped at his pate, the pain causing sweat to bead on his brow. His lungs wheezed as he breathed deeply and said, 'I'm glad you're here.'

Anavi took her sword from where it leaned against the wall and buttoned up her armour. *Nothing is more uncomfortable than trying to sleep in these leathers. Everything feels squashed and out of place.*

'Where are youse off to?' Magnus asked as he threw the covers from the bed.

Should I tell you that I plan to go after Xylac to kill him, finally putting an end to Lanik's misery, and for what they did to you? If I don't, it's just another lie. If I do, you're going to persuade me to stay, and this time, you just might win. Not meeting his gaze, she said, 'I, uhm, have to let Lanik know you're awake. He and Ladriana have been terribly worried about you. I told them you'd be fine, but you know them.'

Magnus grabbed her arm with his one good hand as she passed, holding it tight. 'Please come back to me.'

No more words were needed, as they both knew the truth of the matter without having to confront it.

* * *

'Up! Down! Up! Down! Only a hundred more to go! Run a lap around the lake and finish the rest of the hundred.' Link peeled an apple with his knife as he sat, shouting instructions to Blanka, who was by now sweating like a pig in a pastry factory.

Off he went for the run, his lungs burning and his heart feeling as if it wanted to explode. Blanka's arms felt numb, and his legs could barely keep him upright, but he would not quit. He needed to rebuild his muscles. The more he exercised, the more his memories made sense.

'Hey! I said run, not lag like an old cow! Those kids are running faster than you.'

The sudden appearance of the assassin running next to him made Blanka's legs wobble and almost made him lose control of them. He couldn't focus on anything except putting one foot in front of the other, and now the assassin was toying with him, jogging backwards faster than he could run, shouting encouragements along the way. Faster and faster he pushed himself until the end drew near. *Oh no!* A wobble in his pattern, and his legs were uncoordinated. Unable to keep up with the momentum, he dived forward, skidding on the ground face first. From the dirt, Blanka rose, coughing and spitting, as he heard Link's laughter in the distance and saw the assassin illustrating the dive and the facial expressions to the kids. Blanka's anger flared, and he opened his mouth to shout, but an enormous ball of flame burst out instead, his face scaling up and turning black at the mouth.

Link dived into the lake, narrowly avoiding the fireball, to resurface a while later. Soaked to the bone as he got out of the water, he cursed as he looked at Blanka, seeing him laughing and illustrating the dive and facial expression he'd made.

'I'm sorry, Link. I don't even know how I did that, but the result was pretty great.'

Link walked out of the pond, water sloshing from his shoes and clothes as he reached dry land. 'That was not funny.'

Blanka set off to complete his lap around the lake as Link shouted instructions again.

* * *

The constant movement and pressure on his stomach made him sick as he woke. Ganda'har opened his eyes to see the motion of Untara's buttocks and immediately shouted as he smelled the warrior's behind, 'Put me down, you lummox!'

'Yes, sir!' Untara shouted back, and slid the captain to the floor.

'What happened? Bring me water,' Ganda'har said as he stood, and felt his legs buckle beneath him before he caught himself, then looked back down the line of soldiers. 'How many have we lost?'

Talgar came from the front, handing him a water pouch, and said, 'Good to see you back on your feet, Captain. We've lost fifteen so far. Stilts estimates we've travelled over two-thirds of the way. But sir, there's something down here with us, and it's not happy that we're here.'

The cool water quenched his parched throat. He was hard-pressed to force himself to stop drinking, but did so, as they had a limited supply. 'What happened to me back there?'

'We think you started hallucinating, maybe too little air, then passed out. Untara and Stentor took turns to carry you over their shoulders for most of the march. We've rested twice since you were out. Stilts said you were asleep, but he'd seen nothing of its like before. There was a worry in his eyes, but he said no more.'

Ganda'har extended his arm, gripping Untara's, and said, 'Thank you. I can't believe I now have to thank that woman...' He cocked his head, and said, 'Sshh!' Gestures flew from his hand and sound fell away as the word spread to the back of the column. Intently staring at the cave dome up high, then at the myriad of tunnels now clear to him, he looked to the left and saw the edge of a cliff, the drop seeming endless as the pitch black swallowed the bottom. With eyes closed, he listened to sounds echo in the cave. Water dripped to the right, and faint sounds of rushing wind echoed in the distance down the left railway. He opened his eyes and ordered Untara, 'Take some men and gather some water not too far down the right tunnel. We'll wait for you and then move down the second from the left, as that leads out.'

Stilts joined them and turned to his captain to ask, 'How did you know that? I can barely keep track of the routes using magic to see where the workers used to move about. Yet you did it so effortlessly.'

'Yes, you have a habit of reminding me how useless you are,'

Ganda'har snapped.

A piercing cry erupted from the top of the cave, followed shortly by a large, sleek bat-like creature moving extremely fast. Blending in with the darkness, it was nearly impossible to follow, its huge head the shape of a ship's anchor split down the middle, revealing its gum-line and dagger-like fangs as it grabbed a soldier by the head and dragged him into the air. His screams echoed as they loosed a few arrows, then abruptly ceased.

'Quiet!' Ganda'har roared as he sought the animal, focusing on the sound of the creature's passage through the air. Suddenly a change occurred to his vision, with everyone taking on a bewildering array of colours from red to blue, orange to yellow. Far above them, to the right, sat the creature, tearing away at the soldier it had nabbed. More movement came from his right, then to his left. More of the animals dived at them. *Snake's tits! They're everywhere.* 'Move! They're coming!' Soldiers streamed past him as they ran into the tunnel. He looked back up to see another and another and another swooping down. *Oh, this is not good.*

One flew low, heading straight for the exit tunnel and his soldiers, until the sudden weight of the captain pushed it towards the ground when he leapt on it. It ripped and snapped at its back, trying to reach its attacker when red hot talons ripped into its neck and pulled free a chunk of its throat; it plummeted to the ground, skidding for a distance before they rolled on the rocky floor. Before Ganda'har could get up, another of the monsters rushed in with a gaping maw and ripping claws extended, eager to get hold of his deliciously soft flesh. The immense warrior-woman, Stentor, leapt from the side, burying her axe deep in its skull and dragged it to the ground with a shout of anger. Dark blood sprayed out as she wrenched the weapon free and extended her arm to her captain. They ran as fast as they could down the dark tunnel, not looking back as the cries of the creatures neared. Light streamed in from the mouth of the tunnel in the distance as they ran past the shield wall erected by his soldiers, who were standing firm, bracing for the impact to follow. Ganda'har and Stentor turned immediately, each grabbing a soldier to support. A mighty crash followed as the creatures slammed into the shields, pushing them back a few feet. Sharp teeth and claws scraped against the iron shields. Step by agonising step, they moved back, growing ever closer to the exit.

Talgar held firm to his shield and shouted, 'Hold! Hold! Move!' Then he took one step back, the line falling back in place as they all shouted in unison, 'Hu-ha!'

The onslaught was relentless, one step at a time, as the creatures threw themselves at the shield wall. One creature breached the shields, snapping its teeth at a nearby soldier until Talgar drove his daggers into the side of the thing's head. 'Die, you forsook vermin!' After it fell to the ground, a brief respite was achieved as its brethren stopped and fought over the carcass, ripping it apart.

Edging back step by step, Talgar shouted, 'They're cannibals! If we wound them enough, they'll attack each other!'

Finished with their meal, the creatures looked back to the soldiers, spread their wings, and flew at them. Using their talons, they pulled at the shields. One of the lighter soldiers held on for dear life as his shield was lifted into the air. Outraged, he screamed as he swung his sword at the creature, but couldn't reach it. Ganda'har jumped out and grabbed the man by the legs, pulling as hard as he could to bring him back to the ground; Untara swung the axe up high, cutting a foot off the creature just above the claws. It fell to the ground and flopped around in clear pain, unable to stand as its own kind moved in for the kill.

The bleeding creatures attacked one another, providing more relief for the Kamatayons as they slowly retreated. Tired and sore, they continued backing up and cutting. One soldier, Obbe, turned around and saw sunlight in the distance, and broke formation as he ran for the exit.

Talgar shouted at the man, 'Wait, not yet! Shit!' The hole in their defences would make it virtually impossible to withstand the onslaught.

Ganda'har saw the inevitable outcome approach as another soldier turned to run, and shouted, 'Run! Everyone!'

As fast as their legs could carry them, the soldiers pushed for the exit. Passing Obbe, Talgar heard the screams just behind him as a creature ripped into the man's flesh. To his right, he saw another dragged down and feasted upon. There was nothing he could do. The exit was so close now, they couldn't give up. Moments later, he stepped to the side of the cave mouth, into the exultation of the sun's rays, daggers in hand, ready to strike. But nothing followed him. Ganda'har and Stentor stood on the opposite side of the exit, panting as they waited.

Untara rolled out of the cave, his arms around the neck of one creature, strangling it from behind. He hammered down his arm and broke one wing as it thrashed about in his death grip; a final jerk of his arms, and the creature stopped moving. Six more men came running out of the cave. Finally deciding that the creatures would not come out into the sunlight willingly, Talgar gestured to the men to retreat, keeping a keen eye on the exit as they did.

Some distance from the cave, Ganda'har looked at his few remaining men as they lay on the ground in exhaustion. 'Come on, men, set up camp for the night,' he ordered. 'Tomorrow we march to get the hell out of here.'

* * *

The streets were hard to move through with his splinted leg and the crutch digging into the ground, getting stuck most of the time as he put weight on it. To get his right hand aligned properly, the healer had been forced to break his fingers again, then cast them in splints to keep them rigid. His fingers throbbed every time he lowered his arm. The long, arduous walk just to cross the road made him feel like he was about to fall and die on the kerb when a friendly fruit merchant recognised him as he passed with his wagon, heading for the castle, and pulled on the reins as he said, 'Hey — Magnus, isn't it?'

Magnus looked up at the man and said, 'Aye.'

'You heading to the castle? I can give you a ride.'

'That would be mighty fine of youse. Thanks. Can't walk with these blasted things.'

The young merchant jumped down and gave Magnus a hand up onto the back of the wagon before setting off.

Down in the market, they rounded the last corner, and he looked up at the castle in all its splendour, wishing he had never come back. Life was so simple back in Kobo. *This place only causes suffering.* The Flying Squirrel had been a dream come true for him: having a good time with the lads as they came and went from the inn, not having to worry about marching to some godforsaken place to do battle with people he didn't know, killing them for political reasons not even his own. He'd realised long ago that lives didn't matter to the kingdom; only outcomes did. Sighing, he furrowed his brow and bit on his lip as he chewed a dried fruit. 'Blasted monkey's arse! My teeth hurt so bad.'

'Here,' came the merchant's voice as he tossed a green fruit the size of an orange to him and continued, 'Try the jaga-jarra. They're soft, with lots of juice. It's one of my favourites.'

Magnus bit down into its skin, the soft, sweet flesh filling his mouth as the juice ran down his beard. 'This is incredible. Thank youse.'

Upon arriving at the castle, they were greeted at the gates and escorted in. The young merchant shouted at the guard, 'Bring the invalid's chair. This man is a part of the royal house!'

Immediately, one guard saluted and ran off. The sun was already high, and Magnus felt sweat running down his back. Sounds assaulted him from all sides with no ear to focus their origin points; the only relief was the bandage that softened the noise some. As they pulled the cart around to the back near the kitchen, the guard returned, running as fast as he could with the heavy chair, its front wheel locking up on the gravel, nearly flipping it over. Magnus eyed the contraption, lifting his brows as he said, 'I ain't gettin' in that thing. I'll make my way on this infernal crutch.'

The guard drew near and shouted, 'Your chair, sir.'

'Nope. Not happening.'

The merchant and another guard helped Magnus down from the

cart before he took up the crutch and said, 'Where's Lady Ladriana?'

The guards saluted and said, 'In the garden around the corner. Should I announce your arrival, sir?'

'No, thank youse. I want to surprise her.'

Step after agonising step, he made his way to the back gardens and saw Ladriana shooting her bow, as always. 'That's not the way a proper lady behaves, my dear!' Magnus said as he neared.

Her face lit up with joy as she turned and saw him hobbling closer and shouted, 'You presumptuous old bastard! It's good to see you. When did you wake up? Aren't you in pain?'

The agonising stretch to get his behind to go down to the bench took a while as he lowered himself slowly. Ladriana moved in to assist, seeing the struggle taking place, but was stopped as he quickly gestured with his hand. 'No, this is on me, my dear.' Finally sitting down, he continued, 'Hurts like hell. But I needed the air. Woke up this morning very early. Anavi said she would let youse know.' His shoulders seemed to sag after his last words.

'I have not seen her for a while. I believe she's been at your bedside for quite some time now.'

'Aye, I know, always with the quests, that one. Could never get her to sit still.' He stared at the woman next to him in her fine white dress as the hems brushed the paving. Tears welled in his eyes as he said, 'I'm so sorry, dear. They broke me in that crypt. I tried not to say anything, even after they poked a hole in my chest and beat me half to death, but when they broke my leg the second time, I squealed like a cowardly pig. I put everyone's lives in danger.'

Ladriana wrapped her arms around him and said, 'No no no, Magnus. They would have come eventually, whether you told them or not. If it weren't for you, so many more would have died. A lesser man would have broken instantly. I would certainly have been killed, and we wouldn't have been able to warn anyone here of the attack. They would have been unprepared. Many more would have died. In my book, you, sir, are a hero.'

'Can youse please do me a favour?' he asked as he held her hand.

'Yes, of course, anything.'

Magnus pursed his lips and wiggled his beard. 'Please tell Lanik youse two are welcome to visit me anytime. I'm leaving for the inn immediately. I have nothing left here for me. Tell him I'm sorry, but my duties are complete.'

'Are you sure you don't want to tell him yourself? I am more than happy to go get him for you.'

The push on the crutch nearly defeated him as he struggled to get to his feet. Ladriana grabbed his arm, helping him a little as he said, 'No, my dear, I do not. I fear my current mood would be a burden most unwelcome. Goodbye, and all the best to youse two. It would be nice if youse came to visit sometime soon.'

'I promise we will, Magnus. I'll arrange a horse and carriage for you. They won't be missed,' she said as he wiped a tear from her face, and added, 'Just so you know, you would never be a burden to us, no matter the mood.'

'Thank youse, dear.'

* * *

Chickens ran around randomly, clucking their dismay at the world. *Yeah, I'd also be angry if one of my friends got cooked every second day.* Khanaseri hopped out into the street with a bandaged face, legs, and chest. Smoke drifted up from one building down the street. *Must be a blacksmith or a baker,* he thought. Green grass and small wooden huts were lined up to his right. To the left, fields of corn ran far and wide. Acres and acres of the popular crop grew in the area. Sounds of children laughing and cheering guided him down a muddy old road to pass a butcher's shop as two men hauled in new beef.

Cheers went up as Blanka finished his run around the lake, only to jump in and swim across to the other side. As he got out, he fell to the ground and started doing push-ups.

To the left, Link stood eating an apple, laughing with some children at the panting Blanka while more of the annoying young monsters crowded Khanaseri, blocking his path as they stared at the near-mummified man. He was pushing the kids aside to pass when a half-eaten apple splattered against his back. Annoyed, he turned to scowl at the children, and more fruit was flung at him in succession, all half-eaten or nearly finished.

Blanka sat up to see what the new commotion was about, smiling as he watched the warlock trying to defend himself against the children's barrage of fruit. Link walked over to the children and said, 'Okay, okay, that's enough. I think he learnt his lesson. Hey!' An apple splattered against the side of his head, and the children scattered in all directions.

Khanaseri hopped over to Blanka and lowered himself to the grass, waiting for the assassin to join them. He looked up at Link and said in a serious tone, 'The guild will come for you now.'

Link threw the apple core into the lake and watched it get gulped down by a large fish, then said, 'I know. But if this is the way the guild does business, I'll have no part of it. I'll be ready for them. I'm done being someone else's lapdog.'

Khanaseri removed a roped leather necklace with a large fang at the end from around his neck and handed it to the assassin. 'I want you to have this. It's from a bear I killed when I was nine years old. It was a warm spring morning, and we still lived in the countryside, far from the city. I'd sneaked into the woods after my father explicitly told me not to that day. I know right, not very smart, but can you really blame me? A beautiful mob of brumbies stood in the field and I was mesmerised by the black stallion when it attacked out of nowhere, scattering the horses. Luckily, I was carrying my bow. Arrow after arrow hit the beast, but it didn't stop. Even as the arrows hung from its face, it just charged on through the field, coming for my life.'

'What did you do?' the assassin asked, standing with arms folded.

'I kept sending arrow after arrow and with a bit of luck hit the bear dead in the eye, skewering deep into its brain. It dropped to the ground, skidding to my feet in a hail of dust and gravel. It was so close, I could feel its last breath on my face. I pulled out another arrow and thrust it into its head for good measure. For a while, I laid on the ground on my back, just staring at those lifeless eyes, knowing how close death had been. But then I noticed my father stood off to the side, watching me, and nodded when we locked gazes. He was there the whole time, ready to jump in and help if I needed it. I keep this as a reminder that he was always there to help if the time came, and so I would like for you to have it. When the time comes, come and find me in Artorea. My door is always open to you.'

The tooth was nearly as long and wide as his index finger. Link turned it in his hands and said, 'Thank you, Khan.'

Blanka swept his hair back to get the sweat out of his face and said, 'You know I was there too, right, Khan? I mean, you would probably be dead right now if it weren't for me.'

Laughing wholeheartedly, the warlock said, 'Yes, yes, yes. I know you were there. Don't let it go to your head.' He shifted his weight to the other buttock and winced as it hurt, so he laid down instead.

'How are you feeling?' Blanka asked as he made to stand.

Miserable, tired, and weak, but most of all, angry. It was careless to get caught by those assassins. 'I'm doing better, Blanka. I've focused most of my energy into healing my body, and it's proving very useful. My feet are almost healed. Oh, and I've decided to shave my head. Those scars will never heal completely.' He shifted his weight again. Lying on his side, he continued, 'How's the training going?'

'Hold that thought,' Link said, then walked to the children and pulled out a silver coin. 'Whoever can run around the whole village and be the first one back here gets the coin! No cheating, I'll know!'

The children pushed and shoved at each other as they darted off in a widdershins direction, tripping one another to get the lead as they shouted and ran.

He laughed as he returned the coin to the pouch and said to the warlock, 'You know, if you want to thank me, you should give me coin. These kids are making me poor.'

With a grunt and a shrug, Khanaseri replied, 'It's not my fault you can't think of anything else but coin to get rid of them. You should have

213

just said something like, "I heard they were giving away sugar cane at the market." Or something like that.'

'Why didn't I think of that?' Link frowned and muttered to himself, then turned to Blanka. 'Okay, they're gone.'

The warlock watched as Blanka moved back a few steps. A golden refulgence swirled around the man, beaming out brightly, and as it faded, a colossal black dragon stood in his place. A huge flame exploded from his mouth into the air, the heat so extreme that Khanaseri and Link had to shield their faces. Its sinuous neck snaked down and around until its head hovered before the warlock, then opened its maw with a piercing cry, shaking the earth beneath their feet, forcing them to cover their ears. Khanaseri stared at the sword-length fangs in awe and thought, *Well, this is something you don't see every day. I could probably fit in its mouth.*

Around the corner, laughter caught their attention, and Blanka quickly veered back to himself; then they saw the first child running toward them for dear life. The men shouted and clapped to cheer him on to win the coin.

The young boy grinned, gap-toothed, as Link presented him with the silver penny. As the rest of the mob surrounded them, shouting in disappointment, Khan turned to Blanka and said, 'Get your things in order; we leave at dawn.'

'Oh, come on! You can barely walk. You have holes in your hands and legs. Your face is burnt, and *still* you just want to plough ahead? How long have you known Beuneth?'

Khanaseri smirked at his tone of voice and said, 'Oh, it's not like that at all. It feels like I've known her for decades. She helped me unlock my abilities and took me into this dreamlike place for what felt like years to train me. When I awoke, only a couple days had passed.'

Juice dripped down Link's hands as he cut up another apple and asked, 'Who's this Beuneth?'

Blanka adjusted himself as he sat on the grass, then cleared his throat as he said, 'Well, we grew up together. Me, her, and a bunch of other kids were sold to this sorceress in the mountains near Terenore.

We grew up living in that godforsaken cave day in, day out, forced to train to become thieves and assassins for her. Beuneth, more than me, just wanted to get out. To live a normal life, away from it all. One night at dinner, she'd had enough. And that's when things started changing...'

Chapter Eleven

Tand here is no louder shout than a hall filled with silence. Even the slightest of stifled sounds echoes its wilful intent to destroy the silence, just aching to break free of the torment.

Sounds travelled well in the vastness of the cavernous dining hall, the light fickle as the lanterns flickered and died, the air ripe with the smell of cooked meat. With every screech from a knife or fork on the dinner plates, Vandalor's head came up, watchful as children stuffed themselves with wild boar and vegetables.

Vandalor stood from her high-backed throne overlooking the children and called, 'Silence!' A period of awkward stares occurred before Vandalor continued, 'Beuneth, please stand, my child.'

Immediately, all the stares turned to her, and slowly she rose from her seat next to Blanka.

'All of you who sit here tonight feasting on this exquisite boar should give thanks to Beany for how she accomplished her task.'

Blanka saw Beuneth bunch her hands into fists and reached out to stay her rage.

Vandalor glided over the rock floor to stand before Beuneth, and stroked her face as she said, 'You should all take note that results get rewarded, and you all benefit from it. Now enjoy this feast in honour of

Beuneth.'

She glided back towards her chair and stopped when she heard a voice from behind: 'What about Lefty?'

'Who said that?' Vandalor closed her eyes and gritted her teeth.

Beuneth stepped forward and yanked her hand from Blanka's grip as she demanded, 'What about Lefty, Mother? Or did you already forget about him? Speared from two hundred feet away, he died instantly when it struck his heart, pinning him to the ground like a rat! He died trying to steal for you! But you don't reward *that*, do you?'

Vandalor marched up to Beuneth and backhanded her across the face as she said, 'Enough! Lefty was an arrogant fool of a child! He never listened and thought he was too good to be caught. As for stealing, dear girl, how do you think you are clothed, fed, and kept warm with your blankets and beds? Where do you think the coin comes from to keep things running around here?' Her gaze slipped past the girl as she saw Blanka rise from his seat, and pushed Beuneth aside as she said, 'Oh, what have we here? All grown up, you even have a beard forming, but you're still the scared and pathetic little boy you always were!'

A savage blow rocked Vandalor from behind, sending her stumbling to the ground. Eyes wide, she quickly got back to her feet in time to see another rock hurled at her head. Dodging the rock, another came, and then another and another. The chanting began as a murmur, but grew loud enough for all to hear. Rocks were drifting into the air and rocketing towards Vandalor from every direction. Even so, she evaded most of them. Children were all scurrying under the tables to escape the rocks. A loud thud and a yelp sounded as Sister Agacia tackled Beuneth and held her to the ground.

Beuneth gasped for air as it was knocked from her lungs. Dazzling lights exploded in her vision as dark spots emerged, filling her sight. *One day, I promise, Mother, I will gain my freedom and live my own life. I will not be young and weak forever. And when that day comes, Mother, you'd better be ready.*

Vandalor rose to her feet as the rocks stopped and fell to the ground. The shock of the surprise attack was clear on her face as she wiped a cut on her cheek and cried, 'Lock her up! Maybe I should hand you in to the guards of Terenore with a note that *you* stole the amulet from the archives, girl! See you beheaded, you ungrateful whelp!'

Blanka rushed forward and flung himself over Vandalor and Sister Agacia, freeing Beuneth as he screamed, 'Run, Beany! Run!'

Dizzily getting to her feet, Beuneth ran as fast as her legs would allow to get out of the cave; but as she rounded a corner, the back-end of a spear swung into view and splintered as it hit her on the chest, expelling the last bit of air she had from her lungs. Vandalor picked Blanka up by the throat, keeping him dangling in the air as she said, 'You just made a grave mistake. Take them away and strap them down. I will be there shortly.'

* * *

Deep in the bowels of Mount Erliat, sound echoed off the walls as screams of pain and torment filled the air. Most of the children were in bed, pillows covering their ears to ignore the cries for help, but it didn't work; the cries pierced their very souls.

The smell of urine hung in the air as Blanka and Beuneth sat bound to wooden chairs in the middle of the room. Vandalor paced up and down in front of them and said, 'Does this make you happy, Beany? Seeing Blanka in this much pain, pissing himself like a two-year-old?'

'I told you to let him go! He did nothing. It's my fault,' Beuneth snapped back, trying to wrench her hands free of the chair, but the ropes just pulled tighter, burning her wrists as she struggled.

'Well, I suppose that this is your punishment, my dear daughter, more than his. Maybe now you'll learn that we're a family here, and what happens to one impacts others,' Vandalor said as she grabbed the ink-filled bamboo stick and pierced Blanka's face over and over to finish the assortment of lines, circles, and swirls she'd started.

'No! Please stop that! I'll do anything you say, Mother! I'll obey! Please, just let him go!'

'Almost done, my dear daughter. You wouldn't want me to leave him halfway done, would you? He would just look awful.'

Eyes darting back and forth, Blanka's shouts filled the room as he reeled to get away, sobbing as he lay in the clutches of the four magnadons, his face bloody and blue from the ordeal. Vandalor finally stopped and moved to Beuneth as she said, 'I need you to understand that this is all because of you, my dear. His fate was completely in your hands. We could have avoided this, but you just had to throw a tantrum, didn't you? That is what I admire about you, though; you don't really care about others, and that will get you far in life.' Vandalor turned around and said, 'Untie them and take them to their beds.' With a wave of her hand, she was gone, leaving the four magnadons alone with Beuneth and Blanka.

Her pleas fell on deaf ears as the magnadons ignored her sobs. 'Do you four really condone this? Sister Agacia? Sister Ti? Sister Veambrose? Sister Preda? Once nuns of the Caltrate.' Seeing the shock on their faces, she continued, 'What? Did you really think we didn't know who you are or were? I wonder what the Caltrate order would say about four of their own holding kids hostage, turning them into thieves and assassins for their profit.'

The four women looked at one another as they untied the children. Sister Agacia drew closer to Beuneth and whispered, 'You might know something about us, but we know everything about you, you little shit! You best be very careful about what you say about us and to whom you say it.'

That's it, come a little closer, just a little more. A vicious head-butt sent blood spurting out of Sister Agacia's broken nose. As she staggered back, the sister lashed her hand across Beuneth's face, sending the chair with her on it to the ground. The tied-up girl had no hopes of protecting herself as Sister Agacia rained down punches on her face until the other three magnadons dragged her off.

Sister Ti shouted, 'That's enough! She's learnt her lesson. Come, let's go. They can get themselves free and back to bed.'

Beuneth stirred, moaned, and coughed up a little blood from the cuts in her mouth as Blanka untied her, feeling his way around the ropes and chair. The slurred speech that came from him was almost unrecognisable. 'Cme, le go ed.'

She reached out to his face but pulled away before she touched him, afraid that it would hurt him, and said, 'I am so sorry, Blanka. We need to clean you up first, otherwise you'll get an infection. I know where they hide the wipes and alcohol.'

'Yu ne'er sto. Du?'

'No, I do not, Blanka. Come on.'

* * *

The wind blew gently from the east, rustling the leaves of the forest's trees as Blanka lay flat on the edge of the cliff overlooking the valley and the castled vault structure standing tall in the distance. A sudden weight landed on his back as he heard, 'If I were a Kingsguard, you'd be dead.'

'If you were a Kingsguard, you'd be one sexy dragon,' he said, as he flipped over under her and grabbed her back.

With a laugh and a shrug, Beuneth cocked her head as she wiggled her body and said, 'Oh my. Are you happy to see me, or is this valley just that beautiful?'

'Oh, shut up and kiss me already,' he said as he pulled her closer, their lips locking as they embraced. She tugged her white shirt over her head, revealing her golden-brown skin, taking his breath away as he looked at her firm breasts. He stared at her in wonder as he said, 'You're not the young girl you once were. How am I this lucky?'

Beuneth gently caressed his tattooed face, but embarrassed, he pulled away from her and said, 'Don't look at me like that; I'm hideous.'

She scowled at him as she said, 'You can never be hideous to me, you idiot. I love you.'

'But I can be an idiot?' He received no answer, only a smile. Over the years, they had grown to be complacent with what they had, following Mother's rule, accepting their fate. Years had drifted by since the night Mother tattooed Blanka's face. It had broken them both. Subjugated them.

Beuneth chuckled as she undid his shirt and trousers, then teasingly pulled down her pants. Unable to contain himself anymore, Blanka grabbed her hand and said, 'Stop toying with me, woman. I'm about to burst. Come here.'

A gasp left her mouth as she lowered herself onto him, feeling him deep inside her. Sweat trickled down their naked bodies, entwined as the sun beat down upon them with its glorious rays. She toyed with him as she slowly moved up and down, the moment of ecstasy drawing near. Blanka planted his hands in the dirt, grabbing handfuls as his muscles spasmed. Unable to contain it any longer, he grabbed hold of Beuneth with his dirt ridden hands and pulled her closer. Moaning and groaning, she released a scream that sent animals scurrying. Blanka turned her over on to the ground and thrust into her, over and over, until she grabbed his back, driving her nails into his skin.

A lightning strike arcing up to the heavens from the cliff's edge interrupted a somewhat cloudless day. He panted as he slid off her and looked up at the blue sky, and said, 'Is that going to happen every time? 'Cause it's going to draw attention, you know.'

Covering her face as she laughed, she said, 'I couldn't help myself. And don't you dare puff up your chest.'

Frowning, he said, 'What, not even a little after that performance?'

'Okay, maybe you can a little.'

The sky was beautifully blue, with two stray clouds roaming above. Beuneth thought about how she got to this point. *For twenty years I've been with you, Vandalor, you cruel old bitch. You at least gave me one good thing in my life: this man next to me. And one day, we'll be free of you completely.*

'Hey! Beany! Are you even listening to me?'

She shook her head and said, 'Wait, what were you saying?'

'I said that we could be free from this life, Bean.'

'What do you mean? Until she's dead, there is nothing we can do.'

'Yes, there is. Every few years, after a Kingsguard falls, they run the marathon up the mountain, and the winner gets to enter the halls of the elite. It's the only time that the Vault of the Balamuths is opened. What if I could get in and bind with one? They would have to make me a Kingsguard. And it just so happens that the next marathon is in three days. I'm not strong enough to take on Vandalor as a mere man, but as a Kingsguard—'

'No!' Beuneth said as she jumped up from the ground, and continued, 'Don't you even dare think about that again! Do you understand me? They'll kill you! Nobody has ever got out alive. No, I forbid it.'

Blanka rose to his feet and held her tight as he said, 'Okay, forget I said anything.'

* * *

Cold air brushed his cheeks as winds howled over the mountain's summit. Snowflakes whipped about, riding the current as far as the eye could see. Moonlight shone through the trees of the forest. 'You'd better look before you move, Blanka,' he muttered. 'You don't want to get seen by the Kingsguard.'

He shook his head with indignation as he rejected his own claims and whispered, 'How dare you? I have never been caught, and I'm not about to start now.' The wolf-skin cloak warmed him, and he pulled it tighter about him and edged his way closer to the Vault, moving silently as he hugged the trees for cover. The massive walls loomed ahead. Years of wear and tear had seen some mortar and stone get dislodged in places, *a perfect way to get up and over.* Scanning the walls, he marked out his route and edged forward into the clearing, then dashed back to the shadows as he heard a voice drawing close.

'Oh, come on, you miscreant. There's no way you can pull that off,' said one guard to another as they passed by Blanka, the cover of the wild brush and snow concealing his whereabouts.

The other guard replied, 'How would you know, you worm? I'm

telling you the truth; this is going to happen.'

The handholds were treacherous in the cold, his skin tearing easily from scraping against the rough stone wall. A high-pitched squeal shook him from the right as a dragon settled on the front gate tower, observing to the east, down the mountainside. In an instant, it veered, and the Kingsguard moved to the edge to get a better view. The guards were all gathered at the front, hoping to glimpse the first competitor to make it to the vault, neglecting their duties in the process. At this stage, they would have been running for about two-and-a-half days since the start of the event. They would be tired, thirsty, hungry, and cold. Near death, probably.

Not so sure if this is a good idea anymore. I'm pretty sure I can't get away from that thing. A guard approached from his left on the wall, and a patrol moved by down below. His only way was through the window and into the hall of the vault. There was no turning back now. He slipped through and dropped to the floor down below.

Massive dull-grey stone pillars lined the light-blue marbled hall, the slight contrast making him think back to the time when he was still living with his real parents. *Oh, how I miss that house. Chasing Temper around and around until she would eventually turn and growl. It was always a fake growl, but it still sent a few shivers down the spine. That blue and grey barn...*

'Dear boy! When did you get here?'

He was so transfixed as he marvelled at the exquisite craftsmanship of the hall — the symbols etched into the walls telling stories of previous Kingsguards — that he hadn't seen the old man shuffle close. 'I said, when did you get here? Are you the first?' the geezer asked as he placed a monocle before his left eye.

Startled, Blanka looked around confusedly, trailing his eyes over the old man. When he was slow to speak, the old man rapped Blanka on the head with his cane and said, 'Are you so dehydrated that you cannot speak? Or is this what we are getting nowadays? I tell you, it is getting worse by the year. No one will sing songs of glory in your name, dear boy, if you do not start speaking.'

'Uhm,' Blanka said, and cleared his throat before he continued, 'Yes, sorry. I'm so dehydrated. Can barely think. I am the first.'

'Then show some joy for winning, you imbecile. Follow me.' They walked over to the big vault door, the old man muttering the entire way. 'Nothing makes you young ones happy anymore. When I was young, I was all too happy to play with a few sticks, maybe a hoop here and there. But no, not you lot. Even being bound with a dragon isn't cause for joy anymore. And why is there no other soldier here to congratulate you? They usually carry the winner in on their shoulders. Everything is becoming disgraceful, simply disgraceful.'

The old man placed his hand on the vault door, chanting loudly. Symbols all over the door and his wrinkled body came to life, glowing until eventually Blanka could hear the door unlock and slowly swing open. He licked his lips, his heart pounding furiously in his chest as he said, 'I don't know. I didn't see any of the guards when I came through the gate. Must have just missed them as they patrolled.'

The old man scratched his chin through his thick beard and squinted at Blanka as he said, 'That is strange. Usually they barely patrol, as they all wait for the first to arrive. What is going on here?'

Quickly grabbing the old man, Blanka swung him around, and in an instant had his knife against the old man's throat. 'Look, I don't want to hurt you. I just need to be bonded. I need to be a Kingsguard. Now, get into the vault and close it behind us.'

The old man did as commanded, shuffling into the vault steadily before closing the door behind them.

* * *

'No!'

The shout escaped her lips even before she was awake. Cold sweat ran down her back as she felt for the usual warmth of body heat next to her. Rummaging through the entire bed, hoping he was playing a trick on her, she finally conceded the fact that he wasn't there. 'I'm going to murder him, if they haven't already,' she vowed. She grabbed her clothes and chain whip, and as she moved to the door, heard a voice in the dark.

'Where are you going, Beuneth?'

'Blanka is in trouble. I can feel it. He went and did something really stupid. And he did it for me. I have to go,' she said as she pulled the door to close it, but hit a foot instead.

'Then I'll come with you.'

She watched the man squeeze between her and the door. Irritation overtook her, and she bit her lip as she said, 'I'm sorry, Setha, but this I have to do alone. I just hope I'm not too late. Take care of the rest while we're away.' Shoving him out of the way, she ran through the cave as fast as she could. Over the years, she'd come to know the cave well, not even needing a torch to navigate its dark halls. But every year it grew bigger, expanding as they brought in new kids. Floors had been put in over the years, the walls plastered. They had even brought in some ornate doors. Heck, some even got their very own rooms, like Beuneth and Blanka.

The more you offered Vandalor, the more you were rewarded. But no reward can be a substitute for freedom.

The woods were quiet in the dead of night. A howl, far in the distance, took her attention for a moment before she opened a portal and stepped through. A few miles further, she stepped out in the middle of the forest. Looking around, she found the direction of the Vault and opened another portal that took her to a large, open field. A few squirrels and field mice scattered as she emerged. Blood seeped from her nose; she wiped it away with the back of her hand, then shook her head and said, 'I should have done more practising; this is rough on me.' Her ability to travel through the portals had increased a lot, but not enough to jump the whole distance. The castled Vault was now at least in sight, but still at least two jumps away. She opened another portal and stepped through.

Frigid air enveloped the area and froze the grass and leaves solid as the portal opened, feeding off the earth as she staggered through. With trembling legs, ragged breaths, and a pounding heart, she knew she couldn't open another portal without killing herself. *Guess I'm running the rest of the way.*

Twice she collapsed on the cold ground before stumbling on.

* * *

'You cannot escape, young man. They will not allow an uninitiated to be bonded and made a Kingsguard. They will kill—'

'Enough, old man, I need to think.' Pacing up and down, Blanka continued, 'How does this work?'

The old man scowled at him as he lowered himself to a golden bench and said, 'Look around; take the gold, the diamonds. That they might let you live for. But not the Balamuths.'

Blanka spread his hands, pleading with the old man, 'Look, what do you care if I live or die? I have no need for jewellery and coin. I need this. Now, please.'

'It will be your pyre that burns in the night. Go stand in the centre of the ring and don't be afraid.'

The old man cleared his throat and said loudly, 'Heed my call, all Balamuths. I, the Gatekeeper, summon you to seek the heart of the next follower. Find him just, find him worthy of the bond and bind with him to be one, forever to roam the lands again. Find him unworthy and burn his soul into damnation, to roam the world lifeless, never to be whole again.'

From all over, voices filled the chamber, speaking Dragovian. Blanka looked around confusedly and shouted to the old man, 'What are they saying? I can't understand them.'

'Oh, they are deliberating your fate. Some seem to think you have courage. Go figure. Some think you are nothing but a thief. Others feel your heart is pure, but broken. Interesting.'

One voice rang out, silencing the rest of the Balamuths as it floated up to hover before Blanka. A swirling mist flowed through the sphere of red and black. In wonder, he reached out to the sphere. As he grabbed hold, it turned into a mist, flowing down and enveloping his being. Wide-eyed, screams erupted from him as memories filled his head from the dragon: from the moment of ripping the amniotic sac and taking its first breath, to siring a newborn and its inevitable enslavement, imprisoned in the sphere for centuries. A deep, guttural voice filled his head: 'I am called Belgarr. I find you worthy.'

The internal burn spread throughout, his skin turning as red as the fruit of the jakka-jakka. Pain coursed through his body as his face purpled. Slow movements from the old Gatekeeper saw him edging closer to the ring, and he reached out to support Blanka as he said, 'Oh, he is going to burn you alive. Do not resist him. Let him in. Join with him. Remember, it is a mutual relationship.'

Eyes closed, he breathed deep, ignoring the pain, and invited Belgarr in. A soothing calm flowed over him, as cold as ice. Tensions eased, and his skin returned to its normal tattooed brown. The strangest feeling occurred then, almost unexplainable: an irrevocable step of acceptance, as if his body and mind were torn apart, but still intact. He could feel the new life course within him. Rapid, ragged breaths escaped him as he turned around and stared at the Gatekeeper, and said, 'What was that?'

'You didn't think there would be a cost, did you?' Hands clamped together, the Gatekeeper said, 'That was your soul being torn in two—'

Louder than he intended, Blanka jumped forward and gripped the old Gatekeeper by the shoulders and shouted, 'My *what?*'

'Well, more accurately, your soul and mind were torn in two and shared between you and whoever—'

'Belgarr.'

'Oh. Him. Uhm, Belgarr, then.'

* * *

Torga paced up and down on the wall above the big gate, then stopped to pull a cigar from his pouch to hold it before his mouth. Vivid red eyes came to life, shining in the dark as his throat glowed dull orange-red from within until he blew a small flame, lighting the cigar. From his right a guard asked, 'Doesn't that hurt your throat?'

Brows raised, Torga looked around at the dozen men surrounding him and said, 'Hurts like hell, but I like my cigars.'

Suddenly Torga doubled over, feeling like he'd been punched in the gut. In his mind, he saw a bonding taking place. He felt a dragon emerge from its captivity. *No. Not possible. No one came through yet. I would have seen it.* A sizzle and a smell of burning flesh followed as he crushed out the cigar against his hand, making the guards next to him wince on his behalf. He smirked as he shouted, 'We have an intruder. Go down and surround the Vault. Be careful; although he is still weak, the intruder has already bonded, and will be stronger than the average man. Let nothing happen to the Gatekeeper.'

Guards ran all over as orders were shouted, getting into place to capture the intruder.

* * *

'Oh no, you idiot! What did you do? If they don't kill you, I will.' From her vantage point, Beuneth could see the door to the Vault hall, surrounded by a picket. The lantern lights were dim, and the moon had already departed for the night, making the darkness oppressive. Suddenly, a loud crash sent splinters flying from the door, splitting it open with immeasurable force as two men rolled on the ground, locked in battle, throwing punches at each other's heads. Blanka jumped to his feet, as did the Kingsguard. Circling one another with raised fists, they charged in.

Beuneth gasped as she saw the blood streak on Blanka's face. *Well, here I go.* She unhooked her chain whip and ran in under the cover of darkness.

* * *

Blanka pleaded his case to Torga as they circled each other. 'Please, brother! I just want to join the Kingsguard. I'm not an enemy!'

Torga rushed in and grabbed Blanka by the throat, lifting him into the air as he snarled, 'Brother? Just because you have one of my kin bonded with you doesn't make me your *brother*. In fact, it makes me furious, as I now have to kill one of my own. You've sullied our creed. We accept only the best of the best, not petty thieves who crawl at night.'

Blanka looked down into the glowing red eyes before him, struggling to breathe as his windpipe was slowly crushed.

To his right, a scream of pain erupted from a soldier as he crumpled to the ground, clutching his left ankle as his foot hung limp. All the other guards milled around, searching the area, and Torga threw Blanka aside like a rag doll as he said, 'Well now, what do we have here? There,' he said, pointing to his left as he advanced on their attacker.

Lightning arced from up high, searing into the chest of another guard and throwing the man off his feet.

Blanka launched himself at Torga and grabbed him around the throat with his arm, squeezing as hard as he could. An elbow cracked into his ribs, then another. The Kingsguard jumped backwards, smacking Blanka hard against the wall of the hall, loosening his grip and allowing Torga's escape. Guards were falling like flies being swatted as Beuneth sent her chain whip slicing through their Achilles tendons or sword arms, maiming them just enough to take them out of the fight.

A massive gust of wind whirled out of nowhere, and Beuneth found herself suspended in the air, the life being squeezed out of her by the thick black tail wrapped around her chest and neck. Too exhausted to do any magic, Beuneth struggled to breathe, and could only watch Torga break Blanka's arm as he readied a death blow with his dagger.

A voice rumbled through the area from the one holding her. 'Torga, stop!' With a flick of its tail, the massive black dragon sent Beuneth flying into the wall behind Blanka, where she fell limp to the ground.

She and Blanka shuffled closer to each other in their bloodied state. Beuneth grabbed hold of his hand as tears rolled down her face, and said, 'I'm sorry, Blanka.'

'Why do you always have to spoil my fun, Caryk?' Torga growled as he walked closer to the dragon as it veered, then looked up at his captain and continued, 'He needs to die for what he did.'

Caryk pushed Torga aside and stalked up to the two lying on the floor as they mumbled their pleas to be spared, and said calmly, 'You have brought shame upon us, Belgarr. Yes, I can smell you in there. How could you bond with this heretic?'

Blanka's face was grey with pain as he struggled to straighten, then knelt before Caryk and said, 'I know this is unconventional, but there was no other way to show that I am the one who must be bonded. I may be uninitiated, but I will serve. I will fight for the kingdom.'

'No. You're nothing but a worthless criminal, seeking fame as the first to break into the Vault. I can't allow that. What message would it send?' He turned and gestured carelessly with one hand, then said to the guards, 'Take them away and throw her in the witch pit. I can sense the sorcery radiating from her. Spread the word; in two days, we'll have a public execution, and she'll be made to bear witness.'

Frantically, Beuneth jumped at Blanka as she opened a portal. A loud crack, and pain radiating through her skull, was the last she remembered.

* * *

Crowds gathered early on the day of execution, wearing thick, long coats as the frosty morning air gusted through the streets and alleys of Terenore. Shouts and cheers rang out over the city square as the whip came down once more, taking another piece of flesh with it. In the middle of the square, produce was being thrown at Beuneth, who stood in a cage, inscribed symbols all over the iron bars. She shouted at the top of her voice for them to stop this madness, pleading with the king and the three Kingsguard next to him, but they ignored her.

'Blankadu Valkus. As retribution for your crimes, you shall be crippled and flung into the bottomless pit. Do you object to the case made against you?' Wearing a great red dragon's hide as armour, fire coursing through its very existence, the king's voice echoed from the open hall and throughout the square. A hushed crowd now waited in anticipation. The only sounds were the winds howling through the alleys, Beuneth's screams from the cage, and the rustling chains around Blanka. His hands were throbbing inside the cast-iron gloves. The constant chafing had eaten through his skin, and blood flowed down his arms to the ground. The inscribed chains bound around his body were burning his very soul. He could feel Belgarr writhing inside of him, unable to come out.

Cold sweat ran down his face as he looked at the king in front of him, and said, 'Yes, Your Grace, I do. With all my heart, I do. All I wanted was to become a Kingsguard, to serve you.' Hoping for a shred of mercy, the tiniest sliver of compassion, he shouted out, 'Please, Your Grace, at least spare the girl!'

The king gave one last insult as he slapped him across the face and said, 'Your time is up.'

Two guards moved in from the side, one grabbing him by his broken arm, the other dragging him by the collar of his shirt. The floor was slick with blood underfoot and sent the guards sliding as they approached the raised stone slab. They threw him hard onto the stone top and the crowd gasped as his body spasmed before going limp, thinking that it could be the end. For the longest of moments, there was silence in the square. Slow movements from the prisoner satisfied the crowd with the prolonging of their entertainment as he regained consciousness. Arms shackled to his sides, he lay with his back on the slab, his feet raised a few inches by a vice block, holding them firmly in place. The old Gatekeeper came into view as he ascended the stairs to the stone slab with his hands behind his back and gazed at the witch in the cage, shaking his head in disappointment. Upon noting the bloodstains on his new white robe, he let out a curse and stared down at the prisoner as he said, 'I am sorry, this will hurt a great deal; I told you to take the gold instead. The Balamuth will not separate unless your senses are a complete mess.' The Gatekeeper gestured a guard forward.

This was the moment the crowd had been waiting for: the tearing out of the Balamuth. A big guard walked up to him with a massive two-handed warhammer and placed it on his shin, just above the ankle. Feeling the weight of the cold steel pressing against his skin, Blanka said a quick prayer as he closed his eyes. With a mighty swing, the guard shouted as he expelled the force of the blow. The loud crack of bones reverberated through the square as shouts of pain filled the sky. Beuneth was rattling the cage bars, pushing and pulling, throwing herself at them, but nothing budged. They had warded the cage; her magic was useless. She could but only watch in horror as they tortured her love. The guard shifted to the other leg and rested the big hammer on the shin. Blanka was sliding in and out of consciousness by then, the fever of pain assaulting his mind.

The sickening crunch sounded again as the hammer came down with brutal force. Some people in the first row of the square hunched over and vomited, unable to contain it any longer. As the guard moved away, the old Gatekeeper moved closer, waving his hands above his head, chanting as he did so. Blanka shook violently as the Balamuth left his body, tearing his mind and soul in two. He could feel the ghostly claws of the dragon holding on with everything it had, trying not to be sundered. But Blanka had no more fight left in him. A steady flow of mist left his body, forming a sphere above his head. The Gatekeeper placed a cloth over the sphere and plucked it from the air. Walking to the pit a few feet away, he unceremoniously tossed it in and watched it disappear in the darkness of its depth.

A Kingsguard called Ragian pushed the bile rising from his stomach down and clenched his teeth as he whispered, 'Are you sure there was no other way, Caryk? I have memories of Belgarr. He fought valiantly to save other dragons from enslavement. We could have used a dragon like him.'

Cold eyes stared back at him as Caryk said, 'It needed to be done.

Now, keep watching.'

They left a trail of blood on the floor as they dragged Blanka towards the pit, his feet hanging limp. A crimson river flowed from his torn back, over the feet of the staring crowd. The whipping had taken more than just blood.

The guard dragging him along dropped him to the floor twice as he said, 'You should be glad I wasn't the one to torture you, or you would be dead already.'

'Then I wish you were the one to torture me,' groaned Blanka as he spat blood onto the grainy floor.

With a vicious motion, the guard threw him from the stage as a whip cracked to draw more blood, tearing deep into his skin even before he hit the ground. Outraged and in great pain, Blanka screamed almost silently as he hit the cobbles, the wind knocked from his lungs. Limp, his consciousness came and went. He pleaded once more, 'Please do—'

The guard rolled him over the edge of the pit with his boot. 'One last sting to remember me by,' then there was only darkness as he fell.

* * *

'And so, I fell through that pit for what felt like a lifetime, just waiting for death to take me.' Blanka shifted closer to the fire and stared at the two men, then continued, 'Instead I woke up in a pool of blood next to the pit inside a cave, crippled and with no memory. And I'm sure, now, that the time I spent falling through that pit stole years from my life.'

Khanaseri stuffed his mouth with another bite of the rabbit, breaking the leg off for further enjoyment. The crunching sound of the bones splitting apart made Link turn to him, then to his own piece of rabbit in his hands. He tossed it in the bush, and asked, 'What happened next?'

Rubbing sand over his hands to clean off the fat from the meat, Blanka raised his brows and said, 'I crawled. Luckily, before long, a man came by and found me slithering through the woods. He got me to a healer. I spent months with the healer as he helped me get back on my feet. After that, they employed me to scrub the decks on a boat. I crossed the ocean, and I ended up in the village for a few years before he,' he pointed at Khanaseri, 'found me.'

Khanaseri sucked a piece of meat from between his teeth and said, 'Sounds like they really did a number on you. Sorry, my friend.'

Blanka cleared his throat. 'So, now that I've regaled you with the tale of how I know Beuneth, can you tell me what happened to her?'

The sudden attention caught Khan by surprise as he sat with the rabbit's leg dangling from his mouth. He took it out. 'Uh, yeah. They imprisoned her for a few years.'

Silence fell over the camp as the two men waited in anticipation for the story to continue, but Khanaseri went back to pushing more of the rabbit into his mouth.

'Wait a moment! Was that it? I told you my entire story, sparing no details, and *that* is what you come up with in return?' Blanka was on his feet, pleading with the man.

With the shocked look of a cornered deer, Khanaseri said, 'Uh, okay. So, she was imprisoned for a few years, like I said. Then she escaped and jumped down into the pit, actually trying to commit suicide to be with you in the afterlife. Except she didn't die. Obviously. She searched for you and the Balamuth for a long time. Oh yeah, she ran into my father, and they fought. I was pulled into the mess when I tried to kill her. Then she trained me. And here we are.'

Link stared at the big warlock and said, 'Wow. You are *not* good at telling stories.'

Blanka stomped off, muttering to himself, and lay down for the night, turning away from the other two.

Chapter Twelve

Another day dawned as Khanaseri awoke to the crows of a rooster sitting perched at the top of the healer's house, curses following its long cries through the streets. He'd been told that once a month, all citizens of the little village would wake up early, before the rooster's first crow, waiting in the street with nets and ropes ready. It had become something of a sport here in the village. No weapons were allowed, though. At the first sight or sound of the rooster, everyone leaped into action, climbing the healer's home to get to the infernal animal. Today was such a day and Khanaseri, perturbed as he was, laughed at the people as they clambered all over each other and up the side of the house. *The fools probably wouldn't even kill it if they caught it. They enjoy this too much. I wonder how many times they've tried to catch this rooster.* He stared out the window from his bed and said, 'Okay, so what am I doing back here?'

The door opened and in walked Link, with a bag slung over his shoulder. 'Glad to see you awake. How are you feeling?'

'To be honest, a little confused. How did I get back here? We were down at the lake, talking around the fire, and then I woke up here.'

Brows raised, Link put the bag down on the bed and said, 'Well, you just dropped like a rock. We were still talking when you got up from the ground; next thing I know you're back down and barely breathing. We carried you back to the healer. He said your body was exhausted. Looks to me like that healing magic is taking a toll on you. You've been asleep for two days. Oh, yeah, I went back to the mountain to get you these, and I returned with your mounts, too. Least I could do. Loyal beasts you have — they never strayed far from the campsite where we took you.' Link opened the bag and pulled out the massive axe and a brown leather pouch.

Khanaseri gathered his equipment and said, 'Thank you, Link. Is Blanka ready to travel?'

'He's been ready for the last two days. I think he's eager to see his Beuneth.'

The big warlock grunted and smiled as he slung the bag over his shoulder. 'Aye, judging from the stories he told, I can't blame him.'

The sun peeked over the hills, lighting up the staircase as the warlock made his way down. Laughter echoed in the house as the healer stood, smoking a pipe at the window as one after another, people fell off his house to injure themselves. 'Oh, that's a nasty spill. One more patient for me. Ooh, and another. Better get my tools ready.'

The sound of the footsteps made the healer turn to see the warlock, his face scarred and scabbed, but healing. 'I see you went for the bald look. I like it. Let me see the wounds on your back.'

As he moved toward the big man, Khanaseri raised his hands and said, 'No need, thank you. I'm fine.'

The healer stopped and tipped out his pipe as he continued, 'You healed quickly. Some would say *too* quickly.'

'I come from hardy stock. I have to go, but I wanted to thank you for all your help.'

Khanaseri pulled out the leather pouch, fished inside, and handed a couple of gold coins to the man, who gripped his hand and said, 'Just remember, there's much more to wounds like yours than just the scars they leave.'

Khanaseri nodded, and he and Link left the house.

Dogs barked at them as they made their way through the slow and unencumbered lives of the village. Khanaseri slapped the assassin on the back and asked, 'What will you do now?'

Link tilted his head as he looked to the sky, 'Well, I heard some rumours about a temple high in the mountains that teaches enlightenment through the art of battle, using various forms: sword, longbow, bo staff. I heard they were being harassed by some bandits. Maybe I'll make my way there.'

Khanaseri grinned and said, 'The path to enlightenment is a long and arduous one. At least, that's what my teacher used to say. It was a goal that I couldn't obtain. How about you, Blanka? Have you found enlightenment?'

'*I* am enlightened, especially regarding what time we said we would meet up,' Blanka said as the two men approached. 'Can't say the same about you. You're only two days late. "I'm all healed up," he says, only to drop like a turd to the ground.'

Khanaseri patted Flintlock on the neck and packed his belongings in the saddlebags before pulling himself up with some effort. 'I'm here now, aren't I? Let's go. See you around, assassin.'

'Call me Codar. I am sure we will meet again, warlock. Be safe.' They nodded with a smile and turned their mounts. Link watched them ride out of the village before turning away, and let out a long sigh as he muttered, 'Can't stay too long. The guild must know my location already.'

* * *

Hooves thundered across the plains of the Urangatu, just before the icy mountain pass of Galbadore's Eye. The grey mare's muscles bounced, pulled taut with every landing of her hooves, sending ripples across her body. Anavi lay flat at her neck, driving her hard to catch up with the Desert Dogs. Aqueous vapour escaped the mare's nostrils as she leapt across a fallen tree, the figurative hellhounds on her heels. Anavi knew she couldn't keep riding the mare so hard, or her heart would eventually give out; but anger fuelled her drive for vengeance.

The Desert Dogs won't be moving as fast. Knowing them, they'll probably drift apart, each making their way at their own pace. Another bright flash came from behind, followed by the thunderous snap of lightning drawing closer, and it inevitably soaked her with its bountiful, wet kiss. Night was approaching with the wind and rain. She scanned the area and saw an old hut to the left, by the looks of it abandoned. Dismounting, she tethered her horse to a tree branch and walked up to the door. She could barely hear her knocks, and eventually slammed her palms against the door, but there came no answer.

The wooden frame had bulged from the rains over time, causing the door to stick; it would not open as she leaned and hammered on it. She untethered the mare, led her to the door, and turned her back towards it. A quick slap on the rump and the mare kicked with both her legs to send the door flying open, almost breaking the hinges as it hit the wall on the inside.

'That's a good girl, Lexiphene,' Anavi said as she patted her on the neck and led her into the little house. 'I don't want you catching a cold out there, ol' girl.' Moving the old and dusty furniture out of the way, Anavi kept patting her neck and gently spoke to her to put her at ease. 'We'll rest here for the night, ol' girl. What do you think, Lexi?' The mare brayed her agreement and pushed out her lips, asking for an apple. 'You deserve it, girl. Hold on, I'll get food and water for the both of us.'

The last person to have left the cabin was courteous enough to have filled the hearth with wood in case of a weary traveller passing by. From her pouch, she took some tinder and stuffed it under and between the logs, then lit it with a piece of flint. Slowly and precariously blowing at the tinder, she guided her hands to the sides to stop the excessive winds rushing down the chimney from killing the burgeoning flame. Once the crackle of the flames filled the room, she rummaged through the little house and found a bucket with a home-made rain catcher.

Given the pouring rain, it wasn't long before they had ample water. Anavi fed the mare some carrots and apples as she herself took a few bites of the bread she'd bought back at New Runswick. She removed her saddle and pack from the mare, and quickly examined her for any foot-sores, then rubbed her down before covering her with a blanket she found in the back. Anavi dusted off some old pillows and made a pallet for herself, then lay down as Lexi nudged her for more carrots. 'Okay, okay. Little pushy today, aren't we?' She rose and pulled a bag of horse feed from the pack and wet it in a bucket. Lexi voiced her gratitude and dipped her head into the bucket. Tired and wet, Anavi removed her clothes and hung them to dry near the fire before returning to the pallet. Sleep came and went as dreams constantly woke her with their strangeness: seeing Magnus made king and sending her away; Lanik being a babe in the arms of her mother; and terrifying creatures roaming the sky, patrolling the world beneath them.

* * *

An illicit brothel had taken over occupancy of the dilapidated green house to his left, attracting the most obtrusive of clients. One by one, they sneaked into the building, glancing around, hoping no one watched as they lusted for the sexual attention of the bought girls and boys. Blanka spat at the ground in disgust, then turned as he pulled his hood over his head and strolled down the street. Rounding the corner of the fisher's market, the street was suddenly alive with a buzz in the air as people shopped while the merchants shouted out their wares to attract new clients. Boats coming and going after offloading their catch for the day. He smiled under the hood as he found the person he was after standing at a stall, negotiating a bargain for a child's toy.

'I'll pay one silver and nothing more. Take it or leave it, you old bastard. Should be ashamed of yourself, stealing from people like this.' Suri took out the coin and flung it on the table as the merchant shook his head in annoyance. He collected the small wooden sword to sheath it in his belt and turned around just as a hooded stranger walked into him, sending him to the ground. Quick on his feet, he felt for his pouch and sword, then looked at the stranger babbling on for all to hear while weaving through the mob, 'They're here! I've seen them! Men turning into beasts. I have seen them.'

Suri shook his head. 'Ozo! Is that you?'

The man didn't turn and kept walking through the crowds, keeping just ahead of the trailing Suri. As they moved away from the busy streets of the fish market, the crowds thinned and Suri ran up to grab the man at the back of his cloak as he shouted, 'Stop!'

The man removed the hood as he turned and stared at the young guard.

'Sorry, sir, I thought you were someone else. My apologies.'

The man smiled and said, 'No apologies needed. We're all searching for something in life. I heard you calling this Ozo. Is he a friend of yours?'

Suri looked at the man, furrowing his brow. 'Yes, he is. You have an uncanny resemblance to him. Not to mention the markings on your face. Who are you?'

With a wide grin, the man said, 'I told you there were unnatural things in this world.'

Suri's eyes went wide as he gazed upon his old friend in wonder. 'Ozo? But how?'

'I have much to tell you. Come, join me at my old cabin.'

Dumbfounded, Suri's mouth hung ajar. Not knowing what to say or do, he simply nodded, his eyes glancing back and forth until Ozo reached out to give him a hug as he said, 'I've missed you too.'

The walk up the side of the mountain to his old home was a familiar one as they talked about everything that had happened and as they reached the ruins of the house, Suri saw the warlock next to a fire, cooking a small deer. Upon seeing the new scars on the warrior, he pulled a face stated, 'You looked better when I saw you last.'

'Yeah, well, the other guy is dead. You know, Blanka here saved my life. If it weren't for him, I'd be dead too,' the warlock said as he added some more wood to the fire.

'Who's this Blanka?'

With a deep sigh, Blanka turned to Suri. 'There is no simple way to say this, so I'm just going to say it. I'm leaving with Khan here for a while. I finally have my memories back, Suri. My real name is Blanka. And I have things I need to take care of.'

'You're leaving again so soon? But Senri still needs to meet you.'

With a smile on his face, Blanka said, 'And so he will, someday. Just not today. I can't wait to meet him, and that alone will get me back here for a visit. But I have to do this.'

The three sat around the fire for the better part of the evening as they talked and laughed, enjoying each other's company a little while longer.

Khanaseri rose and rubbed his stomach as he moved away to peer at the setting sun, then started drawing patterns in the sand. 'We have to go, Blanka. Say your goodbyes.' He started chanting.

Blanka laid his hand on Suri's shoulder and said, 'You're a good man. Thank you for everything you've done for me over the last few years. I won't forget you.'

The wind howled as it cut through the remnants of the cottage, picking up speed as Khanaseri continued with his chants. Great, vibrant blue lightning bolts arced to nearby metal objects, the thunderous claps resonating through the area. Suri winced at the lightning strikes and looked for cover as the two men climbed on their mounts. Abruptly, a portal tore open big enough to fit a wagon, and through the swirling chaos, Suri could see a world away.

Barely audible over the howling wind and thunder, Blanka shouted to Suri, 'Take care, boy! We'll see each other again.'

The pair entered the rift astride their mounts and disappeared from Suri's sight as it snapped shut. A sudden calmness enveloped the area, making Suri feel empty inside as the howling winds died instantly and the lightning ceased its rage. He looked around at the vacant lot and sighed before heading back home.

* * *

The smell of petrichor graced their noses in the cold of the cabin as they woke. 'Time to go, Lexi; the sun is almost out, and they'll be ready to march soon enough,' Anavi said as she removed the blanket from the horse's back and led her outside to graze. Quickly gathering her gear, she stuffed it into the saddlebags and fitted them to the mare, checking twice to ensure the billet straps were secure. She then climbed onto the horse's back and set off, taking in the sun's rays as it peered over the horizon, lighting the few remaining clouds in the sky with fiery orange and pink. A narrow footpath ran through the trees approaching the mountain; Galbadore's Eye loomed before her. The shortcut had won her a lot of ground, and she knew they would have no need of taking it. They would march back languidly, enjoying the sun's warmth, feasting more than walking. Slowing her horse, she loosed an arrow and heard a squeak as it hit. 'Seems we have lunch, Lexi.' A quick trot over and she retrieved the arrow and the rabbit.

For the past three days, she'd struggled to get up in the mornings. The riding had been hard on her back and legs. Now, as she rocked to the sides — nearly falling as Lexi stumbled over rocks going up the steep mountainside — she winced from the lancing pains in her back. Anavi clenched her jaw and pushed through the pain. She brought her hand up to check whether Lanik's stupid throwing knives were still in the vest she wore. *How many times has he pestered me to learn how to use these things? Stupid little knives.*

Lexiphene's pace slowed drastically as she climbed the mountain pass, the cold air alone already making it hard for the animal to breathe. They passed a stand of trees to the right. Lexi stopped and flicked her ears back and forth as she lifted her head and curled her upper lip.

'What's the matter, girl?' Anavi asked as she scanned the area, seeing nothing but the thin layer of snow forming on the ground as flakes drifted gently from the sky, obscuring her vision. Bushes lined the right side of the path, with some small trees farther down. Squinting against the glare of the snow, movement — cleverly concealed between the bushes and the snow — caught her eye behind them as she looked over her shoulder. To the right, more movement, flat to the ground, slowly creeping closer. *Wolves.* Anavi drove her heels hard into Lexi's flanks to send her bolting up the slope. Two wolves gave chase from behind. A third joined in from the left, one that would most likely have proven successful in flanking them had she not bolted.

Taking aim from the back of a frightened horse, one trying to climb a rough mountain pass over rocks while being chased by wolves, proved difficult. She leaned into the bow and guessed more than anything when to release the string as she bounced up and down and side to side. The arrow sailed through the sky, slicing into the back leg of one of the wolves, sending it toppling to the ground. Another arrow flew, hitting stone and skidding away. Rocking heavily to the side, she was almost thrown and grabbed on to the saddle horn. She righted herself and took a deep breath, then loosed another arrow. A wolf's legs buckled underneath it as the arrow sank into its chest. The third wolf turned around, heading back down the mountain as it lost its reinforcements. Anavi pulled on the reins and slowed her mount, taking a deep breath as she relaxed. A big alpha came suddenly from the left, leaping through the air from a boulder to crash into her and throw her off the horse. Lexiphene bolted up the path.

Anavi bounced off a tree while she tumbled down the mountainside, then through some bushes before she reached for her sword, slashing wildly as she came to a stop, and heard a faint yelp. On her feet now, she saw a trickle of blood running down the side of the broad head of the wolf, which was standing a distance away. *Almost had me, didn't you?* The wolf growled and snarled at her as it moved to and fro a few paces away, hesitant about this prey.

She sheathed her sword and slowly bent down to pick up a rock and throw it at the animal, hoping it would run. But it stood unflinching, with death and hunger in its eyes. Pebbles went flying as its claws dug into the ground, charging at her. Anavi retreated and slipped on a wet stone, trying to draw her sword as the wolf leapt through the air, its canines ready to sink into her throat. The piercing of flesh and bone reverberated through the sword as the wolf crashed into her. Shocked, the wolf frantically ripped at her throat, not understanding what had just attacked it. Leather vambraces protected her arms as she covered her face against the vicious, slashing teeth. Reaching farther past her head, she pulled an arrow from the quiver and plunged it into the side of the wolf's head. The howl could be heard for miles as the animal staggered away and breathed its last, collapsing to the ground as its legs gave way.

Angry and regretful, Anavi stood and shouted at the dead wolf, 'Damn you! I didn't want to kill you!' She set off towards the path, then walked down to pick up her arrows, knowing she would need them in the coming fight. To her right, she saw the animal she'd shot in the chest and walked over. 'Sorry, furred one. This wasn't my idea.'

After the bilious act of yanking the arrow from the beautiful wolf's chest, she wiped it on her pants and placed it back in the quiver before hearing a faint yelp to the left. Quickly she ran and saw, not too far distant, the other wolf slowly hopping away, one leg dangling in the air where the arrow was pinned in its muscles.

'Come on, big boy,' she said, trying to coax the animal closer. A most beautiful creature, it was pure white with blue eyes and a grey patch on its chest. *He must stand taller than me.* Growls left the wolf as it bared its fangs, snapping at her as she moved closer. Anavi spoke gently and slowly lowered herself next to its injured leg. 'You shouldn't have tried to come after me, big boy. I had to defend myself, you know. Now look at this mess.'

The growling was slowly replaced by panting as she spoke. The arrow hadn't hit bone, but had gone straight through the right leg's biceps. She reached for the arrow and said, 'I won't lie to you, this will hurt.' With a quick break of the shaft, she pulled it through its leg as the wolf lashed out and tried to bite her.

Quick on her feet, she sighed as she looked back at the wolf, knowing it would probably die because of this wound. Anavi walked up the slope to her horse to retrieve her bounty and jogged back down.

'Here you go, big boy. You can have this one. I'll get another,' she said as she threw the rabbit at the wolf's feet.

* * *

The flicker of the fires below the low-lying ridge was easily visible; voices carried far into the quiet night sky. Men stumbled around, slurring songs in their drunken stupor. One nearly fell into the fire, dragged down by the invisible threads of the alcohol, tugging him back just when he thought he'd won a step forward. Roughly twenty men must have straggled from the main column, too drunk to keep the pace with the rest. *Four tents, five soldiers each.*

Snoring soon replaced the drunken hymns as they retreated for the night.

By their direction of travel, she deduced that they were heading to the Ottiva caves, not to their hideout in the mountains. Cautiously heading down to the campsite, taking care to avoid any dried brush or twigs, Anavi drew an arrow as she heard snores under the tree to her right. The guard had his arms wrapped around his body, trying to keep some of the heat inside. Nocking the arrow, she aimed and released. Not a sound escaped the guard as the arrow penetrated his skull. Another guard wandered out towards the horses. Whistling as he walked, he didn't hear the soft crunch of leaves under the feet of the killer swiftly moving in with sword in hand. Grabbing him from behind with an arm around his throat, Anavi pushed the sword into the man's back and through to the chest, severing his aorta. The cold steel slid out of his warm body, spilling his blood on the snowy mountainside.

Four ropes each. As fast as possible, she moved around the tents, cutting the ropes to send the tents crashing down on the soldiers. Sudden entanglement and confusion reigned; efficacious. Her sword hissed through the canvas, stabbing and slicing. This was a massacre. At the farthest tent, men were spilling out, looking for their attacker. In a trance of murderous rage, she didn't notice them approach as she hacked at the ones before her. *This is for all the hurt you have caused, the suffering you've wrought in this world.*

An arrow hissed past her, nicking her shoulder as it drove into a man about to bludgeon her with his mace. Snapping out of the trance, she turned and sliced through another soldier's scapula, half severing his arm. She kept low and swept the sword around, cutting another's feet cleanly off, sending him to the ground with a crash. Screams of horror filled the skies as pain languished in the air for a while longer.

Knives flew from her hand into a charging warrior's neck and chest just as another arrow flew past her, killing a soldier to her right. A man crashed out of the bushes and jumped on the back of a Desert Dog who was fighting to get to his short sword. With his arm wrapped around the soldier's thick neck, he wrenched his arms and a loud crack followed as the soldier slumped to the ground.

A war cry came from a soldier charging at Anavi, who was fending off a man swinging a piece of timber at her. A savage blow landed on the back of her head. Stars flashed before her eyes; her legs buckled under her weight. She stared up at the man towering over her and saw him raise his mace. Momentary panic rampaged through her before he fell on top of her, his eyes suddenly went wide and fearful, gurgling blood from the blade lanced through his throat.

The newcomer reached out his hand and helped Anavi to her feet. Her legs were unsteady, and she leaned on him to stabilise herself.

Ladriana moved out of the darkness to stand with them.

'Should've known it was you,' Anavi said as she peered at the cut on her arm, and continued, 'you still shoot like shit.'

Ladriana shrugged as she said, 'I suppose you can't have it all — looks *and* skill. I guess that's why you're such an excellent shot.'

Anavi laughed and walked over to the man screaming on the ground, bleeding out from the stumps of his legs. She looked down on him as he crawled, and said, 'Meet your family in hell, cur!' The sword sank into his back. She twisted it and ripped it out.

'I still prefer arrows, but the knives did their job,' Anavi said as she took off the vest and threw it to Lanik, then continued, 'There's two in those men over there.'

Bodies lay sprawled all around them, bleeding into the ground, the nature of humankind unveiled once more, showing the violence in our hearts.

Numb and blue, Anavi rubbed her hands together and blew into them as she said, 'Come on, let's burn them. We don't want animals getting a craving for human flesh. Then we need to find some shelter. I'm freezing.'

* * *

Dragging a piece of timber through the woods to their makeshift camp, Lanik thought of so many things he wanted to say to the two women in his life. He closed his eyes and saw Anavi stabbing through the tent, murdering those Desert Dogs in cold blood; it haunted him. *I want revenge just as much as she does, but not like that.* As he neared the cave they'd taken shelter in, he heard the women talking and decided not to intrude, staying quiet for a time.

'Magnus has gone back to Kobo to run the inn you know, crutches and all. He wants you by his side. I could see the hurt in his eyes when he realised you had left. Why don't you go to him?' Ladriana asked, as she lit the tinder shavings. Smoke hung in the camp, stinging their eyes for a while until the logs dried out enough to burn.

Anavi dabbed a piece of wet cloth to the back of her head to get rid of the clotted blood in her hair as she said, 'Maybe after this is done, I'll join him. But I can't stop now. For Magnus and young Grey Cloak, I need to end this.'

Ladriana smirked. 'I've been meaning to ask. Why do you call him Grey Cloak?'

A loud groan came from the mouth of the cave as Lanik pulled the log to the fire and set it down, lowering himself next to it. 'This should last us the night.'

Anavi loosened the ropes from the four rabbits she'd shot, spicing only three of them. The fire crackled, and as she pushed a stick through the rabbits, Lanik asked, 'Why four? Surely three is enough for us.'

She cut a piece from the fourth rabbit and walked to the cave-mouth as she said, 'Because I have a big, shy stalker.'

The two in the cave looked at each other quizzically from around the fire, enjoying the warmth and turning the rabbits over to send sizzles through the air. Ladriana glanced up as she heard the horses getting restless.

Anavi gently said to them without turning, 'Calm the horses, please, and don't make any sudden movements.' She tossed a piece of rabbit out of the cave, then moved stealthily towards the fire, placing small pieces of meat on the floor every few steps. Lanik stood by the horses, petting them, talking soothingly to calm them. An involuntary gasp escaped him when he saw the massive wolf hopping on three legs to enter the cave, the fourth bleeding slowly. A chill ran through his body as he met the beast's eyes and thought: *The comforting heat of the fire and the aroma of the meat must have coaxed it in.*

Without looking at Lanik, Anavi brought up her finger to show he must remain silent. The wolf moved closer, a low rumble in its throat as it neared the fire. On her feet, some distance away, Ladriana nocked an arrow and trained it on the wolf. Canines flashed as the wolf barked at her, a growl deep in its throat. Anavi quickly interjected, as she jumped between them. 'Don't even think about it, Elle.' Anavi stared intently into the eyes of the wolf and tore another piece off the rabbit, casting it to the beast.

Piece by piece, the rumbling softened as the wolf enjoyed his new-found companionship. Slow and steady, Lanik and Ladriana made their way closer to the heat once more. Afraid that any sound might set off the beast, they sat in silence, just watching the woman feed the animal over and over until at last only the bones of the rabbit remained. Anavi tossed the carcass to its feet, and said, 'Oi, you'd like a bone, wouldn't ya?'

The sounds of bones snapping under the force of its bites made Lanik and Ladriana even warier.

Watching Anavi laugh as she fed the wolf brought a lump to Lanik's throat. It was as if they'd been friends for years, with no fear between them. When it was done with the rabbit, the beast yawned and closed its eyes, licking the last bit of flavour from its lips.

In hushed tones, the two jumped at the opportunity, talking over each other. 'Are you crazy?'

Ladriana fell silent and let Lanik continue: 'That thing needs to go.'

Anavi stared at the beautiful animal, watching the rhythmic rise and fall of its chest as it breathed, sleeping peacefully. She sighed softly and said, 'I'm sorry you feel that way, but he's not going anywhere. Until I say otherwise, he's in my charge.'

* * *

Dust clouds puffed into the air as he slapped his chest and shoulders, his clothes chafing him all over as sand settled in every crevice. The Tergaron tundra was no Artorean desert, but it still got very dusty when the wind picked up to blow over the flat plains, and few places got as cold at night. Khanaseri looked at his surroundings and coughed as the dry air filled his lungs. The sun hung low over the horizon, preparing the day for the heat it would receive. It was dry, with little greenery in sight; a few scattered acacia trees stood nearby, giving the little shade they could for the wandering souls who needed it most. Under one such tree lay a few taktan — a small burrowing creature the size of a dog — enjoying the fresh air with its young cuddled up close.

Blanka hawked and spat as the dust swirled into his face. A *miserable place indeed*, he thought, as he patted his horse's neck. Having emerged a few miles back in a forest so green and rich with life, he couldn't believe his eyes as he stared at the vast, open plains before them, dotted with little else but shrubs.

Khanaseri turned around at the ghastly sounds of Blanka still spitting in the wind and said, 'It's going to be a long day. Sun's coming up.'

'What? It was setting when we went through the portal. Guess it makes sense, losing time as you go through the portals. Assuming that's what happened to me as I fell through the pit.' Finally ceasing his violent spitting, he looked up and saw the sun in all its glory as it rose.

'Aye. That tells you how far we've travelled, and why I feel so weak. I guess the farther you go, the more time goes by. In the dream-state training I did with Beuneth, she had me doing portal exercises for years before I attempted one for real. But in there, I had no real way to tell time, so I never noticed it. We'll rest tonight before we get to the tunnels. We have far to go today.'

Khanaseri peered at Blanka and said, 'I've been meaning to ask — how come you aged so much more than Beuneth? I assume this,' He pointed at Blanka from head to toe, then continued, 'is what you looked like before you went into the pit?'

Blanka's response was slow and thoughtful. 'Yes... When I bonded with Belgarr, we shared more than just a body. It is the complete package; we're intertwined with every fibre of our beings. So when they tore us apart, I believe we still shared some things between us. He took some of my youth and I took those abilities. Now that we're whole once more... Well, you get where I'm going with this.'

'I do,' Khanaseri said as he turned forward in his saddle.

They pushed their mounts over the plains and watched as big cats stalked them in the distance. An uneventful day passed while they were stuck in their heads, thinking of what was to come and what had already come to pass. Blanka thought back to his incarceration and eventual execution, wondering if he could have changed the outcome had he done something different. Wondering what he had put Beuneth through with his actions.

* * *

'I need twenty men to search the cave for the chest of gold. The rest of you can wait out here. Be merry, gentlemen; once we find that chest, we're officially rich!' Xylac raised his hands to the air and laughed as the cheers went up. 'Tonight, we eat the best meats and drink the best ale!' More cheers arose as he turned and headed for the cave mouth.

To no one in particular, Xylac spoke as he neared the entrance, 'I hate caves! Always so dark. I don't understand why that witch prefers living in one.' He gestured to one of his men to get a torch from the wall and light it as he moved deeper into the darkness. Thoughts of riches already ran wild in his head. He didn't care about their banishment anymore.

Xylac was already making plans to run away with the gold as his men slept off their drunkenness tonight.

* * *

'Looks like they haven't been here long,' Lanik said, passing the spyglass to Anavi.

'Yes. They seem to be just sitting around, waiting.'

Ladriana slapped herself on the back. 'Ouch! Fucking ants! How many are there?'

'How am I supposed to know that? Probably thousands?'

'Ha-ha, hilarious. You know I'm talking about the men down there.'

Lanik chuckled and said, 'Must be about half the remaining Desert Dogs — maybe twenty.'

'Hold on. Look over there. Who's that?'

Anavi peered through the spyglass and said, 'Never seen them before. A big bald guy with a beard and a smaller one; black hair and facial markings. Peculiar couple. Wait, they're dismounting now. Looks like the Desert Dogs are saying something to them. Like chasing them away or something. The big man is shaking his head and pointing at the cave. The smaller one has moved closer. Looks like they're shouting at each other now. More Desert Dogs are joining in. Trying to shove them away. Holy blistered balls!'

'What was that?' Lanik asked as he saw smoke rise in the distance.

Eyes wide, Anavi said, 'We have our distraction. The smaller one just shot a fireball through the air, taking out two men, and the big guy pulled a massive axe from his back and nearly chopped three men in half with one blow.'

Staring at each other, the silence grew before Lanik said, 'Okay. So best we try to avoid those two. Let's leave them to finish with those outside while we sneak in. Move.'

* * *

'Move *quietly*. Don't you two know anything about being stealthy?' Anavi rolled her eyes at Lanik and Ladriana as they made their way into the cave, darkness swallowing them as they crept deeper inside.

In hushed tones, Lanik said, 'In our defence, we never had to be sneaky. We went in and did our job, then left. Easy. No sneaking.'

'Shh. You'd make a terrible assassin.'

'Shut up, the both of you. I think someone is coming towards us from the mouth of the cave.'

They jumped to the right to hunker down behind a massive stalagmite as one of the Desert Dogs came running past, followed closely by a ball of fire that smacked into his back, hurling him to the ground engulfed in flames. More footsteps drew closer as a man walked by, his eyes ablaze with fire as he spoke to the hulking man with the axe behind him, 'I feel the Dragovian blood burning hot in my veins today.'

Their voices trailed away as they heard the big man answer, 'Aye, I can see it in your eyes. Do not let it consume you...'

Lanik wiped the sweat from his forehead and whispered, 'I think it's safer if we trail them.' The others nodded their agreement and the three set off once more, following the trail of carnage to the vast open hall that surrounded the pit. Glow-worms lined the ceiling of the cave with their magnificent display of glittering blue and green luminescence. A strangled voice pleaded from the right as a man clutched at his throat, trying to breathe through his crushed windpipe. Anavi jumped over him and said, 'They'd better not get to Xylac before I do.'

'We.'

'Fine. We.'

They peered out from around the corner to see the two men walk into the hall, and heard the shorter one say, 'Where is she?'

Xylac stood up from the back as he rummaged through Beuneth's belongings, overturning everything to find the gold, and sauntered over to the two intruders. He sucked something out from between his teeth, and said, 'Now, who do we have here?'

Again, they heard the smaller man's voice, filled with anger, as he repeated, '*Where is she?*'

'Where is who? Your mother? Not too sure. I left her a thank-you card, though.'

The headbutt came suddenly, and Xylac staggered back as blood gushed from his nose. He shouted, 'Get them!'

All the Dogs rushed at the two intruders while Xylac jumped out of their reach.

Keeping to the dark, the three had moved closer to get to Xylac when the big man threw a Desert Dog on top of Anavi, taking her to the ground with him. More of the Desert Dogs noticed them and rushed at them. Arrows flew from Ladriana's bow, skewering a Dog about to stab the big man in the back.

Khanaseri turned and saw the man lying on the floor, then looked up and saw Ladriana holding the bow, and nodded his thanks.

In a blur of motion, knives flashed from Lanik's vest, slicing into a Desert Dog's throat and chest. He spun around and narrowly evaded a sword thrust as Anavi tripped the man and jumped on him as soon as he hit the ground.

Scales formed over Blanka as he doubled in size, talons flashing on the ends of his fingers as he ripped open a man's chest; then jumped to another on his right, dropping the corpse behind him.

Lanik saw Xylac running for the exit and sent a knife flashing through the air. A dull thud sounded as the blade sank into his target's left thigh, hitting the bone. He smirked as he heard the scream from the now limping Xylac. Leaving the violent fray behind him, he slowly followed Xylac out of the chamber and rounded the corner from the crude hall. He watched his old Kremagshi from the back; the wiry frame of the man buckled beneath the pain of the blade in his leg.

Lanik said, 'I've waited for this day for most of my life.'

Xylac glanced back and hopped as fast as he could and said, 'What did I ever do to you? I took you in and gave you a seat at my table. I taught you everything! This betrayal is unwarranted!'

'No. It is very warranted. I let you train me. I let you teach me your crooked ways. I let you groom me, all so this betrayal could be more devastating.'

'But why?! I cared for you like a son!'

You took everything from me! You murdered my entire family in cold blood!

Another knife flashed through the air, slicing deep into Xylac's shoulder, sending him to the ground. Painfully, he pushed himself up from the rocky floor and hopped on again. 'What are you talking about? You came to me with no family!'

'Exactly!'

Another knife flashed out, sinking into Xylac's other arm.

Lanik dragged another knife from his vest and said, 'Nearly the entire royal line of New Runswick was murdered by your assassins twenty-two years ago. Do you even remember that? I only survived that night because of your men's laziness.' The knife flashed out. Xylac doubled over with the knife stuck in his back.

Crawling over the rocks now, Xylac could see the sunlight in the distance. 'I'm sorry, Lanik! It was just business! Nothing personal!'

Another voice echoed from close by: 'And what about the man your Dogs tortured in New Runswick? Was that business too?' Anavi appeared from the shadows and climbed on top of Xylac's back as he crawled, drawing her knife over his throat, not waiting for a reply. She dropped his head to the floor and let him bleed out, then spat on his back as she walked away and said, 'It's done. Let's go.'

Retrieving his knives from the corpse, Lanik said, 'Yes, let's get Ladriana and get out of here.' The walk back to the hall was silent, barring the brief scream from the last Desert Dog as Ladriana sent an arrow into his chest.

Blanka walked up to her as she lowered her bow and said, 'Thank you, but who are you?'

'We had some unfinished business with this group of thugs.'

Lanik interjected, 'And now that it's done, we'll be on our way.'

The air suddenly grew cold, the walls of the hall freezing over as a portal opened. Stepping out, Beuneth closed the portal and turned to regard them.

Shock registered on Ladriana's face as she saw the woman who had nearly killed her standing a few feet away. She pulled an arrow from her quiver and loosed it. Khanaseri, Blanka, Lanik, and Anavi were all slow to react, all wanting to jump in and do something — but none knew exactly what that was.

'Stop!' Bringing back childhood memories, Beuneth stared at the pendulous arrow in front of her face and looked around her.

Frozen stiff, Ladriana moved her eyes to follow Beuneth as she walked up to Blanka and Khanaseri to lay her hands on them. She saw them relax as they came out of the spell, moving their muscles to ease the tension, and the big man said, 'What was that? How does she know you?'

'Oh, that's a long story. Don't do her any harm, though, she's been through enough.' Beuneth looked over at Lanik and Anavi. 'We'd better get a move on. The spell won't last forever.'

Not having had a chance yet, his heart about to explode with joy, Blanka looked at Beuneth with a smile on his face and said, 'Beany.'

Shocked, she only now looked back at him and saw the change in his appearance. 'I haven't heard that name in years. Blanka? Are you truly whole again?'

Blanka embraced her and lifted her into the air as he said, 'Yes. Yes, I am!'

Khanaseri cleared his throat and said, 'Sorry to interrupt the reunion, but they *are* starting to move. So best get on with it.'

'Oh, no. What did they do to you?' Beuneth asked as she pulled away from their embrace and stared at the big man.

'I'm fine, Beuneth. Someone got the better of me, but I survived.'

'Come with us, Khan,' she said as she reached out to him.

'My home is here, and I need to account for the man I killed in the gaol. I can't run forever.' He sighed as he looked at them and continued, 'Hopefully one day, we'll meet again.'

She nodded and took Blanka's hand as she held her knife and said, 'I need to do this so you don't age as we travel through the portal.' Beuneth cut an archaic symbol in his hand and quickly covered it with hers as she muttered a few unrecognisable words. A warm glow emanated from her hand, and soon the cut was just a scar. 'Are you ready?'

Blanka immediately turned to Khanaseri and said with a smile, 'I was right about the ageing,' then winked as he turned back to her. 'Yes, I am. I just want to say goodbye to this big oaf, then we can go.' Blanka embraced the man before he could say anything, holding him tight. 'Thank you for making me whole again, my friend.'

They walked over to the pit and jumped, vanishing into the darkness as they fell.

Khanaseri stared down after them and whispered, 'Take care,' then turned to exit the cave, leaving the other three still frozen where they stood.

Chapter Thirteen

Merchants shouted their wares to the public as people perused the stands for bargains, the streets buzzing and crowded. Laughter sounded as a mime mimicked the actions of some passers-by. Others were sitting on the short wall surrounding the great pit in the middle of the square, enjoying the festivities and entertainment, when Beuneth and Blanka came flying out of the pit and into a large man as he waddled through the stalls. Like bowling pins, people succumbed to the weight and force of the rolling fat man, and flopped down onto the ground as he rolled into them. Their outraged shouts followed his eventual stop as he struck the rickety frame of one of the stalls, causing it to collapse. The straw roof neatly covered the fat man as he lay sprawled, ragged breaths escaping him in quick succession before he shouted to the merchant, 'Help me up, you tit!'

Blanka and Beuneth rose from the ground, dusted themselves off, and tried to blend in with the crowd as people shouted, 'Who was that! What just happened?' They weaved through the excited mob and left the square before someone took too much notice of them, even as guards ran into the square to investigate the disturbance.

'In here! Quick,' Blanka said as he pushed Beuneth down an alleyway.

Out of the bustling streets, they finally stood alone. Beuneth burst out laughing as she looked at him and said, 'Oh, that was fun. I've missed getting into trouble with you.'

He smiled and leaned in to press her against the wall, then kissed her. 'Where are we going next?' Blanka asked as he pulled back.

'I thought we could go pay a visit to Mother. I think it's time we had our last talk.'

'Beany, please. Let's just leave that life behind us.'

'We made a promise to free the rest of the children in her care. Let's fulfil that.'

His shoulders drooped, and he sighed as he said, 'Fine, but after that, we're done with that life.'

A prickle in her head made her shiver as a voice reached out, causing her to stumble into his arms. Blanka grabbed her and asked, 'Are you okay?'

Her head was spinning, thoughts running amok as she righted herself. 'Yeah, I think so.' *Gatekeeper!* A bombardment of voices filled her head, unrecognisable as they screamed over each other. The only word she could make out was *Gatekeeper!* As if she'd walked into an invisible wall, Beuneth fell backwards, clawing at the air until she hit the cobbled path. Slowly, the voices faded.

'Beany?!'

'I'm fine, really,' she said as she pushed Blanka's arm away and got back to her feet.

Concerned for her well-being, he made a mental note to bring up the occurrence later. He knew her strong-willed nature would only cause a fight, and right now, that would attract attention they didn't need. Resigned to defeat, he said, 'Let's go, then.'

* * *

Winds rushed up the cliff side, his body buffeted as the powerful currents pushed him back. Ganda'har turned to see Talgar edge closer to the drop, nervously glancing over as he said, 'You were looking for me, Captain?'

The captain turned back and looked over the area. The sheer drop of the cliff reached far down before the majestic trees of the forests jutted out to be seen swaying on the winds. To the right, a little way past the forest, were the gigantic walls of the city, stretching far and wide, encasing it in their protective bosom.

'What do you think that is to the left there?' Ganda'har pointed to a vast structure rising out of the mountaintop. He shouted, 'Stilts! Get over here.'

'Yessir!'

Talgar scratched his beard. 'I don't know, Captain. But our way back is in that city. Isn't that right, Stilts?'

The young warlock stood for a moment in silence before he said, 'Yes, our way home is definitely in that city.'

Ganda'har curled his upper lip in disdain at the warlock as he said, 'We're going north to that structure in the mountains. You have your pull, warlock; I have mine. Talgar, let the men know my decision. Get them ready.'

'Yes, sir,' Talgar said as he turned and left to give the orders to the men.

Stilts found himself unable to walk away, and instead asked, 'Why do you hate me so?'

Utter annoyance immediately had its hands around Ganda'har's throat, the irritation startling even to himself. He looked down at the pale warlock and said, 'I don't hate you, Stilts. You just remind me of Galvos, except infinitely more pathetic; like if he were a babe, still suckling from his mother's tit. You're infantile.'

Stilts shook his head, then turned to leave and suddenly shouted, 'Who are you?!'

At the outburst, men near him whirled around, staring at the boy sitting on a rock a few feet away. The boy laughed and said, 'You lot would make for easy pickings. Been here so long I got bored. Not very attentive, you. Name's Scallywag, or that's what Mother used to call me.'

With a raised brow, Ganda'har signalled Untara with his eyes. In a flash, the boy hung in the air, shouting his outrage at the big man. 'Hey, put me down, you fat freak!'

'Permission to throw this scrawny little shit off the cliff, Captain?'

'No, just shake it to see what falls out. I think this here is a little thief.'

Small fists landed blows on the big man's arms. 'I stole nothing from you!'

'But you *are* a thief?' Ganda'har inquired as he approached the hanging boy.

'I'm whatever I want to be! I'll tell you about that structure you so dearly want to go to. All I want is the mage's sword.'

Ganda'har saw the stares from the nearby men. 'A cheeky little bastard, isn't he? Where are you from, boy?'

'We live in the mountain.'

'Stilts, your sword,' Ganda'har said, with his arm extended to the warlock. Then he continued, 'I'll let you go on two conditions. One, you tell me about that place, and two, you tell me how to get into the city unseen.'

The warlock had unsheathed his sword, but clutched it as he whispered to Ganda'har, 'Sir, this weapon has been magically altered. It's not just any sword. Not to mention it's a family heirloom. You can't—'

'Did I ask for your opinion? Now hand the scrawny lad your sword and step back.' An icy stare from the dark brown eyes of the captain accompanied his words.

'Yes sir.'

* * *

'The forest seems just like I remember it. As if nothing has changed.' Blanka picked up a little rock and tossed it into the bush as he said, 'I've been meaning to ask. Why did you live in that cave? You hated living in the cave here.'

Beuneth fell silent as another amalgamation of voices suddenly filled her head, drowning out her thoughts. She could feel her legs buckle beneath her and composed herself as Blanka steadied her with his hands, a concerned look on his face. She looked around and saw they were close to the entrance of the cave. 'Oh look, we're here. Don't worry. I just need to eat something.' They walked out of the forest and she gasped. 'Wow! This is new.'

A big, newly built home had been erected to cover the entrance of the cave. The high-towered building stood proud above the outer walls, with windows lining the front. She walked up to the dark wooden door and knocked as she peered through the windows.

'Looks like the only way into the cave is through the house,' Blanka said as he moved around to the side. They could hear footsteps coming down the stairs, the wooden floors creaking with each footfall. The latch to the door fell away and swung open to reveal Sister Preda standing in the doorway. 'Well, well, Beuneth and Blanka. Ever the pair. I did not expect to ever see you again.'

'Spare me the talk, Sister. We're here for Mother,' Beuneth said as she pushed open the door and moved into the house, shoving the sister against the wall with some force. The contempt in her voice was clear as she shouted, 'Vandalor! Come out, you cowering old crone!'

'Things have changed here, Beuneth. Vandalor is no longer with us.' Finally recovered from the shove, Sister Preda calmly closed the door and turned to them.

Children came out of their rooms, standing on the stairs, watching to see what the commotion was about. Blanka was looking around at all the unfamiliar faces when one called out from the top. 'Beany! Blanka! Is that really you guys?'

A toned man wearing no shirt made his way down the stairs and embraced the two, picking them up one at a time as he said, 'It's so good to see you. I thought you were dead.'

Back down on the ground, Blanka looked at the man and said, 'Setha? It's good to see you, too. What happened here?'

Setha gestured to them to follow him outside, and said, 'It's okay, Sister, I'll talk to them.'

Birds chirped in the trees, the leaves rustling in the wind as they walked through the forest. Setha looked around as he walked ahead of them and said, 'Things have changed completely. For one, I run the orphanage now. We still have our underground business, of course, but it's now completely voluntary. And we actually help the kids who come our way. Give them a home, food. In return, they help out around the house.'

Beuneth swatted a fly away from her face as she said, 'That's great, but what happened to Vandalor? I was looking forward to having a good old-fashioned punch-up with her.'

Setha released a deep sigh as he stopped and turned to them. 'I know you were, Beany. Look around you. I brought you here for a reason.'

Everywhere around them, the trees were flattened, no undergrowth visible, with black, charred rocks starting from the centre of the clearing and spreading out, the char fading as it did. The ground and rocks were marred with deep scars. Branches from the still-standing trees on the edges of the clearing were torn off, looking maimed.

'I know you hated her, Beuneth. And for a very long time, so did I. But after she died fighting to free you from that place, my hatred for her faded away.'

Blanka moved closer as Beuneth said, 'She did what?'

'Yeah, shocking, I know. She stood right there,' Setha smiled as he pointed to the blackened stone and continued, 'and took on Caryk for your freedom. Almost had him, too. It was a night of thunder, lightning, and ravenous fire. She rained down hell upon him. But in the end, she was getting old and slow. We watched from the mountain as he flew up and melted her bones to the ground. There was nothing left but ash.'

Silent and despondent, Beuneth sat down on one of the charred rocks. Blanka scratched his chin as he said, 'So...could we stay at the house for a couple of days? We just got back and don't have a place yet.'

'I thought you'd never ask.'

'She *died* for me?' Beuneth asked, pulling their attention back to her, then continued, 'After everything I said and did to her, she went and died for me?'

'Mother had her way of showing love, Beany. It just wasn't what we expected,' Setha said as he sat down next to her. 'Come, let me show you your rooms and the house. I'm sure the kids would love to meet you two. I've often spoken about my old friends. Most of the older children left us after Mother's passing.'

* * *

Hunted to the very ends of the earth, the Dragon Wars saw to the extinction of the beasts. When captured, they were placed in the magical spheres known as the Balamuths, to serve mankind when called upon, doomed to an eternity of imprisonment and servitude.

Beuneth crossed the bridge as it floated in the clouds, attached to nothing but air, watching a colossal dragon rise above the cloudscape to hover before her. Its eyes locked on to hers as it spoke. 'Gatekeeper! You will bear witness to what this imprisonment is doing to our kind.'

A rush of wind pushed against her face as she suddenly fell, the bridge having vanished in the blink of an eye. She screamed as a sphere rushed ever closer at a terrible speed. Not sure if the sphere was growing or if she were shrinking, Beuneth closed her eyes as she fell into the swirling mass.

'Open your eyes, child.' The deep, guttural voice of the dragon was so close she could feel the heat from its mouth warming her stomach.

'Who are you?' Beuneth asked as she stared at the red dragon, his right eye dim, a scar running through from the top down.

'I am Ormarr. Look upon this ravaged world we now call our home.'

Beuneth stared out over the wasteland – a world of stone. No greenery, no water, no life, just stone as far as the eye could see. 'What do you want from me?'

The great red dragon turned his face away as they stood on the mountain overlooking the world. His rumbling voice shook the earth, shifting the mounds beneath her feet as he said, 'Look at my kin beneath you, Gatekeeper. You stand on the bones of a thousand dragons.'

Only then did it sink in that the mountain was not made of rock or sand. She gasped as she precariously shuffled her feet on what might be a rib, mixed in with various other bones from other dead dragons, blackened by time and the intense heat of the world. An uncontained tear rolled down the side of her face, and she felt the pain of the magnificent beast before her.

'Why do you think there is so little magic left in the world? Why so few can still perform it? Without us, it does not exist. And we are dying out. You are the key to our freedom, to our survival. Never has there been an Ageian Gatekeeper with your power. And when you bind with me, we can finally free my kin. I will be the willing sacrifice.'

Her lungs burned from the dry air as she breathed vigorously and said, 'This is a lot to take in. I thought I would be more afraid in your presence.'

Gills on the side of his neck reverberated, shaking as he breathed. 'You know this to be a dream, though. Gatekeeper, we haven't been with our kind in a thousand years. We will not survive the next thousand.'

'The voices in my head?'

'Yes. The price you pay for being the Gatekeeper; hearing all our pleas. Reliving our pain, over and over.'

Beuneth cocked her head as she said, 'In all honesty, I became the Gatekeeper because I wanted to destroy all the Balamuths. Never did I realise you were still alive in there, that you could ever be freed from this prison. I will do my part, Great One.'

The dragon bowed his head at her and took to the sky, winds buffeting her frame as he lifted higher. The image of him flying away slowly faded to darkness.

Her eyes blinked rapidly as she woke, then smiled as she realised she lay next to Blanka, and listened to the sounds of his snores filling the room. In small, incremental movements, she got up from the bed and tiptoed around the room to get her clothes and chain whip. Glancing back at Blanka, she sighed as she closed the door. Carefully placing each step, she headed downstairs and stood in the lounge area. A portal burst open before her as voices streamed into her thoughts to consume her mind. She fended off the onslaught to her sanity and stepped through the portal to vanish from the room as it closed.

* * *

Why did I begin this journey again? Oh yes, at the behest of the king... For his entitled arse to gain more power. Snivelling sack of putrid swine. Good men and women have died for this. Ganda'har drew the animal pelt tighter around him as the freezing winds blew through to the bone. Step by agonising step, they climbed up the mountain, fighting the belligerence of the weather. Back down the column of soldiers, a man slipped and fell on his face, sliding down the mountain somewhat before grabbing hold of a vine sticking out of the ground. His fellow soldiers could only watch and shout at him to grab something to stay his fall. Their relief made clear as their eyes relaxed upon his crawling return to them. It would be a most undesirable end if one were to fall down the side of the mountain. Ganda'har looked back at his soldiers and breathed deeply, nearly losing his footing in the thin air, and said, 'Fight the sleep, men, and watch your footing. It's a treacherous affair.'

The sun doused its rays as it disappeared over the mountain ridge, making the biting cold much more unbearable as they trudged through the snow under the guidance of the full moon. A bestial roar sounded through the mountain, echoing as the soldiers tried to place the origin.

'Shit! Head for the ridge; run!' came the shouts from a soldier at the back. Gathering their reserved energy, they ran up the mountain as branches broke at their backs. A desperate cry sounded as the soldier's foot caught on some rocks and sent him tumbling on the ground. He looked up and saw behind them a white-furred creature in the dark — at least twice his height, with huge tusks protruding from its mouth — crash through the tree line and charge them with an apish roar. The ape picked the man up by the legs and hurled him over the edge of the mountain. His screams disappeared in the fog as he fell.

Arrows sailed through the sky to slice into the big ape's chest, barely penetrating its thick hide. But it definitely stung as the creature retreated to the forest, its chest fur matted with blood. They wasted no time waiting around, instead hurrying further up the mountain as fast as they could.

Every so often, they would glimpse the creature in the tree line, never straying far away. 'Keep your eyes peeled, men!' Talgar shouted as he kept watch on the trees to their right.

A long, narrow bridge of ice connected the path over a steep drop-off from the snakelike mountain range, too narrow for even a horse. Slowly edging over, step-by-step, they made their way across. Some men stood with arrows nocked, scanning the tree lines for any signs of the creature as they waited for their turns to cross.

The pathway up the mountain became very narrow, with a steep cliff face to their left that sent blocks of ice crashing down every so often onto their path. Not much lived this high up the mountain, except maybe a few crazed mountain goats and a snow leopard stalking them in the distance. *To venture a guess, I don't think even that ape journeys this high up.* Ganda'har looked at a mountain goat as it scaled the rocks, thinking how effortless it made it look. *It doesn't even have hands. How do they do it?*

Finally, as they reached the peak, Ganda'har saw on the spine of the serpentine mountain ridge a walkway only three feet wide. At the very end of the range, in the distance, was the vault of the Balamuths.

'Quiet!' The militant discipline of the soldiers immediately took effect as the conversations died abruptly. All items that could make noise or rattled in their packs were suddenly muffled. Talgar had his hand in the air, and said, 'Listen. Captain, I hear screaming.'

Tobacco sailed out of the captain's mouth as he spat down the side of the mountain. 'That makes it a good time for us to drop in unannounced, then. Either way, we'll have an ally.'

* * *

Beuneth placed the blood-slicked chain whip back on her hip, her hands trembling from adrenalin as she pushed on the door to the great hall, which was at least ten times the height of a man. She leaned into the door as she thought back to the night of their capture, pushing as hard as she could. Her muscles ached and trembled from exhaustion; her skin was numb to the touch. The climb up the mountain was harder than she remembered; the cold tore through her body to the bone. More men were approaching. She could hear them running into the fort behind her, then the screech and clang of metal on metal sounded. Screams erupted as the fighting behind her intensified. But she didn't care about that. Her goal was in front of her, not whoever was behind her. Slowly, the door creaked open and gave way as the wind pushed from the back. A blast of snow streamed into the hall as she turned to close the door. The dull wooden thud echoed as the massive door slammed shut.

Lanterns hung on the walls, fires burning brightly from each, heating and lighting the hall. She slid down on her backside and panted as she took in the warmth, waiting for her muscles to thaw. A long corridor of stone and mortar, devoid of any furniture and ornaments, with a lone steel door in the centre of what looked to be the end of the hall, was all that she could see.

'Come out, Torga!'

Her hands ached as she pushed herself up from the floor, leaving a small smear of blood behind. She walked to the massive steel door, listening to her footsteps as they echoed through the hall and ran her hand over the cold metal standing flush with the walls. No visible handles existed, no way to grab and pull on it.

A voice echoed from the right. 'How did *you* become Gatekeeper?' It suddenly changed, becoming ancient and deep. 'How are you even alive?'

'Ah, Knucker, so you *can* see me,' she said as Torga moved out of the shadows, his eyes glowing red.

Smoke trailed from Torga's nostrils as Knucker spoke through him. 'What is it you want, Gatekeeper?'

She let out a soft curse, then shouted, 'I'm not here to *get* anything. I'm here to free all your kin, Knucker! We don't have to fight.'

Torga drew his sword as he said, 'We will never allow that!'

A ferocious growl came from Torga as he charged and brought his sword down on Beuneth. She dived to the left and spun her chain whip to both sides with ease, parrying the blade before it got near, the whirl of the chain a blur before her eyes.

Lightning erupted from her hands, scorching the marbled floor before hitting Torga in the chest. The thick bolt coursed through him, driving him back and to his knees. His shirt fell away in charred tatters, his chest a charcoaled piece of meat. Contemptuous laughter rang out as he threw his sword to the ground; the black around his chest scaled and spread out as he veered into the massive dragon. Knucker stood on his hind legs, glaring at her with huge, bestial eyes as he scraped his bull-like horns against the walls. Deafening screeches sounded as he sharpened them.

A creak sounded at the entrance of the hall as the door swung open and soldiers streamed in. Ganda'har watched as the black dragon spewed fire over the woman cowering behind a shield of magic before it and shouted at his men, 'Stay back! This is my fight!' Confused by the statement, his men wanted to follow at first, then stood back as he shouted again, 'No! Trust me!'

Ganda'har rushed in and veered into a massive red dragon as he saw Beuneth collapse soon after the flames died down. Caught by surprise, Knucker backed away quickly as Ganda'har crashed into him, driving the talons on the ends of his wings into Knucker's sides. The hall shook as the two beasts collided with the wall on the far side.

Knucker roared in anger and pain as he fought off the massive, snapping fangs aimed at his face. With a shake of the head, he pushed one of his horns into the chest of the attacking dragon. Blood sprayed to the ground as he ripped it out, only to stab it into Ganda'har's arms.

Ganda'har set the room alight as he fell back, the gills on his neck vibrating as the flames funnelled through his throat to scorch Knucker's face, arm, and wing as he shielded himself. Talons ripped into Ganda'har's midsection while Knucker kicked with his legs and flung him across the room. One of Ganda'har's wings folded under him as he got to his feet and saw that Knucker's left eyeball had popped from the heat; half-blinded, the dragon thrashed about in anger. A bloody tongue hissed out as Knucker said, 'You will die here today. If not by my hands, then by my brothers'.'

Ganda'har gauged Knucker and paced a distance away, lips trembling, showing fangs as the dragon roared, 'Ingrate! Let her free our kin!'

Both charged. Ganda'har swooped his spiked tail from the right, driving it deep into Knucker's chest. A piercing cry sounded through the hall as Knucker staggered back, ripping the spikes from his flesh. Blood sprayed from the wound. Ganda'har was quickly on top of him, biting down into the wound and ripping out chunks of meat. As Knucker's body fell to the ground, Ganda'har roared to the sky and pulled the heart from Knucker's chest with his fangs — then swallowed it.

From the corner of the hall, his men all squirmed in disgust as he veered back and walked up to them, his mouth slick with dragon blood. A wide-eyed soldier at the back dropped his pack and ran for the door, leaning against its weight to open it. Untara shouted to the man, 'You have to pull, not push, you daft dimwit!'

The soldiers demanded answers and raised their weapons as they shouted their concerns. 'Who are you? What have you done with our captain?'

Talgar threw the captain a rag and said, 'Clean yourself up, sir. You're frightening the men.'

Ganda'har caught the rag and wiped his mouth as he said, 'You're not afraid of me?'

'Seeing what you became back there, I believe that if you wanted to kill us, you could have already. So I have to believe that you're you.'

'I see you had a hearty meal there, Cap'n,' Untara said, furrowing his brow as he looked over at the men and women surrounding them, then continued, 'Uhm, not that it's any of our business, but how did you become that thing?'

Fear of the unknown is an interesting emotion. Through battles and wars they had always fought side by side, and now, suddenly, they backed away as the captain neared.

'It was back in the mountain when you thought I was hallucinating. I was, in fact, bonding with this creature.' Ganda'har saw the fear in some of their eyes as he looked at the men, and said, 'I'm still myself, just stronger. And now that we've seen what's out there, we have a better chance of getting back home with me like this. Oh yeah — Untara, that was a terrible joke. Go fetch that moron you helped get out of the hall before he lets the entire world know we're here.'

'I thought it was pretty good.'

'No. It wasn't,' Talgar said as he slapped the big man on the back.

His men relaxed as he turned and walked to where the woman sat, leaning against the wall. Her breathing was ragged as she clutched her chest and stared at the soldiers in the distance. Ganda'har tossed her a water canister, and said, 'Who are you exactly, Gatekeeper?'

Cool water ran down her throat, staving the burn she'd felt earlier. Eyes closed, she said nothing. Using the wall to push herself off the floor, she walked towards the vault door and said, 'I'm here to free them. The dragons. They're all dying in there.'

With his beard all slick with sweat, he worked his fingers through the knotted hairs and continued, 'Yeah, I heard you the first time. I guess we can help with that, if you can help us get out of this place.'

Exhausted and pained, Beuneth turned to him as she stood in front of the door and said, 'You mean your bonded heard me? You don't remember me, do you, Captain?'

'There's something about you, yes, but I can't place my finger on where I saw you last.'

'I'm the servant girl you took along to Artorea after the battle with King Madock.'

Eyes wide, Ganda'har gasped as he said, 'I thought I knew you! You're no servant girl!' His sword hissed from his scabbard as he shouted, 'How do you fit into all this mess!? Speak! Did you kill Galvos? Where is Khanaseri?' Adrenalin surged through his body, making his muscles jump as he stared at her.

Backing up slowly with her hands up in surrender, Beuneth said, 'Calm down, Captain. Remember, you falsely accused me once before when I helped Galvos in the back of the wagon. I was the one who stitched him up and saved him, made it possible for him to reach Artorea in the first place. I would not have killed him. And yes, I helped Khanaseri escape and taught him how to use his gifts.'

'Where is he, then!?' the captain shouted as he saw his men converge around her, making ready to attack.

Beuneth followed his gaze, keeping an eye on the surrounding men, and said, 'He's not here in this time. We parted ways a few days back after he helped me get what I needed to return home. Last I heard, he was heading back to Artorea to atone for his killing of the guard during the breakout. You might help him still if you hurry back. What I want to know is how you ended up in this time, Captain.'

Ganda'har gestured to his men not to attack and said, 'We were following Khanaseri to bring him back to the city, and our warlock, Stilts, tried to reopen the portal Khanaseri generated to wherever he went, but instead, we ended up here. Nearly killed Stilts to open that damn portal. We thought someone, like you, had tampered with it.'

She dropped her hands to her sides as she cocked her head and said, 'No, but I used his portal energy to come back the same way as he went. I believe my imprint on the portal might have been what brought you here, and not to Khanaseri. May I say — Stilts, was it? Very impressive, opening that portal to this side. Most would have been killed instantly.'

The warlock nodded his thanks and said, 'Aye, sir. She speaks true. It's very possible her unintentional influence on the portal could have been the reason we ended up here.'

Ganda'har sheathed his sword. 'Can—'

'Can't be too careful nowadays, I know, Captain,' Beuneth said as she interrupted him. She drew near as she saw him relax. 'I'll tell you how to get home.'

The captain greased his hair back as he said, 'Stand down, men.'

'Trust that what I'm about to say is the truth, no matter how crazy it sounds. You need to make your way through to the city square. There you will find a great pit. It should be unguarded, as they do not know of its power. If you jump into the great pit, you will be transported through time back whence you came. But I'll need to perform a ritual with all of you, unless you want the pit to steal years of your life. So, if you help me carry all these Balamuths out of the vault, I'll help you get back home.'

Over his shoulder, he shouted, 'Form a line to the door, men!'

She touched the great metal door and cleared her head as she said, 'I am the Gatekeeper. Open to me.' With an ungracious give, the steel doors slid open, grinding on the stone floor as a screeching noise echoed throughout the hall. She stepped through the gap and saw the plethora of Balamuths, lying in wait for their vessels. Ganda'har gasped as he looked upon them, and could for the moment not believe what he saw.

'I have come for you, Ormarr! The time has come for dragons to roam free once more.'

Far up in a distant corner, a Balamuth lifted from its shelf, floating towards the door. The sphere hovered above her, pitch black, the darkness stretching beyond this world. In her head, she heard the Dragovian voice speak. 'I am ready.'

* * *

With a quick look and a beckoning with his head, Ganda'har gestured Geolas over to him as the bonding took place before him. Beuneth was hunched over in pain as the dragon seized its vessel. A quick jog, and Geolas stood next to his captain and said, 'I don't know if we should trust her, sir.'

Not taking his eyes off Beuneth, the captain stood with arms folded and whispered, 'Yeah. Me too, Geolas. I need you to take a couple of men you trust to be good at stealing and not getting caught.'

'Oh sir, we do not—'

'Spare me the mendacity, soldier. Take those men and ensure we get at least ten of these Balamuths. Make sure they don't stick around here. We'll meet them farther down the mountain on the way to the city.

Now get back to work before she suspects something.'

'Yes, sir.'

They had formed a long line, each standing just far enough apart to pass the Balamuths to the next person, all the way to the courtyard and outside to the gates, where they spread the Balamuths apart. From a distance away, one of his soldiers screamed as he dropped to the ground, still clutching a Balamuth with his bare hands. Soldiers surrounding the man gripped the Balamuth with their gloves as it tried to seep into the veins of the man. Scars appeared on the soldier's arms, like those of talons ripping into him, grabbing hold of its prey. A train of soldiers pulled on the sphere with all their might, slowly getting it to release its grip on the man.

The soldiers all hit the ground as the Balamuth came away to roll on the ground until it stopped. Stilts ran up to the man and placed his hands over the wounds, chanting until the blood stopped flowing from the tears in the soldier's arms as a thin layer of skin formed over them and blood trickled out of Stilts' nose.

Ganda'har pulled him away and shouted, 'That's enough! He'll survive.' He looked back at the soldier on the ground. 'Felter! I told you to wear gloves, you imbecile!'

'Aye, sir, but my gloves are ruined,' the short, stubby man said as he slowly got back to his feet to re-join the men. He looked to Stilts and nodded. 'Thank you, warlock.'

'Felter, you can't join the men. Go to the vault and see what you can find in there that we can use for our trip back home.'

'Aye, Captain!'

* * *

'Captain, I would like your squad warlock up front with me. Just in case some of them harbour a grudge and try to burn us alive,' Beuneth said as she stood outside the hall, looking over the multitude of spheres in the courtyard and outside the gates of the vault, aligned in neat rows spaced as far apart as the area would allow. She covered her eyes as she looked at the sun slowly making its way over the mountain ridge, the early morning air crisp, yet warmer than the day before.

The pale warlock was making his way past the men when Ganda'har grabbed his arms and whispered, 'Is this a good idea, letting all these dragons free?'

'I had my doubts as well, sir, but from the conversation I had with her, it makes sense. This might have been the tipping point for magic at one stage. I believe this could benefit us in the future, but I'm no soothsayer, sir.'

I really hope this is the right thing to do, Beuneth thought. All the stress and tension in her body made her muscles tight. Deep breaths escaped her as she stretched her limbs and closed her eyes, then said, 'Mage, be prepared for some fire. If they turn on us, we need to shield everyone from the heat.'

Arms raised to the sky, a Dragovian voice roared out of Beuneth. Ganda'har jerked his head around, shocked that he understood her words.

'All dragons hear my voice! For the first time in a thousand years, we finally have the key to release us from these prisons. These men and women have fought for our freedom, lest we forget their sacrifices for our gain. As the Dragovian Gatekeeper, I release you from your prisons!'

An exponentially growing white light emanated from her, growing fiercer as time passed, until a shock wave left her body and rippled across the Balamuths, cracking their exterior shells as light poured from each. One after another, the spheres lifted to the sky and exploded, expelling the dragons to their freedom. Massive scaled bodies clambered over each other as they tried to escape in haste, flames billowing up every so often. A few times, the flames got close to the soldiers, hitting the shield wall created by Stilts.

One can never be too cautious; that's what father always said. Stilts channelled magic through himself to protect every soldier in harm's way, waiting in anticipation for the next blast of flames to hit them, to be attacked out of pure, misplaced anger.

Beuneth burst out laughing, raising her hands up to the sky as she celebrated her victory. One and all, the soldiers slowly joined in with the celebration, knowing full well their time to go home had come to pass.

* * *

No, this can't be happening! This shouldn't be possible! No one has the power to do this. Not only having a dragon bonded with you, but to also have all that magic coursing through your body and a Gatekeeper's soul thrown in the mix? That should tear you apart!

'I cannot say that I am unhappy about this, Caryk,' Uldronth spoke to Caryk's mind as he glided high above the vault with Isaluth next to him.

'*I understand, Uldronth. But I still have a duty to our king. We will have to salvage this somehow,*' Caryk said to his bonded dragon. They focused on the group before the hall from up high. *I see you standing there, girl. So you're the one who caused all this mess.*

'We will be ripped apart if we go down there. They will not be imprisoned again,' Isaluth stated in agreement with his bonded host, Ragian.

Locked in a staring contest with Isaluth, Caryk could feel the vestigial hatred for humans growing from the beasts. They banked to the right and headed back to the city, knowing it was too late to intervene.

* * *

Flintlock walked languidly as Khanaseri sat hunched over the saddle, barely holding the reins, lost deep in the labyrinth of his thoughts. *Was I too quick to give her my help after Father's death? Should I have avenged him still? Was his death really an accident, or was I justified in calling her a murderer? I still feel so angry, but I don't know at whom.*

Shifting uneasily on the horse, he looked up at an enormous tree with long vines hanging down from its branches all the way to the ground. Wrapping his calloused fingers around one, he tugged on it. *Strong. Wonder if it would hold my weight. What do I do now? I'm a little concerned that I don't feel as much when I kill someone anymore. Is that a problem? Should I feel more? Have I always been like this, or just since the magic started?*

'Hey, you! Stop riding and get off your horse.' The voice came from a man at his back. 'And don't even think about reaching for your axe. We have arrows trained at your head.'

'Finally, something interesting. Hold your horses, I'm getting off. But no one touches Flintlock. I really like him.' The scabs on his face were irritating him, itching all the time as the injuries healed. Picking at a burn mark on his neck, he flicked the scab away and lowered his axe to rest on his foot. 'You know, I was just wondering why I don't feel anything anymore when someone's life slips away as I release their bodies. Maybe you can help with this. What do you want?'

'Look, we're not here to fight. We just wanted to know why they jumped. I mean, no one kills themselves like that. Especially not clinging to someone like they did. What was going on there?'

Disappointed, the warlock said, 'Oh, well. No, they're not dead. They went back home. Now, if you will excuse me, I have to slowly walk to nowhere and do nothing when I get there.'

As he turned to get back on Flintlock, Lanik said, 'Listen, how about we buy you an ale and you tell us what happened?'

'I could be persuaded to drink. Tell those two to get out of the bush first, then lead the way.'

'How did you know it was two?'

'You just told me. And it's not like I didn't just see you in the cave back there with your two hussies, trying to kill Beuneth.'

In a swift motion, Khanaseri kicked his axe up and spun it before his face as an arrow sliced through the air to break against the steel of the blade. Lanik quickly stepped back, thinking the man would attack. Anavi crashed through the bush, shouting, 'Who are you calling a hussy? I told you we should kill him!'

'Oh, so emotional. Got you out of the bush, didn't it? Lead on.

Take me to the ale.'

* * *

Birds chirped as the morning sun rose, warming the room as Blanka opened his eyes. An empty bed was not an occurrence unknown to him, and he didn't immediately realise that Beuneth wasn't in the bed, nor in the room. Clothes lay scattered, with his tunic lying on the floor on the far side near the window. Reluctant to get up, he sighed as he threw the sheets from his warmed body and moved to the window to retrieve his woollen top. Far to the left, he saw the head of the sun as it poked out from behind the mountains, the sky a dull grey. He squinted his eyes. *Wait, that's not the sun. What is that? That looks like fire.* With tunic and trousers donned, he opened the window and climbed out onto the roof for a better view. In the distance, he saw a swirling mass floating up into the sky.

Belgarr spoke to his mind, excitement in his voice. 'Look through *my* eyes. The day has finally come!' Blanka's vision sharpened as his pupils became slitted. The mass he saw in the distance suddenly didn't seem so far away anymore.

'Dragons! All of them, taking to the sky. What is this, Belgarr?'

'They have been freed!' The crazed emotional mixture of happiness and sorrow in its voice nearly rent Blanka's soul. He'd never thought about the possibility of freedom for the dragons. It had never even registered until now.

With a deep, encumbered sigh, Blanka said, 'So if I'd never shown up at the great hall, you would have been free as well? Belgarr, for what it's worth, I'm sorry.'

'Mhm. No. Events happened like this for a reason. If I hadn't bonded with you, it's possible they would not be free today, for I believe you to be the key that led to this point. It is as it should be.'

The jump to the ground barely hurt his feet, and he quickly turned to regard the height. *At least five men's height.* 'Do you think humans are in danger because of this?'

A low rumble sounded in his head as he heard, 'I believe most dragons will get away fast and far. Some might think of vengeance, but that will fade when they see that they're alone in their quest for it.'

'I wonder who freed them...' It was awfully quiet. He focused his hearing. Soft snores came from the house and the bugle of an elk from the west, but he couldn't hear Beuneth anywhere. *Maybe the cliff edge she used to frequent.* Not all his memories were terrible from the time they grew up in the cave; some were actually fantastic. Thinking back to the day they met on the cliff edge, he shook his head and smiled as he ambled through the forest, then cocked his head and asked, 'Belgarr, when you said I was the key, what did you mean?'

It took a while before the dragon answered, 'Mhm, I believe you know exactly what I meant. Where is the one you love so dearly this morning?'

A cold chill filled his bones as he whispered, 'Oh no.' Then he started running.

* * *

'This is incredible. I don't feel the weight of the magic, the draining effect it has on the body anymore.'

Ormarr stirred awake in her mind, and said, *'Yes, this is a fortunate side effect of our bond, child.'*

'I am not a child!'

'I am thousands of years old. To me, you are not even a fledgling.'

The last of the dragons broke free of their prisons and took to the sky. A strong, pungent smell hung in the air as they departed.

'Well, Captain, you held up your end.' Beuneth unsheathed a dagger from her side and said, 'Give me your arm.'

An unimaginable event had just occurred, one these soldiers would never forget. To them, dragons were a fairy tale, so long extinct they didn't even scratch the surface of actuality. Confused emotions plagued them, along with the fear and the excitement of the ordeal. The reality of the occurrence proved too much for some as tears just rolled from their eyes. No sobbing, no words, not even mocking from fellow soldiers. Just tears.

Ganda'har looked around at his men and shouted, 'Stop crying! You are the Kamatayon! The elite! Now, fall in, and let's get this over with.' He rolled up his sleeve and held out his arm as he continued, 'What's your real name?'

'Beuneth, Captain. I never lied about that.'

Ganda'har winced as the cold steel sliced into his arm to carve the archaic symbol into his flesh. No one wanted to lose years of their life for no reason.

'What does this symbol mean?' Untara asked from behind his captain.

Beuneth muttered a few words as her hands covered the symbol on Ganda'har's arm, then said, 'It doesn't really have a meaning — more of a function. We need to speed this up, so no more questions. The Kingsguard could be here at any moment.' *I'm finally done. Free of this weight. Blanka, I'm coming home.* One by one, the soldiers moved forward to have the symbol carved into their hands or arms.

A shout came from a soldier as he rummaged through the back of the vault. Alarmed, Ganda'har ran to the great steel door, followed closely by Talgar and Untara, and shouted back, 'What is it, Felter? Speak up, man!'

From the back of a pile of golden goblets and silverware, the marine poked his head out, silver and gold falling from his pockets as he fumbled to keep them in place. 'Aye, sir, a water fountain at the back here. Best tasting water I have ever tasteded...tastededed, sir.'

The captain gestured to Talgar and said, 'Get the men to fill their canteens when Beuneth is finished with them.' He handed his canteen to his lieutenant and continued, 'Fill mine as well.'

Icy blue water, as sweet as nectar, bubbled over itself in the golden fountain, ready to quench the thirst of the Kamatayon soldiers. The rush to get their canteens refilled outweighed their eagerness to get back home as men and women shoved at each other to get to the fountain.

'The Spring of Ananathia. It is said to cure the ails of man.' Beuneth watched the soldiers scurry about, then eyed Ganda'har next to her and said, 'I wish you well with your travels, Captain. I would not linger here for long, were I you.'

The dagger spun between his fingers as Ganda'har twirled it round and round. He cocked his head and sheathed the weapon. 'Why am I still bonded if you freed all of them?'

'Ah, yes. You and the dragon have shared your souls and minds, Captain. One can't live with half of either of those. If separated, you might not die, but neither of you would ever be whole again.'

He stared at her for a while with his brows raised, then said, 'Aye, thank you, and safe travels to you too.' He turned from her and shouted, 'Kamatayon! Fall in. We're going home.'

As the men readied their gear, Beuneth walked from the hall and veered, taking to the sky as the red dragon Ormarr.

Chapter Fourteen

'What do you mean, they've all been freed?! That's preposterous! Where's Torga? I should have his head on a spike!' King Turneroth Brajuck slammed his fists on the table, scattering the various foods and fruits on the stone floor as the bowls bounced off the flagstones.

'That will not be needed, my king; I fear Torga has fallen protecting the Balamuths. I cannot sense him anymore. They have broken their chains. I saw it with my own eyes, sire.' Caryk stood with his hands behind his back, unflinching before the king's tirade.

With all the precision of a wobbling duck, the king picked up a plate of chicken and hurled it at Caryk's head, but it fell short. The metal plate bounced and skid past, the chicken smearing the floor with its fat. Caryk sneered at the thought of wasting good food. *Many in the kingdom have starved with nothing to fill their stomachs, and yet the king can throw his excess on the floor.* A servant girl came running into the hall from the kitchen and started picking up the waste from the floor. The king shouted, 'Who said you could pick that up?!'

Shocked, the servant girl said, 'Sorry, my king, I thought—'

The high-back chair skidded back and fell to the ground as the king jumped up and said, 'You thought! Oh, heavens forbid. You thought?'

He ran to her and grabbed her by the hair as he continued, 'Get down on your knees and eat. Get!' Caryk watched as he forced the poor girl to the floor, pushing her down to eat the food. Awkward moments passed before the king noticed the stares from the guards, then let go of the servant girl and stomped back to his chair to pick it up. 'Caryk, I want the head of the person responsible!'

'Sire, if I may,' Caryk said as he walked towards the king and continued, 'I think you are not seeing the opportunity we have here.' Icy blue eyes met his, locked in a battle of wits.

The king whisked his silver-streaked black hair back behind his ears as he said, 'Oh, and what is that, Caryk?'

'For one to set them free, that person needs to have significant power. It is the trifecta, my Lord; a powerful Ageian sorceress, become Gatekeeper, bound with a powerful dragon, one with authority.'

Eyes squinted and brows furrowed, the king demanded, 'Meaning?'

'Meaning, she can force the bond between yourself and the Alpha...'

Those icy blue eyes opened wide as realisation finally sank in. 'Will it work?'

'I don't know my Lord, but it's worth a try.'

* * *

The streets of Terenore were crowded, bustling with people, cats, and dogs. Two pigs even ran down one street, with a butcher trailing close behind. Fed up with trying to catch the pair, he flailed his cleaver about, hoping to kill or cripple them as he ran. People jumped out of his way as the crazed butcher dived at one pig, crashing head-first into a fruit stall. Guards were quick on scene, ushering the butcher away as he pleaded, 'They're today's meat! Please, people will complain.'

Trying not to attract attention, the Kamatayon soldiers all had their hoods drawn up over their heads, wearing long coats to hide their weapons and the Balamuths they'd stolen. Scattered throughout the market area, they stood at various stalls, keeping a keen eye on each other from a distance. Stilts signalled Ganda'har from across the street, raising a long coat slightly. The captain took his time, staring at the crowds as he slowly made his way to the other side of the road.

'Here you go, Captain. I think we've bought all the long coats we could find. We have a ways to go down this street. I believe the pit will be easy to spot once we're through the thick of this market.' Adjusting the bag filled with the Balamuths over his shoulder, Stilts looked down the street and continued, 'It looks like we're blending in quite well.' A few stalls back, he watched as two Kamatayon stood feigning interest in the merchant's wares. Every few heartbeats, they would glance back to the captain, waiting for the signal to move. Ganda'har nodded to Stilts and turned down the street, leaving the warlock to watch their backs.

Casually walking, the captain whistled to signal his men, and one by one they joined the separated train towards the pit. Stilts fell in at the back of the line, keeping his eyes on two guards conversing with each other to his left. One turned his head to look directly at him, then pointed at them. *Shit.* No time now to take any chances. Stilts whistled twice, and all the Kamatayon picked up the pace to a brisk walk.

A guard came from the right to grab Stilts' arm and shouted, 'Hey, you! What do you have there?'

'Nothing!' His words had not yet faded when a tear opened in the bag at his side, big enough for one of the Balamuths to fall out on the ground. In awkward silence, the two men stared at the rolling sphere before their eyes locked again. The guard stood with his mouth agape, and asked, 'Is that a Balamuth?'

Bright lights and thunderous percussions attacked the guard's senses as Stilts chanted. Freed from the guard's grasp as the man reeled back, clasping his hands over his ears, the warlock ran for the pit, leaving the Balamuth behind.

Alerted by the screaming guard still clasping his ears, more guards converged from the sides, quickly making up the distance to the Kamatayon. 'Stop them!' came the shouts from the guards, but the civilians gave way instead, not wanting to get involved in the drama.

The pit was finally in sight, and Stilts saw his fellow soldiers jump in without looking back. People stood stunned all around the square, believing they were witnessing a mass suicide of some zealous apocalyptic cult. One civilian shouted his indignation as Stilts neared: 'Go kill yourselves where it doesn't bother us good folk!'

Stilts had just pushed off with his legs on the parapet leading around the pit when a guard hit his side, knocking the wind from him as he fell. He looked up at the guard and saw the man clutching the bag's strap with one hand, his other holding on to the top of the wall. Entangled in the bag's strap pulled taut across his chest and arm, Stilts reached up and grabbed the guard's legs and yanked. Using the side of the pit as leverage, he pushed with his legs against the rock-face to pull the man down with him.

The rough surface of the rock wall tore the skin from the guard's hand as he hung from the side, shouting for help from his fellow soldiers, but they were too far away. Unable to hold on, they both plummeted into the pit as the guard screamed, believing death would come soon.

* * *

'Has anyone seen Stilts? Has he come out yet?' Ganda'har walked past the soldiers and moved back to the pit, scanning the cave. It was littered with dead bodies.

'I don't know, Cap'n, but I *would* like to know what happened in this cave,' Geolas said as he knelt, inspecting the dead. 'Fire and powerful blows killed them. Their limbs are shattered more than cut...a heavy weapon and a powerful man did this. Those to the right have cutting wounds.'

The stench made Ganda'har twist away for a heartbeat, and he pulled his face into a sneer just before a scream erupted from the pit and two men came flying out to fall on the stone floor. The young guard from Terenore was quick on his feet, hands trembling as he grabbed a knife from his belt and shouted, 'Stay back!' He edged closer to Stilts, who still lay on the floor. Forming a half circle around the pair, the Kamatayon soldiers took a step closer, then another. 'I'll kill him! Stop moving!' the guard shouted.

At the centre of the half-moon, Ganda'har took another step closer, and shouted, 'No one threatens one of my soldiers!' He jumped at the guard, his arms reaching for the man's throat.

The guard's eyes went large. Fear had driven him back, and he stumbled over a rock, losing his footing. Screams echoed through the cave as he fell into the pit, shouting, 'Not agaiiiiiin...' His voice trailed away as he disappeared.

'Poor lad just lost a whole lot of life worth living,' Untara said, as he reached out to Stilts to help the man up from the ground.

'He was going to kill me, Untara. What about that?' The warlock gestured with his hands in the air, questioning the big warrior's statement.

'Oh, he was a nice boy. He wouldn't have killed anyone.'

Ganda'har picked up the bag of spheres and jerked his head to the big man and said, 'What makes you say that?'

Untara walked to where the guard had stood and went down on his knee to pick up an item. 'For one, he dropped his knife.' He held the knife by the blade and showed it to the surrounding soldiers, then continued, 'with the inscription, "Love Ma". And two, he soiled himself when he saw us. Could see it in his face.'

Ganda'har rolled his eyes as he turned around, walked away from the pit, and said, 'I really thought your explanation would be more profound, Untara. Now, I don't know what happened in this cave, but it stinks to high hell. Let's go home.'

A loud voice echoed from the back, 'Hey, Tiny, why don't you brush your face with my boot and stop wasting everyone's time?'

Untara was held back with a gesture from Ganda'har, then shouted back, 'Shut up, Stentor, or I'll brush your face with my face!'

An awkward moment of silence lingered before the men burst out laughing, then turned to leave the cave.

* * *

Forceful winds lifted Ormarr higher as he soared through the sky. *This deluge of human population has left no space in the world for us. They will hunt us again and again. It will never stop.* As he soared over the villages, high enough not to spook anyone, he thought back to the times he was free, the world vast and open, uninhabited by the little monstrous creatures known as humans. Life was better back then. Simpler. *We hunted and killed for nourishment and to feed our young.* Unlike these creatures, who killed for sport. *Did we do the right thing setting all of them free, only to be hunted again?* Thoughts raged inside their heads as they descended, flying low over the treetops towards the rock jutting out from the cliff edge. With great talons extended, he gripped the rocky ledge as he settled down. The veering was instantaneous, almost too quick, as if Ormarr had retreated to a dark cave to get away from the light, causing Beuneth to fall forward onto the stone surface. The sudden veering made her heart drum in her chest. *What was that, Ormarr?* No answer came.

'Beany? What's going on?' Blanka asked as he emerged from the forest, looking down at her on the ground.

'Blanka! I am *so* glad you're here. How did you find me?'

Cautiously approaching, Blanka said, 'You always come here if you're troubled. In saying that, I'm a bit troubled myself. Where were you last night?'

'Consequence and perspective, Blanka. That's where I was last night.' She looked back at the great vault in the far distant mountains, then continued, 'As a consequence of their actions — imprisoning us, your near execution, the life we lived as rats in a cave — I relieved them of their greatest bargaining chip. They will never threaten anyone ever again with dragon fire. I have freed them all, my love.' She looked at Blanka and saw the worry in his eyes. 'I know our perspectives differ. You might think us safer if I had done nothing. And you might be right. But there are things you don't know. Things hidden behind closed doors.'

Stunned, Blanka shouted, 'Great Thenesian tits! Are you mad?' *Here we go again. Does this woman never stop? It's just one thing after the other. I can't do this anymore.* Hands in his hair, Blanka sagged to the ground, holding firm to the belief that her act would be their undoing, and said, 'They'll hunt us to the very ends of the earth.'

'The dragons were dying, and without them, all magic will disappear from the world! The king should never have had this much power to play with. Don't you see?'

Alarm bells sounded from Terenore in the distance.

Twisting around, Blanka stared in horror as he said, 'Dear gods. They'll be slaughtered.'

Three dragons flew towards the city, two branching off to hit from the east and west, while the other headed straight in. Fire erupted from its mouth as it neared; its tail violently whipped down on the wall, shattering the stones and mortar, sending large blocks crashing down on the streets below. People ran for cover as screams rose from the city. Great ballistae on the wall launched enormous bolts at the dragons to take them down. One ballista exploded with part of the wall as the beast above it spewed its fiery vengeance over the area.

'What have we done?' With the focused hearing of Belgarr, Blanka could hear how children wailed as they ran through the streets. He could smell burned flesh and wood as the dragon set everything ablaze.

A shout from Beuneth stunned him: 'They deserve it, Blanka!'

Tears streamed from his eyes as he shouted, 'There are innocent children in that city!'

Beuneth stormed forward. 'Innocent? They all stood in that square watching, laughing, throwing food at us as they tore you to pieces! They enjoyed every moment as they watched you die! As I screamed for mercy for you, they laughed and mocked! They loved it! Do you really want to tell me they don't deserve this? They imprisoned me for years as they tried to rape me, to make me their plaything! My teeth rotted, I was beaten senseless every day, and I never bathed. I remember picking maggots out from under my skin! Have you ever felt a creature burrowing into you? It's disgusting! But sure, they don't deserve this!

Well, to hell with them!'

The disapproval was obvious on his face as he stared at her with wide eyes. Conflicted, he wanted to hold her tight and beat her senseless at the same time. Blanka knew the argument would have gone nowhere. He walked to the edge and silently dropped off. Belgarr rose to the sky and headed for the nearest dragon.

* * *

Talons ripped into the back of the dragon as Belgarr collided with the beast, to fall from the sky entangled and crash on top of buildings, collapsing them with their weight. Stone and mortar rained from the sky, crushing an ox and its cart down in the streets. Fangs snapped out from Belgarr as he wrapped his mouth around the juvenile dragon's neck, biting down hard enough to stop the flow of air. Blood ran down the olive-green scales of the younger dragon as it struggled to free itself from Belgarr's deadly grip. Sudden heat engulfed Belgarr's back as he was set ablaze by one of the other dragons hovering above him. Ballistae bolts sailed through the sky, and one sliced through the wing of the hovering dragon. A shrill cry sounded from the beast, followed by an eruption of flames that spewed over the wall where the men stood with the dreaded weapon. The force and heat of the burgeoning fire exploded the wooden structure, melted steel, and incinerated the soldiers.

Men below on the ground grabbed the trailing rope from the large bolt, trying to pull the beast down. Instead, they were lifted to the sky. Four men dangled on the line as the beast took them higher and higher. Fear and common sense did not see them letting go of the rope.

The body of the juvenile dragon had gone limp under Belgarr. He kicked it aside and pushed himself off the toppled buildings. To the west, the remaining dragon turned and fled the city, trailed by another dragon. *Must be the Kingsguard.*

A glint in the corner of his eye caught his attention. *Beuneth.* As fast as he could, he flew towards the cliff. Lightning arced on the edge as two figures circled each other. Beuneth swung her chain whip at a man as he dived to the side. Quick on his feet, he parried another blow from the whip with his sword. A vicious kick from Beuneth sent him flying before hitting the ground. With unimaginable speed, he was back up on his feet and lunged at her, pushing her to teeter on the edge of the cliff. He soon had his hands around her neck, squeezing hard.

Strong winds buffeted the two on the cliff's edge, pushing them away from the drop as Belgarr turned his wings to stop. Caryk backed away with a smile on his face and stared at Belgarr as he settled down on the rocky outreach. Teeth gleamed as he pulled his face into a snarl. Burning saliva dripped from his mouth, scorching the earth, his lips trembling as he moved forward.

'Whoa, big guy. Let's talk.' Caryk moved back as Belgarr advanced, then said, 'I can let Uldronth come out to play. But I would rather we just talked for a bit. What d'ya say?'

Belgarr looked to his side, noting that coughing fits still racked Beuneth as she lay on the ground, clutching her bruised throat. A shimmer revolved around him as he veered back to human form. Blanka stood in silence as he stared at the man who had captured him all those years back. Spiked black hair, sharp nose, firm jaw, and deep-sunken, dull-grey eyes. The man hid a very muscular body beneath his garb.

'That's better. You two should join the Kingsguard. We could use someone like you,' Caryk said as he moved closer, staring intently at Blanka, then at Beuneth, and continued, 'Wait, how are you alive? I remember you now. Both of you, actually. You both went down the pit.'

'I *wanted* to join the Kingsguard that night that Knucker broke my arm and threw me in the dungeon to be executed the next day, like a common criminal. You had no need of us then. We have no need of you now. Leave us be, or I will rip your heart from your chest and feast on it.'

'That was back then. Now, thanks to your little tease over there, we have no more cards in our deck. I'll tell you what; I will give you the day to think about it. But know that if you don't accept, I will hunt both of you for the rest of your miserable lives. Let's meet back here tomorrow and continue our discussion.' Caryk veered and took to the air, leaving Blanka and Beuneth on the cliff.

'I know you're bonded, Beuneth. Why didn't you transform? He could have killed you!' Blanka stood with arms folded, one hand covering his mouth. Angry and disappointed, he did not want to meet her eyes, and instead walked from the clearing into the forest, hearing her footfalls behind him as she ran to catch up to him.

'Wait, Blanka. I wasn't hiding it from you,' Beuneth said, as she grabbed his arm to turn him around.

'What?! What do you want from me, Beuneth?!' His shouts came much harsher than he intended. 'We have to leave this place. Again!'

The sudden outburst stunned her. 'I don't know why I couldn't transform. It was as if he didn't mind dying. As if Ormarr had retreated into a cave to never come out again, just waiting for death to take him.' Beuneth released his arm and continued, 'And you know what? The first time wasn't my fault! I remember it was *you* who caused that one.'

A long sigh escaped him as he took hold of her arms and said, 'It just seems like we'll never get a break. We're not even back for a week, and we're on the run again. I think we need to go back through the pit. There, they won't hunt us. Let's just forget about this life.'

Suddenly light-headed, Beuneth grasped at the air, trying to right herself as she stumbled forward. A few drops of blood dripped from her nose, down her mouth, and chin. Her eyes went wide and turned bloodshot as she doubled over, clutching her head as pain exploded in her skull. Blanka grabbed her as she fell, shouting something, but she couldn't hear. Inside her mind, she asked, '*Ormarr! What are you doing to me?*'

A voice not from Ormarr spoke to her mind. '*You will rue the day you lied to me, child! I shall tear Ormarr from your body and destroy you from the inside!*'

'*If I die, you die. You, Gatekeeper, should never have imprisoned the dragons in the first place!*'

In a moment of lucidity, Beuneth gripped Blanka's hand and said,

'Khanaseri. Take me to Khanaseri,' then convulsed as foam bubbled from her mouth.

* * *

'Sire, this is the guard I was telling you about.' At the back of the hall, a man stepped forward as the sentry gestured for him, the angst in his face delineated by his wide eyes and jittery movements. The king eyed the man as he slowly made his way closer. Silver streaks ran throughout his hair, his face pockmarked with baggy eyes.

'What is this? Are we now recruiting the elderly?' asked the king with utter annoyance at the state of his soldiers.

'Sire, I know this man. He's a friend. This morning, he was a much younger man. He plunged down into the pit after those bastards that stole the Balamuths—'

'Hush, Vegul. I want to hear it from him. What's your name?' King Turneroth stepped forward from the dais, standing close to the man, waiting for the reply.

'I am Rook, sire.'

'I thank you for your sacrifice, Rook. Now tell me what happened.'

'We spotted suspicious activity in the square, sire, and followed them. When one of us called out to them, they started running for the pit. There were a lot of them, probably sixty. A guard grabbed the one trailing at the back and this dropped from his bag.' He opened the bag slung around his chest, revealing the sphere.

The king stayed his own hand as he reached for the sphere, knowing full well what would happen if he touched it. Nevertheless, it called to him. 'How many did they have?'

'I can't be sure, sire, maybe two or three, but I saw others carrying bags as well.'

'What happened then?' Intrigued, his fullest attention was on the old visage of young Rook.

'Something happened to Guran – the guard who had grabbed the man. He fell to the ground writhing as if being attacked, but I saw nothing. I ran in and lunged at the man as he jumped for the pit. We collided in mid-air, and I grabbed the bag's strap. I held on to the wall for as long as I could, but he managed to pull both of us down. It felt like we were falling for a lifetime, sire.' The gesture from the king saw Rook unslung the bag and hand it over to him, then he continued, 'I thought I was going to die...'

Engrossed, the king stared at the Balamuth, then realised Rook had stopped talking. 'Yes, that sounds terrible. Continue.'

'I was thrown from the pit into a dark place. I cannot say where it was. But all those men stood before me. Just staring at me like I was crazy. I panicked as one of them reached for my throat, and I tripped on a rock and fell back into the pit. I could feel the life draining from me as I fell, sire. And now here I stand, years older.'

King Turneroth turned to the sentry and said, 'Vegul, get me Bohan. The old sorcerer is probably holed up in his cabin in the mountains. Get him down here. We need to investigate that pit.'

* * *

'Listen, I can't tell you what to do. But consider the fact that she was *not* the one that actually hurt your friend. That was all the doing of those Desert Dogs, as I understand, and I believe we dealt with them properly.' With a furrowed brow, the warlock continued, 'Mind you, I was worried that we overreacted to their disinclination to let us pass, but now I am more content. Thank you.' Khanaseri stared at the three sitting across at the table and gulped down his ale.

Mugs jumped into the air, spilling some ale as Anavi slammed her fists on the table and said, 'Stop being so rational! She was the head of the snake. She killed your father and crippled our friend. End of story.'

A loud belch sounded as the warlock finished his ale. 'Rarely are things that black and white. There are several caveats to this story to make you doubt the crimes you accuse her of.' Leaning back in his seat, he sighed as he said, 'There's not enough blood in the world to satisfy a vengeful heart...'

Ladriana sat back, twirling her hair as she said, 'What does that mean? We should just forget and move on?'

'It was something my father always said, and I only recently realised the truth of it. Yes, she was instrumental in his death. But she didn't take his life. He took it himself. In fact, she didn't want him to die, because she needed his help. As for your friend, you don't even know if she was there when they did what they did to him. As you said, he mentioned nothing about a woman. She did what she needed to do to get back what she'd lost. All of us would have done the same if we were in her shoes. Anyway, as much as I'd like to talk all day, I have to get going.'

'He's right. I'm done with all this anger.' Lanik rose from the table, followed by Khanaseri and Ladriana, leaving Anavi to drum her fingers on the wooden top as she said, 'Goodbye, warlock.'

With a nod to her, he left the inn. Lanik looked down at Anavi and said, 'I'm heading to Kobo to visit Magnus before I return to New Runswick for the coronation. I'm sure he would appreciate it if you were to join us.'

The awkward moment of silence that followed stretched out as Anavi — unwilling to look at them — kept picking at the loose strands of wood sticking up from the worn table. 'Fine. I'll go with you. Give me a few and I'll meet you out front.'

Fresh air filled their nostrils as they opened the door and walked outside. Lanik took a deep breath and said, 'Great mother-of-pearl. I'm surprised we're still alive — that place has no airflow at all.' A few feet from the door, the white wolf waited for them, baking in the sun's heat as passers-by gave him a wide berth. The wolf lifted its head and looked at Lanik and Ladriana, a low rumble coming from its throat.

Anavi pushed open the door and laughed as she saw them frozen in place, staring at the wolf. She unwrapped a piece of raw meat and threw it to the wolf, saying, 'There you go, Bogar. Let's go.'

'You named him?'

'Of course I did, Ladriana. What, should I just keep calling him wolf?' Bogar tore into the piece of meat, ripping it to pieces and swallowing, keeping a keen eye on everyone close by. 'Looks like his leg is healing up nicely,' she said as they untethered their horses and waited for Bogar to finish eating before setting off.

* * *

Now it seems the adventure is at an end. Father, how I wish I could speak to you right now. What awaits me back in Artorea? Will I be strung up for the death of that guard? It was an accident. Up ahead in the distance, he saw tents being erected and sighed as he saw the black-on-white eagle-crested flag waving from a branch, then urged Flintlock closer. The air was humid today. Sweat ran down his brow as he took in his surroundings. Enormous trees surrounded them, with copious shrubs hiding their bases. The clip-clop of Flintlock's hooves echoed in the forest as he rode into the encampment. The eyes of all the soldiers scanned his movement with every step the horse took; a long, awkward moment of silence occurred then.

Leaning on a shovel, Ganda'har said, 'Well, well. Look who we finally have here. What happened to you? You look, uhm... Well, you look terrible.'

With a nod, Khanaseri reined in and dismounted. 'Ganda'har. You lot also look a little worse for wear.' Soldiers started gathering around the warlock and their captain as he continued, 'Are you heading back to Artorea?'

Ganda'har whistled and shouted, 'Stilts, bring the bags!' Returning his attention to Khanaseri, he said, 'Yes, we're on our way back. The king wanted you, your head, or these Balamuths.' Stilts opened the bags, showing the nine remaining spheres in all their splendour. 'Now that he'll get both you and the spheres, I think your head will stay firmly connected to your body.' Ganda'har turned and looked at all the faces staring at them and said, 'Come on, get back to work. Nothing to see here. Talgar, take his horse away to graze and watch over the men. They're starting to slack now that we're heading back home.'

'Yes, sir.' Talgar slapped the warlock on the back and took the reins as he said, 'It's good to see you, Khanaseri.'

'Here I was, fighting for *one* of those, and you return with nine.'

A shadow fell over Khanaseri from behind. He could feel someone pressed up close to him and turned around to look up into the eyes of the big man. Untara rolled his shoulders and said, 'Finally, someone uglier than Geolas shows up.'

'Still not uglier than you.'

A sickening blow to Khanaseri's ribs landed out of nowhere, followed by a quick right and left. The warlock ducked to get away from the blows as the men surrounding them scattered. Some fell over equipment lying on the ground and cursed as their efforts were in vain. Untara was out for blood, and shoved his fellow soldiers out of the way when they weren't quick enough to move, sending them flying as he pursued the warlock, shouting, 'Forty-three men died on this search to find you! What do you have to say about that?'

A blow glanced off Khanaseri's right arm. Spinning around, he hit Untara in the face with the back of his fist. The giant of a man staggered back and spat out two teeth before rushing forward and grabbing the warlock.

Suddenly in the air, Khanaseri was thrown into a tent's walls, collapsing the tent and tearing the fabric. Staggering out, he said to no one in particular, 'What do you *feed* him?'

'That's enough!' Ganda'har stepped in front of Untara, holding the shovel ready as he said, 'One more step from either of you, and I'll end this my way.'

The warlock panted as he stepped closer and said, 'I'm sorry for all your loss. I am. But I'm not the one you should be mad at. I didn't put you on this journey.'

Untara turned and stalked off as Khanaseri stood next to Ganda'har, nursing his ribs.

'He got you good with that first blow. Think he broke a rib?' the captain said with a smirk on his face.

'I'll be fine. He's one tough bastard, though.'

The rest of the squad had moved away, disappointed that the fight was over. Ganda'har planted the shovel's head in the sand and turned to his tent. 'You'll sleep in my quarters tonight. We can have a long conversation about what's transpired over the last few weeks.'

'But you also want to keep your eye on me until we get to Artorea.'

'Can you blame me?'

'I suppose not.'

As night fell, they sat around the fire, talking about all that had occurred and what they had endured. Later, Khanaseri sat with his head in his hands, knowing that although he wasn't to blame for their tragedies, he was the reason they were out there in the first place. Sleep did not come easily for him that night, as he found himself, eerily, in a position he figured was similar to Beuneth's.

Chapter Fifteen

The last few days of walking back to Artorea had proven uneventful. The slow pace gave Ganda'har too much time to think about his coming meeting with King Naka. Brooding as he walked and thought about the scenarios that might play out, he was fearful for Khanaseri regarding what was to come. He glanced to his right to look at his friend's son as he led his horse next to him. *How will I get him out of here if the king isn't happy with the outcome? Maybe we can fight our way out? No, we need a better plan. There are too many soldiers around. Oh, yeah – I can fly now. That's what I'll do. And they will hunt us down... We can't run forever, but I can't fail Galvos again by losing his son like I did him.*

Little heed was given to them as they walked through the gates of Artorea. With their mission never made official or public, few knew of it, save for the few family members of those in the ranks. They received salutes from the guards stationed at the gates and pressed on through into the streets, where people milled around, going about their business. Ganda'har stopped and turned to regard the men, then commanded, 'Go to your families. Give them the reassurance that you've returned. In one bell, I expect you to be at the barracks, where we'll go over the mission with a historian so this journey will never be forgotten.'

The soldiers drifted away to their places of refuge and family. As Khanaseri turned to leave, Ganda'har shot out his hand and grabbed hold of his arm and said, 'Not you. We go to the king. Let's get this over with.' The warlock nodded and followed the captain up the path to the castle.

The doors opened to the Great Hall, and they were escorted in by the sentries standing guard. Khanaseri strode in as calmly as a drugged mule. *If he's not worried, then I shouldn't be. Right?* thought Ganda'har. *Why am I anxious? He's not even my kid.*

King Naka rose from the steps of the dais and ambled forward to meet them halfway. The sentries stood nervously looking at each other. This was not customary. Bright eyes glistened with excitement as the king said, 'Khanaseri. I'm glad you decided to come back home. You caused quite a stir with your escape.'

'I am glad to be back, sire. I regret my actions led to the death of that guard. It wasn't my intent. I will accept whatever punishment you deem fitting.'

The king rubbed at his chin through his beard and said, 'Can you demonstrate your powers now?'

'Surely, Your Highness. What would you have me do?'

The king stepped away from them and walked back to the throne, then gestured to the sentries as he said, 'Stop these men from killing you both without touching them. Sentries, attack them!'

Momentary hesitation and doubt settled in the sentries as they looked upon the captain and the legendary Galvos' son, before they rushed in with swords and spears raised.

Khanaseri made movements with his hands, as if he controlled them like puppets. Ganda'har could feel the power generated by the warlock as a wave struck him and the sentries. He could feel the pressure on his body as he was forced back by the warlock. Involuntarily, he sagged to his knees, then looked up.

Yanked from the sentries' hands, their weapons coalesced into a single unit, melted together to fall harmlessly on the floor in a heavy pile of unusable twisted metal. One and all, the sentries stood frozen, then drifted into the air, just floating aimlessly around in the hall. Terrified, they screamed for the warlock to stop.

'I will not kill them, Your Highness. If this doesn't satisfy you, then I'll take my leave from this city for good.'

'Aggh, fine. Bring them down.' As Khanaseri lowered the sentries to the ground, the king said, 'Your service will be extended for an additional ten years as a company warlock; and afterwards, if we need your help, you will be obliged to give it. Understood?'

'Yes, Highness.'

That went better than expected. He will be ecstatic with these, Ganda'har thought, as he unslung the bag from his shoulder.

'Ganda'har, did you find it?'

'Yes, I did, sire. In fact, I think we've exceeded your expectations. Please do not touch them without gloves, sire. They will tear you apart from the inside if you do.'

A flicker in the king's eyes sent a shiver down Khanaseri's spine. He could see the excitement and eagerness to have these Balamuths at his disposal. 'Them? What do you mean "them"?' King Naka grabbed the bag and undid the straps. Colours of the cosmos swirled in the spheres to light up his face. 'One, two, three, four—'

'Nine in total, sire. We can't force a bond; one has to choose you. They are a wondrous find.'

'Sorry to interrupt, Your Majesty,' Khanaseri said politely. 'May I take my leave? I would like to visit my father's grave.' Khanaseri stood with hands behind his back, awaiting the king's answer.

So entranced was he by the beauty of the spheres that the king took a while before looking up at the warlock. 'Yes, yes, of course. You may go. Ganda'har, you stay. Tell me everything about them.'

* * *

'Caryk, there's been a development,' said Ragian, after he veered to stand next to his captain on the high walls overlooking Terenore.

The two walked along the outer walls, hands behind their backs as they looked down upon the residents below. Caryk turned to look at the empty Vault in the distance, and said, 'We might be the last of our kind, Ragian, unless we get her to join us.'

'That might be more difficult than first thought. I did what you asked and watched from a distance, not intervening and staying out of sight. Something happened to her after you left. She doubled over in pain as blood ran from her nose. Belgarr scooped her up and headed for the city, then dived into the great pit at terrifying speed.'

Without turning back, Caryk said, 'It's as I feared, then. Her body can't maintain its hold on three souls. It's breaking down. We'll need to speed up the process. Go speak with Bohan, and find out what he's learned of this pit.' *If we can't fix this soon, the king's predilection for violence will become prevalent to our nation.* 'Ragian,' said Caryk as he looked over his shoulder. 'Bring me some good news I can take to the king.'

* * *

Belgarr looked down at the unconscious form of Beuneth lying in the clutch of his claws as he soared through the sky, heading for Artorea. Below him, the landscape changed from the grassy greens of the forests to the red sands of the Artoklian desert. *Head southeast. Pity Khan couldn't be more specific.* He flew as low as possible, so as not to be seen from afar. *Would higher up be better? How am I going to descend into the city without being seen? It's a blasted desert. I'll be spotted from miles away. I can't carry her all the way. It will take too long. Aha, I've got it. I'll wait for dark; it shouldn't be long off... No, don't be a fool, then I could just as well walk. A distraction, maybe? That might work. Yes.*

In the distance, approaching fast, was Artokla. Its high black walls surrounded most of the city except for a few outlying areas that had been built over time. Only a few folks lived on the outskirts, hoping to make an income by farming the harsh desert lands. *Must be a hard life, trying to farm the desert. There's always a water shortage; it's always hot. Crops get burned by the sun's rays. An admirable conquest to make food from nothing.*

Alarm bells sounded from the wall; men shouted orders as they saw the black dragon swoop in just past the city gates. Fire erupted from the beast as it neared a farm with a great barn some distance off, burning everything in its path as it closed in. Soldiers streamed from the gates, heading in the direction of the dragon as it disappeared behind a wall of fire. Their hearts pounded as they neared the flames, and ran past a man blackened by soot carrying a woman in his arms as he shouted, 'Please help! Dragon! Please help. She's injured!'

The soldiers ran past them towards the now-dying fire wall. Smoke faded away as it drifted out on the wind's current, revealing the empty field behind the barn. Confused and filled with enough adrenalin to swim across the great seas of Telementhia, the soldiers stood staring at each other with swords in hand, as if disappointed by the dragon's disappearance.

One guard ran up to Blanka, took Beuneth's left arm, and lifted it over his head, saying, 'You take that side. We'll move faster together. It's a bit of a ways still. They'll bring a horse soon. What's your name, stranger?'

Caught by surprise, he almost dropped Beuneth as he said, 'Blanka.'

'Tamerick. Here comes the horse.' He whistled and gestured at the young guard on the horse to hurry.

Dust and pebbles flew from under the horse's hooves as it skidded to a halt before them, making it hard to breathe and see for a moment. The young guard dismounted and removed the saddle quickly. Blanka coughed, trying to rid his mouth and nostrils of the red dust as they lifted Beuneth on the horse, then said, 'I go with her!'

'I'm sorry, Blanka. But that will slow them down.'

'Give me the horse! Please! I will return it, I swear.' Blanka grabbed Tamerick by the shoulders as tears welled in his eyes.

'Oh, fine. Just give her a slap on the rump when you dismount, and she'll find her way back to the stables.'

Blanka shook his hand fervently. 'Thank you!'

Now that the dust had settled and his nerves had calmed a bit,

Tamerick looked at the woman. *Really strange garb for a farm lady. No one can work in that. It's way too tight for a farmer's wife.* 'Hey, Blanka, why is she wearing such dubious garb? It looks like it belongs more on a harlot witch than a farmer's wife.'

With a shake of his head, Blanka furrowed his brow as he said, 'Shame on you, young man! My wife likes to play dress-up. I am a very lucky man, is all.'

A dust cloud formed as he rode off through the gates of Artorea, alarm bells ringing all around while people frantically got out of the streets to find shelter should the disappeared dragon return. Fear had its talons in them. Dragons hadn't been sighted for generations before now; and with its sudden disappearance, the thought of it having a lair nearby didn't sit well.

Unwilling to push the horse into a full gallop for fear of dropping Beuneth, Blanka held on to her and the reins as he rode through the streets. *How am I going to find his house in this place?*

Whispers came from Beuneth, and he saw her eyes looking up half-glazed as she said, 'Head north through the market, and towards their Hall of History...few houses down the street to the left...white arch.' Her voice was groggy, barely a whisper. A concerning gurgle came from her throat as she breathed.

'We're almost there, Beany. Just hold on.'

* * *

Twelve mages stood in a half-moon on the rolling fields outside Terenore, chanting as Bohan drew symbols on the ground before them. King Turneroth stood off to the side, scratching his beard as he looked upon the volunteers he had received. *Promises of fortunes make the most unwilling eager to take part.* 'I am very disappointed with you, Caryk — letting them escape like that.'

With a sigh of regret, Caryk said, 'Yes. We'll have to go through and bring them back soon.'

'Really? What do you think we're trying to accomplish here? Your insolence is wearing on me. How long will this take yet?'

A spark lashed out from Bohan, growing bigger and bigger as he stood at the front of the twelve. Lightning erupted from his hands. Before them, a rift appeared. The king could feel the warmth being pulled from his very being to feed the growing portal. His hands trembled, turning blue as he looked around. Animals had suddenly quieted. No more birdsong sounded. He heard a thud to the left and saw a dead crow on the ground. *Was that there before this started?* Glad that he wasn't the first to go through, the king shouted, 'Send the first!'

The scrawny man at the front of the volunteer line stepped forward, glancing at the wizard and back to the king to receive a nod from his lord, then stepped through the rift.

* * *

He scowled as he set foot upon the scorching sands of the desert, burning his feet. There was no time to worry about that right now. He looked up from the sand and saw a city in the distance through the heat waves forming on the surface. A barren land with scattered small trees and bushes, all looking very dead, spread out far and wide. Rolling dunes spread to the left, with little else to the right.

Tired, the man stumbled forward, feeling like all the energy had been sapped from his body. *Time to go back.*

His feet were unwilling participants. He staggered as he brought his hand up to wipe his nose, leaving a smear of red on the back. Dazed, he fell backwards into the rift.

* * *

Laughter, harsh and abundant, filled the inn as Lanik finished his story about why Magnus didn't eat in front of the patrons anymore. Even Magnus was smiling at the humiliating story.

'Oh lad, do youse really have to go back already? I'll miss youse two so much,' Magnus said as he slung the counter cloth over his broad shoulder. The inn was quiet still, being too early for the usual patrons to wake from the previous night's bout with the bottle. Only a few had come in and taken their seats, listening to the stories told by the four sitting around their table. Never had Lanik wished more that he could just stay with his old friend at the inn, but he had his destiny to fulfil, a crown to take up.

'I wish I could, Magnus. I really do. But it's time for me to stop running and become the man I was born to be. Besides, you have Anavi here now.' He cupped his hand around his mouth and whispered, 'But you might want to chain her to the bed this time. Seems she has a knack for running.'

A slap rocked his head as Anavi suddenly stood next to him and said, 'I will castrate you like a mule. I really don't care if you need offspring to further your reign.'

Soft giggles came from Ladriana, as she couldn't keep her laughter in. 'Please, Anavi, you'll be doing me a favour.'

Lanik winced as he rolled his eyes and said, 'Might not be a bad idea to get these two away from each other, Magnus. They'll drive both of us crazy.'

Oh, dear boy! Do youse never learn? 'You're on your own on this one. I ain't getting close to that,' Magnus said as he pinched his face and pursed his lips.

The women launched their assault at Lanik, the indiscernible words coming so fast from the two women talking over each other that he could understand none of it. But he knew it was bad.

Anavi eyed Magnus and whispered, 'Smart move,' before turning her attention back to Lanik. 'You're right, though. I think it's time for you to grow past your history. It's time to leave it behind.'

'How are your injuries faring, Magnus?' Ladriana asked as she toyed with her drink.

'Oh, the leg and my chest hurt the most. Can't do too much before I'm winded, but I'm getting stronger.' He swung his injured leg from under the table and said, 'Here, look at this new... What did he call it? Tecn... Tecnolgy. Impressive, ain't it? These here bolts and pins push my bones to straighten, while the wood keeps everything in place. The healer says I should try to keep some weight off it for a bit. So I'm hopping around like a pegleg pirate who had his leg stolen by Armiranean wood traders.'

More laughter sounded and Lanik smiled as he said, 'I'm glad you have your spirits lifted.'

'Aye, laddie, nothing can lift my spirits more than havin' youse lot with me.'

'We'll visit again soon. I promise. Take care of yourselves,' Lanik said as they stood to leave the inn, then took one last look around him and sighed before he continued, 'Farewell.'

'Aye, youse too,' Magnus said as he pushed himself to his feet, leaning heavily on the table as Anavi quickly grabbed his swaying frame.

'Be careful, you lummox!'

Lanik and Ladriana chuckled and looked at each other as they heard Anavi's voice fade away as the door to the inn closed, then felt the brisk morning air on their skin.

* * *

You didn't think your life would end with you roasting over a fire, did you piggy? Don't worry, little one, you led an honourable life. Be glad. You did what you were born for, unlike me. I have failed in my path. Failed at getting vengeance for my father. Failed at being a dutiful son. Even failed at being there at the end, at his funeral pyre. Forty-three Kamatayon dead because of me. The sweet smell of the roasting pig drifted through the air as Khanaseri took another big gulp from his ale. His head was swimming in alcohol, his mind drowning. It was bliss. Streams of the bitter liquid flowed down the sides of his mouth, spilling onto his pants. The stars glowed brightly tonight, the moon a sickle harvesting the lights in the sky. He stared up at the stars as tears blurred their brilliance, and lifted his mug up high.

'To you, Father.'

A shout came from the front of his house, disturbing his solitary bereavement. 'Khanaseri! Open up!'

'I'm at the back! Come around!' Unsteady on his feet, the world pushed him left and right as he reached for the cask of ale he'd brought home earlier. Fingers straining to reach the ever-distant cask fell away when he heard someone crashing through the bushes on his right. Startled, the world went spinning as he tripped over a log, and sent him crashing down on the ground. A groan escaped his mouth as he looked up at the spinning stars, blinking his eyes as he drawled, 'That really you, Blanka?'

'Yes, it's me. Get up, Khan, we need your help!'

Slow and steady, Blanka set Beuneth down on the log Khanaseri had been sitting on earlier. 'Hold on, Beany. Don't fall.' He grabbed the warlock's hand and pulled him up from the ground, only to see him fall forward, this time face-planting in the dirt. 'Get up, you mule!' Blanka growled.

'Hey, there's no need for that.'

'Beuneth is dying, Khan! Now sit up!'

'Wha... Okay, I'm getting up. Come on, help me!' The weight of the warlock became clear as the alcohol took his balance from him, making Blanka strain his back muscles to move the big man.

Oh, to hell with this. 'Open your mouth, Khan.'

Like a baby taking orders from its mother, the warlock opened his mouth, then closed it and said, 'Wait, no. I'll bite—'

Before the warlock could finish talking, a hand was thrust down his throat and pulled out quickly. Blanka turned him over on his side as ale and bile spilled from his mouth. Contorted, he hunched over and heaved to get the alcohol out of his stomach.

Finally finished, the warlock sat and stared at Blanka, trying to keep the man in one spot as he drifted in his vision, and said, 'What happened?'

'Let's get inside. I don't want everyone to hear or see us. And go drown yourself in some water. I need you sober.'

'Yes, yes, yes. Put her...on the table.' The modest little house had little in the way of furnishings. A couch, some kitchenware, weapons hanging on the walls. As gently as he could, Blanka laid Beuneth down on the kitchen table, staring into her blood-red eyes, the pupils fully glazed over like a blind woman's – or a dead woman's. 'Beany, can you hear me?' Blanka gently caressed her cheek; then she stirred, barely breathing as she struggled to blink her eyes.

Khanaseri entered the kitchen, his head and clothes dripping water on the wooden floor. 'Okay, Blanka, tell me what happened.'

'Oh please, don't sound too concerned, Khan.'

'I don't have the same level of feelings for her as you do. She's still the reason for my father's death. Or have you forgotten that?' *I could let her die. It wouldn't be my fault.* Wiping his face with a cloth, he moved to stand over Beuneth.

'Oh yes, I remember now. I apologise, Khan. Please help her. She disappeared one night back in Terenore and headed for the Great Vault. When she came back the next morning, I could sense a dragon in her. She's fully bonded. But then she doubled over after she told me she freed all the dragons—'

Khanaseri jerked his head around and said, 'She did *what?* To free but one would tear you apart. To free all would be impossible! Unless...' He closed his eyes and mumbled a few words.

Blanka pulled on his arm as he shouted, 'Unless what?!'

The warlock's eyes shot open, and he stared at Blanka with dread. 'She's bonded with not just one soul; she has a second in her wreaking havoc – the Gatekeeper – and he's not happy with them. Hold her down. This might get a little ugly,' Khanaseri said as he rummaged through a drawer and pulled out a brown leather bag. He quickly undid the knot at the top and drew a candle forth. 'Here, light this?'

Blanka cupped a hand over the candle. A small flame burst into life, dancing on the candle's wick. Exhaustion took Blanka as he sat back in the chair, feeling heavy and discontented.

Still woozy, the warlock straightened and focused to pull the alcohol from his blood, clearing his mind. Froth appeared from his mouth at

first, then he bent over the sink to let out a steady stream of alcohol —
not vomiting, just flowing up, commanded to retreat. He wiped his
mouth and said, 'I need her body exposed... Oh, don't look at me like
that. You can cover up her bits.' The warlock handed Blanka a knife
that lay on the kitchen counter and said, 'Cut.'

The chant started as Khanaseri dripped hot wax onto her bare skin.
What looked like a hand pressed from the inside of her stomach,
stretching her skin as if trying to escape. Blanka jumped back and stared
at the warlock, but said nothing. Another appeared, but it seemed more
reptilian. *They are fighting inside her.* A creak sounded from the chair as
the warlock sat down, slumped back, and closed his eyes. The kitchen
disappeared...

*Lightning rained down with a mighty crack as it hit the ground, revealing
the torn grey landscape. Winds swept through the unending waves of rain,
pushing them against the warlock as he stood in the darkness. 'Beuneth!' he
yelled out with his hand over his eyes so he could see. A gigantic form flew in
from the dark, red eyes brimming with fury as fire erupted from its maw. The
heat was intense as it flowed over the protective shield encompassing Khan, but
he remained unfried. 'Whew. Thought I was done for.'*

Beuneth shouted, 'Warlock! Run to my voice!'

*As soon as the fire died down, he ran in her direction and heard her yelling
at the dragon, 'Ormarr! Not him! He's a friend.'*

*A friend? Khanaseri thought as he neared, and demanded, 'What's
happening here, Beuneth? They're killing you!'*

'Thanks for the information, yes. I hadn't noticed.'

'Really? Sarcasm right now? It's unbecoming.'

*'Look, the Gatekeepers are Elder, ancient even. They're the only ones who
have the knowledge and power to enslave the dragons, and these two aren't
happy to be in the same cage. It's just unfortunate that I am that cage. Why do
you think it's so dark and chaotic in here? It's the Gatekeeper.' The howls of the
winds made it almost impossible to hear, even shouting as loud as they could.*

'I have one question for you. Do we lock them all up, or do you prefer one?'

'Lock up the Gatekeeper; he's of no use to me anymore.'

As soon as she said his title, a lightning bolt hit the ground near them and sent them flying. Steam rose from Khanaseri's body as he tore away his burned and tattered shirt, throwing it on the ground as he shouted up to the sky, 'Come down, Gatekeeper! Or better yet, just get in the cage by yourself.' Ormarr flew overhead and settled behind Khanaseri, blowing flames up to the sky. Beuneth moved closer and looked to the warlock as he whispered, 'I have already begun construction of his cage. We need to lock him up for good.'

* * *

Fists hammered against the door, accompanied by shouts from a man calling for Khanaseri. Reluctant to leave the two alone in the kitchen, Blanka cursed as the man didn't leave, and rose from the chair. 'What do you want?' he shouted as he stood before the door.

'Open the damned door before I break it down!'

The lock fell away, and the door swung open. A big man stood in the doorway, and demanded, 'Where is he? Khan!' Pushing past, Ganda'har stalked into the house, looking around searchingly as Blanka shouted from the back, following him.

'He's in the kitchen, but you can't wake him now. You might just kill them both!'

As Ganda'har entered the kitchen, he looked upon the half-naked Beuneth and the unconscious warlock sitting slumped in the chair with his head hanging to the side. Ganda'har spun around and grabbed Blanka by the throat, then pushed him up against the wall, leaving his feet to dangle in the air. 'What have you done to them?'

Fighting the urge for Belgarr to take over, hot steam escaped Blanka's mouth, the heat rising over Ganda'har in shimmering waves. 'I've done nothing to them! He's trying to save her life!'

'Why did she come back here?'

Words came out in between breaths. 'I...brought...her.'

Gravity took over as Ganda'har's hand left Blanka's throat, sending the smaller man to the ground. 'You are the dragon they saw. I heard the rumours. You gave the people quite the scare.'

'How do you know her?' Blanka asked as he regained his composure.

'We were with her when she freed the dragons back in your era.'

Ganda'har leaned over and peered closely at Khanaseri. A loud crack sounded as he slapped the warlock across the face, hoping to wake the man, and shouted, 'Wake up, Khan!'

'Stop that!' Blanka grabbed the captain's hand as he brought it down for another slap, catching it in mid-air. His eyes glowed red as his voice took on a deep, guttural tone. 'I said *stop that*. I will send him to you once he's done.'

With a shake of his arm, Ganda'har freed himself from Blanka's grip and said, 'A rift has opened outside the city. We need to close it. Send him immediately.'

The door slammed shut as Ganda'har left the house, leaving Blanka to look over the unconscious pair once more.

* * *

'Send in the second volunteer!' King Turneroth turned to one side and settled his hand on the young boy standing next to him, saying, 'Remember this day, little Moseroth. We are carving our names in the stones of history.'

An ageing man stepped forward from the volunteers, the second in line, ready to do his duty for king and family. As the man approached the rift, it flickered slightly before the man vanished. Time dragged on as everyone watched in silence.

One of the mages feeding the rift collapsed to the ground and lay unmoving. With a gesture from the king, two men ran forward with a stretcher between them to haul the mage to the healer. Vomit spewed from the first man's mouth after he turned the mage over and backed away. Berated by the other stretcher-bearer, he picked up the arms of the mage as they lifted him onto the stretcher.

From the front, near the rift, Bohan cried out in pain as his hands turned black, and the thick odour of burnt meat hung in the air. A figure stumbled from the rift moments before it closed as the mages one and all collapsed to the ground. Some stirred; some did not. Men ran in, bringing water to ease their pain, followed by more stretcher-bearers.

The man from the rift walked past the line of volunteers and was caught by one as he stumbled, his energy depleted. Old and grey, his skin aged and wrinkled, he stared into the faces of the men standing in line waiting for their chance to serve. All who could see his eyes at that moment knew what he was trying to say without having to mouth it. King Turneroth shook his head and called out to Bohan, 'What went wrong? This man has aged years instantly.'

The old sorcerer walked up to the king with his hands and arms bandaged, blood seeping through the rags. 'Your Majesty. This is a setback, I agree. We are not well versed in the ways of opening portals of this magnitude through more than a hundred generations to lock them in place, especially not one big enough to fit an army through. My hands will be healed before the day is done, and I will work out the issue soon.' A small flicker brought Bohan's attention down to the child, and he said with furrowed brows, 'I did not know Your Majesty had magic in your blood.'

The king looked at him with disdain on his face and pulled little Moseroth in behind his legs as he said, 'We don't. I don't care what you have to do, Bohan, but get it done. Do you understand me?'

Without waiting for an answer from the sorcerer, the king turned and picked up Moseroth and left the area, closing his eyes momentarily as the sun's warmth returned.

His skin grey from pain, sweat beading his forehead, Bohan watched as the king strode away with the little boy in his arms.

* * *

Armour rustled in the distance, and the darkness lifted as the chain mail-wearing warrior revealed himself, walking up to them while dragging a broadsword behind him. He snarled, 'Sacrilege! You pulled a veil over my eyes, child. You took what we have guarded for centuries and dishonoured our name in a day. I trusted you to carry out our sacred duty. Now they will destroy everything.'

Beuneth stepped forward and said, 'Yes. I played you for a fool, because you are a fool. Keeping them locked up was killing them. Their death would have been the end of magic in our world.'

'And would that have been so bad?'

'Some say that waking up in the morning is a bit of magic. That the blossoms of a cherry tree opening in spring are a bit of magic. That finding love is a bit of magic. And you would see it all killed.'

'Oh, you are pathetic, child.'

Khanaseri reached for the axe on his back and charged at the warrior. The blade sang as it sliced through the air to hit the warrior in the chest, biting deep into the scaled chain. The blow sent the Gatekeeper flying. He hit the ground and rolled a good distance away.

'I thought you said we'd lock him up, not kill him,' Beuneth protested.

'Oh, he's not dead yet. That armour's too thick.'

Ormarr swooped in overhead. Billowing fire engulfed the Gatekeeper as he lay on the ground. Khanaseri stood with his hand covering his eyes to shield himself from the insane heat and said, 'Well, he wasn't dead. Not so sure anymore.'

A fierce roar sounded as Ormarr buffeted them with the wind of his wings and settled on the ground next to them, celebrating the defeat of the Gatekeeper. But the celebration was short-lived. Khanaseri silenced them and pointed to the fire as he saw a glint of metal moving to rise in the blaze.

Sword tip dragging on the burning ground, the Gatekeeper walked out of the conflagration to stand before them, his metal helmet blackened by the heat. 'We were born from fire. Do you really think this will hurt me?'

The warlock charged at the Gatekeeper again, swinging his axe. The clangour of metal on metal resonated as the broadsword parried blow after blow. Then a blow from the back sent the Gatekeeper staggering forward as Beuneth launched her own assault, the chain whip's blade biting into the armour, but not deeply enough to reach his flesh.

'Resorting to sneak attacks...so childish,' said the Gatekeeper as another *blow came, but he ducked and caught her fist in the air. He squeezed hard with the metal gauntlet, feeling her bones want to break under the pressure. From the side, Khanaseri stepped in and brought his axe down.*

In a blur, the Gatekeeper had moved to stand behind Khanaseri, the sword slicing through the air and deep into the warlock's back. Blood flowed as he fell to the ground and rolled out of the way, so that the sword came crashing down on the earth next to him. A massive, spiked dragon's tail came suddenly into view, hitting the Gatekeeper in the side, lifting him into the air and sending him into a wall a good distance away.

With great effort and trembling hands, the Gatekeeper removed his helmet and grabbed hold of the protruding spike. One should never have to fight alone like this. Where are you, my brethren, in this time of need? *he thought as he pulled the spike from his side. Blood trailed behind him as he moved closer to Khanaseri and Beuneth. Enraged, he rushed in with sword held high, swinging left and right, cutting up and down. Beuneth fell back as a wild cut nearly severed her head from her body.*

The Gatekeeper grabbed the warlock by the throat and threw him a dozen feet to the right. Before Khanaseri could rise, the Gatekeeper was on him, bringing down the sword with tremendous power. The warlock rolled out of the way just in time; the sword hit the stony surface with a loud clang.

This is our chance, *Beuneth thought as she chanted. Great chains raced out from the darkness to wrap around the Gatekeeper's arm. Turning his attention on her, he ran and lunged at her as another chain came from the opposite direction to wrap around his other arm. He screamed as he pulled with all his might at the chains, stretching them to their breaking points. More chains rushed out of the darkness to envelop him. Encased in chains, he hung in the air, unable to move. Beuneth and Khanaseri chanted together, pulling the chains tighter and tighter around the Gatekeeper.*

'You will regret this!' *the Gatekeeper shouted, spittle flying from his mouth.*

Beuneth sank down on her knees and stared at Khanaseri as she asked, 'Do you think it will hold?'

'It has to. If it doesn't, we'll have to do this all over again. Tough bastards, these Gatekeepers. Are all of them like that?'

'Ageian... My father's race. Most of them were. But I don't even know if *they still exist. They left Terenore so long ago in my time. Thanks for your help again.'* She suddenly looked up and cocked her head, focusing with eyes closed, then said, 'You have to go; something is afoot.'

* * *

The city square had been cleared of civilians as the twelve mages took up their positions around the great pit. A curfew had been established by the king, and if found wandering, the offenders were promptly thrown in with the soldiers to head through the rift. Bohan walked the grounds, inspecting the air and feeling the magic ride the currents of the winds. He pointed to his left, his gesture telling one mage to move more to his left, then gestured for him to stop. Another he motioned to come closer to the pit.

The old sorcerer walked and chanted, writing on a piece of parchment as he neared one of the mages, then tore the piece of parchment and rubbed it over a mage's face. As he spoke his words of power, the little piece of parchment burned to a cinder, slowly dissolving to ash as the edges glowed red hot. Once the parchment had disappeared, he continued to the next and repeated the process until all the mages were so anointed.

The city was eerily quiet as he listened intently. Far away, he could hear the chants of the mages on the outside of the city getting ready for the portal to be opened. Bohan walked to the centre of the square and spoke aloud in his magical tongue, *'Veile anomus porta vanhoseker.'* Dark clouds rushed in to cover the city as all the mages started up the chant. One by one, they were engulfed by a great blue light from the portal in the pit, until all of them pulled power from the source.

Unnatural groaning sounds came from the earth as the blue light of the twelve joined to form one massive source, and shot up in an arc over the city to where the rest of the mages were chanting on the outside to open the rift. Rain poured down on them with the hellish anger of the gods as thunder drowned out all other sounds. Bohan looked to the sky and mounted a horse to ride to the gates of Terenore; the king would need him soon.

* * *

Exultation filled him as he opened his eyes to the sunlight peering through the windows, fresh air rushing into his nostrils as he breathed deeply. Blanka woke with a start and jumped from his seat, grabbing a glass of water to hand to the warlock, and said, 'Drink. You must be thirsty.' Only then did Blanka see the blood pooling at the base of the chair. His eyes grew large as he pulled the groaning warlock forward to the see the massive gash on his back.

A wince of pain escaped the warlock before he said, 'I'm fine. It should be healing already. She'll need some rest, though. Her body took a beating. But she'll be fine.'

'Thank you, Khan! That's twice I have to repay you now. Before I forget, there was a big, burly soldier type here looking for you earlier. He said you needed to join him immediately. Apparently, there's a rift open outside the city, and they need you to close it. I told him to leave.'

Bitter despair replaced Khanaseri's fleeting moment of joy as he said, 'Will this never end? Can't I just have one day with no problems?' With a heave, he rose from the chair and walked out the back to the pig still hanging over the now-dead fire, and looked back to Blanka as he shouted incredulously, 'Really? You didn't even bring in the pig? Unbelievable!' He picked up the roasted pork and placed it under his arm as he strode around the side of the house and into the street, tearing off pieces and shoving them into his mouth. He knew that if Ganda'har was anywhere, it would be on the western wall of the city.

* * *

A massive undertaking had seen the forest's trees cut down to make way for the thousands of men, women, and even a younger selection of sturdy youths — soldiers all — standing ready to do battle. On the outskirts of Terenore, they waited for the rift to open.

'How are the preparations going, Caryk?'

'Sire. Preparations are going well. We have five battalions, comprising around five thousand each, ready to march. We'll have plenty more lining up soon. From what we heard, it sounds like there's a desert on the other side, so we have extra water and food carts. All the weaponsmiths have been working around the clock to bring more weapons down the line. I have one concern.' He cocked his head to the king and continued, 'It seems we're going to burn out our mages to open this rift. Which means we won't have their backing in the battle, and we don't know the sorcerous capability of the enemy.'

'Bohan has assured me it will only take fifty strong mages to lock the rift in place and avoid the ageing process.'

'Fifty!'

The outburst and shock on Caryk's face made the king wince and look around to see if anyone had heard. 'Can you keep quiet? They weren't informed, you know.'

Outraged, Caryk stared at the king in disbelief and said, 'What have we become? This is going too far, Your Majesty. Those men are dying as we speak, just for you to get your bond. This is not—'

'Get a grip, Caryk! This is what war is. Sacrifice!'

And what exactly have you sacrificed, Your Majesty? Caryk looked back to the array of mages chanting, with Bohan at the forefront, the blue-light energy feeding them from the pit in the city. A thunderous crack sounded from Bohan as he tore the rift open with the lives of the mages at his back. 'It's time, Caryk!' the king said excitedly. 'Get Ragian and the new guy. What's his name?'

'Varik.'

'Yes, of course. Get them ready. Tonight, we go through.'

Chapter Sixteen

'I want those ballistae bolts ready by next bell! Move it, you swine-loving meat bags! We've dragons warming up for a fight, so let's not disappoint them by giving them an easy meal!' Ganda'har moved between the men as they frantically ran about, preparing for the coming battle. 'Talgar, get over here!'

The lean warrior jogged over to his captain. 'You called, sir?'

'Get to the other side of the city and make sure they're preparing the ballistae bolts. You've seen those beasts in action. You know what they're capable of. The soldiers there must be pissing themselves for fear of what's coming. Take over preparations if need be. If Captain Kornek has any problems with that, tell him to come and see me. Take Geolas with you.'

'Yes, sir,' he said, then whistled at Geolas and gestured for the man to follow him as he set off through the buzz of activity on the wall.

Men tipped enormous pots filled with a slimy black liquid over the wall to coat the sides and fall to the base, filling hastily dug trenches.

'Sharpen your blades, people! There's plenty of slicing to go around!' Ganda'har shouted as a messenger arrived.

The messenger saluted the captain, then stood with his hands on his knees, breathing deeply to catch his breath. The run up the stairs to the top of the wall had been a vigorous one. 'Yes, speak,' Ganda'har said as he looked at the wheezing boy.

'They have set up their camps, sir. We have riders approaching.'

Ganda'har walked to the parapet and looked over the distance at the three approaching riders. *Their king and probably two bonded, unless the king is the third bonded we saw coming through the portal.* 'Tell the king to be ready for an audience. I believe they want to talk.'

Khanaseri approached them with the roasted pig still in his hands and shoved it into the arms of the messenger as he said, 'Here, you look hungry.' The warlock turned to Ganda'har, and continued, 'What's this I hear about a rift that needs closing?'

'You may go.' Ganda'har sighed and gave a half-hearted salute to the messenger.

Unsure what he should do with the pig, the messenger looked around, hoping that someone would call out to him for it, but no one did. Then he disappeared as he went down the stairs cut into the wall, struggling to keep his grip on the half-eaten swine.

The older captain gestured for Khanaseri to follow and led him to the parapet overlooking the vast army still marching out of the gigantic rift in the distance. A camp had been established to his right, north of the rift, where they could see smoke drifting up, and the trailing dust of the three horses as they rode for the city. 'There's no need for that anymore. Stilts, my company's warlock, assures me it will be near-impossible to close a rift that size. We saw three dragons come out of the portal first, followed by all those men. I'm assuming the three approaching are their king and two bonded, leaving the third dragon in the camp, unless the king is also bonded.' Ganda'har turned to the warlock, the guilt in his eyes clear as he glanced away.

With a cock of his head, Khanaseri said, 'You know why they're here, don't you? You stole those Balamuths from them.'

Yes, and all the death that follows will be on me! 'Yes, Khan. But I didn't think they would travel through time to get them back.'

'Why not? You went there to get them, didn't you?'

'That was by accident! We didn't plan it. But we also might have helped free all the other remaining dragons.'

'Gods below, if *that* is not an act of war, then I don't know what is.'

Ganda'har thumped Khanaseri on his chest. 'You're one to talk! You harbour the woman responsible for all this in your home. So don't come knocking on my door just yet!'

Another messenger came up the stairs and halted before the two arguing men, then said, 'Sorry for the interruption, but the king is ready to ride. He waits at the gate.'

Ganda'har nodded and gestured for him to leave. An awkward moment of silence followed between the two men as they glared at each other, before the warlock turned his head away and said, 'No no no. I am *not* going with you and King Naka. This is your mess.'

'Oh yes you are...'

* * *

'If anything untoward happens, Ganda'har, kill their king first,' King Naka said over his shoulder.

Ganda'har was silent, staring at the three men as they approached at a trot. He felt the presence of the two bonded flanking the king and said, 'I would advise against any threatening action until such a time that this meeting prevents a safe outcome, Your Majesty. The two on the sides are bonded.'

'So are you, remember.'

'Still, two on one—'

King Naka snapped at him. 'What is Khanaseri? A paperweight?'

'Of course not, Your Majesty,' the warlock chimed in. 'He was merely pointing out that if I have to fight as well, then nobody is left to protect you.'

The three riders drew near and reined in to stop a few feet from them. King Naka's voice rang out to break the silence. 'I bid you good day. I am King Naka. Who, may I ask, has come calling at our gates?'

'King Turneroth Brajuck of Terenore and his hundred thousand soldiers,' the other king bellowed out as loudly as he could without having to shout. He smirked as he heard a few gasps and mutterings from the wall, and knew his words had put fear and doubt in the minds of the enemy.

'Ah, you believe by giving me your numbers you'll scare us into submission. You will find, Turneroth, that we Artoreans do not scare so easily. What is it you're doing on my land?'

Khanaseri looked over his shoulder and saw the wandering eyes staring down from the great wall, and winced at the failure of the men's discipline.

King Turneroth pulled tight the glove on his left hand and said, 'I want the girl and the Balamuths you stole.'

Cynical laughter rang out from King Naka before he said, 'Girl? I will give you a hundred girls. But I don't know these Balamuths of which you speak. Are they to help you with the girl? We have some great herbs for that, you know.'

Tensions rose instantly. Only King Naka laughed as the rest of the men stared at each other, waiting for the first sword to be drawn.

'Maybe you shouldn't be insulting the person who stands ready with an army at your door.' The three men wheeled about and rode off as King Turneroth shouted over his shoulder, 'You have until tomorrow morning to comply. If by dawn I don't see a cart riding out with the girl and the Balamuths, we will attack. You've been warned.'

* * *

'One of you had better be able to tell me what girl he was referring to,' King Naka said as he rounded on them after they entered the gates. 'I dislike being left in the dark. Now, if we know this girl, we should just hand her over to him and be done with it.'

Khanaseri looked sidelong at Ganda'har, waiting for him to answer.

'I do not, sire, my apologies. We will find out, won't we, Khan?'

'Yes, of course we will.'

'Good. Ganda'har, your anecdotal experience will guide this battle. Make sure we come out on top.'

What are we to do with that woman? A guard walked past and Khanaseri shouted, 'You there. Soldier. Go to my house. I have friends there; tell them to meet me on the wall immediately.'

Baffled, Ganda'har asked, 'What are you doing, Khan?'

'They outnumber us four to one, Captain. We need the help, and they might just give it to us. Your Majesty, have any of the Balamuths chosen a warrior to bond with?'

'None. I believe you brought me duds,' King Naka said with a sneer on his face, then continued, 'They do not even want to bond with me, a great king!'

The guard lingered a bit to ensure there were no other tasks being handed out before turning to run down the street as fast as he could. Ganda'har stared after the man for a while before he answered, 'No, sire. Not duds, just fussy dragons.'

'We have one day. Figure this out!'

'Yes, sire,' their voices rang out in unison as they saluted their king before he turned and stomped off to his horse.

Ganda'har waited until the king was out of earshot, then said, 'Khan, what are you doing? Naka will hand her over in a blink of an eye.'

'Not if he sees her helping us. She's powerful, Ganda'har. We can use her in this fight.'

A shout came from the top of the wall: 'Ballistae! They bring ballistae, sir, and trebuchets!'

Ganda'har wanted to punch something. He wanted so badly not to be in charge of anyone right now, but here he stood, with the eyes of all these soldiers on him. 'This is going to be a long day,' he muttered.

* * *

'Those were his actual words?' Blanka stared down at the proliferating

321

camp. Perturbation had its hold over him as sweat dripped from his face.

'Yes, that's what he said. They're looking for her specifically. The question is, are you two going to run forever, or are you going to take a stand and fight? Unless we stop them here, you'll never be safe.' Khanaseri picked up some dirt from the floor and rubbed it in his hands.

Soldiers were busy carrying up bags of dirt on their shoulders to strew on the walkways atop the wall, to a depth of about an inch. Blanka wondered at this and pointed at the working men, then asked, 'Why are they doing this, Khan?'

Answering unwillingly, Khanaseri struggled to get the words out, 'It's...for when the blood flows. Dirt soaks up some of it, so it isn't as slippery. It won't last long, but it helps in the beginning.'

Beuneth settled a hand on Blanka's shoulder and said, 'Let's leave, Blanka. If we go, they'll follow us and leave the city alone. We'll give them a fighting chance.'

'No, they'll destroy us before going after you,' Khanaseri asserted. 'Just being on our lands with that army is an act of war. They can't take the chance that we would strike from behind. They have three bonded; we only have one. With you two with us, we at least stand a chance.' A gnawing thought pulled at him. *What if nothing we do will be enough? What if we all die? What if I'm sending the both of you to your deaths?* 'Look, ultimately, it's your choice. There will be no judgement from me.'

For all her beauty, you would think her hands soft as silk; but Blanka was reminded of her ability with the chain whip when Beuneth touched his arm with a calloused hand as she moved even closer and said, 'We're not soldiers, Blanka.'

He released a deep sigh as he stared at her. *His eyes seem so old,* she thought, unable to pull away from his gaze.

Blanka's head dropped as he closed his eyes and said, 'No, we're not soldiers.' Beuneth smiled before he continued, 'But we *are* fighters. We're assassins, thieves, hunters. We've been training from a younger age than any of these soldiers. Like it or not, Mother groomed us for war.' He took her hand in his as he continued, 'I beg of you, go. Leave this place and be safe. But I'm going to stay, my love. I'll see this through. They won't hunt you; I won't allow it.'

He had tugged at her heartstrings; she felt the deathblow hitting her chest, like a cannon ball finding its target. The slap was quick and harsh, leaving a red handprint on Blanka's face. 'How dare you even say that, after everything I've gone through to get you back?!' She wheeled around, and before he could stop her, she walked through a portal to disappear. Blanka turned to the warlock and said, 'Where do you want me?'

'I'm sorry, Blanka. It's not fair that I ask this of you.'

Blanka nodded, unwilling to comment, and just stared at the warlock as he chewed the inside of his cheek.

Khanaseri felt the moment grow, then said, 'Just be ready. They'll surely test our steel with the first encounter. Like I said, they have three bonded, so they could come from any side.'

*　*　*

The sun rose over the mountains, blinding the soldiers on the walls as they tried to search the horizon for the army's approach. Chants and war drums could be heard approaching when a dragon loomed into view from the east, blocking out the sun and revealing the thousands of soldiers in their march to the city. Fire flowed onto the wall, igniting soldiers and sending them tumbling down the sides as they searched for a quick end. Great arrows the size of an ox cart were fired from the ballistae on the wall at the dragon, making it flee as the army drew near. Archers fired from the walls as gigantic elephants trumpeted and raged forward, drawing ramps behind them.

An entire battalion had moved in during the night to flank the city from the east. Trebuchets from the ground catapulted rocks into the sky, sending soldiers scurrying for their lives as the boulders crashed down upon the wall.

Belgarr took to the air when he saw the dragon approach again to give cover to the war elephants as they neared the wall with the ramps. He sped forth and crashed into the attacking dragon as it clutched the side of the wall, spewing fire and incinerating everyone too slow to get out of its way. The collision shook the wall and sent men hurtling to the ground. 'Uldronth!' Belgarr raged. 'I should have known!'

Fangs and talons snapped and clawed as Belgarr drove the foreign dragon to the ground outside the city, leaving them both to roll down a large dune. He bit deep into Uldronth's thick leg, the black blood of the beast coating his mouth. A piercing cry brought his attention around before another dragon ripped into his side with its talons, trying to lift him off Uldronth.

The sound of clashing metal rang through the air as the fighting began, with the men from the past streaming up the ramps and onto the wall. Archers from the watchtowers loosed their arrows at the horde of men exiting the ramps, killing them in droves.

Back at the main wall, Khanaseri shouted orders to the men as the chaos ensued. 'Fire!' Ballistae bolts sailed through the sky, narrowly missing the dragon up high as fire rained down upon the walls.

Ganda'har shouted to the warlock, 'Get on my back — Blanka is in trouble!' He veered and stood before them in all his red magnificence. Khanaseri had not seen Ganda'har transform before now and had to shake his head to stop staring, then climbed aboard its broad back. The two had just taken to the sky at great speed towards the eastern wall when Khanaseri squinted and said, 'Is that another dragon coming from the city?' He watched as blue fire erupted from Ormarr to engulf the beast pulling on Blanka before it struck. A ferocious bite to the neck pulled the beast off him. It devolved to a jumble of dragons as they clawed and bit at each other, tearing at flesh with their talons and fangs.

Ganda'har pulled up and banked to the left, heading back to the dragon at the main wall as Khanaseri shouted his joy at Beuneth's return to the fight.

Fighting a war on all fronts, from the skies and from the surface, soldiers died in scores on both sides as those from the past stormed up the ramps. The oil on the outside of the wall suddenly ignited, setting fire to the ramps and soldiers as they tried to gain access to the parapets. The soldiers of Terenore could only look on in horror as the fire rained from the sky and sprang up from the trenches below, roasting them alive.

On top of the wall, stretcher bearers ran in, carting off dozens of injured to the healers in the city as quickly as possible, making space for the remaining soldiers.

'Are you ready, Khan?' asked the dragon form of Ganda'har in his roaring voice as they flew above the green, fire-breathing beast below.

Without an answer, Khanaseri leapt from the back of the beast, high in the sky, holding his axe out with both hands as he fell. *This is not a good idea.* A cry of pain came from the green dragon as the axe tore through its right wing. The warlock held on for dear life as the axe cut all the way through the wing to slip down its side. The world spun as the dragon flapped the broken wing uselessly about, trying to stabilise itself in the air.

With no more wing to cut, Khanaseri fell free of the beast, plummeting toward the wall below, and shouted, 'Ganda'har! A little help here!'

Massive talons plucked him from the sky and settled him to the wall before veering. Ganda'har stood at the edge, ready to jump again as he shouted, 'Khan, throw me your axe!'

'Be careful! It will drain you...' the warlock shouted as he did so, but Ganda'har had already taken to the sky once more. With no weapon in hand, Khan muttered, 'Great.' A man rushed at him with a big hammer, swinging for his head. Khanaseri stepped in and shouldered the man in the face. He could feel the man's nose break against his arm. It might even have been more than just the nose. The Terenoran staggered back, dazed and blind, as tears streamed down his face. The warlock grabbed the hammer from the man and pushed him over the parapet to plummet to his demise, killing three others as he fell on top of them. Khanaseri jumped into the fray, swinging the hammer left and right, and saw swords shatter as it clashed with the enemy's blades. He shouted to the surrounding men, 'Their steel is weak! It will not hold against ours!'

Thunderous cracks echoed and deafened those nearby as explosions rocked the massive gate, shattering the hinges. Pieces of wood and stone went flying into a smattering of nosy Artorean citizens of who had been unwilling to hide, as the gate succumbed and fell open.

King Turneroth's soldiers stood ready, waiting for just this moment, and charged in, hurling small metal balls through the gate. Explosions erupted; limbs flung everywhere as a concatenation of blasts sounded.

A few Artorean soldiers remained steadfast, fighting with the horde trying to gain entry. Untara was among them and dived as a boulder flew past from a trebuchet to smash into the building behind him. Stones from the collapsing building crashed down on his fellow soldiers as he was flung from his feet. He scrambled back up, grabbing the nearest attacker, and threw him up into a spike sticking out of the ruined building, impaling the man.

'Grab shields! Form a wall!' Geolas shouted as he joined in. The shield wall pushed the attackers back, but then more of the explosive silver balls were flung at them. Detonations rocked them and sent them flying. Dazed and bloodied, his shield damaged from the blast, Geolas looked up, waiting for a sword to end him, but to his surprise, saw the attackers wheel about as they were attacked from the rear. Blood ran down his temples and face as he rose from the ground, shouting, 'Get up, men! Fight!'

At Ganda'har's command, Stilts had taken a couple hundred soldiers through the secret tunnels under Artorea, leading out behind King Turneroth's soldiers at the gate. They started their extermination from the back, hacking their way forward. The horde was thinning as they continued their onslaught. Stilts felt something coming, drawing closer with the pull of magic as he hacked at a man's arm. Thrusting his blade into the dismembered soldier's throat, he looked around and felt the earth beneath them quake. Dread filled him then.

The men of Terenore fell back as the ground beneath them suddenly erupted, and a deafening wail covered the field of battle. From the deep, dark depths below, an Algare demon emerged from the ground, summoned by Terenore's mages. Fire blazed from the creature like molten lava roiling through its body as the creature swung a massive hammerhead on a blazing chain, crushing torsos and breaking limbs. It towered above even Untara, using its reach and strength to kill mercilessly.

* * *

One could barely see what was happening as the two black dragons became entangled high in the sky with streams of fire bursting into life occasionally. Uldronth — being the bigger of the two, with much larger horns on his head — slashed his talons through Belgarr's wing and ripped a gigantic tear to destabilise him. Belgarr kicked Uldronth away to fall to the ground at great speed, with Uldronth close on his tail as he gave chase. Fire arrows and ballistae bolts shot up from the wall at them as they neared. Unable to identify which black dragon was on their side, firing on both seemed the most logical conclusion. Belgarr aimed his fall to crash in the street, to avoid hitting the wall or the soldiers and do the least amount of damage possible. He watched with his keen vision as a ballista bolt was released, speeding towards his head. His timing was perfect. Just before the massive spear-like bolt could penetrate his skull, he spun to the right. A cry of pain sounded behind him, and he looked back to see the bolt pinned through Uldronth's leg as he turned to fly back to his camp.

Belgarr stopped his fall mere feet from the ground, straining his damaged wing, and veered back to human form, hitting the ground and rolling until he came to a stop against the wall of a building all bloodied. Soldiers quickly surrounded him, ready to spear him as he shouted, 'Where's the healer? I need a healer.'

A soldier pushed through the men and said, 'Lay down your weapons! He's with us!' Tamerick helped him up from the ground and walked with Blanka to the healers' tents, draping the man's left arm around his neck for support. Blood streamed down a large gash in Blanka's right arm. He felt lightheaded and ready to collapse as Tamerick guided him to an open bed, then shouted for a sewing kit. Madness ensued in the tents. Healers ran around trying to get to everyone in time, hoping to make a difference between life or death. Flies buzzed around the decrepit beds and tables the injured or dead men and women were lying on. The smell of death stung Blanka's nose; then he saw the dead being wheeled out on carts. He looked at Tamerick and said, 'Thank you for helping again. That's twice I owe you a debt.'

Tamerick fumbled with the sewing kit, pulled out a curved needle already supplied with thread, and said, 'When Captain Ganda'har addressed all of us earlier to tell us about these Balamuths, the bondings and dragons and all that, I must admit I found it a bit fantastical. But then I remembered you and went to investigate the area outside the city that was burned by the dragon. It was some terrible aiming on its part, as it missed every house, person, and animal. You two were the only ones needing help, and yet, there were no burn marks on you.'

Blanka chuckled and said, 'Well, I couldn't really come knocking on the gates as a dragon, now could I?'

'No, I suppose not.' Tamerick laughed and held out the needle, then said, 'Sterilise it.'

Holding the needle, Blanka blew on it until it turned bright red, waiting for it to cool before handing it back to Tamerick. He placed his leather belt in his mouth and bit down, holding his breath as the soldier pushed it through his skin repeatedly to close the gash under his biceps.

After Tamerick wrapped his arm with gauze, they walked outside and looked to the sky just in time to see Ganda'har descending rapidly on the main gate. *Gods, he's going far too fast to stop.*

A piercing cry sounded to his right from the wall, and Blanka saw Ormarr triumphantly rip the heart out of the green dragon's chest to throw it into the air before snatching and swallowing it. *Ugh, that's revolting. Uncooked dragon heart.*

Belgarr sensed his disgust and spoke to his mind, *'This is the way it has been for generations. The victor pulls the heart from his enemy and feasts upon it in a grandiose display of victory.'*

'You never heard of ale? That works just as well for celebrations.'

* * *

Everyone fell back as the Algare moved forward, exacting its revenge and hatred on the soldiers for their freedom and its incarceration in the underworld. Blood sprayed as it tore their limbs from their bodies. Lightning arced from Stilts, burning the demon's chest, pushing it back a few steps. It shrugged off the burn and advanced again, its hollow eyes locked on the young warlock.

Untara picked up a spear from one of the fallen and hurled it at the creature, slightly penetrating its thick hide before the weapon burst into flames from the heat radiating from the beast. *I need a bigger weapon.* A sabre sliced the air from his left as another attacker charged at him. Untara jumped back and grabbed the man's sword arm before he could reverse his thrust. The snap of his arm was quick, his death swift as Untara used the man's own arm to thrust the sword into his chest. *That's it. The ballista bolt.* He turned around and shouted to Stilts, 'Keep him busy!' then ran through the gate towards the stairs leading up the wall. The climb was exhaustive as men spilled down: stretcher bearers carrying wounded, broken warriors trying to escape the onslaught, and Turneroth's men advancing, hacking at everyone. One by one, he moved out of the way to let them pass or threw them from the hundred-foot wall. Finally reaching the top, he shouted over the chaotic scene on the wall at the men who worked the ballista, 'Aim for the demon at the gate! The gate! We're losing the gate!' Slowly, the construction turned as the men leaned in to move it. *Stilts won't last out there alone. This is taking too long.*

From above, Ganda'har saw the Algare at the gate and dived at full speed, seeing only one man left trying to defend against the beast.

Stilts threw fireballs, lightning, and gusts of wind to thrust the demon back, but he wasn't strong enough. The Algare broke through his defences to grab the young warlock by his collar and hurl him into the wall. His head bounced off the stone, leaving a splash of red behind. His vision drifted. A great pain suddenly ripped through his chest as his senses returned to him. He felt his feet dangle in the air and looked down to see the spike protruding from his chest. Gasping for air, Stilts pushed with his palms against the building, screaming as he felt the metal bar scrape the inside of his chest. The pain was surreal. With a last heave, it tore his back open as he slid off to collapse on the ground. Blood gushed from the wound at his back as pink froth bubbled at his mouth. He looked up, his breathing ragged, and saw his dragon captain dive towards the demon faster than anything on the field. If one blinked, they would miss him.

Halfway down, Ganda'har veered and grabbed the axe, holding it high in wait to bring it down upon the creature. Shouting as he fell, a blue light started emanating from the axe. He could feel his power being drained as the axe readied itself. With all his might, he brought it down on the demon's back.

Flesh, bone, and steel met with a thunderous crack, creating a shock wave strong enough to throw the surrounding soldiers from their feet. The ground trembled beneath the whole battlefield, and warriors stopped to look around before continuing their fight.

The massive dust cloud dissipated, and the warriors saw the Algare slowly rise to its feet and climb out of the crater. It staggered as the battle axe hung from its back, the blade completely sunk to the haft. Ganda'har lay off to one side, unmoving, as the beast turned to him, swinging the hammer on the chain.

Up on the wall, Untara pushed a soldier out of his way and took over the ballista. He clenched his teeth as he moved the structure on its base and lined up the shot. Guards were at his back, protecting the big man as he grabbed the heavy, thick ropes to cock the weapon. Usually it took three men to achieve this, but alone and charged with adrenalin, Untara lifted the ropes in place and fired. The bolt bucked through the air and sliced into the Algare's right leg, sending it to the ground with a scream of rage.

'Load another one trailing a long rope!' he shouted as he moved the ballista a fraction more. He saw the creature get up again, then break off the bolt in its leg. It would not be deterred as it lifted its arms to swing the chained hammer towards the unmoving captain.

The sound of the massive bow releasing the arrow was like a drum being beaten in Untara's ears as he watched it fly true. Time slowed for him as he willed the arrow through the demon's head. Brains and black, viscous matter splattered to the ground as it toppled and fell for good. He jumped up, swinging his fist in the air as he shouted his joy.

Cheers went up from the guards around him as one asked, 'What was the rope for?'

Untara turned to him, relieved, and said, 'I ain't takin' the stairs again.'

Ganda'har blinked open his eyes and crawled towards the fallen Stilts as he lay dying. Soft groans escaped the warlock's mouth as Ganda'har cradled the young man's head and said, 'Don't speak; everything will be just fine. We'll get you some help, soldier. You did a fine job. I couldn't be prouder of you.'

Shaking terribly, Stilts pulled a parchment from his pocket and handed it to Ganda'har as he said, 'Mmmyy...o o ww wi nn g.'

His last breath released the tension in his body as Ganda'har stared down at the young man and sighed, then closed the glassy dead eyes with his fingers, and said, 'There's a good lad. It's all over now, it's all over.'

Great cracks tore open the ground, a most foul odour spilling from them as a plethora of creatures of the underworld clawed their way to the top to wreak havoc on the city. Creatures with no eyes and sinewy, skeletal figures squirmed out of the cracks, taking flight with their ghastly decayed wings. Their sharp talons and fangs ripped into the flesh of the defending soldiers, sending them scurrying for cover. Bigger demons crawled out with spikes threaded through their chest muscles. Attached to these were long chains with gigantic, skinless, hound-like creatures at the other ends. The hellhounds snarled and growled, pulling on the chains to be released. They wanted to feast on all the fresh meat.

High above, the sun beat its rays down upon them, making all weapons slippery as the sweat collected in their palms. Ganda'har quickly surveyed the area as he ran to pull the axe from the fallen Algare, and saw his warriors charging toward the demons with Stentor in the lead, shouting her war-cries as she swung her axe to cleave one demon in half. Geolas fired arrow after arrow while Talgar commanded his men to a flanking position on one of the bigger demons. Untara ran in with no regard for his own safety, grabbing any creature close by and crushing it with as much power as possible. Captain Kornek joined the fight at Geolas' side to aid the warrior as he got separated from his group. More and more men joined the fight against this new threat.

A big demon pointed at Ganda'har and let loose his pet monster. The ravenous creature's jaws snapped and talons ripped at Ganda'har's face as he jumped to get out of its way. He brought up the axe and sliced through the beast's scapula, then quickly brought it back down to lop off its head. Its groans faded as it died. The demon ran in, twisting the chain of the fallen hound around the captain, and pulled it tight. A second beast attacked, lunging at Ganda'har's throat. Blood ran down his face as he struggled to break free. Dropping to his knees, he gripped the axe and loosed a cry for power; the axe glowed brightly as he pushed his chest and arms out with all his might. One by one, the links started melting, giving way until he heard a loud *snap*. The chain suddenly fell limp to the ground, and the axe tore into the demon-hound before him, splitting it in two as black blood sprayed all over him. He reached down to grab the chain and ran at the big demon as it staggered back from the sudden release of tension. The chain sailed over its neck and he pulled the beast to the ground with so much force the earth shook beneath his feet. He twisted the chain around the creature's thick neck, pulling and pulling until a deep crunch sounded as the demon's head fell away, spilling its viscous blood over his feet. Exhausted, he collapsed. For a few heartbeats he lay on the ground, catching his breath, as there was no immediate threat to him. From a distance away, he heard a loud voice shout, 'Oi, Cap'n! No time for naps now! We got some killin' to do!'

Ganda'har sighed as he mumbled, 'Oh, shut up, Stentor, just shut up.'

* * *

King Turneroth stood in the shade under the pergola, conferring with his generals as they moved chess pieces around on the crudely drawn map of the area. A voice came from his right. 'We need to pull the men back, Your Majesty. It's a mess out there, and we're gaining no ground.'

The four men around the table stared at Caryk with their omniscient demeanour. 'You think us stupid, Caryk?' one demanded. 'We have destroyed their gate! We *can't* stop pushing now!'

Caryk's eyes glowed red as he hobbled closer to the stocky General Viseth on his bandaged leg and growled, 'We've lost Varik. His heart was ripped from his chest and *eaten* by one of their bonded. Ragian lost his wing and can barely fly. They skewered me with one of their ballistae bolts. They have superior weapons! Our blades are shattering against their steel. Our men are getting slaughtered by the thousands!'

King Turneroth interjected, 'Caryk, if we stop now, they will repair their gate and we'll have to start all over again. Thousands more would be slaughtered.'

'The men are exhausted!' Caryk slumped and sighed deeply. 'Apologies, my king. I did not mean to yell.' He rubbed at his eyes and gestured for Ragian to join them.

Ragian jogged up to the pergola, his arm bandaged and in a sling. A deep cut to his torso saw his clothes stained red as blood seeped from the wound. A high-pitched wail sounded from above as Ormarr flew over their advancing army in the distance, sorcery rolling out from him in waves as he descended on the troops in the front line. Men turned on each other, trying to get out of his path as lightning followed his flight. The constant flashes and thunder drowned out all sounds as it hit ground and man alike, exploding everything it touched. Fire burst forth from Ormarr's mouth, incinerating the ones left standing.

'Pull the men back! Pull them back now! Where's Bohan? Bring the sorcerer to me!' the king shouted as he stared at the slaughter taking place on the battlefield.

Chapter Seventeen

B lanka screamed in pain as Caryk slowly drew the knife across his wrists, cutting to the bone. Blood streamed to the floor as he hung upside down, gravity doing its work. 'Oh, I don't know how long he'll last, Beuneth. Better hurry, dear! Belgarr can only heal him so fast, you know,' Caryk said with a smirk.

'Blanka! Let Belgarr out, burn them to hell! Why are you just hanging there?' she shouted, reaching out to him. 'This is all lies!'

His face was a mess, his eyes swollen shut and bleeding from multiple wounds. Searching for her voice, he mumbled, 'Beany! Is that you?'

Caryk laughed. 'The fool came in the night, begging for your life and for the fighting to stop. Oh, don't look so disappointed. He never stood a chance.' Caryk moved to stand under Blanka and brought his knife up to the man's throat, pressing hard enough for blood to trickle down.

'No! Stop! Please!' Beuneth started forward. 'What do you want from me?'

Caryk smiled as he said, 'You, Beuneth. We want you. You can make all this stop.'

* * *

Startled and shocked, her hands trembled as she woke up in the sweat-stained sheets and realised that Blanka wasn't next to her. *No! This can't be happening again.* She gathered her gear and hurried outside. The stars were still out, but the roosters would crow soon.

Ormarr took to the sky, his wings sending gusts of wind roiling over the ground to stir up the dust. He sailed over the city in silence. Men and women saw the red dragon and felt calm as their protector patrolled the air. Gliding over the western wall, he looked down at the enemy soldiers scurrying about, preparing for the next attack. The main gate had been repaired and drawn closed as masons and smiths worked tirelessly through the night.

In the distance, fires blazed throughout the camped army's grounds; and off to the left, the portal raged on. Unnatural cold rolled over him as he neared the portal and banked to his right. The portal seemed to flinch outward. Dark clouds rolled overhead as lightning continuously struck the earth in its vicinity. *Something isn't right with that portal. It needs to be closed,* Beuneth thought. '*I can feel your animosity, your hatred bubbling forth, Ormarr. I want to see them all burn as well, but I can't take that chance with them having Blanka.*'

A low rumble reverberated through his neck. 'Yes, child. I feel your love for the man. But I fear it will be our undoing.'

She was silent then.

Shouts went up in the camp as he glided over the lit-up area. Blanka was hanging upside down from a wooden gibbet in chains, his face red from the blood spilling from his wounds.

'*This will be a trap, child,*' Ormarr said in her mind as he descended into the clearing a few feet from where King Turneroth stood with his hands behind his back. Melancholy settled in, followed by rage as she saw Blanka all beaten up, struggling to breathe, chains wrapped tightly around his chest. Burning saliva dripped from Ormarr's maw, creating sizzling sounds as it fell to the cold sand. Lightning coursed around her as she veered to stand before them. 'Let him go!' Dozens of soldiers surrounded her, with arrows following her every move. Men with swords and spears, axes and hammers stood ready to charge at the first sign of a threat.

King Turneroth stepped forward calmly as Caryk drew the knife closer to Blanka's throat and said, 'Oh, so hostile. Let's be civil.'

His infuriatingly calm demeanour sent dark thoughts racing through her head. Pushing them aside, Beuneth said, 'What is it you want?'

The king moved aside to reveal a pedestal covered with a red satin sheet. He pulled it away and flung it to the ground. 'All I want from you, as Gatekeeper, is to force this bonding. If you do, I will spare his life. If you don't...well, I guess I don't have to complete that thought.'

'Don't do it, child. Something is not right. A bond should not be forced! To form this bond, you would need to release the Gatekeeper. He will tear us apart!' Ormarr shouted in her head.

'We can kill one more dragon. Now, hush! I need to think.'

Blanka shouted as he hung from the chains, 'Beuneth! Don't do it!' The sharp knife slid across his wrists, and an exuberant amount of blood streamed to the ground. His pale visage made the tattoos on his face look like veins.

'No! Please!' Beuneth started.

'Listen to me, you pestilent woman,' said the enemy king. 'You took everything from me. Because of you, all the neighbouring kingdoms will now seek to overthrow me. There will be war upon war, and we have no defences. You have left us vulnerable. At least with the threat of the dragons, we could abstain from war and have a peaceful life. But you couldn't let that be.' King Turneroth walked forward, pointing his finger at her, then said, 'You and your selfish desire wrought suffering on us all. All this blood is on your hands! You, Beuneth, are the harbinger of sorrow. Caryk, cut his throat. She will have to live with this forever.'

As Caryk drew the blade against Blanka's throat, ready to cut, she shouted, 'No! Stop!' Her thoughts ran wild, the world spinning. *So much destruction. So much death. All because of me. The king is right. I need to atone.* 'I will grant your bond. Just let him go.'

The king smiled as he said, 'You have my word. He will be let go unharmed. Now, what do we do?'

* * *

'Khan, why haven't they attacked yet? Daylight has come, and I see no troops lining up,' Blanka said, peering over the parapet as the sun warmed their backs.

The warlock stroked his beard and said, 'A good question indeed, my friend. Maybe we bloodied them more than we thought yesterday.'

'One can only hope. Have you seen Beuneth? I left her early so she could sleep a little longer, but I thought she would be up by now.'

'Hey, use those dragon eyes of yours and see what's going on there in the centre of their camp. I can't make out what that is.' Khanaseri squinted as he looked in the distance and cursed under his breath.

'It looks like they've strung up a man to a gibbet. I can't make out the woman. Wait. No! Beuneth!?' Angst grabbed him, constricting his throat as he backed away and said, 'What is she doing? Is that a Balamuth?' He veered and took flight. Khanaseri shouted and tried to grab him, but he was too late.

The warlock turned and shouted down the line, 'Get Ganda'har up here! Now! And everybody better get their gear ready. Things are about to get rough!'

* * *

'*Forgive me, Ormarr.*' Deep inside her, she saw the Gatekeeper still in chains, struggling to break free. 'Gatekeeper, I am breaking your chains for a bonding to occur. Heed my summons and officiate this bonding.' She felt the chains snap and saw the enjoyment of the Gatekeeper as she freed him.

A voice in her head declared, '*You know I have no choice but to heed this summons. But I warn you, performing a bonding between unwilling parties could go very wrong.*'

King Turneroth stepped forward and stood before the Balamuth, loosening his limbs as if readying for a fight. Beuneth took hold of his hand and placed it on the Balamuth as she said, 'Great serpent of the skies, make yourself known to us.'

Power radiated from the Balamuth as it awakened, her head ringing as she heard, 'I am Belroc. Who dares awaken me from my slumber?'

King Turneroth flinched as he felt the power come alive, and for a moment seemed unsure of his actions. He glanced at Caryk, still holding the knife over Blanka's throat, then looked back to Beuneth.

She pushed back at the colossal power and said, 'We seek to assuage your penance with a bonding to our King Turneroth Brajuck, so you can fly free once more and assert your dominance along with the ruler of Terenore.'

'I will not be party to your game, Gatekeeper. No mere mortal can contain me. Now leave me be.'

The king shouted, 'I am not some mere mortal, you arrogant beast. I am a king! And you will bow before me and pay homage to your true ruler!'

Beuneth felt Belroc blatantly ignore the king as he crawled back into his cave. Chanting under her breath, she felt her mind touching Belroc's.

An instant eruption of anger surged through the dragon as he felt the entanglement happening without his authority. Unwillingly pulled from the cave, he clawed to stay hidden. The sheer weight of the beast made her legs buckle as her mind staggered at the task. In her mind's eye, she finally saw the beast revealed. All pragmatic sensibilities left her as she reeled at the thought of having this beast trapped in her.

The sphere dissolved to mist as it hovered before the king, surrounding him and seeping into his skin. Laughter rang out as the king saw the improbable become a reality. He'd never thought he would live to see the day of the awakening, and not in the least for him to be the host of the Alpha.

Beuneth opened her eyes as the last of the Balamuth entered the king, and said, 'My part is done, king. Brace yourself as I release him in you. Are you ready?'

'More than I have ever been.'

She let go of the king's hand, and said, 'Belroc, I release you from your prison.' Movement caught her eye to the right, and as she looked up, she felt the sting of a blade slicing through her back. *How can this be? Blanka, how are you in two places?* Beuneth looked at the man hanging from the gibbet and saw that he now had another face. *A simple mirage spell. How did I miss that?*

Fire suddenly surrounded her as talons picked her up from the ground and lifted her to the skies. Arrows and spears sailed past as Blanka weaved through the air, racing as fast as he could to the healers behind the wall.

* * *

Pandemonium erupted as the black dragon settled Beuneth down next to the healers' tents. Blanka veered and picked her up as he shouted, 'I need a healer! Come quickly! Please!'

Men streamed out of the tents and took Beuneth from his arms, taking care not to jostle the scimitar still protruding from her stomach. Blanka pulled at his hair as he paced up and down, watching as she convulsed on the little wood-framed bed. Healers worked frantically on her, trying to calm her body. They injected her with a yellow substance to ease her, but the fits just got worse.

Khanaseri came running around the corner and skidded to a halt before him. 'What happened, Blanka?'

'Those fuckers tricked her, Khan. Used my face to lure her out. I think she had to perform a bonding with their king. I'm going to rip their fucking hearts out!'

The warlock's face sagged as he listened to his friend, and said, 'That means the Gatekeeper is loose in her again. He's what's tearing her apart, not just the sword.' Khanaseri immediately chanted as he stared at her, seeing her body grow calm so the healers could work on her. Steadily, they pulled out the scimitar and threw it to the ground.

The clangour of the metal resonated in Blanka's ears, drumming as it flopped on the stone floor, scattering drops of her blood over the hem of his grey robe. As they stemmed the bleeding, Khan pushed them aside to get to her. Touching her mind, he searched for her. The moment of silence stretched out like an agonising lifetime for Blanka. After a little more time, the warlock opened his eyes slowly and looked away as he said, 'She's gone, my friend. I'm sorry.'

'No! That can't be!' Blanka ran forward and took her hand as he stared into her lifeless eyes. 'Beany! Wake up! Come back to me!' A healer tried to pry Blanka from her and caught a fist to his nose. Blanka bent back down and shook her at the shoulders, tears and mucus running down his face as he shouted her name. A horrible cry roared out of him as dragon and man screamed and cried together.

The warlock found it unbearable to just stand by and watch the suffering Blanka was enduring, so Khanaseri pushed him aside as he reached out to her. Blanka dropped his head into his hands as he looked on. The warlock chanted at her side, trying to bring her back, but there was nothing — not even a spark.

A shout came from the right. 'Wait!' Ganda'har held out a canteen as he ran to them and shouted, 'Give her this! It's water from the spring of Ananathia. I brought it back from Terenore.' He handed the canteen to the warlock, and continued, 'Beuneth said it cures all ills.'

Blanka's eyes brightened with the little hope given as he watched Khanaseri slowly pour the beautiful blue liquid down her throat, then hold her mouth closed, mumbling under his breath. A gasp escaped him as he saw the wound on her stomach slowly close and heal. 'I can't believe it.' Blanka rushed forward to her side, shaking her as he said, 'Beany! Beany, come back to me!' But she did not open her eyes.

Khanaseri lay his hand on her forehead, and after a while he stood and said, 'The spring of Ananathia only cured her physically. She's still gone from us. Again, I'm sorry, my friend.'

Blanka sagged to the ground, sobbing as he did, then jumped up and pushed past the watching men and women. He grabbed the scimitar from the ground and took to the sky as he veered, throwing the healers to the ground with the gusts of his lift-off. As he passed over the city walls, he felt a great weight settle on him, driving him to the ground. Ganda'har was above him, pushing down. Belgarr blew a burst of flames past his head as the dragon captain said to his mind, *'I know it hurts, Blanka. But you can't go in there alone. They will kill you, and we need you still!'*

'I don't care if you need me! They must die!'

'Just look, Blanka – you can't defeat that alone! You'll throw away your life for nothing!' In the distance, he saw King Turneroth veering, a much slower process than for them. *That's odd; it shouldn't take that long. Might just be his first veering.* At last, a charcoal-grey dragon with red streaks covering his body stood in the centre of the camp, at least twice their size. A mighty, piercing cry went up to the sky as it stared at them. *'It's Belroc. He has awakened. We have to get out of here. Belgarr, you know I speak the truth. Turn back, brother.'*

The cries from Belroc went unabated as the two turned and headed back to the city. A thunderous crack sounded to their right, and as they looked upon the unstable portal, a dragon flew through. Then another. And another.

'He's summoning his kin! This is bad. We need to get to Khan.'

* * *

Women and children ran for the underground crypts as dozens of dragons streamed out of the portal, one by one. Khanaseri stood on the wall, chanting as loudly as he could, then turned and shouted to a soldier running past, 'Bring all the warlocks and mages you can find! Anyone who can use the arts, however weakly!' He continued his chant until Ganda'har and Blanka joined him on the wall, and momentarily stopped as he asked, 'What *is* that thing?'

Memories of the last summoning burned bright in Blanka's head. He had been powerless to resist the pull of the Alpha then. As a mindless drone, he had worked his way to the beast and did its bidding, killing and destroying cities. The war had raged for years, with so many deaths on both sides. Now he was his own master. The bonded weren't affected by the call of the Alpha as much as the unbonded. They could resist the urge. 'That, my friend, is Belroc, the king of the dragons.'

'Ganda'har, we need to close that portal!' Khanaseri called out.

The captain was shouting orders to the surrounding men, then wheeled on Khanaseri and said, 'We can't afford to waste our resources on the portal with that army coming for us!'

'That portal is becoming self-sustaining. It's feeding off the world to keep itself alive. It could grow and devour the world if it's not closed. The quicker we stop it, the fewer dragons we have to deal with. That should be our priority!' Khanaseri had to shout now to be heard over the roars of the dragons in the distance.

Ganda'har turned away slightly as he thought, then nodded to the warlock.

A deafening war-cry sounded from the Terenoran troops as they charged the city. Khanaseri hung over the edge of the wall with half his body, holding onto the pole of one of the now-scorched black-on-white eagle-crested flags of Artorea to get a better view. 'Get ready, men! This will be our last stand! Protect the mages and warlocks at all costs! Everyone, soldiers included, repeat after me! *Emas nhuly amas naghte, amanus vaghte!* Again!' He jumped back on to the wall as sorcery rolled out from them in waves, buffeting the portal. Archers moved to the front of the wall, sending volleys of arrows into the stampeding Terenorans. Scores of men fell beneath the trampling feet of their brothers-in-arms as the arrows sliced into them.

Arrows sailed up from Turneroth's men from below, only to hit a wall of shields as infantry soldiers stood ready to protect their mages and warlocks. Few arrows made it past their shields, slicing into an arm here, a leg there; but nothing fatal.

With the ramps all burned down, ladders were now being pushed up against the wall as the attacking army braced for the arrows raining down on them from the wall. Their small wooden shields were barely big enough to cover their bodies and they relied more on the hopes that someone next to them would be hit, like a flock of birds attacked by a hawk. They streamed up the ladders to gain access to the wall, dying by the dozens as they attempted to secure a foothold. Bodies fell from up high on the advancing men and women. Farther to the east, the clangour of metal on metal sounded as they gained a beachhead there, and shouted their cheers to their companions, urging them on.

Khanaseri watched the slaughter unfold, keeping his focus on his chanting even as he saw Artorean soldiers topple off the wall with arrows in their guts or chests. An opening appeared before them, and enemy soldiers climbed up with weapons drawn. Infantry stepped in to block their path, slicing up and down, left and right with their swords. Bodies fell to the ground, spilling their blood, soaked up by the dirt on the floor. Ganda'har threw a man off the wall and into the nearest ladder, snapping it in half, as the sudden weight was too much to bear. Another got impaled by the stump of the broken ladder as he fell.

The captain stood watching the circling dragons and knew it wouldn't be long before they accepted Belroc as Alpha once more. Although the Alpha had considerable power over them, there was still the matter of the *Fov-lak*: a chance given to any dragon strong enough to resist the urge and take on the Alpha for leadership. But he knew none of those he saw would dare try. They would come soon to join the fight.

Mages and warlocks lined the walls of Artorea, chanting with Khanaseri to close the portal as more dragons flew through to join the dozens already circling their Alpha. The portal flickered and shuddered for the briefest of moments as it closed and reopened, cutting a dragon in half as it came out at that instant. The front half of its body fell to the ground in the distance to roll over the sand dunes to the bottom of the hill. 'It's working!' Ganda'har shouted over the chanting in the background. Everyone chanting could feel a shift in their bodies, as if moving a little slower. The spell was sapping their energy to close the portal.

Two dragons broke off from the maelstrom above the Alpha and headed for the wall. A pure white drake with a yellow tinge under its wings was in the lead, trailed by a blue beast with colossal horns.

Ganda'har nudged Blanka and said, 'Are you ready for this?' He looked into the bloodshot eyes of the man, and saw the hatred in them. 'Looks like you are. Here, take this sword.'

Blanka shook his head and said, 'No. Today I kill with my bare hands.'

Both men leapt off the wall to rise in their Dragovian forms.

A few moments later, a fierce cry was heard by all over the fighting and dying of the warriors on the wall. Shouts of panic sounded through the air as another dragon spewed fire over everyone in his path, melting their flesh to get to the mages and warlocks. Nobody had seen it coming from the rear. Khanaseri screamed and charged at the dragon as it reared up from the wall. It had death in its entranced eyes, and that saddened the warlock. The beast spewed fire as the warlock leapt from the wall with his axe held high. Sorcery from the blade shielded him from the heat as it scythed through the flames. Khanaseri suddenly burst through the roiling fire. The blade cut deep into the side of the dragon's face as it turned away, thinking the warlock was dead. Enraged, it howled and staggered as it tried to pry the warlock from the axe. It crashed into the wall and tumbled over into the streets of Artorea.

Thrown from the beast, Khanaseri clutched the axe and hit the ground hard, skidding some distance away from the beast as it thrashed on the ground. It struggled to get to its feet, comically kicking the air to shift its weight like an overturned turtle. The beast thrashed about until it finally flipped over and stared into Khanaseri's eyes. Heat radiated from its mouth, then fire erupted as it charged. Khanaseri dived to the left to avoid the flames. As he rose, a tremendous tail-slap to his chest sent the wind rushing from his lungs as he hit the top of a broken-down wall, flipping him over to the other side. Green and silver flashed through the street as the dragon bore down on him in an instant, baring its fangs as Khanaseri scrambled for cover. The enormous beast drove him into a corner, pressing him back. Swinging the axe left and right, he staved off the inevitable crush from the powerful jaws. Fire enveloped the area as it opened its maw. The warlock stood with the axe in front of him, forming a shield of magic to repel the heat from the blast. Trying to get out of the corner, he ran and leapt over some rubble as fast as he could, but the gigantic tail crashed into his chest again with tremendous force, throwing him back to the wall.

Soldiers had converged on them by then, throwing spears and loosing arrows at the beast, but its scales were too thick to penetrate.

Khanaseri struggled to open his eyes and saw the blood on his shirt. As he rose, more ran out of his mouth. A coughing fit racked him as he spat to the side to get rid of the taste then looked around with his right eye and saw the axe some distance away. His left eye was swollen shut, his face burning from a deep gash.

The dragon towered above the warrior and growled. It sounded like laughter rumbling from the beast. It bore down on him at great speed, and he waited until the very last moment to jump out of the way. He grabbed the axe and hurled it as hard as he could at the beast. It thudded against its thick neck, the blade of the axe sinking deep, emanating a blue light that seemingly burned the creature. Off-balance and in pain, it staggered to its right, wailing as it tried to pull the axe from its neck with its teeth and talons. Soldiers scrambled underneath its feet as they threw spears and loosed more arrows at the reeling beast.

Another massive form sailed over Khanaseri and crashed into the dragon's flank, taking it to the ground, but it wouldn't keep it there long.

The warlock surveyed his surroundings and shouted at Talgar, 'Ready the men! Get those chains from those big, stinking demon creatures. We're going to kill us a dragon.' Standing in the middle of the street, he shouted as loud as he could, 'Come and get me, you overgrown eel!'

Belgarr was thrown off the beast and into a pile of rubble before fire engulfed him. The green-and-silver dragon turned its focus on the warrior in the street waving his hands in the air, and charged in. It was so focused on Khanaseri, it didn't see the chain snap up in front of its feet.

Ballistae bolts the size of three spears were fired into the sky, trailing thick chains. Piercing screams rocked the city as the first bolt thundered into the dragon's leg, then others into its wings and its other leg, and were pulled taut by the pulley systems used to load the massive bows. The dragon thrashed about, but couldn't break the dozen chains that pinned it to the ground. Khanaseri ran up the dragon's wing to stand on its head and shouted down, 'Throw me the axe!'

Fire burst out from the beast as it lay strapped to the ground, melting the earth to glass before it. Untara walked up its side, to where the axe was still embedded in its neck, and brutally yanked it out and threw it up to the warlock. Blood gushed from the severe wound. Khanaseri looked down with his axe in hand, ready to deal the death blow, and in his mind, he heard the dragon say, *'Finish it.'*

Shouts from his right rang out. 'Khan! Wait!' Blanka ran closer and said, 'Go finish with the portal. I have to try to reason with it. It's not their fault. They're as much unwilling participants in this war as us. I have to believe Beuneth wouldn't have wanted them free just to die in this war.'

The warlock jumped down and said, 'I hope you know what you're doing, Blanka. Wars can't be won by sentiment.'

'Yes, me too,' came the whisper from Blanka.

Khanaseri turned and ran for the wall, leaving Blanka to deal with the trussed beast.

* * *

'I hate this blasted desert. There's no middle ground. You never walk through here thinking, "Wow, this is nice." No, it's always burning you alive or freezing you to death.' Lanik fed an apple core to his horse and stroked its neck.

'You're right, Lanik, but something feels off with this temperature. It feels malignant. Volatile, somehow.' Spurring on her horse, Ladriana made her way up the side of a dune and called back down, 'Hey, come look at this.'

The horses were spooked as they drew close to the top and reared, shaking their heads in fear. Lanik dropped to the ground and said, 'Take them down to the road. I'll see what's going on.'

Through his spyglass, he saw swirling clouds spinning around the massive rift as lightning thundered down around it. Warriors advanced on Artorea in the distance. A siege of epic proportions was taking place. Too far away to hear anything, he could only see the movement of soldiers as they gathered in the distance. Dragons burst out of the rift, one after the other, and Lanik gasped as he dropped to the ground. He waited a while for his heart to calm and stood again to see. He saw another reptile glide out of the breach, then another, to circle the tear in the universe and finally settle down on the ground in the midst of the attacking army's camp.

Is my mind playing tricks on me? 'Not your problem, Lanik. Go home, be a king... Oh, who am I kidding?' he said to himself as he descended the dune and vaulted on the back of his mount.

'What did you see?' Ladriana asked, as she handed him the reins.

'Death. I saw the coming of death,' he said, as looked at her with pure exasperation.

Ladriana rolled her eyes as she stood with her arms to her sides and said, 'Do you always have to be so dramatic? What does that even mean?'

'Dozens of dragons and still more coming through a portal, with an army of tens of thousands at their backs.' He shook his head and cursed, then continued, 'There's a mountain up north. We stopped there a while back when I was with the Desert Dogs. There are some stone formations with carvings on them. I need to go there, now.'

Ladriana stood frozen for a time before she marched up the dune to look for herself, then muttered, 'Dear gods, what is this madness?'

* * *

Bustling with crowded mobs of soldiers, the chaotic line to the rift was a constantly moving wyrm over the sands of the desert. Ragian stood, watching the injured soldiers and the dead being carried back to Terenore. Thousands had gone through already, and more were streaming in. He took his arm out of the sling and moved it around, slowly rotating his shoulder to get some blood flowing. From above, the wails of the summoned dragons fighting to resist the Alpha's command – which he knew to be pointless – made Isaluth recoil deep within him. A forceful gust of wind suddenly buffeted him from the back, waving his shoulder-length brown hair to obscure his vision. He sighed as he looked back and saw the black dragon settle down and veer.

'What are you doing out of camp, Ragian? I could feel your animosity for what's happening a mile away,' Caryk said as he ambled up the dune to stand next to the man.

'We can't do this, Caryk. We're murdering an entire city and sending thousands of our men to their deaths. For what?' Ragian spoke with his hands behind his back, composed on the outside while turmoil reigned within. He continued, 'Is this what we've become? Murderers?' He pointed to the assault happening at their backs, as fires raged and winged beasts descended upon the city, the clash of steel ringing loudly across the desert.

Caryk grabbed the man's arm and said, 'Keep your voice down. Do you want to be executed for treason? He'll burn you alive where you stand. Like it or not, we're in this now.' They looked over to the king as he stared at the burning city of Artorea, overjoyed with his new pets.

Ragian paced up and down on the sand dunes, glaring at his commander, and said, 'You know, brother, what it felt like to be summoned by Belroc.'

'Yes, sadly I do. Now go back to camp, Ragian. They'll need our help in the last push to victory.'

Furious, Ragian veered, took to the air, and flew back to camp.

Caryk smirked as he veered and flew in the opposite direction, heading for the rift.

* * *

The Artorean mages and warlocks were exhausted. Some fell to the ground trembling, barely breathing, as the rift sucked the energy from their bodies. All the dragons broke off from the circle above the Alpha and headed in their direction. Khanaseri froze as he saw the winged beasts drawing closer, and shouted his chant as hard as he could, hoping to inspire the rest of the exhausted mages. The chant slowly picked up again, and he saw the portal flinch. The waves of sorcery hit it over and over as the dragons swarmed them.

Fire burst forth over them as the beasts hovered above. Soldiers ran for their lives, but the mages and warlocks stood their ground. Fire raged around them as some cast a protective barrier to cover the group. He could barely see anymore. Adrenaline was the only thing keeping him going. A blow to his head sent his vision swimming for a moment as someone clubbed him with a mace. Khanaseri spun around and grabbed the man by the throat, twisted his hand, and tore it out.

More men rushed in to meet him. He grabbed his axe, swinging left and right. Bodies fell before him as the deadly axe cleaved its way through flesh and bone. His arms burned with fatigue. Khanaseri knew he couldn't hold out for much longer.

Ganda'har dived in his Dragovian form from above, extending his talons, and ripped into the dragon closest to the mages. Both beasts tumbled to disappear into the torrent of raging fire below.

With the setting sun, they couldn't anticipate the dragons' movements anymore. There were too many of them anyway. *Turneroth's men and the dragons will just keep coming, pushing and pushing until nothing is left standing.* Belgarr climbed the wall despite his broken wing and spewed fire at the dragons and charging men of Terenore. A beast of green and silver crashed into him and carried him away into the darkness. Screams and cries of terror followed in his wake until they faded away into the darkness.

Khanaseri fought with everything he had. His left leg buckled under him as a spear was thrust into his thigh. *Oh, Father. How did you always survive against such odds?!* 'Help me, Father!' He wasn't aware that he was shouting the words aloud. The axe glowed; a blue mist drifting from its blade, enveloping Khanaseri and filling his being. He screamed at the top of his voice as he brought the hammerhead of the axe down to the ground. The wall ruptured beneath him, quaking the earth as an enormous explosion followed by a wave of sorcery blasted outward, throwing the mages and warlocks from their feet. Dragons turned and fled frantically to escape from the rolling sorcery charging with a wave of violence. Some were caught in its rage, their scales and flesh melting from their bones. Charred dragon limbs fell to the ground below.

The blast went outward, doming the city and burning everything it touched. Everyone ran for cover from the deadly blast. Darkness took the warlock then, as his body gave in to exhaustion.

* * *

'These carvings must be thousands of years old, Lanik. What makes you think any descendants, let alone the actual people that carved them, still exist?' Ladriana asked, as she rubbed her arms to bring a little heat back into her body.

'Just keep looking. Anavi saw something here that pointed to them still existing. And by the looks of the glyphs, as far as I can make out, they knew how to imprison the dragons. After they captured the big one, see here,' he pointed to a glyph of a gigantic dragon flying above the men and continued, 'See, it's bigger than any of the other dragons. In the next glyph, it disappears into these spheres. They locked them all away. When all was done, they left. They didn't die; they moved on. Here they are on what looks like a beach. Then gone. Vanished from existence. If anyone can help, it would be them.'

* * *

Birds did not chirp, and the cicadas were silent. None of the normal joyous sounds echoed in his ears. There was nothing to celebrate this day. All he heard was the smouldering of wood, the crackle as it split, the cry of a mother in the background, and the eerie silence of the one or two men's eyes that followed him as he walked by to climb the remaining stairs of the wall.

He stood at the epicentre of the blast and stared down at the area of devastation. Ganda'har had awoken in the dunes some distance away from the wall, thrown there by the blast. *What happened?* Bodies still lay scattered down below in the street. Men and women slowly carried out the dead and covered them with sheets. The city had fallen.

'Khan!' he bellowed. 'Where are you? Blanka! Talgar! Untara!' *At least the portal is closed. That's good, isn't it?* He picked up a blue robe from the ground; it bore the black-on-white eagle crest on its chest, but the inner lining was covered in blood. His heart was heavy. The captain made his way back down and came upon the destroyed statue of Penthis the Great, then read the plaque at the base: "A true man fights for others, not himself. For loyalty and honour." He fell to his knees and sobbed as he clutched the remaining foot of Penthis. Pain lanced through his side, and he pulled at his shirt. Clotted with blood, it stuck to his skin and pulled open the wound, extending from below his arm to his thigh. He winced as he pushed the flap of skin back down and got to his feet slowly. By all accounts, this wound would have killed him were it not for his bonding with the dragon.

A scrawny man, older in years, walked up to him, tears streaming down his face as he said, 'I saw you fight for us, sir. It might not have been enough for victory, but you did your part. Thank you.'

In between his sobs, Ganda'har said, 'Where is everyone? I only regained consciousness this morning.'

The older man said, 'It's been five days since the fall of the city.' He pulled out a water skin from a sack slung over his shoulder and handed it to the captain, then continued, 'Drink; you must be thirsty. Those bastards came in after the dust settled, searching for something, killing all who stood in their way.'

'What of the warlocks and the mages? My squad of soldiers? Did any of them survive?' Ganda'har had grabbed the old man by the collar and pulled him near. Eyes of utter desperation stared at the old man. He released his grip. 'I'm sorry. I didn't mean to—'

'No apology needed. They took away all the mages and warlocks who still lived, although there were few left. Of your soldiers, I'm afraid I don't know.'

'Who can I thank for this water?'

'I am Nigante. And no thanks needed. Today, we need to help any who are alive.' The older man turned and headed back to the bodies to resume his grim duties.

Ganda'har looked back down at the broken feet of the statue, and said, 'Goodbye, old friend. It's time for me to leave this place. I've already had enough killing and fighting for a few lifetimes, but it seems it has just begun.' The captain turned and walked down the street, then shouted at Nigante, 'Do you know which direction they went?'

'West, I believe,' came the shout back.

A strange calling pulled at him, summoning him as he turned to leave. His right hand itched suddenly, and Ganda'har couldn't shrug off the feeling. It came from the left, where he saw a collapsed building. A few strides took him to a door hanging ajar on its hinges. Blocks of stone and charred wooden beams covered the floor. He moved inside, ducking his head under the fallen beam, and stood on a heap of rubble. The pressure on the wound made it hard for him to bend down and shift one of the stone blocks. He dropped to his knees and pulled brick, mortar, and stone away as he rummaged to get to the bottom.

The calling was getting louder now. A brush of leather against his bruised and bloodied hand caught his attention. Then he saw the haft sticking out of the rubble. His eyes widened, and he shouted, 'Khan! Are you there?' He began frantically digging, stones flying from his hands. He pushed with all his remaining strength to lift a fallen piece of the wall, throwing it over to collapse in the street. Onlookers stared at the sudden noise, then returned their attention to the sorrow before them. There was no Khanaseri, but at least there was no body there either. Before him lay the warlock's axe, begging to be picked up by the captain. A humming sound assaulted his senses, radiating from the weapon. He picked up the bloodstained axe and got back to his feet, vowing, 'I'll make them pay, Khan.'

Ganda'har felt something in his pocket and pulled forth a parchment, then remembered that Stilts had handed it to him. He had been too busy, and then too unconscious, to get it to its rightful owner. He walked the streets like the rest of the ghosts who would haunt Artorea forever, watching citizens cry in their despair, holding onto their remaining loved ones. Deeper in the city, far away from the wall, houses still stood. The blast hadn't killed everyone. He walked up to an old, little house on the corner of a street and stopped. Clearing his throat, he then moved up the pathway, past the wilted flowers, to knock on the door. A soft voice called out from the other side, and moments later, the door swung open. Before him stood a woman trying to conceal her tears, but Ganda'har could see the streaks down her face, and her red eyes.

He was a broken man; he had no more left in him. The only words he could utter were on the reddened parchment as he unfolded it. 'Dariah?'

The woman paled and covered her mouth as she saw the blood-streaks on the parchment and said, 'No, sir, I'm Galla. Dariah's caretaker. I will get her quickly.'

The woman scuffled off down the hallway, calling out for Dariah. A few moments went by before quick, running footsteps echoed through the little house and Ganda'har saw a small blonde girl run round the corner shouting, with a big smile on her beautiful little face, 'Is Daddy back?' Her big, radiant blue eyes tore a hole in his soul.

Ganda'har crumpled on the inside as he looked at her. *So innocent, so joyous. And now I have come as a debt collector for that joy. To break her knees out from under her.* Tears streamed down his face as he looked at Dariah and took her little hand, then moved into the little house as he said, 'Let me tell you a story of a great man.'

The End, for now...
To be continued in Book 2 of the Dragon Wars Saga.

AFTERWORD

Thank you for reading Daughter of The Ageian. I really hope you enjoyed this novel. If you have a moment, please leave a review on your preferred store as this will allow me the opportunity to write more books such as this. I would really appreciate it. Reviews are especially critical in today's world. Help other fantasy readers and tell them why you enjoyed this book. Thank you!

* Leave a Review here:

https://www.amazon.com

Want to stay updated with news about my books?

* Join my mailing list at:

https://www.mariushvisser.com/contact

* Like me on Facebook:

https://www.facebook.com/mariushvisserbooks

* Follow me on Instagram:

https://www.instagram.com/mariushvisser

Thank you again, reader. I hope we meet again soon amidst the battles to come in a new adventure.

* Hint, there's a sneak preview of King's Plight – The Dragon Wars Saga Volume Two on the next page…

**King's Plight is the second book in the Dragon Wars Saga.
Below is an excerpt for your pleasure.**

'Sail ho, Cap'n!' came shouts from the crow's nest up above.

Bellof rushed out of his quarters and leaned on the rail as he whispered, 'Bastard's early.' Far in the distance, over the calm, dark sea, hovered a light, disappearing from time to time with the roll of the waves. He glanced around and saw the king's guards rise from the small table they'd placed on the deck.

The first mate shouted at the drunken guards, 'You haven't played your hand yet! No man quits halfway. It's a disgraceful insult!'

One of the drunken guards turned and stumbled over a barrel and said, 'But someoneses is com...ing. Wee haf to fight!'

Another of Bellof's men neared and shouted at another guard, 'What ya say 'bout me mum?!'

Still trying to explain that he had said nothing, the crew jumped at them, and a fight quickly broke out. 'Throw 'em in the brig!' Bellof shouted from the upper deck, and turned to see Tekar walk up to him.

'What is going on, Captain? What are you playing at? Let the men go!' He stormed at the captain, who greeted him with a right hook straight to his face. It happened so quickly, he had no time to evade the blow, and now lay on the wooden deck clutching his broken nose as blood streamed down his broad, flat face. He heard the heavy footsteps of Bellof draw near, and through his teared-up vision saw the captain towering over him.

'I forgot youz didn't drink, lad. Best youz stay on the floor and ignore what's 'bout to happen. Savvy?'

Tekar squirmed to retreat from under the big man and shouted, 'What did you do with the king?' A flash of dark a boot, and his head stung from the blow. Darkness was his friend then.

'Oh, he's fine, lad,' Bellof said while he turned to watch the ship draw near, its grey silhouette outlined by the moon as it turned broadside, then shouted to his crew, 'Pull her near, lads!'

A loud buzz filled the deck as men spun ropes trailing hooks, and sent them across the chasm between the ships to hear the metal thud against the rails and deck, quickly pulling in the ropes to tighten them and secure the hold. More grappling hooks sailed over the chasm from the other side and swung round their taffrail, skidding on the decks and mast to latch into place wherever the sharp metal fingers found a hold. Shouts and curses followed as the two ships collided with a little more force than intended, thanks to the helping hand of a wave. The loud knock reverberated through the ship and sent some of the more inexperienced crew to the deck. Bellof stormed at the floundering men, 'Get yer lazy behinds off the deck and bring the cargo up! Don't leave these friendly folks waiting, or they might not be so friendly before long!'

Men boarded the *Derecho* with hands on their swords, observing the crew while a tall, pockmarked man with a long, sharp nose and beady eyes walked towards Bellof, combing his shaggy grey beard with his fingers as he said, 'I suppose you have the goods ready?'

'Tall Edward,' Bellof said, as he nodded and glanced over his shoulder to see the crew bringing the crates up to the deck. 'Aye. There is the matter of payment.' The man gestured with his head to his men, and they brought a few crates forth.

These exchanges were always a dicey affair, with each side wondering if they would be played for a fool. Bellof indicated to his first mate to investigate the crates and see that the goods were legitimate, quickly receiving a curt nod from the man, then said, 'Youz won't get any finer liquor anywhere on the Beladon Seas.' He uncorked one of the bottles and took a swig, then handed it to Tall Edward, who pulled a face at the harsh smell and swallowed a mouthful.

Everyone stood quietly, watching cautiously around them, until the pockmarked man shouted, 'Aha, that *is* good! Load it up!'

A loud crash from above drew their attention. All the men turned to look up and saw the drunken king wave his sword around as he leapt from the captain's quarters to fall over the railing to the lower deck, losing his blade as it skidded a distance away. Immediately, swords were unsheathed on both sides, and Bellof roared, 'Wait!' Everyone froze and stared at the king as he lay sprawled on the deck, unmoving. He rolled his eyes as he sighed and said, 'He had a bit too much to drink, is all.'

Tall Edward rounded on him and shouted, 'Who is this man? Why did he come from the captain's quarters?'

Bellof raised his hands as he said, 'Just a ship hand who can't take his liquor. Thought it best to stow him away until youz were gone.'

Tension rose as everyone stood ready to swing their swords at the drop of a hat. Tall Edward walked to the passed-out Garidan and turned the man over, feeling his hands, and stared at his face. 'This is no deckhand. He hasn't scrubbed a single thing in his life. What's going on here?' The tall man rose and shoved his finger in Bellof's chest. 'He disrespected me. He needs a flogging.'

'Cap'n?' Vascily whispered on Bellof's right, and saw the quick shake of the head and stepped back.

'It just so happens that I lost my cat-o'-nine-tails. Best youz be on your way. Take the cargo and let's not speak of this again. Savvy?'

'It's a good thing I always carry a spare with me,' Tall Edward said as he pulled a whip from the back of his pants and handed it to Bellof, slowly stepping away from the captain of the *Derecho*. 'You know the rules. A deckhand must be punished if he steps out of line.'

Lanterns swung from hooks every few feet, chasing the dark from the area as the crew stood ready for anything, stretching their shadows and hiding their eyes. Bellof spoke over his shoulder, 'Vascily, stand the man up and tie him to a barrel. Strip him of his shirt.'

'Sir. Are you sure?' the first mate asked, a tone of concern in his voice.

'Aye, get to it. Seems weze gonna have a good old-fashioned floggin'!' Bellof shouted, and quickly glanced up to the quarterdeck, before turning to watch the king get propped up and bent over a barrel.

They tied his hands together and stretched him out before tearing his shirt from him. 'Double-check them knots. I don't want him getting loose. This'll get messy.'

'You're stalling, Captain Bellof! Hit him, or we do a keelhaul.'

King's Plight is available for purchase right now. Join my mailing list for updated information:
https://www.mariushvisser.com/contact.

The world seems to darken with every passing day; the ever-growing threat of the dragon army invading their world and destroying what has taken generations to build. With Artorea sacked, Garidan takes it upon himself to find allies in the farthest reaches of another realm: the world of the Ageians. He never expected the journey to turn out the way it did, to be as fraught with danger…

New Runswick is barely defendable after previous wars and neglect. The walls need to be rebuilt and quick for a chance of survival. Now queen, Ladriana needs to prove her worth to the capital of Elmohria and protect them from the nearing threat, but who will protect her from an altogether new threat?

A professionally trained Information Technology Specialist Marius H. Visser spent the better part of a decade honing his writing skills and pushing the bounds of imagination after his début fantasy novel Mercury Dagger - A Tale From Kraydenia. When Marius H. Visser is not off exploring the wilds of Australia, he is dreaming up new adventures and monsters to cause chaos in a fantastical world filled with twists, loyalty, honour and great and terrible battles.